The White Indian Series
Book XXIV

P9-DDS-442

FATHER
AND
SON

Donald Clayton Porter

THE CACTUS WREN
BOOK EXCHANGE
56336 29 PALMS HWY.
YUCCA VALLEY, CA 92284
(760) 365-6652

BCI Producers of **The Frontier Trilogy,**
The Holts, and **The First Americans.**

Book Creations Inc., Canaan, NY • Lyle Kenyon Engel, Founder

BANTAM BOOKS
NEW YORK • TORONTO • LONDON • SYDNEY • AUCKLAND

This is a work of fiction. While the general outlines of history have been faithfully followed, certain details involving setting, characters, and events may have been simplified.

FATHER AND SON

A Bantam Book / published by arrangement with Book Creations Inc.

Bantam edition / June 1993

Produced by Book Creations Inc.
Lyle Kenyon Engel, Founder

All rights reserved.
Copyright © 1993 by Book Creations Inc.
Cover art copyright © 1993 by Lou Glanzman.
No part of this book may be reproduced or transmitted in any form or by any means, electronic or mechanical, including photocopying, recording, or by any information storage and retrieval system, without permission in writing from the publisher. For information address: Bantam Books.

If you purchased this book without a cover you should be aware that this book is stolen property. It was reported as "unsold and destroyed" to the publisher and neither the author nor the publisher has received any payment for this "stripped book."

ISBN 0-553-29219-6

Published simultaneously in the United States and Canada

Bantam Books are published by Bantam Books, a division of Bantam Doubleday Dell Publishing Group, Inc. Its trademark, consisting of the words "Bantam Books" and the portrayal of a rooster, is Registered in U.S. Patent and Trademark Office and in other countries. Marca Registrada. Bantam Books, 1540 Broadway, New York, New York 10036.

PRINTED IN THE UNITED STATES OF AMERICA

OPM   0 9 8 7 6 5 4 3 2 1

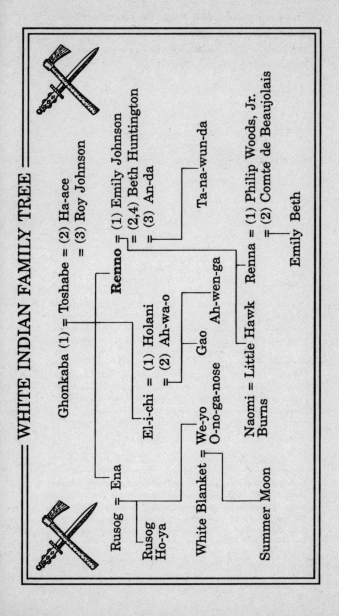

WHITE INDIAN FAMILY TREE

FATHER
AND
SON

Chapter One

They strolled side by side among the looted treasures of continents, two ladies, one mature and majestic, the other vibrantly young.

"Notice the small one, there." The empress Josephine inclined her well-coiffed head in the direction of a statue of a kneeling man. "Said to be a rarity. Brought from Egypt by my husband."

The younger woman turned her ash-blond head. Her charmingly tilted blue eyes lingered on the eager, up-turned face of the little stone scribe, then swept out over the richness of the decor of the immense, elongated gallery. The touch of darkness in her flawless skin came from her father's Seneca blood, the pale hair from her mother.

Together they made an alluring picture: Josephine, although not as seductive as she appeared in her favorite portrait, the full-length, half-reclining masterpiece just re-

1

cently completed by Pierre Paul Prud'hon, the ripened product of luxury and power; the other, who was called Renna, also known as the comtesse de Beaujolais, hauntingly beautiful in pale blue.

Renna had chosen the dress carefully to be an understatement to contrast with the bold colors and styles affected by Josephine. It was not the first time she had been in the Louvre, ancient home of French kings. The emperor Napoleon—the *"petit tondu,"* or little crop head—had bestowed princely titles on members of his family, and—so Josephine had told her young friend Renna—was thinking of creating an imperial nobility. As if seeking legitimacy for his claims to royalty for himself and his family, the emperor made it a point to seek out the few survivors of the former elite. Thus Renna, wife of the younger brother of Louis Philippe, Duc d'Orléans, was a court favorite, for she combined charm, a hint of the exotic, and a title all in one personable and attractive package.

"Do you know what the name of this place means?" Josephine asked, as they promenaded toward the distant end of the 750-foot gallery.

"I have heard," Renna said, "that lepers were kept in the dungeon of the original fortress, and that *louvre* was taken from an old French word for leper."

"Perhaps," Josephine said, "but I like the other story better. It is said that Philip kept hunting hounds in the fortress and, thus, *louvre,* for kennel."

"Actually," Renna said, smiling inwardly as well as outwardly, "I like the current name best."

"Ah, the Musée Napoléon," Josephine said with some irony. "Yes, it seems *he* is determined to outdo all the kings of France in his patronage of the arts."

"I think he has succeeded," said Renna, not mentioning that most of the artworks Napoleon had placed here had been looted from defeated nations.

"Possibly. But think of Francis the First, who bought paintings by Raphael, who convinced the great Leonardo to come to Paris."

"I do think it is touching that the king held the dying Leonardo in his arms," Renna said.

Josephine sighed. "Henry the Fourth was fortunate to have had Rubens to glorify his likeness and that of his queen, while I have only poor Prud'hon."

"But the inspiration of Prud'hon's subject has lifted him to greatness," Renna answered. She was, after all, married to a skilled diplomat, one who, unlike his father, had survived the Terror and the guillotine's sharp blade.

"You are so sweet, my dear," said Josephine, chuckling. "In all modesty, my little artist did not have the challenge that Rubens faced in beautifying Marie de Médicis."

"Yes," Renna agreed, "Rubens had to have been a genius, didn't he?"

Josephine said nothing but took Renna's hand and guided her to a bench, where they sat.

Waiting for the empress to speak, Renna thought of her father, Renno, half-white but all Seneca. He contended that no Indian could be a good liar to another Indian, only to a white. Flattery was a form of lying, she realized, but a harmless one if it helped advance her husband's career.

Beau had risen to a position of responsibility in the empire's diplomatic service, not only because of his title, but because he was truly loyal to Napoleon. A rising star in the emperor's diplomatic corps, he had helped lay the groundwork for the three treaties signed at Tilsit, when Napoleon met Czar Alexander I of Russia aboard a raft anchored in the middle of the Niemen River to divide Europe between them. For Beau's services, portions of the family estates had been returned to him, enough to make Renna the wife of a wealthy man.

Josephine was still silent, and now Renna saw a blankness in her eyes. "Is something bothering you, madam?" she asked.

Josephine shook her head. "It is nothing, my dear. Nothing." She rose, straightened her skirts, and swept back toward the living quarters, where a small dinner awaited the arrival of the emperor and Beaujolais.

As it happened, Napoleon did not join the count and his wife at dinner with the empress. Josephine's mood became black, and it was with relief that Beau and Renna took their leave after desert and brandy in Josephine's sitting room, next to the bedroom where Napoleon had hung Leonardo's masterpiece, the smiling woman without a name.

"The empress seemed preoccupied tonight," Renna said to Beau as their closed carriage, cozy against a chill night, rumbled across the Seine.

"Hmm," Beau muttered.

She snuggled up to him, enjoying his warmth. "Do you suppose something is bothering her?"

"You are the curious cat," Beau said fondly, putting his arm around her.

She leaned to kiss him lightly. "And is my curiosity to be answered? You were with the emperor."

Beau sighed. "If you should ever want to be rid of me, all you would need to do is say, 'My husband tells me everything.'"

"Tell me," she insisted.

"It's simple. The emperor wants a son."

"She was a mature woman with two children by her former husband when he married her," Renna protested.

"She was rather indiscreet with Monsieur Hippolyte Charles while the emperor was in Egypt."

"That's only rumor," Renna said. "And, after all, they were married again, with religious rites, just before he was coronated."

"Ah," Beau said, "but some people noticed—even if the radiant Josephine didn't—that Napoleon had arranged for the absence of the parish priest."

"Oh, no!" Renna exclaimed.

"My naive darling," Beau said, "such men as our Napoleon are above ordinary conventions. He has caught the dynastic disease. He wants a son. At any time he can declare his marriage to Josephine null and void."

"Oh, poor Josephine."

"Well, she has come far, for a colonial woman," Beau said. "I imagine she considered herself lucky when she married a viscount. To be empress, even for a short time, would have been beyond the wildest dreams of a girl from Martinique."

"Lucky? Her husband was sent to the guillotine, and she herself was imprisoned."

"But she conquered the conqueror," Beau said, "and now she is empress of half the world."

Renna was silent, musing on the unfairness of it, on the nature of men. When she spoke her voice was small. "Beau, we had no priest at our wedding."

He laughed. "What of it? We are nonetheless fully wed."

"Yes, and if you ever decided to divorce me, I would see to it that you would never be of use to another woman."

"Ouch!" he said. "And you would, too."

He held her close for a long time. The carriage wheels rumbled over cobblestones, then came to a halt. Beau helped her out. The night was clear and cool, and the stars were bright enough to make themselves seen through the weak glow of the streetlights on the Ile de la Cité. Beau guided her to the entrance of their town house and kissed her as the door closed behind them.

"Renna . . ."

She was alerted by a certain tone in his voice. "Oh, no," she said.

"Do you read me so easily?"

"Yes. What is it? Are you going away again?" She clung to him.

"I fear so," Beau replied. "It is made necessary, you see, by those churlish and stubborn people on William Shakespeare's sceptered isle, and by their allies who tend to disagree that Paris is the center of the world."

"That is why we were invited to the Louvre tonight?"

"Come," he said, "we'll discuss it while we prepare for bed."

Upstairs, as Renna emerged from her dressing room in a clinging, silken nightgown, Beau was already lying under light coverings, his hands behind his head. A warm smile came to his face, and he reached for her as she knelt on the bed beside him.

"No," she said, pushing his arm away gently. "Tell me first." She snuggled down beside him, her head on his shoulder.

He sighed. "You know that I shared with the emperor my personal doubts about his grand scheme to force England to capitulate."

"I hope, dear heart, that you didn't argue with him."

"One does not argue with the little crop head. I told him, however, that his Continental System, his plan to deprive England of her European markets through a blockade of the British Isles, might fail."

"I don't quite understand his reasonings," she replied.

"The idea is to cause unsold merchandise to accumulate in English factories and warehouses. The factories would be forced to close. The unemployed workers would rise against the government and demand peace." Beau's voice changed tone. He was being the diplomat. "The decrees of Berlin and Milan forbid all trade with the British and order the confiscation of all goods coming from England or the British colonies. Under the two decrees, the French navy is authorized to seize not only all British ships, but any ship that has touched the shore of England or her colonies."

"That I understand," Renna said. "He has taken aim at the commerce of the United States as well as that of England."

"Exactly," Beau acknowledged. "But there is a worm in Napoleon's apple. All of the nations of Europe, save one, have agreed to honor the blockade. Only Portugal, England's old ally, refuses, stating that the blockade would mean commercial ruin for them. So they resist Napoleon's order, and this the lord of Europe cannot allow."

"So we're going to Portugal?" Renna asked, lifting her head.

"*I*, my darling, not we," Beau answered.

"Not likely," she said.

"Tonight the emperor told me that he had ordered his armies to move on Portugal through Spain. That means more war, of course, and I could never take you into such an uncertain situation."

"You will *not* leave me alone in Paris, center of the world or not."

"My darling, I have orders to go to Lisbon to speak politely but firmly to the Portuguese government. In effect, I will be threatening the war that the emperor has already ordered. If I arrived in Portugal with a wife and a child in tow, I would not be a very creditable messenger of war."

"Is it not true, my dear, that as a diplomatic representative you can travel to England?"

"That is not in my plans."

She raised herself on one elbow to look down into his face. Her pale hair brushed his cheek. "Perhaps you can put it into your plans. That way Emily Beth and I can visit my uncle William and my aunt Estrela while you are on your mission."

"Out of the question," Beau objected. "The English Channel is made dangerous not only by seasonal storms but by the Royal Navy."

"You'll be sailing under a diplomatic flag."

"Which some overeager British ship's captain might ignore," Beau said.

She shuddered.

"No, no, I will be in no danger," he reassured her.

"You can't have it both ways," she said. "If it is not dangerous for you, it is not dangerous for me and Emily Beth."

"Out of the question," he repeated.

"Then we will go to sleep," she said, giving him her back.

He put his arm around her. "Renna—"

"Good night, *darling*," she said.

"Renna? . . ."

"I am very tired," she declared, "and very angry with my husband."

"Ah, listen—"

"I will listen only when you say that your daughter and your wife will not be left behind."

"I'm sorry."

"Good night, then."

She waited. She wanted to be in his arms as much as he wanted her, but she would not give in to his small caresses. She had never before used denial as a weapon, but she had very special reasons for wanting to be with him: she loved him very much; she was pregnant with their second child; and she could not bear the thought of being alone at such a wonderful time.

She turned to face him, reaching out, and they both spoke at the same time.

"I'm sorry—"

"I'm so sorry—"

Then silence for a time. Finally Beau said, "If you must go to England—"

She kissed him. He could not see her triumphant smile in the dark.

Across an ocean and one-third of a continent, Renna was very much on the mind of her father, Renno the white Indian, as he took his ease on the veranda of the large frame house he shared with his aristocratic wife, Beth Huntington Harper.

Mild weather, unusual for winter on the Tennessee frontier, had drawn Renno outdoors—a blessing, considering the fact that his wife was raising a commotion inside, preparing for the wedding of Renno's eldest son, Little Hawk, to a frontier woman, Naomi Burns. As Seneca and Cherokee from the neighboring villages looked in wonder, Beth had half-a-dozen women—including the bride-to-be —engaged in a frenzy of cleaning, cooking, and preparation, although the great day was still a fortnight off.

Renno had just returned from a successful hunt with his brother, El-i-chi, and his brother-by-marriage, Rusog. Venison was drying in the brash winter sun. Storehouses in the villages were stuffed. The smokehouses of Huntington Castle—as Renno and Beth's home was sometimes called —were aromatic with cured smoked hams and bacon. On the creek behind the two-story house a picturesque mill house rumbled to the rotation of big, stone grinding wheels, turning a bumper crop into cornmeal for bread and a dozen other dishes.

Yet for all this bounty, Renno's heart had an empty place, an ache for his daughter and for the little grand-daughter he had never seen. He was past his forty-third summer, and he yearned to hold a grandchild in his arms. Little Emily Beth—he had been told in letters—had inherited her grandmother's pale hair as well as her name. Renna was expecting another child, but she was thousands of miles away. Fortunately, he was about to have a new daughter-by-marriage, and if the manitous were kind, a baby closer to home would come soon.

He put his moccasined feet up on the porch rail and lit a pipe that had been carved from a gnarled root by his talented Cherokee friend, Se-quo-i. The thought of grand-children turned his mind to the future, which, as he grew older, seemed more and more troubled. The world was changing quickly; things were no longer as simple as they once had seemed. As the son of the sachem Ghonkaba, who had led the people of Ja-gonh and the original white Indian to the south to join their Cherokee cousins, Renno had followed his father's example, leading his people into ways of friendship with the Americans. But some—including Renno's own nephew Rusog Ho-ya—had challenged this philosophy, believing that the Senecas' destiny lay elsewhere, apart from the white man's ways.

These thoughts were broken by El-i-chi, who came up from the creek. He looked around carefully, as if he were afraid of being waylaid into women's work, then sat in a rocker beside Renno's chair. There was a definite family resemblance in the brothers, although El-i-chi was more true to Seneca tradition in his hair styling and his dress. Both were lithe, tall, well formed. Renno was thicker of chest, stronger of arm, and lighter of skin and hair.

Renno puffed smoke. Beth's voice, raised to emphasize an order to one of the household's free servants, came from an open window.

El-i-chi gestured with his chin. "Flame Hair lives up to her name."

"Umm," said Renno.

"Where's the groom?" asked El-i-chi.

"I think they've got him making up a guest list."

"Ummm," El-i-chi said. Then, after a long pause, "Why a list? Everyone in the two villages will show up anyhow."

"Ummmm."

Beth appeared in the doorway, her autumn-leaf hair in disarray, an apron around her waist. "RENN-ooooo!" she called loudly. Then, seeing him, "Oh."

"I hear," Renno said in Seneca.

"Andy Jackson . . ." Beth began.

"So."

"We haven't sent him an invitation."

Renno shrugged.

"Renno!"

"Too late to get word to him now, I'm afraid."

"No," Beth replied. "Roy was in Knoxville a few days ago, and he heard that Andy was going to be there on another court case. If we can send someone to Knoxville with a letter—"

"I'll be happy to go, Mother," said the groom. Little Hawk pushed past Beth and came out onto the veranda, a young man an inch taller than his father, with the bronzed skin and golden hair of his ancestor, the first Renno.

El-i-chi winked at Renno. "I don't see how the groom can be spared, do you, Brother?" he said.

"All those last-minute decisions," Renno agreed.

"I think it will be left to the older generation to go to Knoxville," El-i-chi said.

"Thanks a bunch, Uncle," Little Hawk said with a wry grin.

"I was thinking, Brother," El-i-chi said, "of a quick run to Knoxville, and on the return a swing to the east into the foothills, where the hunting, they say—"

"Thanks a whole heap," Little Hawk said.

Two ran together. Renno and El-i-chi moved at the warrior's pace, that jogging run that covered ground with amazing rapidity. In the past that gait had moved the warriors of the League of the Ho-de-no-sau-nee fifty miles in a day to fight at the end of the run. Perhaps the two did not move with quite the ease and swiftness they had known in the past, but few Indians and fewer white men could have kept up with them as they sped through the woodlands, leaping over patches of lingering snow, pausing only to lap water from a cold, clear stream.

They found Knoxville much larger than the last time they had seen it. Indeed, the white eyes bred like rabbits, and there was no end to their ambition for lands in the west. As they asked for Jackson at the local hotel, a wagon train of settlers rolled past, dogs barking at the heels of the mules, towheaded youngsters chasing the dogs and peering out of the hooded wagons.

Yes, Andy Jackson was due in Knoxville. When? Who knew? Matter of days. Yes, he would be given the letter.

And then it was the long way home, the stalking of deer, a near encounter with a mountain cat. Through all of the sightings, their weapons were silent. Renno's bow stayed on his shoulder, for they had jerky and nut balls in their kits and were not ready—not for the first three days —to kill.

It was good to be free, to move as carelessly or as silently as the situation demanded, good to be in one's own country, without concern for human enemies. It was good to be brothers, to feel the onset of a winter storm, the temperature dropping from sweat-producing balminess to biting cold in twenty-four hours.

The change in weather came with dark clouds rising up from the west in a purple wall laced with jagged streaks of light. Already the roiling mass had eaten the sinking light.

"The spirits are uneasy," El-i-chi said, while the low rumble of thunder came rolling down the sky to surround them as they stood atop a ridge. A wooded valley lay before them. The course of a stream was marked by tall cottonwood trees with winter-barren limbs ghostly white in the gloom descending from the sky-climbing clouds. A fitful, uncertain wind flirted with dead leaves on the ground, sending them skittering and cartwheeling.

Renno nodded toward the creek and led the way down the slope. There was a feeling of tension, as if the air were charged with the dramatic lightning that was so unusual with a winter storm.

Some long-ago wind had bent a large tree to the ground. Twenty feet up the huge trunk, wood had splintered to allow the brush of the top to lean, touch the ground, and rest on sturdy-looking limbs. Between the brush and the tree trunk was an ideal spot to construct a hasty shelter of pine boughs. By the time their home for the night was ready, spits of cold rain rattled on the leafless cottonwoods and made dimples on the surface of the stream.

There would be no fresh meat. Neither of the brothers was eager to venture forth in the cold rain that threatened to turn to sleet at any moment. Renno felt that any self-respecting game animal would be tucked away securely in its den. He satisfied his hunger with a strip of jerky, wincing as he bit down on the dried meat with a tooth that had become tender.

El-i-chi noticed and grunted a question.

"It is nothing," Renno said. "Like an old horse, I have worn out my teeth."

El-i-chi lifted one hand in amused denial. "My brother. So ancient."

"I noticed, Brother, that you did not object when I slacked the pace at midday."

El-i-chi grinned, but made no comment.

"Once I held the warrior's pace from Nova Scotia to the cities of the white men in the East," Renno said, as if in wonder.

"The number of your winters has not diminished you," El-i-chi said. "There is no one I'd rather have at my side when steel clashes on steel."

Renno nodded. "So," he said, to cover his pleasure and his embarrassment at the praise.

The rain came on the wings of a gale that hit the line of trees along the creek like a knotted fist. Both of the brothers heard the wind's howl as it came rushing through the forest on the western side of the creek. Overhead limbs crashed as the great force slammed into them. The last of the old dead leaves whirled away to merge with wind-driven sleet and raindrops. The half-broken tree trunk supporting a great weight of limbs and brush groaned, twisted, and with a loud snap came crashing down toward the pine-bough shelter.

El-i-chi moved as lithely and as quickly as a striking snake, throwing himself toward Renno, who, as his brother reached him, was just raising himself to one elbow. El-i-chi's strong arms lifted Renno and threw him outward. He followed his brother to safety, rolling on the rain-soaked detritus of the forest's floor. Behind them the broken trunk, with a thickness greater than the width of Renno's shoulders, thudded down onto the spot where Renno had been resting.

El-i-chi pushed himself up on his hands and knees, looked at Renno. He was breathing hard. Renno came to his feet, gave El-i-chi his hand, and lifted him.

"Slow," Renno said. "I was too slow."

"I had prior warning," El-i-chi said.

"From the spirits?"

El-i-chi looked away. Water streamed down his face. The wind was abating, the brunt of its initial force having passed.

"If I had been given no more time to evade an enemy's blade," Renno said, "I would be with our father now."

"No, for you would have been expecting the blow," El-i-chi protested. He wiped his eyes and grinned. "You have a long way to run, old one, before you join the manitous."

"Do you suppose it might be a good idea for us to look for some shelter?" Renno asked.

"As always, my brother, you are wise."

"There?" Renno asked, pointing to the mass of brush around the deadfall.

"Given a choice—" El-i-chi said, frowning.

"There," Renno said, pointing toward the ridge on the far side of the valley.

They walked in darkness through a freezing, blowing

rain, mounted the ridge through evergreens, found a rocky overhang facing east. With flint and steel El-i-chi worked the magic of fire, and it was good. Neither of them was ready for sleep.

"It is sad when a man cannot say that his best years are ahead of him," Renno said moodily.

"Nor can you say that your best years are behind you," El-i-chi said.

"I'm tired, Shaman," Renno said. "And the times change. When my own nephew preaches against my teachings, calling for the old ways of bloody war with the Americans, I wonder if, indeed, my time has not passed."

"You have given them your wisdom," El-i-chi said. "Now it is for them to decide, for each man is free to break his own trail. Old Casno told me that as each generation is born, matures, and then passes, the only thing that truly belongs to a man is his own time on earth, and that he should manage that time as he sees his duty. If young ones pay no heed to knowledge gained by years of experience, then there is nothing we can do except pray that when it is time to cross the river and join our fathers, we can say that we served to the best of our abilities."

Renno removed his tunic, shivering as the cold air touched his bare chest. He placed the garment on a flat rock near the fire. Soon steam was rising as the deerskin began to dry.

"Forgive me for being funereal," Renno said in patrician English. "You're right, of course. One can only do one's best." He grinned and winked, reverted to the corn-pone accent of the Tennessee frontier. "And, Brother mine, we got us'en one tree-menjous and bodacious party comin' up when the younguns git spliced."

On the last day Renno and El-i-chi walked the remaining miles to the village, each with a gutted deer hanging over his shoulders. They were waylaid by the *do-go-ka go-go-sa*, the terrible demons of the woods, for the wedding of Little Hawk and Naomi had been set for the eve of the greatest celebration of the year—the feast of the new beginning.

The demons were mostly young, and behind the grotesque False Faces the brothers recognized the voices of their sons, Renno's Ta-na-wun-da and El-i-chi's Gao.

Laughing, Renno went to greet them. It was good to be alive; let the manitous wait.

Beth Huntington well understood and accepted that her Indian family would hold differing opinions regarding her success as a wife to Renno. Renno himself, she was sure, would say that she had been a splendid wife. About her mother-in-law, Toshabe, Beth was much less secure. Perhaps Toshabe would have said that Beth had been a *good* wife—but not a good *Seneca* wife. True, Beth had made a study of Seneca customs, but could she ever persuade Toshabe that she had done so out of respect for the Seneca and love for her husband? She feared not.

She had other things on her mind. A wedding and the midwinter festival were at hand, and she was busy. Still, she found leisure to be homesick. She was beginning a campaign to get her husband to take her to England, to see her brother, and her nieces and nephews who were being turned out in astounding numbers by the prolific Estrela.

"Have I not been a *good* wife?" Beth asked Naomi as they baked for the wedding feast. "Did I not leave my home, my country, and then my business to be with him?"

"I pray that wherever Little Hawk takes me," Naomi said, "I will be content."

"Easy for you to say," Beth answered smilingly. "You haven't been transported thousands of miles away from your family." She paused, realizing her error. Naomi's family was dead, killed by Bearclaw Morgan, a man who had enslaved her and shared her with his two sons.

"I'm sorry," she said quickly.

But Naomi, lost in her own reverie, had taken no notice.

It was as if Beth were talking to herself. "Oh, I'm perfectly willing to spend the rest of my life with Renno in his own country. Didn't I build this house here to be our home, and don't I throw the doors open to all of his people?"

"Yes, ma'am," Naomi said dreamily.

"Perfectly content—*after* I've visited England just once more," Beth said.

Renno was not unaware of Beth's desire to go to England, and he understood it. She deserved to go. Years had passed since she last saw William and Estrela. She had nieces and nephews she'd never seen.

More than once he had considered telling Beth to make the trip to England alone, for he had vowed to stay with his people after his last extended absence. Since she owned several ships, the ocean voyage would be no problem. Her business, the Huntington Shipping Company, under the management of Adan Bartolome in North Carolina, was doing well, so there would be plenty of money.

She *was* a good wife, and it was his duty to grant her wishes. But it was also his duty to fulfill his responsibilities as sachem of his tribe. Too often had he been away from the village, leaving the Seneca without a leader. So his debt to his wife was diametrically opposed to what he owed his tribe, for a trip to England would keep him away for well over a year—if things went well.

To the very day of Little Hawk and Naomi's wedding, Renno was undecided. Then he put the matter resolutely out of his mind, for this was his son's day. Sitting beside his wife and Andy Jackson, Renno listened to a Methodist minister from Knoxville bellow his way through a Christian ceremony. He said his piece at the appointed time, when asked "Who giveth this woman to be married?" He answered in Seneca "I do," while winking at his son.

Little Hawk had never seen a woman look more beautiful than his wife when he lifted her veil and kissed her. Her eyes were moist, her smile was wide. He whispered in her ear, "I thank the manitous for bringing me to my senses."

"I thank God they did," she whispered back.

In a shower of corn—no rice was being grown in the Cherokee Nation—the bridal couple ran to the front door and out into the mild air to wave and shout back at the greeting of people who had not been able to crowd into the house. El-i-chi led a group of men, including Se-quo-i, Rusog, and Ho-ya, to capture Little Hawk and haul him off to the village, where he was stripped of his fancy white man's clothing. Meanwhile Naomi had been taken in hand by Ena, We-yo, and Ah-wa-o. Another ceremony was to be performed in the council longhouse with Little Hawk in loincloth and warrior's kilt and with Naomi dressed demurely in a pure white doeskin skirt and tunic. This ceremony was shorter and was conducted by the tribe's shaman, El-i-chi, but the aftermath was noisier than that of the ceremony in the big house.

It was well past midnight when, at last, Little Hawk took Naomi's hand and led her to that room that had been hers alone in Beth's house. Not once did Little Hawk think of the past. Not once did the shadows of Bearclaw Morgan and his two sons intrude.

He had seen her before, of course, in the sweet time of their first lovemaking after his return from the Far West. But tonight all was changed and new, as if transfigured by the power of their promises to each other. He could not get enough of her—the perfect breasts, her narrow waist, her flickering eyes. He touched, he caressed, he kissed. The tenderness of his lips inflamed her, and their love was consummated with an emotional totality that left them gasping.

"Oh, my dear," Naomi whispered, holding his head to her breasts. "Oh, my dear."

"Is it love when I want to hold you so tightly that you'll melt into me?" he whispered.

"Yes."

"And when I can't get enough of you?" he asked, taking first one then the other of her nipples deeply into his mouth.

She giggled and tried to pull away, stretching one of the nipples, for he was reluctant to free it.

"Mine," he whispered.

"They are attached to me," she said, "so if they're yours, then you'll have to take all of me."

"Gladly," he said.

Her response pleased him.

In the light of dawn Naomi rose—sleepless, sated, warm with love—and stood at the window. A late moon was fading with the morning light. Sparrows cheeped and tumbled on the lawn, looking for crumbs from the wedding feast.

She had known three men, and they had given her shame, pain, and despair. That was all behind her now. Little Hawk's tenderness made her want to weep with happiness, and the depth and force of her response had astounded her.

"Lord God," she prayed in a whisper, "please make me worthy of him. Forgive me my sins of the past, and make me his and his alone."

Little Hawk was dreaming of another girl, a girl with a round, dark face and ebony hair—Twana, the Chehalis girl who had saved his life in the Far West, only to die because of him. Then, in his dream, Twana became Naomi, and he lost her as well—

He awoke suddenly. Reaching for Naomi and finding her absent, he sat up and looked around in a panic, till he saw her at the window.

"There you are," he said. "You scared me."

She ran to him. "I'm so sorry. So sorry."

"It's all right," he said. "I was just dreaming."

He held his wife close, and to his surprise he felt rising between them a sweet lust that demanded completion. Their morning love was slow, slumberous, as exquisite as a ripe apricot, as warm and soft as a September night.

Once again he thanked the God of his mother for cleaning away the filth that had been left in his mind by the Morgans, for showing him his wife as she truly was.

Chapter Two

The next morning, bride and bridegroom arose in time to join the family for a late breakfast.

They found Roy Johnson, Little Hawk's grandfather, at the table. Though he had attended both wedding ceremonies and imbibed more than his usual portion of the nuptial spirits, he was tucking into a heaping pile of pancakes, served with bee-tree honey and soft, rich, freshly churned butter.

Roy and Little Hawk were still eating when the others finished. As Beth and Naomi began to clear the table, Renno rose.

"I think I'll have some fresh air while these animals feed," he said, heading toward the veranda.

Roy winked at Little Hawk. "I hope, boy, that you'll

have more respect for your old grandfather than some people."

"Old Grandfather," Beth called from the kitchen, "are those last six pancakes going to be enough, or should I tell Cook to stir up another batch?"

"Oh, I'll be fine, so long as we have an early lunch," Roy said.

Left alone with his grandfather, Little Hawk put down his fork, rubbed his stomach, and leaned back. Roy continued eating.

"Quitting, are you?" he asked.

"I concede defeat," Little Hawk replied.

"A newly married man needs his energy," Roy said with a grin.

Little Hawk flushed.

"Son, you've got yourself a good woman there," Roy said.

"I know."

"Reminds me a lot of your grandmother Nora, rest her soul," Roy went on. "I always tried to take care of her, and know I don't have to tell you to do the same for Naomi. Sometimes a man can live out his life without finding the right woman. Me, I found two of them, for which I give thanks daily."

As Little Hawk sipped coffee, Roy finished off the last of his stack of pancakes.

"Sometimes a man runs into a conflict between taking care of his woman and doing what he might think is his duty," Roy said. He took a match from his pocket, sharpened the end of it with his knife, and used it for a toothpick. "Like someone I know real well?"

"I'm an officer on active duty in the Marine Corps, Grandfather," Little Hawk said. "Sooner or later I'll have to go to Washington and report to President Jefferson."

"Will you, now?" Roy asked idly. "Me, I'd say that you've done your share, boy. Let's see, you fought yourself a war in North Africa, and then you sailed all the way to the northwest coast and walked home across half a continent with Lewis and Clark. I'd say a man your age who's traveled that far and done so much has done enough service for his country. And if I remember right, any officer has the right to resign his commission."

"Yes," Little Hawk said. "I have served the enlistment that I contracted for, but—"

"But what?" Roy asked. He leaned forward and spoke earnestly. "Look, Hawk, a good marriage goes on forever, or until—as the preacher says—death do you part, but the sweetest time is the beginning. You're young, and that time comes jest once. Now what I want you to do is set yourself down, write yourself a letter to Mr. Jefferson, and tell him, thank you, sir, but I have decided that I'm going to quit being a marine, at least for the time being. Later on maybe, when you've had a kid or two and something comes along makes it look right bad for the United States, you might offer your services again."

"It's a difficult decision, Grandfather," Little Hawk said. "You know there's a crisis brewing at sea, with both the French and British navies threatening our ships. Each ship needs its contingent of marines—"

"They can get along without one little Injun Marine," Roy said, "at least as long as that pretty little girl looks at you that way."

Naomi was standing in the door, her eyes alight with happiness, a small smile on her lips. When Little Hawk turned toward her, she became flustered and whirled to go back to the kitchen.

"Well?" Roy asked.

"I will give it serious thought," Little Hawk promised.

That night Andy Jackson sat with Renno and Beth in the village common for the ceremony of the white dog. The weather had moderated again. Old ones were saying that it was the mildest winter since the Seneca followed Ghonkaba and Toshabe from the northern homelands.

Jackson was amused by the antics of the False Faces and the Big Heads, led by the tribe's shaman, El-i-chi, but he cringed when the little white dog was killed, its body painted and hoisted high where all could see.

Jackson liked dogs, and to see a dog killed for no good

reason was not to his liking. For a moment he forgot where he was.

"Those who argue that the Indian's way of life is worthy of preservation," he said, "have not seen this foolish cavorting of fully grown men hiding behind ludicrous masks. Those who feel that the Indian's culture should be saved for posterity have not heard the death yelp of that little dog."

Too late Jackson realized that he had spoken out of turn. He did not apologize, for that would only have emphasized his low opinion of Seneca customs. Instead he asked Renno, "When do we get to hear this visitor of yours?"

"He comes to us from our homeland, from Iroquoia," said El-i-chi, in introduction. "He, too, is a shaman, and a friend of the Seneca prophet Handsome Lake. He has made the long trek from the north to teach to us the revelations of Handsome Lake."

"A new religion?" Andy Jackson asked in a whisper.

"Hear him and decide for yourself," Renno answered.

His name was Good Hunter. He was short and sturdy, and he wore his hair in the old-fashioned style of the Iroquois warriors, his scalp bare on the sides.

"I have talked with Good Hunter," Beth told Andy Jackson, speaking softly. "This so-called 'new religion' of Handsome Lake's is nothing more than an effort to give the Iroquois a moral code that will allow them to make adjustments for the massive life changes being forced upon them by the shrinkage of their territory. Handsome Lake preaches against drinking and wrongdoing—"

"Good Baptist, against booze and sin," Andy chuckled.

"—and to the old Iroquois concepts of good and evil, of the Master of Life, and of one's orenda, or spiritual power, he adds the notion of eternal punishment. No doubt he borrows this idea from the white man's religion. He puts more emphasis on a Creator and brings in a devil to give the Creator God more importance."

"Hush," Renno cautioned. "He is ready to begin."

Beth whispered hurriedly. "He sets great store in giving public thanks for what he calls 'Our Life Supporters,' corn, beans, and squash; and he talks a lot about Sun, Moon, Wind, and Thunderers, who are the spirits of the dead of the Iroquois."

"Enough," Renno said.

"Incidentally," Beth added, "he condemns the white-dog ceremony."

"He gets my vote already, then," Jackson grumbled.

Good Hunter's reverberating voice filled the council longhouse, immediately quieting the rustlings and coughings of the people of the two villages. Renno listened intently.

"This is what the Four Beings did—"

"Who are the Four Beings?" Jackson asked.

"The messengers from the Creator who appeared to Handsome Lake," Beth answered.

"Shush," Renno admonished, his finger to his lips.

"They told us that we should have love always, we who live on this earth," Good Hunter continued. "Love will always be first when people come together. That is the way it begins. They first have an obligation to be grateful that they are happy. Our Creator said, 'The people moving about on this earth must express their gratitude.' Those of us gathered here, we must be grateful."

"There are those who are ill," a voice said from the audience.

"That, too, is the responsibility of the Creator," said Good Hunter. "Be thankful for one another.

"Now this is what the Creator did. He said, 'There will be plants on the earth. They will have names. They will grow from the earth and mature. They will abound, serving as food and medicines for the people.'

"And this is what the Creator did. He decided that illness would overtake the people, but that the medicine of the plants would always be here for their assistance.

"When we see the sweet berries hanging above the earth, we must express thanks. When the wind is warm on the earth and the strawberries are red, we must be grateful.

"And this is what the Creator did. He said, 'There will be springs on the earth and brooks and rivers that flow, and there will be ponds and lakes; and after I fashion them on the earth, the rains will fall to replenish them. All things will be provided for the contentment of those who move about on the earth.'"

Renno nodded in agreement. El-i-chi glanced at him and smiled. Good Hunter listed other gifts from the Four Beings: forests, the changing seasons, the sweetness of maple syrup, the rising of the sap in the spring.

"And now this is what our Creator did. He said, 'I shall now put animals on the earth, for the warriors whose bodies are strong and for food.' And to this day we have the animals, large and small. And the Creator made the birds to spread their wings on high, to go into the clouds, and to fill the air with their beautiful song."

Although Renno enjoyed the oratory and the imagery, the most important point of Good Hunter's speech, in his opinion, was to relay Handsome Lake's advice to the Iroquois to change with the changing times, the policy Renno had been advocating for years. His people could follow that covenant without any change in the traditional notions of orenda or any alteration of the image of the Master of Life.

Of course the Master of Life made the winds and the sky, the stars, and the moon. Handsome Lake's Four Groups—Wind, Sun, Moon, and Thunderers—had always been present. To have love, one must be given love, Renno thought, and sometimes the best way to assure that love is given—taking love to mean mutual respect among peoples—is to bare the tomahawk and ready the arrow. So it had always been. To be prepared did not necessarily mean a contradiction of his advice to keep the peace with the whites. An Indian nation armed and willing to fight made it easier to talk peace.

When Good Hunter finished, he stood with arms outflung, face toward the ceiling of the longhouse. Grunts of approval were his applause. El-i-chi moved to his side.

"I didn't get all of it," Andy Jackson remarked, "but what I understood made sense. Couple of questions I'd like to ask about things he said."

"Beth will be happy to explain," Renno assured him. "I must go to pay my respects to our guest."

A week later, with Andy Jackson gone, another traveler came from the east, a shaman of the Cherokee who, in spite of white encroachment, had chosen to live among the fog and snows of the Smoky Mountains. He had come seeking wisdom, for he had heard that among the people of Rusog, principal chief of the Cherokee and grandson of the great Lorimas, lived a man who was most learned.

The man whom the visitor sought was Se-quo-i, and for once it seemed that this sage of Rusog's people had met his match, for the eastern shaman, whose name was Bending Tree, had attended a white man's school in North Carolina and had studied the history of the Cherokee Nation.

After long and sometimes heated discussions with Se-quo-i, Bending Tree continued his discussions with a fellow shaman, El-i-chi. Then he was feted with courtesy and ceremony, as befitted a man of his stature.

Beth joined Toshabe, Ena, and the other matrons in preparing the feast in the visitor's honor, and she was present at the ensuing gathering held in the council longhouse.

Standing before the group, Bending Tree did not appear to be a young man, but his back was straight, his limbs unbent, and his voice strong.

"Here we are all brothers," he said in opening. "I know that you will understand when I call you all Ani-Yun Wiga, the Real People. That is the name that the great chief Dragging Canoe gave to his people when he voiced his protest against giving Cherokee land to the whitefaces. Now we can see the wisdom of Dragging Canoe's protest.

" 'Great Chief,' they told him, 'the whitefaces want only a little land, only a small part of the Cherokee hunting grounds.' But Dragging Canoe stated, 'Although it is said that the whitefaces will not travel beyond the mountains, that is a lie, for the whiteface will finally demand the whole country that the Ani-Yun Wiga have long occupied and the Real People, once so strong, will be compelled to seek refuge in some distant wilderness.' "

"Not so," said a young Cherokee. "We will retreat no farther before the whitefaces."

"Ah," said Bending Tree, "but that, young brother, is what was said long ago when the Spaniard, Hernando de Soto, brought his mounted and armored soldiers into the lands of the Cherokee. They were not many, a few horsemen and between five and seven hundred foot soldiers. Only a few. The Real People met them in peace, giving them small-dogs-that-could-not-bark—opossums—and corn to eat. Why did not the Real People fall upon these first whitefaces and slay them? They had, after all, shown their true colors by bringing with them—in collars of iron and in chains—men and women of the Tamemes of Florida. That many of them, men and women, had been purchased from their own chiefs in exchange for looking glasses, knives, glass beads, and caps of yellow satin did not alter the fact that they were of the blood, and that they were enslaved.

"Did the Tamames captives not tell the Real People of the rape of women, of the burning of warriors at the stake? Did our ancestors not see that when a slave tried to escape, the Spaniards set bloodhounds on him so that his limbs were torn? Did our fathers not see the nature of the whitefaces then? That was long, long ago, my brothers, and we have changed so little, we of the Ani-Yun Wiga."

The great hall was quiet. Selfishly, Beth wondered what effect Bending Tree's exhortations would have on her campaign to get Renno to take her to England. It was, she felt, an inauspicious time for the arrival of an agitator crying out in ringing phrases, giving warlike advice counter to all that Renno taught his people. It was unusual for such a one to come from the east. The last one had come from the north, from the lands where Tecumseh continued to call for an Indian union against white expansionism.

"Once the Real People hunted from beyond the mountains in the east to the great river to the west, and now, great Chief Rusog, what is the range of the Cherokee? How goes your hunting?"

"Well," someone said.

"Well for now," said Bending Tree. "But tomorrow, when the white eyes have killed the deer? When did you last have buffalo tongue? For buffalo once roamed these forests. Have you ever been hungry enough to eat dog?" He paused, let his burning eyes cross the faces of all those who sat in the glow of the fire. "Dog is not the preferred meat of the Real People. Perhaps, in times of old, when the snows were deep and game was scarce and men's bellies growled with hunger—but the whitefaces who came in armor and on horseback lived on the meat of dogs, liked the meat of dogs, preferred the meat of dogs. And now if the Real People do nothing, we will eat dog and very little corn. We, like the Tamemes of Florida who were first enslaved by De Soto, will be consigned to the scrap heap of history."

Beth looked around as grunts and comments of approval were heard throughout the chamber. Renno, too, was watching his brothers, his people—Seneca and Cherokee alike. A junior warrior brandished a fist and whooped a war cry. The cry was taken up by others so that the sound rose through the smoke hole and crept outward through the sides of the longhouse.

Renno stood. "So," he said.

"Don't go," Beth pleaded, holding on to his hand as he rose.

He looked down at her, and there was pain in his eyes.

"Go, then," she said.

Renno traveled lightly through the mild winter, which was still being kind. He carried only his bow, his quiver, and the Spanish stiletto that never left his side. He would need no food. His buckskin shirt and trousers and his own exertions would warm him. He turned southward from Huntington Castle, leaped the creek, ran past the winter-barren mulberry tree where once Beth had been cornered by a bear, and in the small hours of the morning he was running through the glades of a woodland that climbed the side of a rocky ridge.

During the run he tried to blank his mind, for he was seeking physical catharsis, a ratification of a decision half-made as he heard the vocal approval of Bending Tree's call to arms from his own people. Then, too, he was, perhaps, running from the knowledge that he was growing older, that his limbs tired more easily, that his lungs seemed smaller.

Over a small, smokeless fire beside a deadfall, he mused over the words of Bending Tree and, for a time, knew doubt.

What if, when the whitefaces from Spain first landed on the shores of Florida, the people had banded together to throw them back into the sea? What if the English whitefaces had not been met with friendliness by the Indians of the northeastern coast?

Idle speculation. Had the Indians of Florida and North Carolina and Virginia and the northeastern areas fallen on the first invaders, slaughtering them, other whitefaces would have come sooner or later. The inevitable would have been delayed only a short while.

He bowed his head and stared into the glowing embers of the fire. He sat without moving, his breathing scarcely detectable, his head down. He looked back on his life, on his youth when he fought side by side with his father, the great Ghonkaba. He thought of the times when he had faced danger with his brother. He thought of his earlier wives, the pale-haired Emily and smiling An-da. His lip curled in anger as he recalled the mutilated face of the evil shaman Hodano; and his skin crawled in revulsion at the memory of Othon Hugues and the witch Melisande.

It was a night for memories, good and bad. Gradually a mass of dark cloud advancing from the northwest obscured the stars, and even as Renno put fresh deadwood on his small fire, a cold wind slammed out of the advancing storm, sending sparks flying and chilling him with an icy breath. He hunched his shoulders against the wind and continued his vigil.

With the morning came snow. Renno moved his dry, foodless camp to the shelter of a rocky overhang on the leeward side of a ridge, and though he warmed the small concave area with a roaring fire, he shivered, his arms clasped on his chest.

Throughout the day he prayed to the Master of Life and to the manitous. He could not adopt Handsome Lake's term for the spirits of Seneca who had gone to the west, refused to think of them as Thunderers, for that name implied threat, and to him the manitous were kind. They came to him at times of stress, the spirits of his fathers and his mothers, offering solace, hope, advice, and courage. His desire, on this blustery day of windblown snow and freezing temperatures, was to be one with the manitous, to inquire of them if he were truly justified in his thinking that it was perhaps time for him to relinquish the leadership of his tribe.

His father, Ghonkaba, had led his people on the side of the Americans in the Great White Man's War, and the son continued the father's belief that the fate of the Seneca lay with the United States. It was obvious, from the tribe's reaction to the oratory of Bending Tree, that his people did not share his convictions.

Still shivering, he put more wood on the fire. Night came, the wind died, and the snow sifted straight down to burden the barren limbs of the trees, settling in front of the shelter. A warmth crept into his limbs. His back straightened, his voice rose in a traditional hymn of praise to the manitous. He was no longer cold. A feeling of pleasant warmth mixed with a fierce joy engulfed him as *her* face began to form in the glow of the fire, pale-haired Emily, his first wife, his first love.

"Honored woman, worthy wife," he whispered.

Her lips moved, but there were no words in his head. He bent forward. It seemed that she was saying, "Renna. Renna." To confirm his impression the face altered slightly, became fuller, younger, darker in hue, and he was looking into his daughter's image with a heart that pounded.

"No, she is not dead," he whispered; for though he had never seen the image of a living person before, he could not accept the implication of Renna's image before him now. The thought that she might have gone to the

Place across the River without his having seen her once more was agony.

Finally the face again became the smiling visage of Emily.

"You must tell me," he demanded.

The manitou's smile faded, and she looked from one side to the other, her eyes wide and frightened, her lips forming the word, "Renna. Renna. Renna."

The import was clear. Renna was in danger. A feeling of helplessness overcame Renno, for his daughter was thousands of miles away, across a wide expanse of the continent and the Atlantic Ocean.

He lifted his arms to chant a prayer for guidance to the manitous. The snowflakes fell in silence. The only sound was the small, cheery crackling of his fire.

In the darkness beyond the glow of this fire something moved.

"Father," he cried as the warrior Ghonkaba stood before him, so seemingly solid that Renno wanted to leap to his feet to embrace him. "My father, guide me, speak to me."

"The story of our small lives, my son, is told by the wind briefly, and we must seize the moment. We must know when the wind blows change."

"I hear," Renno whispered.

"There will be pain. For you, for others. Be strong. The wind blows. Duty is defined by those who are dear to you, not by those who listen not."

The manitou of Ghonkaba seldom came to Renno. He let his eyes drink in the stalwart form, the bronzed skin, the strong limbs clad in traditional Seneca garb.

"I understand, Father," Renno said. "But what of Renna? If I go, will I be able to see her with Europe at war, with French ports blockaded by the British?"

"Consider the Old Ones," the manitou said. "The Old Ones know."

The cold crept back into Renno's limbs, penetrating to his bones. He covered over the remains of his fire, heard the coals sizzle as they, too, were cooled by the snow, and left his shelter to run through a diminishing fall

of flakes, to stretch his legs to their utmost until exertion
stopped his shivering.

When Renno arrived in the village, he was damp with
melted snow and his own perspiration. Gaunt with fasting,
he let Beth fuss over him. She pushed him into a hot tub
and saw to the preparation of food while he bathed.

He ate hungrily, in silence, Beth watching patiently.
She knew he would speak when he was ready. He saw the
joy reflected in her smile when he said, "It will be good to
see William and Estrela."

The Seneca elders gathered that very night. As Renno
entered the council longhouse, he saw Beth seated with
Toshabe, Ena, and Ah-wa-o, for Renno has requested that
matrons of the tribe be present. Rusog was also here, along
with Se-quo-i and half-a-dozen senior Cherokee warriors,
for so closely intertwined were the destinies of the Seneca
with the Cherokee that anything affecting the Seneca had
significance to Rusog and his people.

There was an air of expectancy among the audience.
As Renno rose, an aging Pine Tree warrior—one of the few
who remained who had fought with Ghonkaba against the
British in the Great White Man's War—urged silence.
Slowly the mutter of talk faded.

Renno was dressed as the sachem, in dark buckskin
accented by decorations of white. His hair, which had
grown long during the winter, was in braids, and he wore
the totems of his clan. He had the bearing of a chief, and
when he began to speak, his words were honored by complete attention and silence.

"In the long ago, the prophet Dekanawidah had a
vision. He saw a great spruce tree reaching through the
sky to the land of the Master of Life. He called it the Tree
of Great Peace, and it represented the sisterhood of all
tribes. Its five roots were called by the names of the five
tribes of the Iroquois. He spoke to the people of three
great things, and each of those three was a duality: health
of body and health of mind; peace between men and peace
between tribes; conduct and thought based on right and
justice, and respect for the rights of all."

"So it was," muttered Toshabe.

"But not all of the people agreed with Dekanawidah and his Great Peace," Renno went on. "They clung to the old way, which led to bloodletting among tribes, the killing of brother by brother; and so came Hai-en-wat-ha."

A sigh came from the gathered people, for Hai-en-wat-ha—Hiawatha—was a legendary hero of all Iroquois, and they never tired of hearing of his deeds.

"Now the Onondaga were a bloodthirsty tribe, always at war with the Huron. The strife and the killing of brother by brother filled Hiawatha with sadness, so that he began to travel among the people, from tribe to tribe, speaking of the Great Peace, and of Dekanawidah's Tree. In the end even the fierce Onondaga became a part of the League of the Longhouse People, and there was peace."

"Until the whitefaces came," someone said.

"So," Renno said. "Now there are those who, not unlike Hiawatha and Dekanawidah, speak of peace. You heard the council of Handsome Lake, as voiced by Good Hunter. You have heard Renno, sachem of the Seneca, tell you that our path is that traveled by the wise leaders of the United States."

A mutter of protest began. Renno bowed his head, lifted one hand. "Hear me," he said. "This I have said. You listen, but you do not hear."

"Do you liken yourself to Dekanawidah and to Hiawatha?" a young voice demanded.

"You have said, not I," Renno replied quietly. "I am Renno. My father was Ghonkaba, who led us here to live among our Cherokee brothers and chose the way that we have followed. The blood of my great-grandfather, also called Renno, runs in my veins, and it is the blood of the whitefaces."

He paused. The silence was absolute.

"I have heard that some say I forget that the blood of the people of the great Ghonka also fills my body. No man says this to my face, but it is said, nevertheless. I do not forget, nor will I ever; but the winds of change are blowing, and I have decided that it is time for another to advise you."

"No, no," someone shouted.

"I leave you with this," Renno said. "My brother, my father-by-marriage, and I all saw the results of bad council at the place of the fallen timbers, when the long-knife soldiers of the United States defeated the Indians of many tribes, Indians who outnumbered them greatly. I saw the bodies of my brothers lying among the twisted trees. I smelled their blood, and I do not want to live long enough to smell the blood of my Seneca and Cherokee brothers.

"I have said that I will not leave you again. This promise I will keep, at least in part. I will not leave you while I am your sachem. For this reason I have called the matrons of the tribe here, together with us, for to them belongs the duty of selecting a new sachem."

"No, we will have you!" someone protested.

"I, of course, have no say in who the matrons will name to advise you and lead you," Renno said, "but I think that I do have the right to say that the traditions of Ghonka, Renno, Ja-gonh, and Ghonkaba should be preserved, and so I suggest to you, honored mothers, that you name my brother, El-i-chi, son of Ghonkaba, to follow me in the office that I have not always, I fear, served well."

El-i-chi leaped to his feet. "Renno is sachem of the Seneca," he said, "and will remain so."

Renno shook his head sadly. "No, Brother, it is too late."

"I am shaman," El-i-chi replied. "I do not care to abandon that responsibility. If you are determined in this course of action, Brother, there is another in whose veins runs the blood of the white Indian, another who will make a great sachem, for have not the manitous predicted that Little Hawk, son of Renno, will be chief?"

"Hear, hear!" cried a Pine Tree warrior.

Little Hawk, glancing first at Naomi, seated next to Beth, rose to make his first oration before the tribe as a whole. He swallowed hard, then began.

"I am so greatly honored by my uncle El-i-chi's praise that I am speechless. . . ."

For a long moment it appeared that he had spoken the literal truth. Then he continued.

"I must, however, decline the honor of being considered as sachem. You know I wear the uniform of the United States. Although I have written to resign my commission, I am still a member of the United States Marine Corps until I receive notice that my resignation has been accepted. And I, too, will be leaving you."

Naomi's eyes widened.

Little Hawk sat down.

Toshabe, the tribe's senior matron, came to her feet. "My grandson," she said in even, calm tones, "has proven himself to be a great warrior. Indeed, he has the blood of Seneca sachems. He is worthy of becoming sachem in the manner of the two Rennos, of Ghonkaba, and of Ja-gonh—but not at this time, when his mind is as divided as the blood in his veins. Not when he cannot decide whether he is Seneca or white."

Renno saw his son flush. His own expression remained somber, for he, like everyone else, was surprised by Toshabe's words. In saying that her grandson was not worthy of the leadership of the tribe, she was also striking out at her own son, at Renno himself. He knew well the pain it must cost her to speak thus; he also had to admit that she spoke wisdom.

"It is desirable that we have a sachem with both feet in our world," Toshabe went on.

Though she did not say that a sachem of the Seneca should not have a white wife, Renno caught the clear implication.

"Although it hurts my heart to say the things I have said," Toshabe continued, "I have done so because I am charged by the manitous to serve the tribe to the best of my ability as senior matron. I therefore advance the name of my youngest, El-i-chi, to be sachem. He knows where his heart is."

Renno stood with his head bowed, his emotions riotous but not showing on his face. *So. It has come to this.*

Other matrons and the senior warriors were agreeing with Toshabe. For a moment, when Renno realized that he was no longer sachem, he felt as if he had been ripped out of time and place, as if he were a man without a country; but he was Renno, and he was wise.

It is right, he said to himself.

Each man has the right to determine his own destiny within the will of the manitous and the Master of Life. He had chosen his. He had chosen to counsel peace with the United States, advising his people to learn the white man's ways. But the older generation of Seneca was naturally resistant to change.

He prayed silently. *Perhaps in the long run my teachings will convince the young ones. Perhaps I will not have to smell the sharp odor of the blood of my brothers again.*

Little Hawk rose once more and bowed to his grandmother. "What you have said, Grandmother, is true. I am not yet worthy. For you to have said otherwise would have been against the honor of the Seneca."

Renno saw in his son's eyes that he, too, harbored hurt and felt more than he was saying. Little Hawk had never expressed a desire to become sachem; why, then, had it been necessary for his grandmother, in effect, to call him a white man? Was he not a worthy Seneca?

Again Renno spoke. "Brothers, Mother, honorable Pine Trees, worthy matrons, hear me for the last time. Hear my plea for forgiveness, for it is true that in the past I have spent much time in the white man's world, on the white man's business, without attention to the affairs of my own people. For this I am sorry."

"I will *not* be sachem," El-i-chi declared. "My sachem is Renno."

"Hear me," said a Pine Tree warrior, creaking to his feet with the aid of one of the poles that supported the roof. "We have been led by a descendant of the white Indian from before the time of the Great White Man's War. I fear that without such leadership there will be petty jealousy. Remember the time of the pretender, who, in the absence of Renno, wanted to be sachem. There will be internal struggle for leadership, and this we will not have." He turned to face Renno. "Will you not reconsider?"

"This I cannot do," Renno said.

The Pine Tree faced El-i-chi. "Then it will be El-i-chi who holds the war club of the sachem."

"El-i-chi!" shouted the matrons, almost as one. "El-i-chi is sachem!"

El-i-chi rose and stepped to face Renno.

"Ahhh," said those gathered in the council longhouse, as El-i-chi did something he had never done before and would never do again. He knelt before Renno.

"Thus," he said, in a loud voice, as if daring anyone to make little of his gesture, to call him less the man for bowing to another, "do I swear my loyalty to the true sachem of our people, to my brother, Renno." He rose. "I will serve in Renno's place only until he desires to return to his place."

"So be it," said Toshabe. Only Renno saw the tears beginning to form in her eyes.

Father and son, and their wives, crossed the high passes of the mountains in a time of melting snow. All four were mounted on horses from Huntington Castle, though occasionally Renno and Little Hawk descended to explore the neighboring woods at a run. Some nights they spent with Cherokee families, many of whom had adopted the log cabins of the whites. Other nights were spent under the stars or in whatever shelter could be found. Naomi declared the journey to be strenuous, but bearable because her husband was at her side.

White settlers had pushed farther into the mountains. They looked upon the travelers—particularly the men—with suspicion, until they heard Renno and Little Hawk speak in cultured English tones. It was not all that unusual, they decided, to see bronzed men of the frontier dressed like Indians, and so they accepted the two as easily as they did Beth and Naomi, whose beauty they openly admired.

When they reached the eastern foothills, Beth sold the horses, for stagecoaches—uncomfortable though they were—had become the fastest means of traveling the east-west distances of North Carolina. She parted with her steeds reluctantly, haggling long and hard, not because of the money involved but because she wanted the purchaser to value the horses as highly as she had. She had bred, named, and raised each of them, and she wanted them to be so costly that good treatment from their new owner would be ensured.

Spring met them as they crossed the Piedmont plateau, which was beginning to be quite thickly populated, and descended to the rolling, sandy hills that in turn gave way to the coastal plain. It was warm and sunny as they crossed the Cape Fear River to Wilmington and were greeted with enthusiasm by Adan Bartolome, Beth's brother-in-law and a captain in her shipping business.

Adan could not wait to show Beth one of two new Huntington ships. She lay at anchor in the middle of the river, an impressive square-rigger with the name *Beth Huntington* painted on her bow and stern.

"I didn't authorize this," Beth protested. "You know, Adan, that my ships—"

"*Our* ships," Adan corrected mildly, for he had been buying into the company slowly but steadily.

"Our ships, then," Beth granted, "have always carried a name relating to the Seneca."

Adan laughed. He was aging well, was still darkly handsome with not a trace of gray in his wavy hair. He had the rich coloring of his Spanish blood, sparkling white teeth, and he affected a bushy mustache that hid his upper lip.

"Lady Beth," he said, "this ship, too, is a lady. She's built to engage in the East Indian trade. She can carry huge cargos, and it pleased me to honor you by naming her after you."

"You're very sweet," Beth replied, taking his hand. "I'll admit that I, too, am pleased." She looked at Renno. "I guess this reprobate husband of mine has had enough ships named after him, after all."

"I hope so," Adan declared, his dark eyes creased with a smile, "because we named the new schooner the *Comtesse Renna*."

"Of that I heartily approve," Renno agreed.

"But you haven't told me why we are being graced

with your company," Adan said. "I know Nathan and his family will be thrilled to see you all." He winked at Naomi. "And we'll have to show this young lady the town, won't we?"

"I've already seen so much that I'm dizzy," Naomi said with a laugh.

"And young Hawk," Adan said. "You've filled out well since the last time I saw you."

Little Hawk grinned.

A reunion dinner was held that night at the home of Renno's cousin, Nathan Ridley. Here Renno learned that Nathan's son, James, was captain of the *Comtesse Renna* and would be with them during the voyage across the Atlantic.

Within a few days the second of the new ships of the Huntington Shipping Company came up the Cape Fear River laden with a cargo of rum and coffee beans from Jamaica. Renno and Beth were on the dock with Adan to see the sleek and agile schooner maneuvered skillfully to her mooring place in front of the Huntington warehouses.

James Ridley was a tall, young man in his late twenties. He looked very much like his father and had Nathan's serious manner. He bowed to Beth and took Renno's hand.

"Good to see you, Cousin Renno," he said. "And you, ma'am. It will be my pleasure to show you your new ship, if that pleases you."

"It pleases me very much," Beth replied.

James escorted Beth onto the deck of the *Comtesse Renna*. "She's built like a Baltimore clipper," he explained, "sleek and sharp lined. She can't carry as much cargo as one of the square-riggers, but she's fleet enough to sail away from a French or English cruiser."

"She looks quite yare," Beth commented.

"Built in Baltimore of good American oak," James replied. "Check the joining of the deck planks. True craftsmanship."

"You keep the ship in excellent condition, Captain," Renno said.

"Well, we don't eat off the deck, but I want it that clean," James said. "The crew understands me."

Under heavy booms, the house of the schooner was painted white with adjustable blue shutters over all of the glass. Beth listened with genuine interest as James Ridley talked knowledgeably about the ship's modern pumps and windlasses. The galley, well equipped and gleamingly clean, was the domain of a cranky Chinese man, of that never-never age that lies somewhere between fifty and finality.

"This is Han Lo," James introduced, and the cook bowed, grinning to show gaps in his teeth.

Back on deck, James pointed upward. "She's rigged in the fore-topsail style," he pointed out. "That makes her a bit less weatherly than a fore-and-after rigged schooner, but she has the advantage off the wind and on a reach."

Beth did not need explanations of James's salty terms. Renno didn't bother to ask.

"The mainmast has a hounded length of sixty-one feet, two inches," James went on.

"It soars to the heavens," Beth said, looking up to see the rigging outlined against a clear, blue sky.

"I don't know whether you've noticed, Lady Beth," James said, "but the men have just raised the flag signifying that the owner is aboard. I want you to know that we're honored."

"Will you still feel honored when I tell you that you're going to be saddled with the owner all the way to England and back?" Beth asked.

"Most emphatically," James said, bowing again.

Chapter Three

To Adan Bartolome's surprise, the young lovers Naomi and Little Hawk were on deck as the *Comtesse Renna* left the docks in Wilmington, though the day was made wet and raw by a light, blowing rain. He wondered how long they would remain.

Adan, who had not seen his sister, Estrela, and her growing brood in three years, had switched assignments with young James Ridley and was commanding the sleek schooner as she made her way down the broad, muddy Cape Fear toward the mouth of the river. Over the centuries the river had been called by various names, such as the Jordan and the Clarendon. Once an attempt had been made to alter the name of the barren head that gave the river its name to Cape Faire; but the appellation of dire import persisted, and so it was that the Cape Fear River entered the sea just to the west of the Cape of Fear.

Before making the southward bend into the Atlantic,

the river flowed past tall pine trees looming up through the blowing mist. The newlyweds watched for a while; but then, dampened and chilled, they gave up sightseeing and retired to their cabin. Seeing them go, Adan grinned and felt a quick stab of envy, which he quickly banished from his mind.

Adan had never married. He knew women, of course. In Wilmington he was welcome in the home and bed of a buxom widow, who would have liked nothing better than to hear him say the magic words leading to the altar. But Adan had never addressed the subject at all. If pressed, he would have said that it was too late for him to think of matrimony.

Girls were available in every port for a handsome sailor with money in his purse, but it was not Adan's love of variety alone that kept him dedicated to his single state. The reason was here, aboard the *Comtesse Renna*, in the form of a mature, flame-haired woman. For Adan had been in love with Beth from the first moment he saw her, so many years before. It was not a love that debilitated him and left him frustrated and empty, but it was love; if he couldn't have Beth as a permanent fixture in his life, he would have no woman other than on a purely temporary basis.

Adan, who had hired the crew for the schooner himself, knew each man by his first name and by his reputation. Before turning the new schooner over to James, he had sailed her in a variety of weather conditions, learning her moods and vagaries while training the crew to a crisp efficiency. It was that expertise that saw the ship's sails go up without a hitch, so that *Renna* swept down the broad river under a cloud of canvas. She burst out over the river bar, with the bald head of Cape Fear to the east and shoals stretching southeastward into the broad ocean, where the gloomy day blended sea and sky into a nebulous unity.

It was an excellent day to exit the Cape Fear in safety. Wilmington was not the busiest port on the eastern seaboard, but enough ships went in and out to make it worthwhile for an ambitious English captain to maintain a watch on the river. To confuse the blockading Britisher, Adan sailed straight south, away from the shoals, before turning at dusk toward the east. As expected, he sighted the sails of the British cruiser just off the southeastern end of the shoals. The Britisher put on more sail and gave chase.

Adan ordered a full suit of canvas for *Renna*. She lowered her leeward rail into the foaming seas and drove into the huge, smooth-topped swells with her sails thundering. Even before nightfall, the British cruiser was falling behind. By morning, the sea was empty save for *Renna*.

Naomi felt that her life had begun on the day when she was married twice, once by a Methodist minister and once by a Seneca shaman. She saw everything with new eyes, and it was all made wonderful by the tall, strong man who was constantly at her side.

All except for the seasickness. This, too, was a new thing for her, but it was an experience—she told Beth— that she would gladly forego. After she had been confined to her bed for a day and a night, she let Beth drive Little Hawk out of the cabin so that the older woman could sponge bathe her, freshening her with cool, clean water. At Beth's insistence Naomi took a swallow or two of tea and a bite of biscuit, and to her surprise both stayed down.

"Believe me," Beth said, "you will live, even if at times you think you don't want to."

"I'm beginning to hope so," Naomi replied, covering a burp with the back of one pale hand. She managed a weak smile. "I have so many reasons to live, Beth."

"I know. Isn't it lovely?"

"One reason I haven't told anyone yet, not even Little Hawk."

Beth raised one eyebrow. Naomi placed her hand on her stomach and smiled.

"Oh, my darling girl," Beth said. "Is it true?"

"To the best of my knowledge," Naomi said. "For I have not—" She paused, and her pale face flushed. "I have not blooded since our wedding night."

"But that is wonderful." Beth was reckoning the time on her fingers. "Since you've missed two bloodings, I would say, my dear, that you are very much pregnant. And you haven't told Little Hawk?"

She told him that afternoon. She had been able to hold down more tea and biscuit and she was feeling much better, although the ship continued to go through a disturbing series of motions with each forward leap. Little Hawk's mouth dropped open, spread into a glad smile. He took both of her hands in his and kissed her tenderly, then leaped to his feet with a whoop.

Much to the amusement of the crew and to the puzzlement of the cook, Han Lo, Naomi's glad news sent father and son into a wild dance of celebration and thanksgiving. Beth, coming on deck, got into the mood of it, pounding out a rhythm on a barrel head with a belaying pin, while the two wild Indians whooped and chanted as they pranced around the deck. Naomi, too, came out of her cabin to see what was happening, and the fresh air, the brilliant sun, Little Hawk's evident joy at her news, made her forget her malady.

Fair weather and favorable winds blessed the *Renna* for days on end, until finally Adan called everyone on deck to show them Land's End, the distant southeastern tip of England. In the channel the winds moderated, and fog rose up from the warm waters to engulf the *Renna* in a clammy embrace. With all sails set skillfully to catch the smallest breath of air, the schooner ghosted past a lurking French cruiser. The Frenchman sent a shot after the schooner, but it was a futile gesture; the ball fell two hundred yards astern. And then, slowly, majestically, *Renna* was approaching the docks at Portsmouth.

Adan and Beth were eager to see William and Estrela. Not two hours after the ship was securely berthed, Adan had hired a coach and the party was off for Beaumont Manor, not far from London.

The English weather gave them its best face: a warmth that was unusual, cloudless skies, and pleasant breezes. Little Hawk rode atop the vehicle with the coachman, the better to see the countryside, he said, for the tailored neatness of the landscape pleased him and the thatched cottages alongside the road intrigued him with the mystery of the lives they contained. Finally they reached a graceful country manor sitting on a pleasant slope among wide-branched trees. A million birds serenaded the passage of the coach. A flock of sheep grazed in a meadow.

As it happened, the current lord of Beaumont Manor was enjoying a game of croquet with his wife and children on the front lawn when the coach came bouncing and creaking up the long drive and drew to a halt. Little Hawk, Naomi, and Renno stood aside as brothers and sisters met with shouts of delight and happy tears. The children, the youngest a tiny, blue-eyed, pale-haired moppet of less than two years, gathered around noisily.

William broke away to clasp Renno fondly in a very un-English way and to exchange the warrior's greeting with Little Hawk—expressing astonishment that enough time had passed to bring his old friend's son to manhood. He kissed Naomi's hand and shouted out over the boisterous voices of the young ones to Estrela to come and see the young beauty that Little Hawk had brought to them.

The children, five of them—the two eldest Beaumont siblings were away at school—gathered round to meet their uncle Renno and their cousins.

"Shy little beggars, aren't they?" William said to Renno, smiling fondly. "Not your typically well-behaved English children, I warrant. My wild Spanish wife tells me that I must not stifle their creative instincts and natural exuberance by being the stiff English father."

He took Renno's arm. "Look at them, Renno. Do you see anything unusual about any one of them?"

Renno nodded. "The littlest one," he said, "takes on the coloration and the hair of your English ancestry."

"Not mine," William replied.

Renno raised his eyebrows questioningly.

"*Yours,* old friend," William explained. "The child is your granddaughter, Emily Beth."

"Manitous," Renno whispered.

"By some black fate you have come just weeks too late to see Renna and Beau," William said.

It was not the time for further explanations. Renno knelt, looked into the face of the child, and saw Renna, saw the hair of Emily, his first beloved.

"Hello, Emily. May I call you that? Do you know who I am?"

She looked at him shyly.

"I'm your grandpa," Renno went on. "May Grandpa have a hug and a kiss?"

Emily, who was as curious as she was loving, toddled forward with her arms extended.

Beth, having heard about Emily Beth from Estrela, came to kneel beside Renno. She saw tears roll down her husband's face as he clasped the blue-eyed little girl to his breast.

Childbearing had broadened Estrela slightly, but she was still darkly beautiful as she presided over long, laughter-filled evenings of good food and good talk. For Renno, it was a time for reviving memories, going back to the occasion when William Huntington first saw Estrela as a captive of the Apache Indians of the American Southwest.

Renno's days were involved as much as possible with his granddaughter. She had been left in the care of William and Estrela after the comte de Beaujolais and his family had sailed from France to Portsmouth aboard a vessel carrying the diplomatic flag. Though Renna had originally planned to remain in England with her daughter, William explained, she had prevailed on her husband to let her accompany him to Portugal.

Renno immediately began to think of ways to get to see his daughter, for Beau had said that they would be abroad for an indefinite period.

"As I remember, Portugal is an ally of England's," Renno said.

"An old and honorable one," William agreed, "but if you're thinking of going there on an American ship, you'll still have to run the French blockade."

"Isn't it being done all the time?" Adan asked.

"Where there is money to be made, there you will find English ships," William said. "And trade continues between Portugal and England in spite of Napoleon's edicts."

"A bit of danger enhances profit," Adan put in.

"It sounds as if we're going to Lisbon," Beth said.

"Not 'we,'" Renno countered.

Beth smiled.

William and Estrela decided to give a ball to welcome home the daughter of the manor and to introduce Little Hawk and Naomi to English society. In preparation Naomi went with Beth to London, and they returned with a carriage load of plain and fancy gowns, dozens of pairs of shoes, and boxes of lacy undergarments. Still other boxes contained formal wear for Little Hawk and Renno.

Two days before the big event, the guest bedrooms of the manor were filled, and carriages were constantly coming and going. Naomi marveled at the elaborate preparations consuming the entire household, and she offered her services to Beth, who was helping Estrela manage the extra staff hired for the occasion. But she was told with a smile to go play with her husband—something she was more than willing to do.

At first, after telling Little Hawk that she was pregnant, Naomi had found herself being treated as if she were made of eggshells. But with a little prodding, she soon cured her husband of that, so that he matched her eagerness with his own natural passions. To the fond amusement of all, the newlyweds were always going off together.

They walked the manicured gardens. They explored equestrian trails that Beth and William had ridden as children. Estrela, who had six offspring, told Naomi that riding wouldn't hurt her or the child. Since Estrela had the experience to back up such a statement, Little Hawk "allowed" Naomi to ride a calm and gentle mare, and his reward was the discovery of a hidden, grassy glade where young lovers could practice their favorite pastime under the warm English sun.

On the night of the ball Beaumont Manor gleamed with light. Sprightly music came from the ballroom on the second floor, poured outward through the open windows, and rolled down the stairs to the great room where gentlemen gathered to sip brandy and smoke cigars. Here Renno was presented to Sir Arthur Wellesley.

"Sir Arthur is very military," William had warned, "but I think you'll find him interesting. He is definitely a man on the rise, and I believe we will hear more of him as time goes by."

Wellesley was a distinguished man. He wore his hair old-style, pulled back into a tie at the nape of his neck.

"Sir Arthur is preparing to take a military expedition to Copenhagen," William said as he completed the introductions.

"Indeed," Renno replied, nodding politely in Wellesley's direction.

Wellesley nodded in return. "You have the bearing of a military man, sir," he remarked.

"Oh, Renno and his sister were scouts for George Washington," William explained with a wry smile.

"I say, your sister?" Wellesley asked. "That, then, is why our generals lost the colonies. You chaps cheated by bringing ladies into it."

Renno laughed cordially. "I can safely say, sir, that it would have taken a disproportionate share of General Washington's manpower to keep my sister out of it."

"Well, I happen to be a student of that war," Wellesley replied. "Our problem, you know, was that the king depended too much on mercenaries. Damned Hessians had no reason to fight, did they?"

"At times they fought well," Renno offered.

"And I fear that we did not send our best military minds to the affair," Wellesley went on. "No troops under my command would have been caught by surprise as the Hessians were at Trenton. And I most surely would not have allowed myself to be surrounded at Yorktown."

"I see," Renno said diplomatically.

"Yes, it would have been a different story if I'd been there," Wellesley said.

"Perhaps," Renno replied, "the story would have

been longer in the telling, but the denouement would have been the same."

Wellesley bristled, then he smiled coldly. "Indeed."

William intervened, easing the rising tension. "Well, we'll never know, will we, Sir Arthur."

"Perhaps we shall, if the Americans continue to allow deserters from the Royal Navy to serve on their ships," Wellesley declared.

"I believe, Sir Arthur, that England has her hands full with the little crop head," Renno countered.

"For the moment," Wellesley conceded. He looked up and away, and his profile was hard for a man so young. Renno felt a sense of strength emanating from him, and he agreed with William's assessment that the world would be hearing from this young man.

"For the moment," Wellesley repeated.

Several days after the ball a note from Sir Arthur Wellesley arrived at Beaumont Manor. It was an invitation to join him in a fox hunt.

Renno deduced that Wellesley was feeling a compulsion to prove British superiority to the upstart Americans, particularly Renno himself. The ladies were also invited, presumably to witness the humiliation. Estrela and Beth had to scramble about to find hunting costumes for all concerned, and on the morning of the hunt they arrived at the estate where Wellesley was passing the time before joining his expeditionary force.

After greeting them, Sir Arthur placed Renno and Little Hawk directly at his side, in the fore of the mass of red-clad riders.

It was a glorious day of bright sun and pleasant temperatures. The English saddle was new to Little Hawk, so Renno gave his son suggestions. Little Hawk refused to bounce up and down at each step of the horse. He found that it was possible to take a deep seat even on an English saddle, and he soon learned the little mannerisms of his horse, so that by the time the hounds struck the scent of a fox, he was in control.

As Wellesley put his horse to a hedgerow and lifted

the animal up and over in a smooth flow of motion, Renno and Little Hawk were right with him. Wellesley's astonishment was written on his face. And so it was, over fences, water courses, and stone walls, until at last the pack, with excited bayings and obscenely superior numbers, pulled the fox out of a hole and tore it to bits.

Back at Wellesley's manor, Sir Arthur sought out Renno, Little Hawk, and their ladies. "Well, sirs, what think you of the hunt?"

"A pleasant ride," Renno said diplomatically.

"And you, sir?" Wellesley asked Little Hawk.

"As my father said, a pleasant ride, but, I venture, an exercise in bullying futility, hunting something with dozens of dogs, something inedible at that."

Wellesley fumed, then burst into laughter. He had discovered the Americans to be excellent riders, but he was not to be thwarted.

"Come along, then, all of you, please," he said, "for I have arranged a small entertainment for you. Beaumont has told me, Renno, that you are a good marksman."

On the rear grounds Wellesley had set up the apparatus for a down-the-line shooting contest. From the trap house a spring-loaded device flung out glass balls on different trajectories to simulate the erratic flight of live birds.

"In the last century, when the sport was developed," Wellesley explained to his guests while readying a finely engraved shotgun, "live birds were used as targets. But when the sport began to gain popularity, you can imagine it made severe demands on the avian population."

Wellesley demonstrated. He called out an order, and a glass ball shot out of the trap house, to be broken perfectly with Wellesley's shot. Feathers placed inside the ball floated down to make the effect quite realistic. He broke five balls in quick succession, then handed the shotgun to Renno.

It was, Renno saw, a beautifully made weapon, but it was an unfamiliar one. He hefted it, placed it to his shoulder once or twice to get the feel of it, then nodded when he was ready. He treated the shotgun as if it were a rifle, an extension of his arm. He pointed his finger at the target without sighting along the barrel, broke five erratic targets in short order, and handed the gun back to Wellesley.

Once again Wellesley's chagrin was evident. The man, Renno thought, would never make a good diplomat, for he had difficulty hiding his feelings. Renno decided to rub salt in Wellesley's little wounds.

"It's an amusing game," he told Sir Arthur, "and rather good for training the eye, but there is a sameness to it, don't you think?"

"Judging from your performance, I daresay you've played the game before," Wellesley replied.

"Oh, no," Renno said. "Actually not. However, I find that it is rather a simple matter to knock down such targets when their flight is so predictable and the pattern of the shot spreads so widely."

"Hummph," Wellesley said.

"The American Indian takes fast-flying birds with bow and arrow," Renno went on, continuing to needle Wellesley, for he was becoming a bit put off by the Englishman's superior manner.

Wellesley laughed incredulously. "I would be pleased to witness such skill," he said.

Renno looked at William and nodded. Within minutes an English longbow was provided, along with an ancient quiver holding arrows. Renno selected carefully, for the antique weapon had not been used in a long time and some of the arrows had become warped. When he was satisfied, he pulled the bow once, twice, three times to test it, then nocked an arrow and nodded his readiness.

He knew that he had set himself a difficult task. The glass balls were small. They left the trap-house door at great speed, and their path was—contrary to Renno's statement—quite unpredictable. When a ball flashed out and away, he blanked his mind and shot instinctively. The arrow smashed the ball, sending a waft of feathers downward. Before the next ball could be released, Renno handed the bow back to a servant.

"Amazing," Wellesley exclaimed. "But don't stop now, man."

Renno laughed. "Sir Arthur," he said, "I was very lucky to hit with my first shot. I would be a fool to try to improve on that performance, wouldn't I?"

Wellesley was profoundly impressed. "I'd give my left arm to have a dozen like you with my army," he said.

"Sorry," Beth said, "there's only one of him, and I have prior claim, Sir Arthur."

Little Emily Beth was a delight to both Renno and to Beth, although seeing the child in Renno's arms never failed to remind Beth that she, over the long years, had never conceived. It hurt her heart to think that had God willed, the child in Renno's arms might have been from her own loins, but she accepted the little girl as a granddaughter and showered love on her.

When Wellesley said good-bye and went off to join his unit for the invasion of French-dominated Denmark, Beth could see her husband becoming noticeably more restless. Adan had already left the manor for Portsmouth, where he was amassing a cargo in the holds of the *Comtesse Renna*.

Now the discussion between Beth and Renno reached a point of heated intensity.

"You know as well as I," she argued, "that the Royal Navy dominates the waters around Europe. I am entitled to fly a British flag on my ship, so that there will be no danger to her from British vessels, and precious little from the French."

"I would be more at ease," Renno countered, "if you were here with Estrela and Naomi."

"My place is at your side."

"Not on this voyage."

"Beau took Renna."

"Under a flag of diplomacy."

A similar discussion was going on in the bedroom occupied by Naomi and Little Hawk, for Little Hawk was determined to see Renna.

"If you go I will go," Naomi declared. "I do so want to meet your sister."

"You have other responsibilities," Little Hawk argued, gently patting Naomi's stomach, which was beginning to show slightly. "Look, we'll be back well before it is time for the baby. You'll be here with good medical care, with Estrela—who probably knows more about birthing babies than most doctors—and with Beth."

And so it went.

Renno held his wife close to him. "Wife," he whispered, "it will please me if you will honor my wishes."

"It will be perfectly safe," Beth insisted. "We'll sail down to Lisbon, we'll see Renna and Beau. We'll sail back here and then back home."

"Please," he said. It was at once request and command.

She sighed, giving up the battle. "Yes, if you so ask."

Later, when it was all over, Renno would remember this moment and be thankful that Beth loved him enough to subordinate her own desires to his judgment, for finding Renna and Beau was not to be as simple as she had portrayed it. It was not to be a matter of simply sailing down to Lisbon.

The French cruiser carrying Napoleon's personal representative and his lady had managed to exit the English Channel without incident. Twice, as it sailed south into the Bay of Biscay, distant sails were sighted. Each time the captain ordered the crew on alert, even though the white flag of diplomacy flew from his masts. The war between France and England was an old, festering sore, and in the open sea a British captain, longing for prize money, might be deliberately blind to the little flags. The French captain—making no secret of his distaste for his diplomatic mission and the risks to which it put his vessel and men—explained this to Beau and Renna.

It saddened Renna to see the crew so agitated at the sight of a British sail. "I wouldn't say that they're not brave," she told Beau when the captain returned to the quarterdeck, "but one would have to admit that they *dread* an encounter with a ship of the British navy."

Beau nodded glumly. "In spite of all our efforts, that tiny island dominates the seas," he said. "And that single factor, more than any other, will contribute to our downfall."

"Beau," she said, shocked by his glumness. "You can't mean it. All the brilliant victories, the invincible French army—"

"With all of Europe prostrate before it, the French army could not travel to England's white cliffs, even though, on a clear day, the generals could see the enemy coast with the naked eye."

"Ah, well," Renna said. "We must not think such black thoughts on such a beautiful day."

They were on deck watching the sunset, and Renna had a holiday spirit. The warm weather, gentle breezes, the pleasant loping motion of the ship could bring nothing but optimism to her mind. She was pleased that she had been able to persuade Beau to take her along instead of leaving her in England; she missed Emily Beth, but she knew that her daughter was in the best of hands. Some of the sweetest times with Beau had come to them aboard one ship or another, and it was exhilarating to be off and away on another adventure with him.

"I am my father's daughter," she told him, "for I have his desire to explore the far shores of lands previously unseen."

Beau put his arm around Renna and held her close. She, in her mood of gaiety, felt that the time had come to give him the news she had been keeping from him. The way her stomach was losing its flatness and the way her face was filling out, she would not be able to keep it from him much longer.

"Beau, would you like Emily Beth to have a brother or a sister?" she asked.

"A brother, I suppose," he replied, "although when the time comes, I will not be disappointed with another little one who looks like you."

"Darling, the time is not too far off," she answered, smiling up at him.

He frowned, then burst into a glad smile. "No! Now? When did you know?"

"Before we left Paris," she admitted.

His face darkened. "You tricked me."

"Yes," she agreed, kissing him on the cheek, "for I knew that you'd be stuffy if you knew."

"Then it's—it's—"

"Unless you complete your mission quickly, Emily Beth's little brother might be born in Lisbon," she said.

"And I thought you were just becoming more . . . well, voluptuous. How can it be that I did not guess the truth?"

She laughed. "You never were very observant," she chided. "I fear that you have always wished for one of those women painted by David. I think you'd have no complaint if I became quite fat."

He laughed with her. "It would still be you, my love."

For days the favorable winds held and there were no alarms, but one night the Atlantic struck, sending a howling northwester down upon the cruiser to bury her bow in the sea, to lift her and smash her down, down, into the briny troughs as the winds howled in her reduced sails.

The ship had rounded Cabo Finisterre on the northwest coast of Spain before the storm rose to its full violence and shifted its winds more to the westward. This turn of events put the ship at risk, with winds forcing her toward a lee shore. While the captain cursed the day he had been assigned to transport a French diplomat and his lady, the crew worked mightily, scurrying up the riggings to adjust the sails, fighting to gain seaway away from the shore.

For two days and two nights they fought the battle. In a cold, roaring dawn the captain sought out Beau and said, "I'm sorry, sir, but we will have to seek shelter."

"Short of Lisbon?" Beau asked.

"At Porto, I'm afraid," the captain said.

Beau nodded. He knew little of Portugal, but he had read that the Portuguese called Lisbon their first city and Porto their fifth, with no second, third, or fourth in be-

tween. There would be no communications between Porto
and Lisbon except by sea or by slow-moving coach.

"Captain," he said, "the safety of your ship is para-
mount." He laughed. "Not to mention our own hides, eh?"

It was a tense time when, in gale-whipped rain, the
ship turned her stern to the westerly wind and ran on
short sails directly toward the rocky shore. The transition
was sudden. One moment the ship was climbing the back
of a running wave to drop off the front into a trough with a
thunderous bang, the next she was sailing serenely in calm
waters as she passed behind the protective land shielding
the harbor at Porto from the storm.

The arrival of the French man-of-war caused a stir in
the port. Even as her anchor chains rattled and the hooks
secured her, uniformed men in small boats were putting
out from the pebbly shore and the docks to converge on
her. A voice cried out in passable French, "Ahoy, the
cruiser, you have entered a neutral port. Under the rules
of war you are to be interned. Meanwhile, you will stand
by to be boarded."

"If you will look, sir, you will see that we sail under
the flag of diplomacy," the captain called back as the small
boats drew near. He turned to Beau. "I think it wise that I
call the crew to stations."

"I am on a mission of peace," Beau said. "Let them
come aboard."

It was evident from the actions of the Porto officials
that they were not accustomed to dealing with interna-
tional dignitaries. Beau explained over and over again that
he was on a diplomatic mission.

"A state of war does not exist between your country
and mine," he told the police and local military leaders
who had come aboard. "We are at peace, and I am an
accredited representative of the emperor of France, sent to
speak with your government in Lisbon."

"While it is true that we here in the north are far from
the seat of government," said an impressively uniformed
man of some years, "we are not ignorant of the fact that
your Napoleon is amassing an army to march on Portugal
through the lands of his ally, Spain."

"A state of peace exists between our countries," Beau insisted. "I intend to speak about this with your government in Lisbon. I'm sure, General, that if you will look over my credentials, you will see that it is necessary for this ship to continue on its voyage to Lisbon."

"Perhaps you'd better come ashore and speak with our mayor," the general said.

"Yes, I will go with you," Beau agreed. He managed a word with the captain while Renna was readying herself to accompany him, for nothing, Beau felt, would more effectively prove that his mission was peaceful than having his wife with him.

"Be patient, Captain," he said. "I will be back shortly, and as soon as the storm abates, we will sail to the south."

Just before disembarking, Beau overheard the captain giving instructions to his first mate. "If M'sieur le comte does not return within six hours with permission to sail, we will force that permission ourselves. Prepare the men accordingly."

Beau started to warn the captain, but the Portuguese were at his elbow, urging him none too gently into the waiting boat.

Ashore, Beau and Renna were taken to an old and impressive public building, where Beau tried to make it clear to a series of local officials that he was a bona-fide diplomatic envoy on an important mission to Lisbon.

The mayor of Porto was not available at the moment, he was told. He and Renna were escorted into a small anteroom.

"How long will we have to wait to be treated with the courtesy to which we are entitled?" Beau demanded, for his patience was wearing thin.

It was two hours before a man finally came to say, "The mayor will see you now."

The mayor of Porto, Senhor José Manuel Lisboa de Carvalho, was a man of silver-haired dignity and a hearing problem. He spoke no French. He was moderately proficient in Spanish, so it was Renna who translated Beau's request for an immediate release of the ship and safe passage to Lisbon. But even as she spoke, the rattle of gunfire came from the harbor. The mayor moved to the window and turned to face them, his face grim.

"Come," he said, "and see the results of your peaceful mission."

Beau's anger soared when he saw the smoke of battle rising from the cruiser. Musket and pistol fire were intense, sending up a blue cloud. The Porto police and militia began to scramble back into their boats. Soon the boats, only partially loaded, were being rowed away from the man-of-war at a frantic pace. A man at the stern of one boat suddenly doubled over and fell forward, hit by a musket ball from the cruiser.

"No, damn it, no!" Beau exclaimed. "The fools!"

The fight was a brief one. The well-trained crew had killed several Porto policemen and militiamen and had cleared the cruiser's decks. As Beau watched, helpless, sails went up and the ship beat her way out of the harbor into the diminishing storm.

The place of internment for the comte and his lady was a comfortable apartment in the mayor's mansion. Uniformed police guarded the doors. All that day and into the next, Beau asked in vain for another audience with the mayor. The guards were openly antagonistic, for several of their comrades had been killed by the crew of the French ship.

On the morning of the third day Beau heard mournful music coming from the street. Going to the window, he looked out and saw a funeral procession moving along the boulevard, several caskets draped in black. One of the caskets was smaller than the others—evidently for a child. He called to Renna, and they both watched.

The whole town, it seemed, was in the procession, the women weeping and supported by their husbands. Several people looked up and, seeing Renna and Beau at the window, shook their fists.

A guard came by. "The little casket, it is for my nephew," he explained. "He went with the police without his father's knowledge, he was so eager to see the ship of the famous Napoleon. We are told that it was your captain's own bullet that killed the boy."

Stung by this outrage, Beau stammered an apology. The guard turned away without acknowledging it.

Day after day Beau pleaded, stormed, demanded that he be taken before the mayor. As the days became weeks, he insisted that word be sent to the government in Lisbon.

It was news from the south that gained Beau another interview with the mayor. It was true, he was told, that a French army was preparing to march through Spain toward Portugal because that country continued to refuse to obey Napoleon's edicts against trade with the British. Even the mayor of provincial Porto knew the might of Napoleon. If, indeed, the imprisoned Frenchman was a representative of the emperor, and if, as the mayor feared, the French army would break through Portugal's weak defenses with impunity and suddenly appear on his doorstep, he did not want to be in a position of having defied the emperor's flag of truce.

"We have decided," the mayor said, "to send you to Lisbon."

"Thank you," Beau replied. "I must admit, sir, that it is high time."

"A small coastal schooner departs for the capital city in the morning," the mayor said. "You will be on it."

"Since all of my wife's belongings were aboard the ship," Beau said, "I would be very grateful if, before we leave, you would arrange for extra clothing for her. As you can see, she is with child and must have proper attire. Once we arrive in Lisbon, I can call upon my credit through the French offices to—"

"Your wife, Count, will be treated with all consideration," the mayor said. "The nuns in whose care she will be left will tend to her needs."

"I beg your pardon?" Renna asked, not waiting to translate the statement for Beau.

"Of course, you will not be accompanying your husband, madam—not in your delicate condition."

"Beau," she protested, her face strained, "he means to keep me here!"

Beau exploded. He leaped to his feet and advanced toward the startled mayor. Two burly policemen standing at the door rushed forward to seize him by the arms.

"My wife *will* accompany me," Beau insisted, and Renna translated.

"Consider this, sir," the mayor cautioned. "We have only your word that you are an accredited representative of the emperor of France."

"But you have my credentials!"

"Papers can be forged. Your people have committed crimes against the authority and the citizenry of Porto. Your wife, sir, will be held here until it is determined whether you are a diplomat as you claim, or the pirate that you seem to be, judging from the actions of your crew."

Bluster and protest as he might, Beau could not move the mayor from his position.

"Go," Renna told him. "That seems to be the only way that we will escape this place. Go to Lisbon, present your credentials, and send a ship for me. The mayor says that I will be in the care of nuns. I'll be fine. Go and return for me quickly."

Chapter Four

T he Convent of the Little Sisters of Suffering squatted atop a rocky hill on the outskirts of Porto. The setting was typical of the Portuguese countryside north of the Tagus River: mountain highlands interspersed with tiny plots of cultivated land.

Renna was escorted to the nunnery by two silent and grim sisters in the dark, nondescript habits of their order. Her attempts at conversation came to naught. Apparently the two nuns spoke nothing but Portuguese. Renna had been under the impression that Portuguese and Spanish were quite similar languages; indeed her knowledge of Spanish allowed her to read Portuguese with a modicum of success. However, spoken Portuguese sounded to her exactly like what it was, a foreign language, and she was beginning to suspect that the northern dialect made the speech of the people in and around Porto even more difficult.

When the iron outer gate of the nunnery clanked shut

behind her, Renna looked up to grim walls of gray stone, a dismal pile with narrow windows and massive turrets. In the courtyard was a garden with tiny plots of vegetables, but no flowers to add color to the desolate bleakness of the place.

Renna was led through a vaulted, echoing hallway, past a series of doors. Two sisters coming toward them lowered their heads, as if to hide their faces under the cowl of their hoods. Her escorts stopped in front of a massive carved door, and one of them knocked softly. A voice within barked an order, and one of the nuns opened the door.

Inside, a sere leaf of a woman sat behind a massive desk. Her face, pinched and wrinkled, was that of one who had long since become soured on life. She spoke sharply to the two nuns who had escorted Renna into the room. They bowed quickly and left.

"You may sit down," the woman behind the desk said in Spanish.

"Thank you," Renna replied, taking a large straight-backed wooden chair.

"I am the mother superior. You may call me Mother Manuela."

Renna nodded.

"I want it clearly understood," Mother Manuela said, "that your presence here is not considered an asset to this institution."

Renna's face colored quickly. "I am not here by my own choice," she answered.

Mother Manuela waved one gnarled hand. "Sometimes life offers no choice," she said. "I myself, for example, have long wished to be out of this earthly life, and I pray daily to the Blessed Virgin to relieve me of my burdens and take me to her breast in Heaven. But it seems to be God's will that I continue to do my temporal duty—which, in your case, is this: we will care for you until you have recovered from your present . . . ah, condition—"

"Recover from my condition?" Renna snapped. "Do you mean until my child is born? I assure you that I intend to be long gone before that time."

"Nothing would please me more," Mother Manuela said, "but God will decide. In the meantime, be advised that I know your type well. Ah, yes, you have youth, beauty, and robust health, and you think that the world is yours because of these endowments. And you are of the French nobility, I am told. Let me tell you that your worldly rank will gain you no special treatment here."

"I have no idea why I offend you so," Renna said, "but I promise you that I am as much disturbed by being imprisoned in this convent as you appear to be to have me here."

"Enough," Mother Manuela said, rising suddenly. "Follow me. And if you can manage it, keep your garments loose about you to conceal the obvious result of your carnality. My sisters are not to be offended by the things of the world."

Renna was so shocked by Mother Manuela's twisted attitude toward what was, to her, a blessed state that she was speechless as she followed the mother superior back into the hall and up a flight of stairs. They reached and entered a small cell-like room with stone walls and one slit of a window. The tiny windowpane was glazed over and admitted almost no light. Against one wall was a narrow cot. A rude table held a water jug and a washbasin. Under the table was a ceramic covered pot, whose purpose was obvious. In spite of the pleasant weather outside, the room was chill and damp.

"I was told, Mother Manuela, that I would be provided with clothing," Renna said.

"Our charity is reserved for those who are worthy of it," declared Mother Manuela. She turned to leave, then halted in the doorway. "Your food will be brought to you twice a day."

"I will require exercise," Renna persisted. "I will want to walk in the courtyard at least twice a day."

The wrinkled face frowned. "You may walk before dawn and after dark, so as not to offend the sensibilities of my innocent young ones."

"Thank you," Renna said sarcastically. "Am I to remain a prisoner?"

"Since you have missed the morning meal, your evening meal will be brought to you a bit early," the mother superior said, withdrawing.

The door closed behind her with a sound of finality. Renna tried the handle to find that she was locked in. She walked to the window and tried to clean the glass with her hand. She could see a sliver of courtyard below and, over the wall, a rocky ridge rising toward the blue sky.

The evening meal, delivered by a small, silent nun who kept her face averted, comprised a rich, thick soup and a hunk of dark, coarse bread—nourishing enough, but not in sufficient quantity to fully satisfy Renna's hunger. She fell asleep and slept soundly, in spite of the hardness of her bed, for the coverings were adequate protection against the coolness of the night.

Breakfast, identical to the evening meal, was brought by the same nun who had brought supper. "Wait," Renna said as the little nun turned to go. "Do you speak Spanish?"

"*Sí, señora*" the nun replied.

"*Cómo se llama?*"

"*Me llamo Consuela.*"

"Sister Consuela, the food you have brought to me is good," Renna said, smiling. "Very good. Solid and nourishing. But there is not enough of it." She laughed. "You see, I have to eat for two."

Sister Consuela ducked her head and made a sound of mild distress.

"My child is forming itself," Renna said. "When I was last in this condition, I felt much better when I had milk, cheese, and fresh vegetables, perhaps because they helped the baby to grow. Can you bring me these things? I have seen vegetables growing in the garden plots, and with the dawn I heard the lowing of cows."

"I will have to ask Mother Superior," Sister Consuela said as she scuttled out the door.

"And I was not allowed my morning walk," Renna called out after her as the door was closing.

The door stopped moving, and the small nun peered

round it. Her face was elongated and pointed, her eyes bright. "I will speak to Mother Superior."

Three days later, as darkness fell, two stern, older nuns escorted Renna to the courtyard and stood huddled together, their arms clasped and their hands hidden in their cuffs, while Renna walked around the courtyard. The fresh air made her restless; if Beau did not come soon, she would have to try to escape.

Sister Consuela continued to bring the morning and evening meals. The quantities remained small. More than once Renna told the little nun, "I must have better nourishment, milk and vegetables."

She had been in the cell-like room for ten days, with no chance for escape, when Sister Consuela delivered a jug of warm milk, a mound of raw cabbage, and a small tomato along with the evening meal.

"Thank you," Renna said. "Tell Mother Superior that I am grateful."

"No!" Sister Consuela said quickly. "Do not mention this to anyone."

"Did Mother Manuela say not to give me milk and other things?" Renna asked.

"She said nothing. She merely told me to be quiet and obey my orders as they had been given."

"Then you are taking a chance?"

The nun shrugged. "At home, my mother gave the family four children younger than I, and my sisters have also given birth. They say a mother-to-be needs to eat properly."

"I am profoundly grateful," Renna replied.

In response to repeated requests for books to read, Sister Consuela received permission to borrow tomes from the convent library. She brought books in Spanish, mostly religious treatises by learned men discussing such weighty matters as how many angels could dance on the head of a pin. She also brought two volumes on the history of the Iberian peninsula. These told Renna more about the past of Spain and Portugal than perhaps she wanted to know, but she read them to pass the time. The history of Portugal, in particular, gave her a better understanding of the reasons for the suspicion with which the Portuguese seemed to regard all outsiders: the nation's past was largely a series of invasions.

Originally the Iberians lived atop the mountains of northern Portugal, only to be merged forcefully with Celts in the sixth century B.C. The Celt-Iberians were, in their turn, overcome by the Carthaginians. Roman influence came to Portugal in 185 B.C., when Rome overran the Lusitanian descendants of the Celts.

Later waves of invasions brought the Swabians into northern Portugal, and the Visigoths came in 414 A.D. Then came the Moors, in 711. After the Christian reconquest began in Asturias in 718, the kings of León and Castile ruled Portugal until Afonso Henreque became king and beat the Moors at Ourique, earning recognition for the kingdom from the pope in 1179. But the Spanish influence was not overcome until Nuno Álvares Pereira beat the Spaniards in 1385.

Now Portugal, always at risk from her more powerful and more populous neighbor, faced the threat of a new invasion, this time by Napoleon's troops. It was easy for Renna to understand why a French ship had not been welcome in the harbor at Porto, and why she and Beau had been met with such hostility. Renna questioned Sister Consuela about life in Portugal, and as the weeks passed, began to gain some command of the language.

Consuela was from a maritime province, where her family earned a living by raking the ocean bed for seaweed to be made into fertilizer or agar-agar. She showed a lively curiosity and was fascinated by tales of life in Paris. She was even more interested in Renna's childhood.

Renna told her about life in the Cherokee Nation, of living in a Seneca longhouse. They compared notes on gardening. Consuela's people grew cabbage and potatoes, but she had never eaten corn or okra.

Once the conversation turned to religion. "My mother, who died when I was born, was a Methodist," Renna explained. "My husband is Catholic of course, and my daughter was christened in the Church." She smiled with memories. "My father's people pray to him whom they call the Master of Life."

Sister Consuela crossed herself quickly.

"My father feels that the Master of Life is God, the same God that my mother prayed to, the same God of the Catholic Church."

"Oh, please, don't say such things," Sister Consuela whispered, "lest someone hear you."

"I have discussed all this with our parish priest," Renna said. "He seemed to understand, and perhaps even to agree with my father."

"Hush," Sister Consuela begged. She fingered her beads and prayed, "*Nossa Senhora*, forgive her, forgive her."

Renna did not understand Sister Consuela's agitation, but she could see that the nun was seriously disturbed. She made no further mention of her Seneca relatives' beliefs.

As the days became weeks, Renna depended more and more on Sister Consuela for kindnesses—for the extra food that she brought, and the few minutes of conversation. The older nuns who came to escort Renna to the courtyard twice a day spoke only Portuguese, and although, with Sister Consuela's help, Renna was learning more and more of the language, the other nuns rebuffed all attempts to converse.

"Sister," Renna said, one morning after her walk when Consuela came with a large tray—the usual morning fare plus fresh fruit and a jug of milk, "how can I ever repay you?"

"My reward, if any is deserved, will come in heaven."

"My husband will come for me soon," Renna said. "If there is anything at all I can do for you, you have only to ask."

"I require nothing," Sister Consuela replied. "If your husband so desires, he may give a gift to the convent."

"The convent, as represented by Mother Manuela, has done nothing but make me a prisoner in this dark and chill room," Renna said. "The only kindness I have received has been at your hands."

"Then pray for my soul," Sister Consuela answered, gathering up the breakfast things and turning toward the door.

"With all my heart," Renna assured her.

Sister Consuela reached the door, and as she opened it, she let out a gasp of surprise. Mother Manuela, in the doorway, looked at the empty milk jug, then glanced past the little nun to see the fresh fruit on the table beside Renna's water pitcher.

"So, it is true!" the mother superior said. "You have been giving this foreign woman the food reserved for our own mouths."

"Forgive me, Mother," Sister Consuela said, her voice shaking in terror, "she eats for two and needs milk and vegetables for the young one to grow."

"How dare you speak of such things," Mother Manuela said. She slapped the little nun ringingly. "Leave us! Take your unworthy self to the place of punishment."

"Mother Superior," Renna interposed, "Sister Consuela was merely being kind. If punishment is due, let it fall on me."

"It is not up to you to say to whom or when punishment is due," Mother Manuela snarled, her shrunken lips drawn back. She turned to Sister Consuela. "You're still here? So be it. Perhaps the foreign one will enjoy seeing and hearing what happens to those who disobey." She left, slamming the door.

"What will they do to you?" Renna asked.

"Only the lash." Sister Consuela spoke the words calmly, but her hands were trembling.

"Only?"

"I will pray to *Nossa Senhora* for courage."

"Oh, my dear," Renna said, hurrying to take the little nun into her arms. Sister Consuela's shoulders trembled.

Two of the older nuns came to drag Sister Consuela from the room. The door was left open. Renna started into the hallway, but a nun pushed her back roughly.

Sister Consuela gasped in pain as her hands were

bound tightly before her. Then she was dragged to a place
in the corridor within Renna's view, where she was lifted
to hang from a peg by the rope around her hands. Mother
Manuela ripped the little nun's habit away with the sound
of tearing cloth, exposing the tender, olive skin of Sister
Consuela's back.

The lash hissed and fell. A red welt appeared on the
skin. Again the lash fell.

"Stop it, stop it!" Renna demanded, trying to push
past the nun who guarded her. She was thrust back into
the room, the door closed behind her. She could hear the
hiss of the cruel leather, the slap of it as it wrapped itself
around the little nun's back.

"What kind of people are you?" she shouted.

She sank down to lean her back against the closed
door, and, as the lashing continued—fourteen, fifteen, sixteen—she put her hands over her ears, but that did not
shut out the sound of Sister Consuela's first scream.

"God, God, God," the little nun cried, "help me,
please."

"Animals," Renna shouted, "animals, animals, animals!"

Now Sister Consuela was crying out continuously,
and after a while the hiss and fall of the lash ceased.

Renna heard the hateful voice of the mother superior.

"Have you anything to say?"

"*Nossa Senhora,* forgive me and succor me," Sister
Consuela sobbed.

The lash fell again, once, twice. The little nun
screamed.

"What magic did the foreign one who came to spy on
our country use to induce you to break our rules?" the
mother superior demanded.

"I was being kind. She carries a child."

The lash hissed and snapped.

"What evil inducements were you offered?"

"None, oh, my God, none."

The hiss and fall of the lash caused Renna to scream
along with the little nun.

"Stop, please," Sister Consuela said.

"Confess your sins, then," the mother superior said.

"Mother, I have sinned in not telling you—" The voice was high, strained with pain. The words came in small bunches, between gasps of agony. "—that the foreign woman worships not God, but someone whom she calls the Master of Life."

"Blasphemy!" the mother superior shrieked.

"In worshiping this Master of Life, she and her people dance and chant evil songs."

The lash fell again, and Sister Consuela screamed.

"Stop it," Renna yelled. "She has told you the truth."

There was silence from the hall. Only Sister Consuela's sobbing could be heard. Then came a shuffling, and the sounds of pain faded away, leaving Renna alone.

She could stand it no longer. Whatever the cost, she decided, she had to escape.

When the evening meal was delivered, this time by one of the nuns who supervised her walks, Renna was waiting behind the door. She smashed the heavy water pitcher over the nun's head. The older woman fell to her knees, then to the floor. Renna ran into the hallway and moved swiftly toward the stairs.

The mother superior was on the stairway, a candle in her hand. "What have you done with Sister Maria, evil one?"

"I am leaving the convent," Renna said. "I advise you not to try to stop me."

A strongly built man in the black robes of a priest stepped to the foot of the stairs. "It will not be left to Mother Superior to stop you, heretic," he said.

The man who blocked her way was dressed in a long, heavy black cassock. He was not tall, but the thickness of his torso gave him bulk. His hair was cut in a style Renna had seen in paintings of medieval scenes: a roll of darkness above the ears, the pate shaved. His large nose spread at the tip like a cauliflower, and two tufts of black hair protruded from the nostrils. One of his eyelids drooped, and from the narrow slit a yellowish eye, made the more baleful for being half-hidden, glared out at her.

Renna was not to be deterred. She ran down the stairs

and tried to slip past the priest. But moving with surprising quickness, he seized her upper arm with a grip so cruelly tight that it would leave bruises.

His voice grated like the roll of pebbles in the surf on a rocky shore. "Be still, heretic."

"Take your hands off me," Renna said.

"Consider your words, heathen," the priest replied. "For I have come to save your immortal soul."

"If you are the one who is in authority here, then I demand that you release me from my imprisonment," Renna said.

"Indeed, you will be leaving this place," the priest said. "Come."

"Who are you? Where are you taking me?" she demanded, as he led her toward a small door.

"I am Father Monteiro. That is all you need to know, other than the fact that in the morning I will take you to a place where you will be instructed in the true faith."

Renna was chained in a stuffy back closet for the night, with only the crack beneath the door admitting the air she needed to breathe.

The next morning she was given a smelly woolen cloak against the chill of the mountains and placed upon a mule, with only a thin blanket between her and the animal's back. Father Monteiro rode beside her, grimly silent, while two tonsured monks led the way. Behind Renna and Monteiro came the mother superior, for as Monteiro pointed out, the proprieties would be observed: Renna would have a female chaperone. Two monks riding behind the mother superior completed the party.

It was good to be in the open air. The mule was fat, and the ride was not overly rough. Renna noted the direction taken by the little caravan and memorized landmarks, for she intended to escape at the first opportunity. Behind her, beyond Mother Manuela's nunnery, was the city of Porto, where Beau would seek her. Beyond Porto lay the sea. Ahead were the mountains.

Throughout a long day of travel no opportunity for escape presented itself. The trail steepened, growing narrower as it wound around hills, through valleys, and up and over barren ridges. Renna became more and more exhausted, and she began to fear for the baby.

"I must rest," she told Father Monteiro.

"Soon," he said.

Late in the day they came to a mountain village—called Guarda, she was told.

"We are closer to God here," Monteiro said, "for we are very high."

"I'm very tired," Renna said again.

"Soon you will rest. Look around you. Here you are in my land. Here I was born, and here God came to me to speak to me of my calling."

Monteiro's yellowish eyes glared at Renna, then seemed to go out of focus as he spread his arms wide. "Here God told me that it is a dark sin to abandon the old ways. Here he said to me, 'My son, the methods of purification are not to be abandoned, the purpose of my chosen ones remains.'"

Renna did not understand, but she did not ask questions.

"Here," Father Monteiro said, "are my people, a unique people who are close to God. They pray to him not in Portuguese, not in Spanish, but in a language all their own, a tongue known only to them and to God."

Only Monteiro himself knew the full truth of his statement that the inhabitants of the village of Guarda were his people. His sphere of influence, the area in which Mother Church made his word law, extended throughout Guarda Province and into neighboring Trás-os-Montes. He spoke the language, which some said was derived from Latin, others said was more similar to Basque. He knew the moods of the people because he had grown up among them and had once entertained the same hopes and fears. He also knew the power of the church, and he used the authority of the pope as his own, for there was no one in the isolated provinces to deny him. He had brought back the old ways to instill holy awe in the people. In Father Monteiro's lands, sin was punished as God had intended it to be punished, just as the pale-haired foreign woman

would be punished for her blasphemy . . . after her purification.

Monteiro was looking forward to the time when the
woman would endure her punishment for still another reason that only he knew. He was sorry that the man who had
been with the foreign woman had been allowed to sail
south to Lisbon, for he—more than the woman—was responsible for inflicting a loss on Monteiro that the priest
could not mourn publicly. Among those who had died in
the brief fight with the French ship was Monteiro's bastard
son, a strong-limbed lad, son of a half-witted kitchen maid
at Mother Manuela's nunnery. Monteiro had been fond of
the boy and had been instrumental in obtaining a position
for him with the Porto police force. Now he was dead.
Someone would pay for that, and if only the woman was
available, then she would pay for both her own sins *and* for
the death of the boy.

Monteiro considered himself an expert at his work,
since he was directed and inspired by God himself. He
allowed Renna to try to talk to the people of Guarda as
they passed through the village, knowing that her inability
to communicate—the language, his language, was unlike
any other—would enhance her feeling of isolation, causing
her, as time went by, to turn to him as her only hope of
reprieve. In that case, he might grant her a reward, a few
hours' respite from punishment—in his bed.

The pathway became steeper, taking the group half a
mile higher into the mountains to a grim, gray, granite
building that clung like a swallow's nest to the side of a
sheer cliff. A lone shepherdess in a hooded black cape
watched in silence as the travelers passed her small flock
and came to a halt at the foot of the precipice. Here a
cratelike lift descended and hoisted them, two at a time, to
dizzying heights before it was pulled into a rock-walled
room by two monks.

"Now, heretic," Monteiro said, when the party had
reassembled, "you will hear the voice of God." With the
others following, he took Renna's arm and guided her

through dark halls, lit only by smoking torches, to a chamber of terrors.

The large room, cut from buried rock, had never seen the light of the sun, nor would it ever. Its solid walls dripped water here and there, the accumulated liquid forming dank rivulets across the uneven floor.

Mother Manuela pushed Renna roughly into a small, iron-barred cage. Renna was so tired that she did not resist. She could not take her eyes off the other occupants of the chamber until, with the creaking of a pulley, her cage was lifted to be suspended a full ten feet above the floor. She could not stand inside the cage. The bottom of it, like the sides, consisted of nothing but iron bars at four-inch intervals. From this cramped and uncomfortable perch she looked out upon instruments of torture.

Below her, the priests had secured a pleading young man to a rack. She could not understand the language in which he begged for mercy, but she heard the creaking of the ropes as the priests tightened the rack. The poor man's screams echoed from a devilish device that Renna recognized from illustrations in books: the iron maiden, a hollow, metal humanoid form built to enclose flesh and blood in a terrible embrace.

From the floor below Renna's cage, Father Monteiro spoke in a loud, grating voice. "You see, heathen, the power of God and the wages of sin."

"You animal!" Renna cried out as a new sound came to her ears, a sound of crunching, a loud sound heard even over the screams of the young man, for the priests had stretched him on the rack until his flesh split and his joints were torn apart.

Monteiro said, "Now you will hear the truth."

He translated for Renna as the young man on the rack began his confession. "You see," the big-nosed priest said, "he lied at first, telling us that he merely kissed that whore over there on the cheek." He pointed to a dull-eyed woman in a cage across the room. "It was a devil-inspired lie, for now he admits that he feasted with the scarlet woman on the lust of the flesh."

Renna fainted. When she regained consciousness, she

watched in numbness as the priests took the mutilated young man, who was moaning in pain, off the rack, gave him absolution, and then cut off his head with a huge, double-bladed ax.

She was too frightened to pray, too shocked to cry out. It was as if she had been taken back in time, back through the centuries to the darkest days of the Inquisition.

Beau's trip to Lisbon aboard a Portuguese coastal schooner went swiftly. Here, upon presentation of his credentials, he was greeted with formal coolness. His first act was not to present his message from Napoleon, but to protest his treatment in Porto and, most loudly, the detention of his wife. The name of Napoleon had power, even in Lisbon. Within the day a swift sloop was dispatched to sail up the coast to Porto to bring Renna to Lisbon. Aboard the sloop were two nuns and a doctor to care for Renna during the trip to the south.

Now Beau began his work. At first it went exactly as he suspected it would. He hinted that Napoleon was unhappy with Portugal, and the Portuguese government gave him indication that it would not easily abandon its resistance to Napoleon's demands that Portugal cease trade with the British. That the Portuguese wanted to defer the problem suited Beau's purpose well. His instructions were to state the position of France first, not as an ultimatum but in a way that men of common sense would understand; then, if caution did not prevail with the Portuguese, he was to drag out discussions as long as possible, giving the French army time to move.

Beau knew his emperor well enough to feel that once the army began its march, Napoleon no longer would be interested in a peaceful settlement of his dispute with Portugal. The little crop head had grander things in mind than a conquest of Portugal, for between Portugal and France lay the lands of a somewhat reluctant ally, old Spain. Drained of her vitality, with her best blood having gone to the New World, Spain was a prize waiting to be claimed. The days passed slowly. Beau spent many hours waiting in anterooms, seated in conference chambers, and being wined and dined with scarcely disguised hostility—for word had come from the north that the armies of Napoleon were on the move.

Then came the sloop that had been sent north to Porto. It arrived days later than expected, and the news was that the countess was not to be found. She had been housed comfortably in a convent where she was tended by the Little Sisters of Suffering, but apparently she had run away. A determined search was under way, Beau was told, a search conducted quite fruitlessly by the authorities in Porto.

"My dear sir," Beau told the Portuguese minister with whom he had been going round and round the subject of possible war, "I must break off our talks for the moment while I go to Porto to do what your people can't seem to accomplish; that is, to find my wife."

Chapter Five

Because Renno and Little Hawk were gone from the village of the Seneca and Cherokee, Roy Johnson felt as if a large part of himself had been amputated. He hunted with El-i-chi and the boys, Ta-na and Gao, both of whom called him grandfather, and he spent the lingering evenings in the bosom of a family into which he had been fully accepted. He and Toshabe retired early, often to lie in their bed speaking of things past or to give the lie to the myth that love grows cold in the old. Good as his life was, though, it was not the same without his son by marriage and his grandson by blood.

Thus Roy greeted a visit from Andy Jackson with more than ordinary pleasure. Andy's presence called for a festive gathering, and the ensuing exchange of courtesies and tall tales enlivened an entire evening.

With the morning Roy and Jackson walked out of the village, down past the swimming creek, and into the edge of the forest. After some small talk they fell silent, each absorbed in his own thoughts.

At length Roy spoke. "Andy, you know that you're welcome here at any time and that we're right pleased to see you. But I get the idea you've got something on your mind other than visiting."

"Yep," Jackson replied, "I have."

"I reckon you'll come out with it in your own time," Roy said.

"Matter of fact, I've been called to testify in Aaron Burr's treason trial, up in Richmond."

"So," Roy said. The noncommittal word reminded him of Renno.

"You and Renno warned me once about getting mixed up with Burr's grand scheme, and for that I'm grateful. I ain't asking you for advice in this matter, 'cause I'm pretty sure you'd tell me just to tell the truth as I know it and keep as much distance as possible betwixt me and Burr."

"Yep," Roy said.

"Thing is, I don't know what Burr had planned. Anything I say on that matter will be hearsay."

"I think there's a phrase that would cover that situation," Roy said. "It goes something like this: 'Not to my personal knowledge.'"

"Well, I appreciate that," Jackson said, "but as I said, I didn't come here for advice. I came to ask you if maybe you'd like to take a little vacation and travel up Richmond way with me. Can't think of a man whose company I'd rather have on the trail."

Roy was sorely tempted. Serene as it was, life in the village became monotonous after a while. Though he was reluctant to leave Toshabe and the boys, the idea of a long trip appealed to him mightily.

He talked it over with his wife, trying not to let her know his feelings. Toshabe, however, had been married to a man of action when she was young, and she'd reared two boys who had quite often come down with severe attacks of the "we-go" disease. She understood.

"Husband," she said, "go with General Jackson. The time of planting is coming and you should get out from underfoot. When you return, the crops will be ready for harvest. Then, perhaps, I can get some work out of you—even if you are only a man."

Jackson and Roy set out together on a day of blue skies and warm temperatures. Roy rode one of Beth's finest mares, a horse bred to cover forty miles a day without strain. At first Jackson, the younger of the two, tried to set a slow pace. Roy would have none of it.

"What's the matter with you, Andy, lollygagging along like a schoolgirl on a Sunday outing?" Roy demanded.

Andy laughed. "Just thinking of your old bones, Roy."

"You let me worry about my bones," Roy said. "Just do your best to keep up. What with outdoor life and plenty of tobacco, and a snort or two of good whiskey now and again, I can match any pace set by a young sprout like you."

So at the rate of about forty miles a day, two gentlemen from Tennessee rode up to Richmond.

They found the town buzzing as if with holiday. Aaron Burr's trial was the biggest thing to hit the city since the war. After some difficulty they found a joint room in an inn and for the first time in weeks had a bed under their backs and a pillow under their heads.

Roy, feeling the need for an application of one of those little pleasures of life to which he attributed his health and longevity, led the way into the public room of the inn. A stout but dignified man was holding court at the bar, and Roy and Jackson found a spot nearby. They ordered whiskey, took their drinks to a nearby table, and listened while the man—his ruddy nose and watery eyes symptoms of too much drink—talked of the late war in North Africa against the Barbary pirates.

When the gentleman paused to have his glass refilled, Roy rose and went up to him. "Excuse me, you wouldn't be General William Eaton?"

"That I am, sir, and whom do I have the pleasure of addressing?" the hero of Derna asked.

"The name's Roy Johnson, of Tennessee," Roy replied. "My grandson was with you, General, a marine named Hawk Harper."

"By God," Eaton thundered. "Hawk! Indeed, indeed. Your grandson, you say?"

"Yep, my dead daughter's boy."

Eaton came and threw his arms around Roy with exuberance. "My pleasure to know the grandfather of one hell of a good fighting man," Eaton exclaimed. "If I had had ten like him, I could have conquered all of Africa."

It was evident that drink had deteriorated Eaton, and when a flashily dressed woman, obviously one of the women of the town, came up to him and quickly captured his attention, Roy turned away sadly and went back to his table.

"Well, it comes and goes, don't it, Andy?" Roy whispered, looking in Eaton's direction. "Yesterday's hero, today's fool."

Jackson sipped his whiskey, his eyes squinted and hard. "It will never be that way with me," he answered.

"Plan to be famous, then, Andy?"

Jackson laughed. "Well, you never know."

Andy Jackson was one of the first witnesses to be called by Aaron Burr's defense lawyers. The courtroom was packed to capacity and was—those who were jammed in cheek to jowl were wont to say—"uncommonly hot." The atmosphere was close and fetid. Sandboxes, placed on the floor to serve as receptacles for tobacco juice, did not catch all of it.

Aaron Burr, dressed in a dark, natty suit with gleaming white linen, gave Jackson a thin smile as the general took the witness stand.

"Now, General Jackson," the defense attorney said, "you are here to testify to the good character of the defendant, are you not?"

"That I am, sir," Jackson said. "To my personal knowledge Aaron Burr has always been a man of honor. It is my opinion that he would never knowingly be a traitor to the United States."

"And yet," the attorney continued, "we have all heard General James Wilkinson state that Mr. Burr approached him with a scheme to subvert the authority of the United

States in not only the western territories but in some western states."

"Sir," Jackson said, "to my personal knowledge General James Wilkinson is a paid agent of Spain and has been a traitor to the United States from before the time of the Battle of Fallen Timbers."

Roy was stunned. Jackson's testimony was based on what he and Renno had told him. It was mere hearsay, but Jackson was presenting it as personal, firsthand knowledge. He shook his head in wonder. Then he told himself that it was Andy Jackson's nature to be true to a friend. It was in the man's favor that Jackson would lie to be loyal to Aaron Burr. Burr, with his powdered hair tied behind his head in a fashionable queue and looking very much the Chesterfieldian gentleman, made a sympathetic figure. Jackson's testimony was greeted with sounds of approval from the audience.

Not surprisingly, the defense attorney did not question the source of Jackson's so-called knowledge regarding Wilkinson. The thrust of the defense was to try to make President Thomas Jefferson look like a man bent on persecuting an innocent, idealistic victim.

This was the view taken by Andy Jackson, when, following his testimony, Roy questioned him.

"Andy," Roy said, "it seems to me that James Wilkinson is more on trial here than Aaron Burr."

"As well he should be," Andy growled. "You read what this fellow Washington Irving wrote?"

"Can't say as I have."

Jackson opened a newspaper. "Listen to this." His voice changed to a reading tone: " 'Wilkinson strutted into the court and stood for a moment swelling like a turkey cock. Burr turned his head, looked Wilkinson full in the face with one of his piercing regards, swept his eye over his whole person, and went on conversing with his counsel. A slight expression of contempt played over his countenance.' "

"Mighty high-sounding words," Roy said.

"Thing about it is, the wrong man's on trial here," Jackson said.

Even though it was unlikely that Jackson would be recalled to the witness stand, there was no question of leaving before the trial ended. There was too much to see, too many people to talk with.

William Eaton was called to the stand on a day when Andy and Roy chose to walk the streets of the town, so that Andy could talk national politics with the citizens of Richmond. They were outside the courthouse when Eaton emerged. He was wearing a tremendous hat, with a Turkish sash knotted over brightly colored clothing.

"Howdy, General," Roy said.

Eaton came to a halt. To Roy's surprise his eyes were red with anger and tears of fury were running down his cheeks. "They questioned me as if I were the villain," Eaton said. "As if I were the villain and not that bastard Burr."

"Well," Andy said, as Eaton stomped off, "another little moment in the sun for the hero of Derna, eh?"

It was amusing to Roy to see that Jackson was put out by the lack of a "moment in the sun" for himself. It seemed that everyone—Wilkinson, Burr, Eaton—was getting more attention than the man from Tennessee. After all, Jackson had served his country in both houses of the U.S. Congress. He was a general in the Tennessee Militia. He had sat upon the bench in judgment of his fellow men. Now it was Eaton and Wilkinson and others who were dominating the scene at Richmond. Jackson was not willing to have that situation continue.

On a fine, hot morning, with Roy in tow as an amused observer, Jackson mounted the steps of the capitol building, waved his arms to attract people to him, and began a harangue in which he praised Aaron Burr and belabored both Wilkinson and President Jefferson.

Well, Roy thought, attacking a president was nothing new to Andy. When he was in the House of Representatives, he opposed George Washington's support of the Jay Treaty and was one of only twelve members of that body who refused to vote a cordial reply to Washington's Farewell Address.

When Jackson finished his speech, he came down to

shake hands with people in the crowd and continue his discussion about the trial. Roy bided his time. It was only when they were alone that he said, "Andy, I've known you a long time, and I never heard you sound off that way before."

Andy grinned. "Had to get it off my chest."

"Personally, I think Tom Jefferson has done a right smart job in the White House," Roy said, "so I part company with you when you criticize him."

"Don't blame you, Roy," Jackson said. "I think Jefferson will go down in history as one of the greatest presidents, if not for his political views, then for his purchase of the Louisiana Territory."

"You didn't say that when you were shooting off your mouth on the capitol steps."

"Roy," Jackson said, with a little smile, "a man is known for his enemies more than for his friends." He winked. "And just so you'll understand, my old friend, let me tell you that a big man has big enemies."

When General James Wilkinson was called back to the stand, Roy and Andy had managed to get good seats for the spectacle. Wilkinson entered the courtroom in a splendiferous uniform of his own design. The foreman of the jury, John Randolph of Roanoke, ordered the sergeant at arms to disarm Wilkinson, so the general was relieved of his huge ceremonial sword.

Wilkinson had been recalled to answer questions about a letter in code sent by Aaron Burr. Under intense cross-examination Wilkinson admitted that he had doctored the infamous cipher letter from Burr to hide his own complicity in the proposed expedition against Spanish lands in the Southwest. He contradicted himself repeatedly and asked permission to retract or amend previous statements. More than ever it seemed to Roy that it was Wilkinson on trial rather than Burr.

Jackson had managed to make himself known to both the district attorney, George Hay, and to the jury foreman. After Wilkinson's testimony, Hay told Jackson and Roy—

over a drink at the inn where the men from Tennessee were staying, "I have washed my hands of Wilkinson."

"Since he's the star witness for the prosecution," Roy said, "it sounds to me as if you're saying that Burr is going to be acquitted."

"So I do predict," the district attorney said.

He was right. When the trial was over, Burr had been found not guilty of all charges.

There was one more small drama to unfold, and Roy and Andy watched with interest as John Randolph made an effort to have General James Wilkinson indicted for misprision of treason. It was a close thing, with the grand jury voting against John Randolph's motion nine to seven.

Randolph was furious. He told Andy and Roy, "The mammoth of iniquity escaped, not that any man pretended him innocent. Wilkinson is the only man I ever saw who was from bark to the very core a villain. Perhaps you never saw human nature in so degraded a situation as in the person of Wilkinson before the grand jury, and yet this man stands on the very summit and pinnacle of executive favor."

As was his custom, Thomas Jefferson was spending the summer at Monticello, away from the heat and dampness of Washington. There were those who said that the president should be in the capital, for the nation seemed to be facing the direst threat of war since the Revolution. The British man-of-war *Leopard* had tricked the new American frigate *Chesapeake* into an unfavorable situation at sea while *Chesapeake* was on her shakedown cruise, not fully battle ready. The *Leopard* fired point-blank broadsides into the American until, on orders from Captain James Baron, on board as commodore, the *Chesapeake* struck her colors. Three were dead, eighteen wounded. The British boarded the frigate and took off three American seamen who had only recently escaped impressed service aboard the British ship *Melampus*. One deserter from the Royal Navy was also seized.

Jefferson was following the Burr trial in Richmond with avid interest, but his attention was diverted from that spectacle by mob action in Norfolk, where British sailors were attacked by a crowd. Meanwhile protest meetings were being held in New York and Boston. Jefferson called his cabinet to him, and it was decided to demand that all British men-of-war leave American waters at once.

"Mr. President," said Jefferson's most trusted adviser, Secretary of State James Madison, "it is my contention that we should ignore the demands from some quarters that we convene the Congress and ask for a declaration of war."

Jefferson, still preoccupied with the Burr trial, asked, "How widespread is the call for war, James?"

"It is confined to the usual firebrands," Madison answered.

"Some people would have me believe the whole country favors war," Jefferson said. "Well, I suspect it will —as soon as the people learn that the British are balking over leaving our waters. The British, you know, are insisting on their right to obtain water and supplies at Norfolk. I fear that if we do not agree to their demands, they will place the city under armed blockade; then we will surely have our war."

"There's also the matter of the new demands from Spain regarding mutual borders," Madison said.

The president smiled coldly. "Isn't it convenient of Spain to play into my hands in such a matter?" he asked.

Madison was looking at Jefferson, seeing the man who had doubled the size of the United States with the Louisiana Purchase, and a man who was not content—would not be content—until he had obtained for the United States Spain's other possessions east of the Mississippi.

"I had rather have war with Spain than not," Jefferson said. "Our southern defensive force can take the Floridas. Volunteers for a Mexican army will flock to our standard, and rich pabulum will be offered to our privateers in the plunder of their commerce and coasts. Probably Cuba will add itself to our confederation."

"And England?"

"Another matter," Jefferson said. "We gain nothing by war with England. I want you to send instructions to Monroe in England, telling him to demand satisfaction from the British government regarding the *Chesapeake* affair."

"The demand to be voiced loudly but rather politely?" Madison asked with a smile.

But another incident in Norfolk made war with England seem even more likely. Virginia militiamen seized and imprisoned a British party that had come ashore for water. Jefferson sent an order to release the sailors immediately, and braced himself for an explosion of indignation from the British. Instead, the British fleet, with the freed sailors aboard, lifted anchor and sailed away from Hampton Roads, thus ending the threat of a blockade.

Jefferson nodded in satisfaction upon hearing the news. "Apparently, James," he told Madison, "the British also feel that there is nothing to be gained by war—at least at this time. Proceed with my instructions to have Mr. Monroe protest the affair in London, and on your way out send in my secretary, if you please."

When the secretary arrived, Jefferson asked for news of the Burr trial and then began to list items that he wanted the secretary to order for him from Italy and France. Wines, soft and silky, headed the list; then came *moutarde de Mailly, vinaigre d'estragon,* macaroni, Parmesan, and Smyrna raisins.

Roy Johnson returned home from Richmond to news of joy and sadness. Since Toshabe believed in passing along good words first, she said, "I will be a grandmother again."

"Already?" Roy asked, for he knew that it was impossible for such news to have arrived from Renno or Little Hawk, leaving only Ah-wa-o as the possible mother of a future grandchild. "Little Ah-wen-ga is only . . . how many months old?" He counted on his fingers.

"The manitous have been kind," Toshabe said.

It was true. Ah-wa-o, blushing prettily, was already showing.

"It will be a boy," El-i-chi declared.

"You have regained the sight?" Roy asked.

"I know it will be a boy," El-i-chi said stubbornly. "He is to be named Ha-ace, in honor of Ah-wa-o's father."

"Well, he'll be named after a good man," Roy agreed.

It was only later, after the beaming parents-to-be had left, that Toshabe told Roy the sad news: Ena's twins, Ho-ya and We-yo, were leaving the village to seek new lands beyond the Mississippi River.

At the age of eighteen, Rusog Ho-ya, Fruit of Rusog, was an impressive young man. Although he disclaimed his white heritage, the blood of the original Renno could be seen in his facial features. He took his height from his Seneca blood, and the Cherokee in him made his chest thick and his shoulders wide.

His twin sister, We-yo O-no-ga-nose, Good Water, was a slim, youthful version of her mother, the fair Ena. She was somewhat duskier of complexion than her mother, but lighter than her brother. She had Ho-ya's chiseled features in her nose, mouth, and cheekbones. Giving birth to her one daughter, Summer Moon, had matured her figure.

A few days after Roy's return from Richmond—after the Seneca had gathered in the council house to hear Roy's account of travel in the United States and the nature of the white man's justice in the case of the United States versus Aaron Burr—there was another assemblage that was strictly familial. It took place in Rusog and Ena's lodge.

Since Little Hawk and Renno were away with their white wives, the gathering consisted of El-i-chi and Ah-wa-o—she of the growing stomach—as well as Gao, Ta-na, and the baby girl, Ah-wen-ga. Toshabe and Roy Johnson were also present, as were Ena, Rusog, and the twins We-yo and Ho-ya.

To honor her mother's blood, We-yo was dressed in the Seneca style. She wore a beautifully beaded dress, the *a-kia-ta-wi,* over bright, red, woolen *ka-ris* leggins. Her hair was pulled back and held in place by an *a-te-non-wa-ran-hak-ta* headband. Her moccasins were cuffed, the turned-down flaps highly decorated with interwoven laces of leather.

Ho-ya's costume was a mixture of Cherokee and Seneca, dark red breechclout over an *o-fa-sa*, an Iroquois warrior's kilt. A heavy breast piece of silver and mother-of-pearl, one of Se-quo-i's designs, rested on his bare chest.

It was Rusog who stated the purpose of the family gathering. "My son and my daughter," he said, in his deep, gravelly voice, "are no longer children. Indeed, my daughter is a mother, and my son is a warrior full in strength and maturity. As such, though they owe allegiance to tribe and family, they are free to make their own choices." He looked around, his face set, his eyes slightly moist. "I have spoken."

Ho-ya rose, tall, slim, and strong in his youthful confidence. "I am grieved," he said, "to think of leaving my people, my family, my mother, and my father. And you, Grandmother. But I feel a continuing pain that is greater than that of losing my family; this pain is the guiding force for my decision."

He paused, looked around, letting his eyes fall on his uncle El-i-chi. "You know, Uncle, the source of my pain, and who is to say—only the spirits know—whether I am wrong. Wrong or right I can no longer live in close proximity to the whitefaces. I can no longer see their sly intrusion into the lives of the Real People, to see my own people building houses of logs in imitation of the whitefaces, to see an ancient and honorable way of life being submerged like an old, sodden log in a flood."

"And what will happen to your Cherokee way of life among strangers in the West?" El-i-chi asked.

"If it is altered, it will be altered in a way of the blood, not in the way of the whitefaces," Ho-ya said. "It saddens me, Uncle, to go against your wishes, and against the advice of my uncle Renno. But then has not my uncle Renno become a white man?"

"Renno is Seneca," declared El-i-chi.

"I cannot accept his beliefs or yours," Ho-ya said. "I cannot agree that the only course of action available to us is to bow to the white man's condescension and tyranny, and to become like him."

"Wherever you go," El-i-chi said, "the white man will come to you."

"But later than sooner," Ho-ya said. "I have not come here, Uncle, to argue or to cast blame. I have come, with my sister and my niece, *Ga-ha-neh So-a-ka-ga-gwa*, to say good-bye to those who are dear to me. To say good-bye and to ask your blessings, along with those of my father and mother."

"I can wish you safety and comfort," Ena said. "I will not bless your desertion of all that you have been a part of."

"I accept your good wishes, Mother," Ho-ya said.

Ho-ya glanced at We-yo, who was weeping silently. She had confided to her brother that deciding to accompany him had been one of the more painful experiences of her life.

"And you, We-yo, are you also committed to this folly?" Ena asked. "Once before you left our village with your brother. At that time you went as the wife of the Mingo White Blanket, to join with the Shawnee Tecumseh in his much-promised union against the whitefaces."

"Please, Mother," We-yo said, "you know that I must go."

"As you went before with a man who then tried to kill your own mother," Ena pressed.

"And who died at my mother's hand," We-yo countered. "But all that is past and forgiven, Mother. Be glad for us. Wish us well, for it is a hard thing for me to leave you, even though my heart tells me I must."

Ho-ya's heart took wing to hear his sister's resolve. And he knew that, at this very moment, in other homes in the adjoining villages, similar scenes were being enacted. For Ho-ya and We-yo were not going alone: a total of twenty-two young Seneca and a slightly larger number of Cherokee had allied themselves to Ho-ya's cause. The party included young children and even babies.

"Nephew," El-i-chi said, "I ask you this last time to reconsider. I ask not only for myself, for I will miss both of you, not only for your mother and father, who will miss you more, but for the Seneca people. You take with you a score of our youth, and the departure of even one or two young Seneca is a matter of concern, for we are few and we face the prospect of being absorbed into the Cherokee Nation by marriage and assimilation. Your decision can do nothing but hasten this process."

"They, all those who will follow us," Ho-ya said, "are of a single mind. What does it matter, Uncle, if your Seneca are absorbed and become Cherokee? Better that than become white men with red faces."

El-i-chi bristled for a moment, then subsided.

Drums sounded a slow, mourning beat. Someone was starting a dance of farewell, a dance usually reserved for the dead. El-i-chi, seeing that there was nothing more to say, took Ah-wa-o's hand and led her out into the night. Fires had been kindled in the commons. A group of young people danced, their silhouettes stark and black against the glow of the fires.

The next day was consumed with preparations, and at dawn the following morning the emigrants were ready to leave. Toshabe was with Ena, who was weeping openly. She tried to hold Ena, but her daughter slipped out of her grasp and ran to seize her granddaughter, Summer Moon.

"It is not enough that you tear my heart from my body by leaving me, children of my loins," Ena cried out. "Now you take from me this"—weeping, she kissed Summer Moon—"my only grandchild."

A few of them had horses. Blankets, cooking pots, and other belongings were bundled onto travois pulled behind the animals. Others walked, carrying their few possessions in bundles. Young children, excited to be doing something different, yelled out farewells. A drum beat out the slow rhythm of mourning.

Ena had dried her tears. She stood, tall and strikingly beautiful, beside her husband, and her face was set, her eyes focused on infinity.

At first the travel was easy and pleasant for Ho-ya, We-yo, and their party. The well-trodden paths lay between Cherokee villages, and the nights usually were spent in a Cherokee lodge, out of the weather and on a comfortable bed. In each village word of the trek had preceded them, and some people, mostly young, questioned Ho-ya closely about his plans and intentions. A few of the interested ones joined the migrating group, some bringing their entire families, until by the time the northwesterly route had led them out of the Cherokee hunting grounds, their numbers had swelled past the century mark.

Then came the times that would test the will and the dedication of each member of the group. Although a peace existed between the Cherokee and the Chickasaw nations, Ho-ya's party was traveling alien ground. No longer were the travelers welcome at the scattered villages. What provisions they had been able to bring with them were running low, and because Ho-ya, unfamiliar with the region, did not always lead them through good hunting grounds, the supply of fresh meat was intermittent.

We-yo's bed was the earth, with one thin blanket between her and a mossy bank or a couch of boughs. To her and the other women fell the tasks of gathering firewood for the night and of cooking the evening meal. With three-year-old Summer Moon at her side, We-yo trudged the endless miles during the day, often wishing that she had ignored her brother's disdain for anything that smacked of the white race and taken a horse from her aunt Beth's stable. She canceled that wish when, with the Mississippi still far off and the game scarce, the first of the horses was slain for meat.

The midday sun baked her. Rains made the footing slippery and the nights miserable. Even though they had started eating the horses, hunger was still with them constantly. We-yo and the women dug for roots, scavenged the fields and meadows for summer greens, and encouraged the small boys to bag squirrels, rabbits, and possums.

Each morning she forced herself to smile, even when Summer Moon begged to be allowed to rest.

"No walking today, Mother," the child pleaded. "No walking."

Many times, especially in the afternoons, it was an effort of will just to put one foot in front of the other, and We-yo would carry her daughter on her back. She lost rack of time, withdrawing into her own inner world, as if she were a solitary wayfarer.

Renno and Little Hawk had made their farewells to England and were sailing southward in the Bay of Biscay. The *Comtesse Renna*, heavily laden with trade goods for Portugal, was riding low in the water, her speed reduced. Adan had set a course that carried her directly toward Cabo Ortegal on the northwestern tip of Spain. The weather was favorable, and for days there was nothing for two restless warriors to do but walk the deck, watch the run of the waves, and listen to the thunder of the wind in the sails.

Renno was having difficulty sleeping. With each day he was coming closer and closer to his daughter, and with each night his fears for her safety grew, for his dreams were troubled. At times he was uncertain whether he slept or was awake, for it seemed that he was looking into his own face, only to realize that he was seeing—or was dreaming of—the original Renno. He could only assume that these manifestations of the manitou meant that the danger to Renna was growing.

Through a night that was an eternity, Renna was kept in the iron cage, suspended ten feet above the dank, stone floor of Father Monteiro's torture chamber. Following the boy's death, the sobbing girl had been placed in the iron maiden. After a few hours her whimperings faded, and there was nothing but the drip, drip of water down the solid rock of the walls.

Renna slept little. It was impossible to be comfortable, for the iron bars cut into her legs, her back, her buttocks. She could neither stand nor lie at full length. After what seemed to be ages she was awakened by the scrape of wood on stone as the outer door opened. Priests entered, carrying torches and candles. They took the girl from the iron maiden. She was rigid as if in death, but Renna saw her eyes move, and as the priests carried her to the rack and laid her there, she heard an eerie sound, a low laugh that began deep in the girl's throat and rose in volume to a demented shriek.

Renna was to be spared seeing the ultimate disposal of the unfortunate girl, for Mother Manuela came into the chamber and ordered the priests to lower Renna's cage.

"I'm sorry that you will miss the entertainment," Mother Manuela said as the priests began to tighten the ropes that bound the naked, laughing girl to the rack.

Renna's limbs were stiff. Her body ached from lying on the iron bars all night. She said nothing.

"You have seen, however, the wages of sin," the nun said. "And heresy is the greatest sin of all."

"You are lucky," Renna retorted, "for when my husband and the French army come, you will find that they are more merciful than these so-called men of God. Your death will be a quick one."

"Come," Mother Manuela said, jerking Renna's arm.

Renna had seen too much, ached too much, was too horrified and angry to take the roughness. She slammed her fist into the nun's face and sent her sprawling. As the old woman hit the floor, her dark habit flew up to show skinny legs in dark hose.

Priests rushed to seize Renna. She struggled, but overpowered and outnumbered, she gave up lest she hurt the baby.

"Thank the heathen god you worship that your belly is full," Mother Manuela snarled, as she pushed herself to her feet. "Pray that your unborn child will be born innocent of your blasphemy and heresy and that God deems it fit to live. It is only for the child's sake that we are forced to postpone your purification and your repentance."

The room in which Renna was locked was much like the one at the nunnery: small, with walls of stone, a rude cot for a bed, a pitcher and washbasin on a wooden table, and slop jar underneath. She prayed for her child in the words of her people, and fell asleep with her heart full of Beau.

The coast of Spain lay just beyond the horizon of Adan's vessel when a lookout called out, "Sail ho!"

Adan clambered into the rigging, glass in hand. "Can't make 'er out," he said, as he climbed down.

Renno fingered the handle of his tomahawk.

"Odds are that she's British," Adan said, "but I don't care to chance it. Even if she is from England, we'd make a rich prize."

"But we fly the flag of England," Little Hawk said, pointing upward.

"And we're all about as English as the Stars and Stripes," Adan said. "A less-than-kind British captain would quickly see that we're American, and at the very least he would impress a few of our men. He might also doubt our word that we're headed for a port in a country allied to England, for we are quite near the French coast. It would be easy for the British to say that we were caught while approaching a French port."

"Isn't it possible that the sail is French?" Little Hawk asked.

"Could be," Adan admitted. "In that case, there's no doubt: *Renna* would be seized or sunk for violating Napoleon's edicts."

It was, Renno felt, a hopeless situation.

"Well, we haven't sacrificed *all* of our speed for potential profit," Adan said. He shouted out orders to make more sail, and soon *Renna* was flying before the wind, causing the distant sail to drop back below the horizon. Adan intended to outsail the ship that lay to their west—to approach the Spanish coast and then to sail near it until they rounded Cabo Ortegal. But his intentions were frustrated when another sail appeared on the eastern horizon.

"Well, that one would likely be a Frenchman," Adan decided. He made adjustments in the sail and in the course, but now *Renna* was caught between two ships. The only course open to him was due south, directly toward the Spanish coast.

"This is not going to be as simple as I thought," Adan said, when still another set of sails came up over the horizon to the southwest. "Is the whole French navy in the Bay of Biscay today?"

He called Renno to a conference. "Renno, we're pretty well hemmed in. What I'm going to do is sail more to the east. I'm going to try to run around that ship that is between us and the morning sun, loop back to the north along the coast of southern France, and then northwestward to open water. It will add time to our voyage, but at the moment I see no other choice."

Two of the ships in pursuit of *Renna* were schooner-rigged. Although their guns made them heavy, they were fleet enough to make it impossible for *Renna* to leave them behind entirely.

All day long *Renna* sailed southeastward until, with the coming of twilight, the Spanish coast was a low darkness on the horizon to the south. With full darkness the wind failed, and the sails guttered and flapped. In a total calm, Adan put out longboats to tow the ship closer to the coast.

Soon they could see lights on the shore. "That would be the town of Santander," Adan told them.

There were lights behind them as well, the running lights of two ships that were duplicating Adan's strategy of placing rowers into longboats to move their ships through the dead calm.

Once again Adan called Renno to him. "My old friend," he said, "I think you can see that the chances of our escaping are small."

Renno nodded.

"You know that if the ships are French, it will mean prison for those of us who are aboard."

"This is true."

"Even if they're British, chances are we'll be seized and taken back to England," Adan said. "Many of our crew will be impressed."

Renno's hand was on his tomahawk.

"And maybe some of us would put up a fight and be killed," Adan said. "I was wondering, Renno, if you and Little Hawk might not want to go ashore and make your way overland to Portugal."

Renno had never run from a fight, but he was realistic

enough to know that *Renna* could not resist two or three ships of the line.

"How far are we from Portugal?" he asked.

Adan led the way to the chart room, lit an oil lamp, and walked an instrument across a chart. "I'd say, as the crow flies, that you'd be about two hundred and fifty miles from the nearest city on the Portuguese coast, which would be Porto."

Renno looked over Adan's shoulder, studied the chart. "Mountains inland from Santander, mountains in northern Portugal. Rough going."

"Since you speak the language well, you might be able to get a ship at Santander and sail around the coast."

"Or end up in a Spanish prison," Renno said. "No, if we go ashore, our only choice will be to make our way across country."

"I suppose you're right. To board a ship, you'd have to show papers of some sort, but you can probably travel cross-country without anyone challenging you. I can supply you with gold and silver. You may be able to buy horses."

"And leave you to face the French," Renno said.

It was a difficult choice. Renno slept. He awoke to see a familiar face, the ancestor who was so much like him. There was concern on the manitou's face.

"Is it Renna?" Renno asked.

The manitou nodded and spoke. "There comes a time, my son, when we must put aside our pride and do our duty to those who are close to us."

With the dawn one of the pursuers was so near that it was possible, with the aid of a glass, to see the French flag at her masthead.

"Forgive me, Adan, but we are going," Renno said.

"I understand." He clasped Renno's shoulder. "Look, it's four hundred miles to Lisbon. Don't try to make it all the way there by land. Head for Porto. Travel southwest until you hit the Portuguese border, and then ask for directions. You'll be traveling through some pretty rugged country, so you'll need warm clothing."

"One blanket each," Renno said. "Plus muskets and pistols, some Spanish specie, and rations. That's all."

"My prayers go with you," Adan said, "and now, if you don't mind, I'm going to lower a boat and cast you off, because I have not yet resigned myself to spending the next few years in a French prison."

The wind was still dead calm when the boat was lowered. Renno and Little Hawk climbed down and began to row away from the ship. A strong current swept them toward the west, away from the town of Santander. They were a good distance from the rocky shoreline when a thunderstorm moved in quickly from the sea. Wind came out of the blackened sky in a strong blast and sent spits of rain against them.

Renno looked back toward the *Comtesse Renna* to see that Adan had raised all sails and that the little ship was careening with the wind, making one last desperate effort to avoid capture. Even as he watched, the ship disappeared into the rain and the darkness of the violent storm.

The winds passed the longboat. A steady, driving rain obscured the shore, but after a time they heard the back-and-forth wash of waves on a shingle beach. When the bow of the longboat grated against the pebbles, Little Hawk leaped out.

"We'll pull her well up," Renno said. "She'll be a welcome find for some Spaniard."

It was still raining. They gathered their equipment and supplies, rigged their travel packs, and climbed a limestone cliff to a rocky promontory. Renno led the way through a rugged landscape. He set off toward the southwest to skirt a village that, he remembered from the chart, was called Santillana. The rains continued and the day was long, the going difficult. Renno was thinking that if the entire route was as challenging, it was going to be an extended trip, and his concern for Renna grew.

By nightfall the rain had diminished to a steady drizzle. It was Little Hawk who spotted the almost hidden entrance to a cave. Inside, out of the rain, they found dry tinder. Someone had used the cave as shelter before and had cached firewood. Renno kindled a fire, while outside the rain continued. When the fire had grown hot enough to burn wet wood, they removed their clothing, dried it, and hung their soaked blankets.

When his clothing was dry, Little Hawk decided to explore the cave that extended into blackness behind them. He fashioned a torch out of dry wood, lit it, and made his way carefully into the darkness. He had to crawl over a rockfall that extended almost to the cave's ceiling, and then he found himself in a large chamber. The silence of the place was broken only by the sound of his breathing and by the whispers of the torch as it burned. He moved forward, keeping to one wall, and in the red light of the torch he saw painted buffalo, almost real, captured in motion by some unknown artist in vivid reds, blacks, and violets. He lifted the torch. The roof of the chamber was covered with painted animals. He recognized two wild boars, horses, a deer, and a bull.

Feeling very much alone and intimidated by the eerie silence of the cave, he turned and made his way back to the fire.

"Others have been here before us," he told his father.

"Yes," Renno said, "for I have felt their presence."

"There are things you should see," Little Hawk said.

Each of them carried a torch into the farther recesses of the cave. Together they looked at the wild boars and the horses, the deer and the bull. In another gallery, the flickering flames revealed sticklike drawings of men among goats, cattle, and more horses. An antelope had been captured in movement, and far back to the rear of the chamber six deer heads were engraved in the stone.

They explored and discovered silently. When they spoke at all it was in a whisper, for the cave generated a feeling of peace and reverence. They were very much alone, yet there was a presence, something almost tangible.

"Who?" asked Little Hawk.

The answer came to Renno's lips without thought: the Old Ones.

Consider the Old Ones. The Old Ones know. So the manitou of his father had told him.

"I'm hungry," Little Hawk said.

"Go," Renno said. "I will come soon."

Chapter Six

Renno sat in the dust of the dry cavern floor, legs crossed under him. The sputtering torch burned low. He was far from the land of his ancestors, and the manitous of those of Seneca blood clung close to their own hunting grounds. Still he spoke to them, whispering softly out of respect for the spirits of the cavern. He chanted, and soon to his voice was added the drone of many others, speaking in a language alien to him. He fell silent. The voices spoke, and although he did not understand, he could feel a common thread of concern and a sense of growing danger.

The torch guttered and flamed out. He could smell the smoke and see the glow of residual embers in the Stygian blackness.

Oddly, he could see into the depths. A cold glow, a blue spirit light showed him the approach of short, heavily built men dressed in animal furs. Their hair was black and oily, their beards wild and uncombed. They carried flint weapons, and they spoke to him earnestly, their small black eyes burning with the desire to communicate:

The Old Ones know.

"Help me, old brothers," Renno said in Seneca. "For I do not know your words."

His great-grandfather's image was here before him, blond and bronzed. He, too, carried a flint weapon, a great, smoothly chiseled war ax.

"Grandfather," Renno whispered, bowing his head. "So you still travel to far places as you did when you were in the land of the living?"

The manitou nodded and turned to face the spirits of the Old Ones, listening. In Renno's mind suddenly was engraved a map of lands unknown to him, of mountains and plains and small valleys and rushing streams. They knew, the Old Ones, and they laid out the route past the mountains of the Spanish coastal areas to the northern coast of Portugal so that it was emblazoned on Renno's memory.

"My gratitude, old brothers," Renno said. "And to you, Grandfather."

The cold blue light faded slowly, but the feeling of kinship for the powerfully built hairy ones remained as Renno felt his way toward the brightness of his son's fire.

Little Hawk had opened a tin of ship's biscuits. He looked at his father questioningly but did not speak for a long time. When he did, his voice was soft and full of awe.

"I heard voices," Little Hawk said.

"Yes, that is so."

It was a delicate subject. Little Hawk knew his father talked with the manitous, but he never discussed the matter.

"Well?" Little Hawk inquired.

"The Old Ones knew the way," Renno answered. "Now it is time to rest, for we have far to go."

The fire had burned low before Little Hawk felt the onset of sleep. He had been thinking of the drawings on the walls and ceilings of the cave, and as his eyes grew heavy, he seemed to see them, the Old Ones, short, thick chested, and strong armed. A great stag was surrounded, and as sleep came, Little Hawk saw—or dreamed he saw —the powerful casting of a spear and the dark, red blood flowing from the wounded animal. He felt as if he were there with those men, the Old Ones, who had hunted, loved, fought, and died so long, long ago.

By morning the rains had ceased and it was good weather for traveling. Renno led the way southwestward, setting a pace just short of the warrior's run. He knew from the chart aboard the *Renna* that the mountain barrier along the Spanish coast, the Cantabrians, was sixty miles wide. In such terrain the going was slow and difficult.

When they spotted a tiny mountain village, they made no effort to avoid it. They found the villagers to be withdrawn and slightly suspicious. Their dialect of Spanish was difficult to understand, but that difficulty had one advantage: the villagers took Renno and Little Hawk to be outlanders but not foreigners. The good Spanish silver that Renno carried bought not only food but toleration of their passage. A well-traveled hunter told them that the cave they had visited was at a site called Altamira, and he gave them instructions on the best route through the rugged mountains into the province of León.

Loose rocks on the steep, winding trail made walking difficult. Mountain storms smashed down upon them, causing them to seek shelter. The days were passing.

When Adan Bartolome had put Renno and Little Hawk into a longboat and cast them off toward the Spanish coast, he felt that his future might be in a French prison, for he was surrounded by French ships in a dead calm.

He thanked God for the sudden onslaught of the line of thunderstorms and took immediate action. He ordered sails set, and the *Comtesse Renna* leaped forward with a bone in her teeth, her sails thundering in the gusting winds. A curtain of rain closed in on them and gave them the gift of invisibility.

Adan sailed eastward, directly toward the French ship that had been closing in from that side. The rain was so heavy that visibility was cut to no more than a hundred yards. He posted lookouts on the bow with orders to sing out loudly if they saw the French ship, but not even he was prepared when the enemy vessel loomed up out of the rain directly in *Renna*'s path.

"Port your helm!" Adan shouted, for the two ships were on a definite collision course. The French ship was under half-sail, inching her way westward against the winds. *Renna* roared down on her, bowsprit pointed directly at the Frenchman's side.

As the ship answered the helm, sails thundered with the change in direction. The Frenchman slid by in the rain so close that Adan could see the dismayed faces of her officers and men as they watched *Renna*'s sharp bow miss them by only a few feet.

"*Adieu, mes amis!*" Adan shouted.

There was sudden activity on board the French man-of-war as orders were given to bring her about, but she disappeared into the rain before the change in course could be accomplished.

Now Adan gave new orders. *Renna* came about to sail just to the north of west, past the last-known position of the ship that she had narrowly missed in the rain and north of the ship that had been closing in on her before the onset of the storm.

The wind quartered with the passing of the line of thunderstorms, and *Renna* sailed in a steady rain. The elements continued to favor her as she made for the open Atlantic with all sails set. Adan put her on a westward course throughout the day, and as they sailed out from under the clouds and the rain into a starred night, he turned southward.

"What course, Captain?" the first mate asked.

"Set course for the city of Porto," Adan ordered. "And, Mister Mate, keep a sharp lookout in case one of our friends decides to peer around the northwestern capes."

He was betting the ship, and probably years of his life, that the French ships would seek him to the north after they cleared the rain.

Once again the winds were favorable. The *Comtesse*

Renna loped over smooth-backed swells. The coast of Spain was just below her horizon to the east with the morning sun, and days later Adan's calculations showed him to be directly west of Porto.

"The problem is, you see," he told his mate, "that I set my friends a journey that will take weeks. Shall we go into Porto and sit there awaiting them?" He shook his head, answering his own question.

"Mister Mate," he said, "make course for Lisbon. We will discharge our cargo and take on Portuguese goods and gold, and then we will come back to Porto, quite possibly bringing the fair Renna with us for her reunion with her father."

At the Mississippi River, Ho-ya and his party discovered that there was only one easy way to cross: in the canoes of Chickasaw boatmen, who came from the village just downstream called Chickasaw Bluffs. The Chickasaw, however, demanded payment. The travelers, having no gold or silver, nor any goods that they wanted to trade, were left to find their own way across the river. Using tomahawks, the men cut logs for rafts.

It was slow work. The river was low, and the water lay far out beyond mud banks, so that each log had to be wrestled across what seemed to be miles of boggy going. Finally, when several rafts had been completed and the first groups loaded, the rafts moved off into the current only to be swept downstream, the polers helpless to do much more than edge their rafts slowly toward the far bank. They came to shore far below the point of departure, so that the rafts had to be pulled, pushed, and coaxed back upstream before being launched for the return to the eastern bank.

It took four trips to move everyone. We-yo and Summer Moon were among the last. Ho-ya had been acting as poler and had made each of the crossings. As it happened, We-yo and Summer Moon did not board his particular raft.

It was growing late, and something odd was happening to the river. From the level of the water it seemed that the surface ran upward toward the middle, and far out in the center of the stream, floating things began to appear—limbs, drift, a dead deer. Ho-ya, inexperienced in such matters, had no way of knowing that heavy rains far upstream had sent cascades of waters from the river's tributaries into the main stream, that the river was rising swiftly.

The raft bearing We-yo and Summer Moon was lightly laden. It carried two polers, one of the few remaining horses, and just the two passengers. It was the last to be cast off, because the two men who were to guide it had difficulty dislodging it from the mud.

Ho-ya's raft was at midstream when the raft carrying his sister and niece was struck by the huge butt end of a fallen tree. The vessel tilted dangerously, and the horse, in panic, jumped toward one of the two polers, carrying that man into the water with him. The lightened raft leaped, throwing the other poler into the water as the awkward craft was swept away before the rising water, pushed by the huge, floating tree.

Ho-ya could only watch in horror as We-yo and Summer Moon were swept downstream with no means of guiding the raft, propelled as it was by the mass of the tree. With each minute the river carried mother and child farther away from the landing site on the western bank. He could do nothing, for he still had to help steer his own craft to the bank to unload its passengers safely.

When at last Ho-ya's raft ran aground on the mud bank and the women and children aboard were assisted to dry ground, the shadows had grown long. The rising waters were lapping over the mud flats, and in some areas were invading the flood plain that lay beyond the black mire. Those who had crossed first had found a small rise of ground for a campsite. Fires sent smoke into the sky.

Seeing a young woman carrying an infant, Ho-ya went to her. "I will help you," he said, taking her arm and leading her across the mud. They were nearing high ground when the woman's foot slipped, and off balance, she stepped into a puddle. She screamed in agony. Ho-ya looked down quickly. She had stepped into a nest of rutting water moccasins. Four of the dirty-brown reptiles had buried their fangs in her leg.

Crying out, Ho-ya seized his tomahawk and began to beat the snakes away from the stricken woman, who was now weeping with pain and fear. He jerked her away, killed one thick-bellied snake that chased them, and took the infant from her hand.

"I am dead," the woman said.

Ho-ya nodded.

"Who will care for my son?"

"Come," Ho-ya urged, taking her arm. "We will find you a place to rest."

"I will rest forever. Who will care for my little Jani?"

Ho-ya did not answer. He called to a group of women around a cook fire. One of them came, looked at the rapidly swelling leg of the woman with a gasp, and took the child from Ho-ya's arms.

"Jani," the woman whispered, as she sat down weakly on the damp ground.

Soon the pain began, the woman's body raging with fever as her leg swelled until the skin tore, leaving great white canyons in her flesh.

The woman who had taken the boy, Jani, came to Ho-ya with the infant in her arms. "Who is to care for this one? I have children of my own. Already I have more to carry than I can manage."

"Care for him for the night," Ho-ya said.

"Only for the night."

Jani's mother died in agony before midnight. Ho-ya was at her side, and her last words were, "Jani . . . Jani."

He held her hand. "Don't worry. Go in peace. Jani will be well tended."

Ho-ya's great concern was for We-yo and Summer Moon, but he knew that it would be foolish to try to make his way through the riverside brush and swamps in the dark. His reason told him that We-yo would have chosen her time, would have left the raft to swim to shore, and in all probability she was spending the night in a tree somewhere downriver, uncomfortable but quite safe. He would go after her at first light. As for the boy, Jani, there were several nursing mothers in the group. Once We-yo was back, she could tend the infant, seeing to it that he was fed along with the babies of those women who had milk.

It was early morning before Ho-ya could sleep. He was awakened by loud voices. He leaped to his feet and ran to the point of disturbance.

During the night the river had risen to surround the mound on which they were camped. Muddy waters, moving lazily, extended all around as far as the eye could see.

When the floating tree had slammed into her raft, We-yo reached out for Summer Moon with one arm and clung to one of the raft's logs with the other. She saw a horse and one of the two men who had been poling the raft swimming strongly for the eastern bank. There was no sign of the other poler, and she feared that he had become entangled in the mass of limbs.

She rose to her knees and waved to Ho-ya before he slipped from view far upstream. Then she and her daughter were alone on the river.

"Where are we going, Mother?" Summer Moon asked.

"It seems we're taking a ride," We-yo answered, although she did not feel as casual about it as she sounded.

The raft rode the crest of the rising waters, moving along at a fair clip, judging by the way the banks of the river slid past. She was helpless to influence the direction of the raft's drift. Even if the craft were not being propelled downriver by the floating mass behind it, there was nothing left aboard she could use as a steering aid or as an oar. Both banks were deserted, for she had drifted past the settlement at Chickasaw Bluffs.

She had no way of estimating how many watery miles had been left behind when the river made a strong eastward curve and the natural push of the current brought the raft nearer to the western bank. She did not hesitate, for she had no way of knowing when such an opportunity would come again. Quickly she used her tunic to lash Summer Moon to her back, and as the raft reached a point nearest the shore, just before the current turned to sweep toward the east, she leaped as far out and away from the raft as she could. She went under, came up spitting muddy water, and swam for her life as the trailing brush that had piled up behind the raft bore down upon her.

"I'm cold, Mother," Summer Moon whimpered into her ear.

"We'll be warm soon," she gasped, as she looked over her shoulder to see the raft and the accumulated debris moving away.

She thanked the spirits that she had been what her aunt Beth called a tomboy, swimming and running with her brother until her muscles were strong, sleek, and durable. She needed all the stamina she possessed to fight the current. She did not try to buck it all at once, but instead angled in toward the bank, gaining a little as she was carried into the eastern bend. Even though her head was at water level, she could see that the river opened up ahead, meaning that the channel was turning back toward the south again. She swam harder, for as the river curved the current would carry her back toward the center unless she could reach the shore.

She aimed her efforts at a small group of cottonwood trees that marked a high place near the point where the river curved back toward the south. Her breath was like fire in her lungs. Her limbs were becoming leaden. Her deerskin skirt impeded her movements, and she wished that she had removed it before jumping into the water.

She was not going to make it. She looked around desperately for something to cling to, some piece of floating debris, a log, anything, but there was nothing. The grove of cottonwoods on shore was about to slip past, and she was still far from the shore.

"I don't want to swim anymore," Summer Moon complained.

We-yo now called upon the last of her reserves and struck out directly toward the bank, swimming now against the current. The ache in her shoulders was fire. Her lungs, too, burned. Just when she was about to give up, to relax her effort and float passively while the river carried her and her daughter past the point, back toward the center of the stream, and to their deaths, her feet struck muddy bottom. She stood up, gasping for breath. The current, though diminished, knocked her off her feet. She fought a few more strokes toward the bank and found footing, waded to the mud flat, and fell onto her face. Summer Moon calmly began to try to free herself, chattering away.

"Why isn't the sun out, Mother? I'm cold. Let's build a fire, Mother. Where is Uncle Ho-ya, Mother?"

"Enough, magpie," We-yo said, sitting up to help her daughter loosen the tunic. "We're going to have to walk back to where we left Uncle Ho-ya."

She quickly found that walking along the bank of the Father of Waters was not as simple as the saying. The rising floodwaters penetrated the land, leaving swirling dangerous channels and lagoons that she was afraid to swim or wade in. With Summer Moon in hand, she turned inland and fought her way through dense brush. A startled deer frightened them, leaping up from a brushy bed to crash away through the undergrowth.

They pushed on northward until the light began to fail; then We-yo selected a spot to spend the night. She had no means of making fire, not even flint and tinder. Selecting a giant, fallen tree, she climbed up onto the wide trunk, gathering small limbs and brush to make a nest in the tree's branches. Thus suspended over the boggy ground—safe, she prayed, from snakes and nocturnal creatures—she clasped Summer Moon to her, told the child not to think about food, and, to her vast surprise, went to sleep immediately.

The waters continued to rise around the mound where Ho-ya's group had spent the night.

"I see nothing to do," Ho-ya said, "but to make our way toward higher ground, there." He pointed toward a line of trees that was at least two hundred yards away.

"And if the water is too deep to wade?" he was asked.

"Then we will swim," he replied.

"Some of us are weak."

"The strong must help the weak," Ho-ya said. "We

must go now, for soon I will leave you to go and search for my sister."

"What about this one," said the woman to whom he had entrusted the care of the orphan child, Jani.

"In the name of the spirits," Ho-ya retorted angrily, "would you abandon the child?"

"You, not I, promised his mother that he would be cared for," the woman answered.

"Ho-ya!" someone called.

Ho-ya looked up to see half-a-dozen canoes coming from the direction of the river. In one of the canoes was the man who had swum ashore from the raft carrying We-yo and Summer Moon.

"Ho-ya," the man called again. "I have promised these Chickasaw payment for bringing me across the river."

Ho-ya waited until the man had been landed on the mound. "Then perhaps you will pay them out of your store of supplies and equipment," he said.

"They will carry us to dry ground in exchange for blankets, tools, or weapons," the man said.

"I have none to spare," Ho-ya replied, "nor have the others. Tell your Chickasaw friends that we are grateful for the offer, but that we have no need of them or their boats."

A Chickasaw spoke. "We have come all the way across the river to help you."

"Not at my bidding," Ho-ya replied.

"We will have our payment," insisted the Chickasaw.

"That matter lies between you and the man you brought across the river," Ho-ya said.

"I have nothing," said the former passenger.

The Chickasaw in the lead boat reached for a bow and was nocking an arrow when a musket exploded to Ho-ya's right. The Chickasaw fell, and the young Cherokee who had fired lowered his rifle, saying, "If it is war you want, Chickasaw—"

"No!" Ho-ya shouted at the top of his voice as others of his party readied their weapons.

The Chickasaw canoes were pulling back hurriedly. The boat containing the dead man drifted slowly toward the mound. A young Cherokee waded in and pulled the boat to shore. "We can use this," he said.

"Dump the Chickasaw into the water."

"No, take the Chickasaw to high ground," Ho-ya countermanded. "His people will be back for him, and I can only pray that by the time they arrive, we will be far away. Let us go, now."

Ho-ya himself got into the canoe with a slightly built Seneca, who used a pole to measure the depth of the water, and together they led the way across the flooded plain, toward high ground at the line of trees in the distance.

The last of the people were climbing out of the muddy water onto the shore when a fleet of some thirty canoes, each with two or more warriors aboard, came toward them across the flooded flat. While the canoes were still out of range, a musket fired.

"Men to the front," Ho-ya shouted. "Women and children move inland, find shelter."

He began to place his men, those with muskets to the fore, the bowmen at the rear, as the Chickasaw split their mass of canoes, one flotilla going to the left, the other to the right. Ho-ya was trying to remember all that he'd heard about fighting from his father, from his uncles, from other senior warriors. He positioned his men to guard both flanks and waited.

Hungry and thirsty, We-yo and Summer Moon began to walk at first light. The waters of the river had moved in around them during the night, so they had to wade. Once We-yo saw, in the pale dawn, the vee of water formed by a swimming moccasin. She found a floating stick and hit the water with it to scare the snake away. A raccoon looked down at her from a perch in a sapling.

"You, Brother?" she asked. "You, too, have been captured by the river?"

By midmorning they had waded, struggled, pushed, crawled their way free of the flood and were shoving through high grass toward a line of trees far back from the river. Soon they were walking on dry leaves through scattered hardwoods.

We-yo halted and sniffed. The smell was definitely wood smoke. She eased her way forward until the source of the smoke was visible through the trees: a sod-roofed log lean-to. The structure was, she was sure, the work of a white man.

She waited for a long time before she determined the best course of action. Her instinct told her to skirt the white man's shanty, to move toward the north and a re-union with her people, but more than once she had heard Summer Moon say, "Mother, I'm hungry." She circled around so as to come toward the lean-to from the front. When she was in the edge of the clearing she called out in English, "Hello, the house."

A musket barrel poked out from the open door of the lean-to. "Hold it right there, Injun gal," a voice said.

"I am We-yo of the Cherokee," she said. "I am lost, and my child is hungry."

A lanky old man in torn and filthy buckskins emerged from the inner darkness of the lean-to. His beard was scraggly and yellowed by tobacco juice. He wore a coon-skin hat atop a rank mass of gray hair.

"Any tricks and the gal gits it first," the man called out, looking all around the clearing.

"We are alone," We-yo said. "The raft on which we were crossing the river broke free and carried us down-stream. I'm trying to make my way north to rejoin my party."

"Cherokee, ye say?"

"Yes."

"What's a Cherokee doin' this side of the big water?"

"We are traveling to the west," she said.

"Got enough Injuns on this side without more comin'."

"Please, have you something for my child to eat?"

He scratched his beard. "Little bit of pone. Leftover deer stew."

"I'd be very grateful."

"Any of your menfolks show up unexpected-like, I'll shoot you right in the belly."

"We are alone," she assured him.

Inside, it was dark. The old man lit an oil lamp, dished up two bowls of stew, and plopped them onto the rough-hewn table. Summer Moon ate hungrily. We-yo found the stew to be tasty, if a bit too salty.

"I didn't know there were white settlers west of the Mississippi," We-yo said.

"Too many already," the old man grunted. "Last I heard, over four hundred in Arkansas. Breed like flies. First thing you know, there'll be more of 'em than they is Quapaw."

Tired as she was, We-yo felt like laughing at the white man's complaint, for it sounded very familiar.

"You say you're headed back upriver?"

"Yes. We were crossing just above Chickasaw Bluffs."

"Well, now," he said, moving closer, "I don't see no reason why you should hurry, do you?"

"Yes. My brother will be worried about us."

"Reckon he'll come lookin' for you?"

"I'm sure he will."

"I reckon you'll be safe here with me," he said, putting his hands on her shoulders. "And in the meantime, little gal—" He ran his hand down to clutch at her breast.

She leaped to her feet and moved away from him.

"No reason to act that way," he said. "You're a right pretty little thing, and the way you Cherokee gals cut up with the bucks, you won't miss the little bit you're gonna give me."

"Please," she said, looking around in desperation.

"Now don't be standoffish," he said. "I been livin' here alone for nigh onto five year now, and you're the prettiest thing come along since I left Natchez."

"We will go now," We-yo said.

"You ain't goin' nowhere," the old man said, moving to block the door.

He had left his musket leaning against the wall, and in his agitation, which was evident in the front of his filthy buckskins, he had forgotten it. We-yo was the daughter of Ena and the great-great-granddaughter of the white Indian. She did not hesitate. With one swift flow of movement she seized the musket and backed away as she cocked the weapon and pointed it toward the white man's stomach.

"Now, little gal—" he said, seemingly not at all concerned that she had a rifle aimed at him, "I don't want to have to hurt you."

"And *I* don't want to have to *shoot* you," she retorted. "So we'll just leave."

"You wouldn't shoot," he said, moving toward her. He raised his hand, palm outward. "Hell, ain't this a sign of peace?"

"Just let us go," she said.

His hand moved swiftly, and she saw the glint of a knife as he drew it from a sheath at the nape of his neck. As his hand moved forward, she pulled the trigger. The slug took the old man in the sternum. He fell backward, even as he released the knife to bury its sharp blade in a log supporting the sod roof. His legs kicked once or twice, and then he was still.

"Boom," Summer Moon said.

We-yo stood over the man. His eyes were open, glazed in death. She looked around, found his shot and powder bag and a fire-making kit, and packed jerky in a cloth. She started to take the blankets from the man's bed until, upon close examination, she saw that they were already in use by a bumper population of lice. She left the white man where he lay and, with Summer Moon chewing contentedly on jerky, started northward again.

The firing began first to Ho-ya's left. He rushed through the thinly scattered trees to see that his men were holding their own. Only a few of the attacking Chickasaw had rifles, and their arrows were ineffectual.

"Keep under cover," Ho-ya told his warriors. "I don't think there are enough of them to try to overrun us."

He was thinking that this was nothing more than an advance force, that it was only a matter of time before huge masses of Chickasaw warriors could be gathered. One of their own had been killed; blood called out to blood.

Now scattered firing came from the right. Ho-ya

joined the men there and told them to conserve their powder and shot.

He detailed half-a-dozen men to lead the women and children away from the river. "Move as swiftly as you can," he ordered.

During the next hour, he kept watch toward the river, expecting at any moment to see a fleet of canoes carrying warriors. Instead, he saw one canoe leave cover and move to a point in front of him.

"Cherokee," came the call.

Ho-ya stepped into the open, his musket across his chest.

"Cherokee, you owe us for a crossing, and you have killed one of us."

Ho-ya could not believe it would be so simple. If the dead man had been a Cherokee, in Cherokee lands, only blood would have satisfied his own people.

"I cannot bring back the dead," he shouted, "but, yes, we will pay for the crossing."

The sacrifice of a few blankets, some pots, maybe even a rifle or two, would be far preferable to open conflict with the Chickasaw, a battle his small group was sure to lose.

"Come," he called out, motioning. "Come, and we will settle this matter peacefully."

As he waited, he prayed as his mother had taught him, to the Master of Life, prayed that it was true that the Chickasaw were so degraded from continuous contact with the white man that they would barter a man's life in exchange for a few iron tools.

The Chickasaw who stepped ashore from the canoe wore the feathers of a chief. Ho-ya greeted him with a nod.

"Now you will pay," the Chickasaw said.

"We will pay for the passage of one man," Ho-ya said.

"You cheated us by building rafts. We, the Chickasaw boatmen, provide boats for crossing. You must pay for all."

"Since only one man used your boats," Ho-ya said stubbornly, "we pay for only one man."

"You are few."

"But we have rifles," Ho-ya said. "We will kill many Chickasaw."

"You will pay for these," the Chickasaw replied, holding up ten fingers.

Ho-ya was silent for a long time. Then he nodded. "That is fair. We will pay for ten."

A few of the Cherokee protested when Ho-ya handed over cooking pots, blankets, and iron tomahawks. "Hear me," Ho-ya told them. "Are we not intent on leaving behind the white man and his way of life? Are not these blankets, these pots and iron tools, the things of the white man?"

When the payment was loaded, the Chickasaw boatmen paddled away, toward the main river. Ho-ya, still amazed that the Chickasaw would be willing to forget so quickly the death of one of their own, gathered his forces and sent them running after the women and children. With every fiber of his body he longed to set out toward the south, to find We-yo and Summer Moon, but he still felt that the settlement with the Chickasaw had been too easy. He still feared that the Chickasaw might follow and attack at a more propitious time, when he and his group least expected it. He determined that he would stay with the people until they had traveled beyond the range of a Chickasaw raid. We-yo was, after all, her mother's daughter. She would find her way northward until she encountered the easily followed trail of the group; and as soon as he felt that it was safe, he would backtrack to meet her.

By the time Ho-ya agreed to stop for the night, it was already growing dark. The women had to scavenge by torchlight to find firewood. Soon fires were burning, and those who had meat were making delicious smells as they prepared their meals. Ho-ya posted guards with stern instructions to stay alert. The people were tired. Soon the camp was quiet.

Ho-ya slept, then awoke to an owl's hoot, rose to his feet, and made a round of the camp. A half-moon was falling down the western sky. The first sentinels had been already relieved by those who would watch till daybreak. Ho-ya, after making known to the guards his intentions, walked the back trail until he was out of sight of the dying glow of the fires. He stood looking back toward the river.

Overhead, the lights in the sky wheeled in their great dance. The moon continued to seek rest below the western horizon. A cool breeze sprang up in the false dawn, and from far off a wolf howled.

His sister was alone in a strange land, alone with her child, without weapons, without food. How far had the river carried her? Had she been successful in swimming to shore? He remembered the scream of the woman who had stepped into the nest of moccasins and shuddered.

It seemed a shame to use a musket to kill a little rabbit, but Summer Moon was hungry. The blast of the rifle caused a covey of quail to thunder up from the grass almost under We-yo's feet, and she cried out, "Ahhhh."

She struck sparks into tinder with the fire-making kit, and soon they were both gnawing on the back legs of the rabbit.

She had traveled quite a distance toward the west to get away from the river's flood and the dense brush. The going was much easier now, but she could only guess at how far she would have to travel. She felt sure that she would be able to detect the passage of the migrating group, for that many people left much sign, and in all probability she would cross well-marked trails leading to a spot on the western bank opposite Chickasaw Bluffs. There was water available from a clear, clean creek that ran toward the Mississippi. It was a pleasantly warm day, so she took the opportunity to remove her clothing and Summer Moon's, to wash the river mud away. Summer Moon sat in the shallows and splashed happily.

We-yo let the clothing dry on their backs as they traveled northward.

Ho-ya pushed his people hard, keeping even the slowest of them moving at a pace that put the miles behind them. He had determined that he would leave them at midday to begin his search for We-yo and Summer Moon. His plans were changed when a scout ran back to report that a sizable Quapaw village lay directly ahead, and it was evident that the Quapaw knew of the presence of the travelers.

Ho-ya named a delegation of warriors and went to the edge of the village to be met by a grizzled Quapaw chieftain who spoke to him in Chickasaw.

"I welcome my Chickasaw brothers," the old chief said.

"I thank you for that welcome," Ho-ya responded. "But we are not Chickasaw. We are Cherokee."

"And yet you speak the tongue of the Chickasaw, and we know not these Cherokee."

"We come from beyond the Father of Waters," Ho-ya explained.

The old chief was puzzled. "Have you come to trade?"

"Great chief," Ho-ya said, "you know the whitefaces, I am sure."

The old man nodded. "My people have known the French and the Spanish," he said. "And now here comes a new whiteface who calls himself American."

"Once, the Cherokee hunted many moons in all directions," Ho-ya said, showing the vastness of the Cherokee lands with a sweep of his hands. "Then the whitefaces came and they said: 'Cherokee, our people need land and you have much.'"

The old man nodded wisely.

"And they came again and again, giving our chiefs gold and silver and sometimes not even that, sometimes trinkets, beads, axes of iron; and our chiefs gave them land. Now there are those of us who want to breathe free, who want to leave the whitefaces behind and find new lands where there are none of them."

"I do not understand," the old chief said. "For there are no lands other than the lands of the Quapaw here."

"Surely, brother, great chief, there is enough for all, enough to share with my few people who have left the lands where the whitefaces build their cabins of logs."

"So said the whitefaces to you, to the Cherokee," the old chief said. "They told you, as you have said, that you had much land, and you gave it to them. We have not much land and we do not give it to you."

"Then, great chief, we ask that you let us pass in peace."

"Go where you will," the old man said. "You will have to go far to be away from Quapaw lands. Go there"—he pointed toward the south—"and there are the Caddo. There"—he pointed west—"and you will find the Osage and the Kiowa."

The long journey had not been without its price. The people were exhausted. Some were dead. A man had been lost in the river. A woman had died of snakebite. Some were ill, and the pace that Ho-ya had set had drained them of all desire for making a home in this strange, unfriendly country.

"You have led us far from our homes," the woman caring for Jani complained, "and now we must go farther?" She held up Jani. "What of this one? Do you tell me I must tend this boy who is not mine, that he is to be added to my burdens?"

"I have said that when my sister rejoins us, she will care for him."

"Make your peace with the spirits, Ho-ya," the woman answered. "Admit that We-yo and the child are dead. For the river took them, just as it took the warrior Falling Moon."

A young Seneca warrior spoke. "You said, Ho-ya, that we would fight for land if we had to. And yet you gave blankets, pots, and tools to the Chickasaw rather than fight; and now when the Quapaw tells us we are not welcome in this land, you bow meekly and ask for safe passage."

"Is this land worth fighting for?" Ho-ya asked. "This land, which is so close to the river? The river is the white man's highway. He will have this land as his own soon. We have not come so far to be forced to move again in only a few years."

He stalked among them, glaring, daring them to dispute his leadership. "I did not ask you to come with me. My sister and I said, 'We go.' *You* said, 'We will go with you.' I did not ask. My sister did not ask. You have come of your own free choice. If it is your choice to go back, go. As for me, I go now to find my sister and my niece. When I return to this spot, I will be able to tell by the trail you leave whether you have gone west or east."

"I, for one, will go west," a Cherokee said.

Others agreed, and before Ho-ya turned his face to the east and set out down the back trail at the warrior's pace, the group was skirting around the Quapaw village to return to a westward path.

Ho-ya was traveling light, carrying only his tomahawk and his musket. He moved at the warrior's pace, and the miles passed under his feet steadily. He was proceeding on faith alone, on his belief in the abilities of his sister. He had seen her at work and play, in times of great sadness and in periods of contentment, and he knew that she was not one to give up easily. Moreover, she carried in her arms the greatest incentive toward survival, little Summer Moon. He knew that she would fight the spirits themselves for the life of her daughter, and so he believed in his heart that she was alive, that she had managed to get to the western bank of the Father of Waters, and that she had then turned her face northward.

He reasoned that she would have stayed as close to the river as possible without having to fight her way through the flooded plain and the riverside brush.

The country was flat and scantily forested. By climbing a tree he could see far ahead, and as he came near the flooded areas again, he climbed other trees to study the land. It was almost anticlimactic when, from a precarious perch, he spied We-yo's slim figure coming toward him.

She came walking directly down the trail left by the group, with Summer Moon's hand in hers. Ho-ya, shouting with joy, clambered down from the tree and ran to meet them. He halted a few feet away from them, pausing to thank the Master of Life for keeping them safe.

"We went for a swim in the river, Uncle Ho-ya," Summer Moon said, "and then Mother made a mean man fall down dead."

Ho-ya greeted We-yo with a formal Seneca phrase, and she replied in kind. He knelt and hugged the little girl in his arms, for a warrior was allowed to show love for a child.

He stood with Summer Moon in his arms. "Are you tired, small one?"

"Only a little bit," Summer Moon replied.

"You don't mind if I carry you for a while."

"Well, if you want to," Summer Moon agreed.

"Come then, Sister," Ho-ya said, "we'll have to move quickly to catch the others before they begin tomorrow's march." He would hear about the swim in the river and about We-yo making a mean man fall down dead at a later time, over a campfire, when there was time and energy for both talking and listening.

Chapter Seven

The birth of a child was one of the most joyful events in the life of a Seneca. Twice before the manitous had blessed El-i-chi with children, and soon Ah-wa-o would give him a third.

It was September, and Ah-wa-o's lying-in period was a festive affair. She had chosen Toshabe's longhouse for the great event, causing Roy Johnson to grumble a bit, for every matron who could crowd herself into the longhouse was present, to honor the wife of the sachem at her time of triumph.

In spite of Ah-wa-o's age—she was thirty-five—the birth was an easy one. The infant boy cried so lustily that Roy Johnson heard the ensuing laughter and shouts of approval all the way down by the swimming creek, where he was wetting a hook in the company of Gao and Ta-na-wun-da.

121

"Reckon it's a boy, by the sound of it," Roy said.

"So said my father," Gao replied.

"Your father doesn't have the sight anymore," Roy said.

"And still he said it would be a boy." Gao leaped to his feet and ran with young grace and strong legs to bring back the word that it was, indeed, a boy.

"Humph," said Roy. "It was a good guess. Once he had the sight, but he doesn't have it now."

On a glorious day that the Master of Life himself had made, El-i-chi lifted his child in both hands and presented him to a crowd gathered at the swimming creek where Roy and the boys had been fishing on the day of the birth. He had chosen the name Ha-ace, in honor of Ah-wa-o's father, who had been El-i-chi's father-by-marriage.

"Ha-ace the Panther!" he said, and dipped the baby swiftly into the water. The boy's eyes went wide, but he did not cry out. Instead, he splashed with his hands.

"Ha-ace the Panther," El-i-chi repeated, as he lifted his son.

"Ha-ace the panther kitten," said Toshabe, taking the baby from El-i-chi to wrap him in a dry blanket.

It was the time of harvest. Though Ta-na and Gao were already young warriors in training, they helped Ah-wa-o and Toshabe gather fat, golden ears of corn. Their reward was to feast on a half-dozen dishes made from the pumpkins that had grown to impressive size that year.

It was a good season. Ta-na and Gao were young and full of health and vitality. They had a few chores, among them helping Beth's hands pick crops and tend the livestock, but that still left them plenty of time for hunting, exploring the woods, and—in the crisp, dry, beautifully starred evenings—enjoying another type of exploration that involved the warm tender bodies of maids both Seneca and Cherokee. The maids were willing; the two boys were fair to look upon and the sons of sachems.

Ta-na was content to be with his "brother" in the longhouse of his uncle El-i-chi, who was now in essence

is other father. He did miss his real father, and at times
he longing to be with Renno was an aching void crying
ut to be filled. He wondered why there had been no
mention of his going to England. Not once in the discus-
ons and announcements of plans had anyone said, "So,
ow do you feel about this, Ta-na?" Or, "Ta-na, would you
ke to go to England with your blood father and Mother
eth and your half brother, Little Hawk?"

At such times Ta-na felt almost as if he didn't have a
ather. He became restless, wondering what would have
appened had he chosen to go west with his cousin Ho-ya.
ut then Gao would call to him to go hunting or exploring,
nd Ta-na, forgetting his pain, would shake off his depres-
ion and take up his bow and arrow.

Little by little, with careful purchases of clothing,
Renno and Little Hawk had taken on the coloration of the
ountry through which they passed. Spanish gold coins
ought two horses in a small village in León Province.
Now the travelers put the miles behind them at the rate of
early forty a day, as they angled westward toward the
rovincial capital. They crossed rivers—the Cea, the Esla,
he Porma—and Renno estimated that when they reached
he capital, the city of León, they would have covered
bout one third of the distance between their landing
lace on the northern coast and the Portuguese city of
Porto.

The roads were well traveled, the hamlets many. The
owns consisted of buildings of adobe brick, and the inhab-
tants spoke a dialect of Spanish that was closer to the
Castilian norm than that of the people of the northern
mountains.

They reached the city of León late in the day, and
Renno decided they would spend the night in an inn. After
splendid meal in the inn's common room, they were
ingering over coffee and a richly sweet torte when four
Spanish soldiers entered and ordered wine.

Until now Renno and Little Hawk had experienced
no problems in passing as Spaniards. Blue eyes were not
ommon on the Iberian peninsula, but centuries of mixing

with invading races from the north had produced a few
people with blond characteristics. So in the inn at León, it
was not their looks but their accent that caught the attention of the Spanish soldiers.

Seated at a nearby table, the soldiers were already
well lubricated with wine and in an expansive mood. One
of them offered wine to Renno and Little Hawk. Renno
thanked him politely.

"Ah," the soldier said, "do I detect the sound of the
New World in your speech?"

"You may very well do so," Renno allowed.

"We here are only recently returned from Florida,"
the soldier said. "That is the cause for our celebration.
Join us, friends."

Renno looked at Little Hawk and nodded. Glasses
were produced, wine poured. Renno touched the glass to
his lips, taking a tiny sip.

"And where was your service?" one of the soldiers
asked.

Renno was on dangerous ground, for he knew little
about Florida. He had gone into the Seminole country on
the peninsula when he was much younger, and he had
made one swift raid on the east Florida coast. But he knew
that he would not be able to answer detailed questions
about the Spanish colony, nor could he carry off a lengthy
conversation about service with the Spanish military.

"My son and I have a ranch near Corpus Christi," he
said. He was familiar with the area around Corpus Christi
and to the west from his visit to Julio de Alda's ranch and
from his long trek to the land of the Pueblo Indians with
Beth, William, and El-i-chi.

"Ah, the West," the soldier said. "The Comanche. I
have heard that they are fierce fighters."

Renno nodded. "The Comanche have long since been
driven out of east Texas."

"But there's something else about your speech," said
another of the soldiers, a short, dark fellow with the insig-
nia of a sergeant on his uniform.

"It is my turn to buy the wine, friends," Renno said.
For a moment questions were put aside as a fresh

bottle of wine was brought. Renno managed to pour half of
his onto the mat of grasses that made up the inn's floor
while the soldiers were not looking. To his amusement,
Little Hawk was sipping his wine with obvious distaste.

"Yes, I definitely hear something in your speech," insisted the sergeant. "You are certainly not from León."

Again Renno was on dangerous ground. He dared not
pick another area of Spain, for he was not knowledgeable
about the various regional accents.

"Perhaps you hear the influence of my Indian ancestry," he said, "for my grandfather married a woman of
indio blood."

"I suppose that's it," the sergeant acknowledged.

"It has been a long day," Renno said. "I think it's time
for my son and me to say good night."

"Where do you travel?" asked another of the soldiers.

"To Madrid," Renno said quickly. "I want my son to
see as much of his homeland as possible before we return
to New Spain."

"What kind of Indian?" demanded the suspicious
one, as Renno and Little Hawk rose from the table.

"Creek," Renno said, thinking quickly. "My grandfather traded with the Creek out of New Orleans." He followed Little Hawk from the common room.

As they reached their bedroom, Little Hawk spoke.
"The short dark one saw or heard something that made
him dubious about us."

"So," Renno said. "It appears that we are not meant
to sleep in a bed tonight."

"We are leaving?"

"Not just yet. We'll let things quiet down a bit." He
sat in a leather chair, extended his legs, stretching wearily.
"Lie down, sleep for a few hours."

"You sleep, Father. I will watch."

"So," Renno said, smiling. "The young one looks after
his old father."

Little Hawk grinned. "Old one, eh? Do you feel old?"

"Old enough to take you up on your offer. Wake me
when the moon is at the zenith."

*   *   *

They left the inn through a window. Somewhere in the town a dog was barking steadily. The sky was clear, and the bright moon gave plenty of light as they made their way to the stables. Renno slipped into the building quietly and listened. He heard only the snort of a horse and the movement of hoofs in straw. The stable attendant, fortunately, did not sleep here. In the dim light, it took them a while to find their saddles and to locate their horses among several stalls. The dog was still barking monotonously as they led the animals out of the stable and mounted.

Since the inn was located on the western edge of León, they had to traverse only a short distance on cobbled streets before they were in the countryside. A sign on the high road said that the village of Carrizo was ahead. They rode at a walk until Renno heard the distant sound of horses moving at a trot to overtake them. Selecting a copse of trees, he led the way off the road and waited. Four horsemen rode past, saddle leather creaking.

"The soldiers from the inn," Little Hawk whispered.

"It seems that we are not meant to travel directly west," Renno said. They turned back and took a road to the south that was marked La Bañeza. With the morning they were riding alongside a stream, which provided water for the horses and themselves.

From La Bañeza the westward road led to the village of Destriana. They spent the night sleeping on the ground, hidden among boulders on a rocky outcrop, and rode on toward the village with the sun.

The spire of a little church was just visible when, as they rounded a bend in the road, they saw the way blocked by four horsemen.

"Again, our friends from the inn," Little Hawk observed.

Renno rode forward, considering the ramifications of the situation. To run was out of the question, for the soldiers knew the country while he and Little Hawk did not. On the other hand, he knew they could not withstand persistent questioning without revealing that they were not Spanish.

He pulled his lips back in a grimace that a stranger could interpret as a smile. "Be prepared," he cautioned Little Hawk. "Use your musket only if necessary. If it comes to that, the two to our left will be yours."

"The road to Madrid does not run west from León," said the sergeant. "Nor will this line of travel take you there."

"Ah, friends," Renno said, "we are well met, for I must admit that we have become a bit confused as to the proper direction."

"You will come with us," the sergeant directed. "We wish to converse further about this ranch of yours in New Spain, and about the reasons for your travels."

"I don't understand," Renno said, glancing at his son.

"I think that we understand only too well. You are spies for the French. That is what I detected in your speech, a French accent. Now you will hand over your weapons."

"Os-sweh-ga-da-ah Ne-wa-ah," Renno said grimly, "they want our weapons."

He swung his musket butt first to take the sergeant alongside the head. The sound was a dull thud, like a melon breaking. He followed up with a jab of his Spanish stiletto to the sergeant's heart; the Toledo steel blade, which he had taken from the body of a Spanish messenger so long ago, had come home to its native country.

Little Hawk, beside him, had lunged with his Marine saber and skewered a man to his left on the sharp weapon. Even as the sergeant was falling heavily to the ground, Little Hawk let his musket drop and, rising to stand on his saddle, launched himself at another soldier. The soldier lifted his pistol, but it had not been cocked in advance. He was still trying frantically to prepare it to fire when Renno bowled him out of the saddle and they fell to the ground, Renno atop, the stiletto searching and finding a warm, beating heart as it penetrated between two of the soldier's ribs.

Renno, leaping to his feet to avoid the blood, whirled to see Little Hawk dodging a wild thrust from the remaining soldier's sword. The two were still mounted. Renno readied himself to take the Spaniard from the rear, but Little Hawk moved faster, urging his horse in close and parrying another thrust from the Spaniard's sword. Steel rang on steel, and then, almost faster than Renno's eye could follow, Little Hawk's wrist swiveled, the saber hissed, and a spout of blood gushed from the soldier's throat, which had been opened from ear to ear.

Renno looked up and down the road. There was no one in sight, nor was there sign of habitation. "We can't hide four bodies and four horses," he said, "but we can delay their discovery for at least a little while."

Working together, they carried the dead men one by one away from the road and dropped them into a ditch. The battle-trained horses had not been disturbed at all by the fight. They calmly cropped grass beside the road until Renno and Little Hawk led them to the ditch, removed saddles and bridles to be tossed in with the dead men, and then sent the horses trotting off with slaps on their rumps.

Only then did Little Hawk take time to comment on the swiftness and finality of the soldiers' deaths. "Such a short space of time," he said. "Is life such a small and insignificant thing that it can be destroyed so quickly and so easily?"

"Suddenly or slowly, it makes little difference in the end," Renno commented.

"I expected more resistance," Little Hawk said.

"It is a matter of intent," Renno replied. "They were four. They intended to detain us for questioning. Killing is a thing that requires mental preparation. They were not ready to kill; we were."

"They were on holiday. Home from their adventures. Safe in their own country."

Renno looked at his son musingly. "If you are asking me to give you an excuse for having killed, I cannot."

"It's the way of the world," Little Hawk said.

Renno nodded. "Had I been given a choice—"

"I know. It was just that it happened so quickly."

"I fear that traveling will become more difficult for us once these bodies are discovered," Renno said. "We will put them as far behind us as we can before sunset."

They rode through Destriana without stopping, merely nodding and mumbling greetings to people in the street. Away from the village Renno urged his horse into a ground-covering lope. By nightfall they were thirty miles away from the site of the brief battle.

Renno's suspicions that things would become more difficult seemed confirmed when, shortly after dark, a horseman galloped past their fireless campsite in a small clump of trees.

"Spreading the word?" Little Hawk asked.

"We must assume so," Renno said.

They slept for a few hours. Renno awoke Little Hawk in the still of the night. They saddled the horses and rode at a walk until the sun climbed above the eastern hills, then found a place of concealment for the day. During the afternoon a squad of heavily armed soldiers came jingling and jangling past.

After several nights of traveling in the dark and sleeping during the day, Little Hawk said, "I have a complaint."

Renno looked at him.

"I'm certainly not seeing much of the country," Little Hawk said.

As long as Ho-ya's group of self-chosen exiles kept on the move, they were tolerated by the Quapaw of the Arkansas River valley. If, however, they lingered more than one night in a camping spot, then by the end of the second day groups of armed and painted warriors appeared to offer a silent threat.

The way was ever westward. Because of the women and children and the travois carrying their belongings, the going was slow. Hunting was hit or miss. With no time to preserve excess meat, they wasted food when the hunt was successful and went hungry when game was scarce. To complicate matters, some of the familiar forage foods were not to be found in the strange land. However, We-yo and the other women did find wild onions, and they cooked young nettles for a nutritious green dish. Milkweed pods and blossoms were also a part of the evening meal, though they were not favorites; once We-yo used the last of her cornmeal to make batter in which to fry dandelion blossoms.

We-yo had taken charge of the orphan boy, Jani. He spent the days of travel on her back, riding in a carrying pouch that she had fashioned. A good and patient infant who rarely cried, Jani had three wet nurses—two Cherokee women and one Seneca who were carrying infants of their own.

Jani was the Cherokee equivalent of John. Ho-ya had suggested changing the name, for it smacked of the white man; but We-yo liked the sound and brevity of it, and Summer Moon could pronounce it.

"Is he my little brother?" Summer Moon asked one night while We-yo was playing with the boy, tickling him so that he laughed lustily.

"We are all brothers and sisters," We-yo answered.

"But is he going to be my real brother?"

"He will live with us," We-yo agreed.

"Will he be a pest like other little brothers?"

"I suspect he will, at first," We-yo said, laughing. "We must be patient with him, Big Sister."

We-yo fell into a moody silence. Until Summer Moon had asked her innocently direct questions, she had not given serious consideration to Jani's future. Getting through each day had been enough. What was to become of the boy? Ordinarily, in village life, he would have presented no problem, for any number of families would have been willing to take him in and make him their own. On the march, however, an infant was a liability because food was not always available. By default, then, he was hers.

He was so young, so helpless. He would not remember his blood mother but would look upon We-yo as his mother, Summer Moon as his sister.

Well, she told herself, so be it. She had no man to make a son for her in her belly. She would take Jani as her son and thank the Master of Life for him.

The long, weary days passed. Though summer had given way to autumn, the days still sent sweat in rivulets down their backs. The exiles entered a land of low, rolling, evergreen-covered hills. For weeks now, Ho-ya had been leading them slightly to the north of west, for he had heard from the Quapaw that green mountains were there, and perhaps a few of a people that the Quapaw called Osage. It was good country, rich in game. In the winter the hills would offer shelter from the north winds.

As they traveled on, they saw fewer and fewer Quapaw villages, and then came a time when they traveled for ten days, up and over ridges, through snug little valleys and glens. There was no corn, except for the precious, hoarded supply of seeds that would become their first crop once they were settled. There was no salt, so the hunters kept their eyes open for a salt lick.

"The people are growing restless, Brother," We-yo told Ho-ya one night over their fire. "We have traveled far, and each of us has worn out more than one pair of moccasins."

Ho-ya nodded. "Soon the first north winds will blow," he said. "Before the snow comes, we must have hunted sufficient meat and dried it." He had not needed We-yo's reminder that the people were tired. He knew it was imperative to choose a place to winter, and soon. If he waited too long, they would perish.

To the northwest lay heavily forested mountains. In the wooded foothills he scouted a pretty little valley where a ridge would be a barrier against the chill winds of winter. He ran back, led the people into the valley, and said, "Here we will stay."

"It is a good place," We-yo told her brother.

Ho-ya nodded. What he liked most about the valley was that it was at least two hundred miles away from the nearest white settlement.

It was as if the spirits had smiled upon them. Hunters ranged out and, in another valley, discovered a great herd of buffalo. Soon racks of wood held drying strips of meat, and the smell of cooking flesh was good to the nose. The women found a salt lick that was well used by the buffalo, deer, and other animals. While the meat smoked and dried in the sun, the women worked the hides.

Blades rang out in the golden days of a perfect autumn. The men built lodges of poles, sod, and skins. Haste was necessary, and the labor force was limited. For ease and quickness in constructing shelter for all, it was decided they should return to the old ways of the Seneca, living communally in longhouses rather than in individual lodges such as Seneca and Cherokee had used in recent years. They cut saplings and lashed them together into two frameworks, which were covered with bark to form two long buildings with pitched roofs. Space was provided in the longhouses for a fire for each family and a smoke-hole above each fire. To the right and left of the fires, they built partitions to create rooms offering some privacy.

Many challenges remained, of course. Already some were complaining about the lack of salt, corn, and sugar. There would be no more sugar, and the only salt would come from the lick. Corn would be plentiful, if the spirits willed it, with the next year's crop. There was game, but they had no way to replenish their supply of powder and shot. When they used up what they had brought, they would revert to the ways of the past, carrying on the hunt with traditional weapons, bow and arrow. They would need a level of skill Ho-ya feared some of the men had lost.

So, you wanted to be rid of the whitefaces and their ways, he told himself. *Now you are facing some of the consequences.*

Ho-ya proved that he could stalk and bring down a buffalo or a deer with his bow. He put his musket, powder, and shot away, saving them for an emergency. Others began to emulate him, and he was pleased when several of them proudly brought back game without having resorted to the white man's weapons.

Armed with official papers from the government in Lisbon, the comte de Beaujolais ran up the steps of the town hall in Porto and was soon admitted to the mayor's office. He was given the name and location of the convent from which Renna had disappeared, along with overly sincere regrets that such a thing had happened. He hurried to the convent, where the acting mother superior told him the same story he had heard in Lisbon: that Renna had simply walked away of her own accord.

"She was not, after all, a prisoner here, *senhor*," said the nun. "We did not stand twenty-four-hour guard over her. She left us in the middle of the night, and as you can see, the country here is wild and rugged. We tremble to think what might have happened to her."

Frustrated and feeling helpless, but knowing in his heart that Renna was not dead, Beau left the mother superior and was nearing the outer gate when he heard a small voice calling from the concealment of a clump of decorative bushes.

"Do not look toward me," the feminine voice warned. "Bend to tie your shoe."

He did as he was ordered.

"The fair-haired Frenchwoman has been taken to the monastery of Father Monteiro."

"Who are you?" Beau asked.

"When she was here, I tended the *senhora*. I brought her milk and extra food, though they beat me for it."

"Where is this place of which you speak?" Beau asked in an urgent whisper.

"In the mountains, near Guarda, to the east. I grew up in the mountains, and I heard stories. . . ."

"Why was she taken there?"

"Hurry, *senhor*. Hurry, for her sake."

Beau straightened. There was a movement in the bushes, and then nothing. He hurried back to the city hall and confronted the mayor. "I have been told that my wife was taken to a monastery run by someone called Father Monteiro."

"This cannot be true."

"You know this Father Monteiro, then?"

"Of course, a man of God who lives in the mountains."

"Near a place called Guarda," Beau said.

"Yes, that is correct," acknowledged the mayor.

"I want a guide to take me there."

"I fear that will be impossible," the mayor said. "It is

a difficult journey, and our people are hardworking, with lives of their own."

"Shall I go back to Lisbon, then, and tell them that you refused to help me find my wife?"

The mayor's face darkened. "Perhaps there is one who can lead you to Guarda."

There was one. He was a small, thin man with a luxuriant, black mustache and large, soulful eyes. He seemed to have no name other than Paulo, and he was unwilling to talk about Father Monteiro beyond saying what the mayor had said, that the priest was a man of God.

They reached the village of Guarda on the morning of the second day, rode through as people stopped to stare at them, and then Beau was looking upward to the monastery that sat atop the cliff and extended over the side.

"Here I leave you," said his guide. Without another word Paulo turned his mule, kicked it into motion, and rode back down the trail toward Guarda.

Beau went forward and, halting his mule underneath the sheer wall of gray stone, called out a greeting. The cage that gave access to the forbidding building was lowered slowly. He tied his mule to a bush and climbed into the basket to be lifted to the small room high above. Here he announced, "I have come to see Father Monteiro."

A monk, his face largely hidden by his cowl, nodded and led the way.

Monteiro did not rise from his desk when Beau entered the large chamber that served the priest as an office.

"You are Father Monteiro?"

"By the grace of God, yes."

"I am Beaujolais." He thrust out his papers, the official documents from the government in Lisbon.

Monteiro took the credentials and looked at them briefly. "Very impressive," he said, cocking his half-lidded yellow eye at Beau.

"I have come for my wife."

"We had not even hoped that you would," Monteiro said, "but, after all, God is good."

"She is here?"

"Oh, yes. She is here." The priest rose slowly,

clapped his hands. A half-dozen monks entered the room.
"You are French," he said to Beau.

"Of course."

"You are a Revolutionist."

"I supported the Revolution, yes. I am an official representative from the emperor himself."

"And the Revolution denied God," Monteiro said.

"Yes, God is indeed good." He waved his hand. "Seize him and take him to the room of atonement."

Beau turned and ran directly at a pair of large monks, who were blocking the doorway. One of them reached for his pistol, while from his desk Monteiro seized a marble inkwell and with excellent aim sent it to smash against Beau's skull. Beau fell weakly into the arms of the monks, his pistol dropping to the floor with a metallic clank.

There were other rivers to cross, streams that, as far as Renno and Little Hawk were concerned, had no names, for the map put into Renno's head by the Old Ones of the cave at Altamira was without designation. As the nights of travel became weeks, he knew that mountains lay ahead. The nights were growing longer and cooler.

The countryside changed, becoming less populated, and once again they risked traveling by day. In exchanging greetings with a farmer who cultivated a little plot of ground on the side of a slope, they learned that the range of hills looming in front of them was the Sierra de la Culebra, and that beyond them was Portugal.

When next they reached a population center, in the form of a small mountain village, the people spoke Portuguese and were obviously suspicious of men they thought to be Spaniards.

As they moved on toward the west and the coast, the map in Renno's head was becoming dim and indistinct. No longer was he able to predict what lay ahead. He was traveling blind.

The trail began to drop from the elevations of the Sierra de la Culebra, and a cold wind blew in from the north, bringing with it stinging rain. Little Hawk, who seemed to be good at finding caves, suggested an early halt, and they made camp in midafternoon. There was ample shelter for both themselves and the horses. Apparently Little Hawk needed the rest, for no sooner had they coaxed a fire into burning than he was asleep, curled up in his blanket with his feet toward the warmth.

Letting his son sleep, Renno sat before the fire. Since they had not found game in the hills, he had nothing to eat but dried meat. He took a long slice from his pack, but then he put it away, for he was not hungry.

For an hour he watched the cold, slashing rain beyond the entrance to the cave. The cave itself was small and ended just beyond the area where he had built the fire. The smoke swirled to the ceiling and made its way into the chill rain.

He dozed in a seated position, his back against the stone of the mountain. He awoke to the sound of his name, and *she* was here, pale-haired Emily, the dead mother of his two oldest. She sat on the ground across the fire from him, and her head was bent.

"Speak to me," Renno whispered.

The manitou looked up at him, and her eyes were reddened from weeping. "Renna," she whispered.

Renno leaned forward eagerly. "What of Renna?"

"Listen," instructed the manitou, and in Renno's mind was a scream of terminal agony, along with a vision of a grim, gray, slate-topped building clinging to the side of a cliff like a swallow's nest.

"Hurry, hurry," said the manitou as the vision faded, leaving Renno's heart pounding with fear for his daughter.

Now and then they encountered someone who spoke Spanish. They learned from one man that they were in Beira Alta province and that the twisting, turning trail they were following was called the Excommunicated Way because of its difficulty.

"So, how far are we from Porto?" Renno asked.

A shrug. "I have not been to Porto," answered the man.

"Have you not heard how many days it takes to reach the sea?"

"I have not asked, nor do I know anyone who has seen the sea."

"Do you know of a slate-roofed building anywhere near here, one that is constructed on the side of a cliff?"

The man shrugged again. "I know of no such place."

Two days later, after difficult travel, they asked another man who spoke a bit of Spanish the same questions. He, too, shrugged.

"I have not seen the sea," he said. "But I have seen the building of which you speak. It is the monastery of Father Monteiro. There are men there who have been to Porto, who have seen the sea."

"Where will we find this place of Father Monteiro?" Little Hawk asked.

The farmer looked around carefully before he spoke. "Not many people seek Father Monteiro, especially foreigners in our lands. Perhaps he will find you."

"But if I were looking for Father Monteiro, where would I find him?" Renno persisted.

"His monastery is high in the mountains above Guarda."

"Why is it so important that we talk to this priest?" Little Hawk asked. "We have merely to follow the trails to the east to find the sea."

Renno was not yet ready to speak in detail of his visits from the manitous. "We will travel faster with good instructions," he answered.

They encountered signs that pointed the way to Guarda. Once they were there, Renno asked again about Father Monteiro and the gray building.

"Yes, it is near," he was told. "But you are a fool to seek it out."

"We are pilgrims from far away," Renno said. "We wish to worship in the monastery."

The man of Guarda crossed himself. "Take my advice and pay your tribute to God elsewhere."

"Why do you say that?" Renno asked. "Is not Father Monteiro a man of God?"

"It is not for me to say."

"I take it that pilgrims do not often visit this place," Little Hawk said.

"Not of their own will," said the Portuguese.

"Have others been brought here against their will?" Renno asked.

The man looked around nervously. "I have seen things. I saw a woman . . . a foreigner. . . ."

Little Hawk looked quickly at his father.

"A young woman with hair like the tassels of the corn?" Renno asked.

"Fair she was," confirmed the man.

"When?"

The stranger shrugged. "A summer has passed since."

"Renna?" Little Hawk asked, as they rode on. "Could he have been speaking of Renna?"

Renno did not answer immediately.

"You knew," Little Hawk said. "The manitous? Did the manitous tell you that she was here and not in Lisbon?"

"Even so," Renno said.

Chapter Eight

For Gao and Ta-na the longhouse of El-i-chi, sachem of the Seneca, was becoming too crowded. It was not the ideal place for two young warriors with great matters on their minds. Ah-wen-ga, little sister, had begun to walk, and she was an extremely active child. Everything that was small enough went into her mouth: she chewed on the toes of Gao's moccasins and left teeth marks on Ta-na's bow. She crawled up onto Gao's bed and made a nest for herself, like a small, cooing bird, by wrapping his best tunic around her. And then there was the new one, Ha-ace the panther kitten, who was even more like a bird, since his only accomplishments—other than being rather cute and cuddly—were eating and eliminating.

It was Ta-na who first advanced an idea that did not wholly appeal to Gao. Without consulting his brother, Ta-na said one night, "We had thought, Father El-i-chi, that we would use my father's longhouse in his absence. It stands unused, as you know, and it is quite near."

Gao looked at Ta-na with puzzlement. Though the longhouse *was* crowded, he had entertained no thought of actually leaving his family. But he was loyal to the cousin he called brother, so he said nothing; and when his mother spoke, one of his immediate objections to Ta-na's plan was overcome.

"Near enough, I assume," she said, "so that you two mighty warriors will come across the commons for each meal?"

Gao was relieved, for he had experienced Ta-na's cooking on hunting jaunts.

"Yes, thank you, Mother Ah-wa-o," Ta-na answered. "And Father, it will give you more privacy," he went on. "We know how you like to spend time with the young ones."

"Hmm," El-i-chi said. "And if I needed privacy, why would I not myself stay in the longhouse of my brother who is absent?"

Ta-na's face showed his inner struggle to shift ground quickly. "The roof of my father's longhouse needs repair," he declared.

"It does?" El-i-chi replied. "I had not noticed your concern about that matter before."

Gao, too, had been doing some fast thinking. He decided that it would be good for the brothers to have an entire longhouse just for themselves. They could have their friends in anytime they liked. If one or both of them felt like whooping or some wrestling, just to enliven the day, there'd be no one to say, "Outside with you." Gao decided to support Ta-na's petition.

"It would be easier to fix Uncle Renno's roof if we were living there," Gao said. "We could spot the leaks when it rained and patch them immediately."

"What do you think, little Rose?" El-i-chi asked, turning to his wife.

Ah-wa-o's expression was sad. Gao looked pleadingly at her; if she was sorry to see her sons go, she should remember that they were already junior warriors. In the olden days they would have been expected to count coup in battle before growing too much older.

"It is near," she conceded.

"Thank you, Mother," Gao said gratefully.

"*I* have not spoken yet." El-i-chi's face was stern.

"It *is* near," Ta-na pleaded.

"Very well," said El-i-chi.

It took all of five minutes for the two young warriors to move their belongings to Renno's longhouse. The first night it rained, and the untended roof leaked in a dozen places, so that it was difficult to find a dry place to sleep. When the fire burned down and there was only the sound of the rain and of Ta-na's breathing, Gao felt a bit lonely. But the rain passed during the night, and the sun dried the roof of the longhouse quickly. The two brothers spent the day patching and repairing. Working on the longhouse made it seem more like home to them, and Gao felt no loneliness that night.

Then he discovered that Ta-na had more than one reason for his eagerness to be out of the family longhouse. When his brother slipped away just after dark, without so much as a word, Gao didn't suspect anything at first, assuming that Ta-na had gone to answer a call of nature. But after an hour had passed, he went in search of his brother.

He soon found the reason for Ta-na's disappearance. Her name was Head-in-the-Cloud, for she walked in beauty and serene grace, a rare thing in one who was just fifteen, and she had captured the heart of the son of a sachem. Ta-na was a willing prisoner of her girlish charms. He called her Cloud, and she was as glorious as the white clouds of a summer day.

In the ensuing days Gao said nothing, not even when Ta-na insisted, with disgusting regularity, that they go to the swimming creek, where Ta-na washed both himself and his clothing more often than even Ah-wa-o would have ordered. It was not until Ta-na's fascination with Cloud began to interfere with important things that Gao decided to act.

On a pleasant autumn morning, Gao arose, roused Ta-na, who had as usual been late to bed, and led the way across the commons for a morning meal. Ah-wen-ga met them at the door of the longhouse, arms out to be hugged. She got her due from both boys and then ran ahead of them to the eating area where good things were sending up appetizing odors.

El-i-chi said, as they ate, "I am hunting today."

Gao brightened. He liked nothing better than to hunt with his father. "Where will we go?" he asked.

El-i-chi shrugged, "Which way blows the wind?"

"A slight breeze comes from the south," Gao answered.

"Then we will go south," El-i-chi concluded.

Gao smiled at Ta-na, but the smile was not returned. When they had finished eating, they went back to Renno's longhouse, and Gao began his preparations. "Hurry," he said, "for Father will be ready soon."

"Today I will not hunt," Ta-na said.

Gao halted his activity, looked at his cousin in disbelief. "You will not hunt?"

"No." Ta-na moved toward the door.

"Where are you going?" Gao asked.

"To walk."

Gao made a sound of disgust. "And I suppose you will walk alone?"

"No."

Gao decided that things were getting out of hand. When Ta-na would forgo a hunt with El-i-chi for the sake of a girl, something was seriously wrong. Girls were not exactly new to either of them. They had both experimented with the strong and sometimes frightening emotions that could be engendered by the nearness of a girl. They had, within the rules, known the saucy feel of a breast in the palm of a hand and the forbidden heat that lingered safely under a securely knotted loincloth. They were both the sons of sachems, and not unattractive. No mother in either village would object if her daughter was chosen when the time came for the brothers to marry.

But, Gao thought, it is not time. There were too many other things to keep one busy. The hunt; the practice of the use of arms; a spirited wrestling match; a good, cleansing swim; a run there and back, and it didn't matter much where "there" was.

Gao went with his father to hunt, and for a while he was selfishly pleased to be alone with El-i-chi, since it happened so seldom. Sometimes Gao questioned the fact that both his mother and his father gave as much consideration to Ta-na, their son by adoption, as they did to their son by blood. Such unworthy thoughts did not trouble him often or for long, however. Yes, he enjoyed his time alone with his father, but before the hunt was over and they made their way back to the village with a freshly killed deer on their shoulders, he had begun to miss Ta-na. The brothers had been together from infancy. No mere girl was going to change that.

The deer that Gao had killed was for his mother, for Ah-wa-o liked young and tender meat. Ordinarily, the soft skin, too, would have been for his mother, but this time he took the skin to Renno's longhouse—Ta-na was absent—and cleaned it carefully.

Ta-na came in while he was at his work. "Does Gao do the work of women now?" he mocked.

"At least Gao does something other than moon around after a girl," Gao shot back.

"Gao talks nonsense."

Usually it took more than that to anger Gao, but he had been sensitized by Ta-na's neglect since they had moved into the longhouse. He tossed the doeskin aside and in one fluid leap landed on Ta-na's back. They went to the floor together, Ta-na twisting so that when they hit they were locked together face to face. They rolled, grunting and straining, and almost knocked down one of the house's center support poles. Now Gao was on top and then Ta-na. It had been thus since they were very young. They were so closely matched in size and strength that neither could gain and hold an advantage. So it was that Gao was surprised when he was able to roll Ta-na onto his back and hold him with his shoulders pinned to the ground.

"My brother has weakened himself in his pursuit of this girl," Gao said.

"Let me up," Ta-na demanded.

"I will, when you tell me that you are ready to come to your senses."

"I never left my senses."

Gao released his brother's arms and leaped back, just in case. Ta-na rose slowly.

"We missed you on the hunt, my father and I," Gao told him.

"There will be other hunts," Ta-na replied.

"Indeed," Gao agreed. "Tonight, then, we will take torches and hunt the fat frogs along the swimming creek."

"Very well."

Gao set aside the half-formed plan involving his new doeskin. But he revived it when Ta-na, instead of meeting him for the frog hunt, disappeared just after dark and did not come back until the owls were hooting, replete from their early night's hunt, from the nearby woodlands.

So it was that Gao went, the next morning, to the lodge of the family of Head-in-the-Cloud. It was she who came to the door in answer to his call. He had to admit that she was good to look upon. "I thank thee that thou art strong," he said, in formal Seneca, for Cloud was the product of one of those marriages that merged Seneca with Cherokee. She, like both Ta-na and Gao, spoke both languages, and she favored the Seneca way of dress, the style taught to her by her mother.

"I have brought you this," Gao said, handing her the newly cleaned doeskin.

The fact that a rather ripe odor still clung to the skin did not seem to diminish Cloud's pleasure. Any young girl would covet such a gift, to make a new skirt for the coming harvest dances.

"It is a fine skin, Gao," Cloud confirmed, showing her even, white teeth in a glad smile. Her eyes danced with delight. Her face was the shape of the full moon, and as fair, and the short Seneca skirt she wore showed her legs, long and strong.

"I had thought," Gao said, "that you would walk out

with me. Perhaps the black walnuts are ripe and ready to fall."

"I think it is early yet," Cloud said doubtfully.

"We can see," Gao said, smiling.

She hesitated, looked around uneasily, as if half expecting that Ta-na might appear. But, as Gao knew, his brother was nowhere near; in his place stood another handsome young sachem's son, ready to pay homage to Cloud's beauty.

"Well," she said, "I guess it would do no harm to go and look at the walnuts."

Gao felt very conspicuous as they walked from Cloud's lodge to the edge of the village, but he relaxed when they were safely into the woods. His plan was working quite well. Women were, after all, so easily influenced. A fresh doeskin, a trinket, and they were won.

To strengthen his new relationship, he said, "Ta-na and I are helping the servants take care of Aunt Beth's place while she is away."

"Yes."

"It is we who will be in charge when it is time to harvest the pecan crop."

Beth Huntington's pecans were in great favor and demand with everyone. It was so much easier to remove the big, rich kernels of nutmeat from the thin-shelled pecans than it was to pick it from the little walnuts and hickory nuts that grew wild in the woodlands.

"Would you like to help?" Gao asked.

"Oh, yes, thank you," Cloud said.

So easily were the affections of a girl won. So simply would Gao show his brother that he was wasting his time by spending each evening—and some days—with a girl.

Father Monteiro stood with his hands behind his back looking up in satisfaction at the Frenchman crouched in the small iron cage of the atonement room. At the moment the Frenchman was the only subject for Monteiro's attention.

It was not easy, these days, to root out heresy and mortal sin. In the old days, parish priests aided Monteiro in his dedicated work, reporting to him all deviations from the teachings of the church. Then the atonement room had been busy, supplying constant work for each of Monteiro's six hired henchmen. But lately the local parish priests had grown slack. Not one case of heresy had been reported to Monteiro in over a year, and the last occupants of the atonement room had not been heretics but merely two peasants surprised in the act of copulation by one of the men who manned the instruments of atonement. The two evildoers had been caught not one mile from the monastery walls.

Monteiro looked forward to long discussions with the Frenchman. He had given orders to his workmen in the atonement room to keep the captive in good health until he himself was ready to "speak" with the heretic.

"Are you comfortable?" Monteiro asked, looking upward, his yellowed teeth showing in a grimace.

"I don't understand why I am a prisoner," Beau said. "I am the comte de Beaujolais, ambassador from the French court to Lisbon. You have seen my credentials."

"I have seen your black heart," Monteiro answered. "I have seen that you reject God. For the sake of your immortal soul, that deficiency in you must be remedied."

"Are you mad?" Beau asked. "This is not the age of the Inquisition. I do not deny God. I have been baptized in the church."

"Cease your lies," Monteiro thundered, his half-hooded eye flashing. "It is well known that your Revolution is godless."

Monteiro turned to his assistants. One of them had lowered his hood to show a full head of hair. "Cover yourself," Monteiro growled.

The man looked at him defiantly. "I am not one of your groveling monks, Monteiro," he retorted.

Monteiro moved with amazing speed, putting his sizable bulk behind a blow that knocked the rebel backward into the stone wall, to slide limply to the floor.

He turned to the other assistants. "It is true you are not monks," he said, "but you do God's work. You will keep up appearances."

No one else was prepared to cross him. The fallen man stirred, sat up, and rubbed his chin. Monteiro, chuckling, lifted him to his feet. "Come, my friend, don't let yourself be upset. We will have work to do soon, no?"

He wanted it to begin. He longed to hear the agonized pleas of the arrogant Frenchman. But there was time. Strong ones like the Frenchman came along too seldom, and to hurry the matter would be a sin. He would have to wait.

He left the atonement room and stalked the cold, ringing corridors of the sprawling building to find Mother Manuela in a little chapel reserved for visitors. He waited until she had finished her prayer. When she rose, crossed herself, and turned from the altar, he cleared his throat to let her know of his presence.

"Father," she said, "I didn't know you were here."

"When you are at your devotions, you make a picture worthy of a great painter," he told her.

"I pray for deliverance," she replied, her wizened face showing pain. "I pray to be taken to the bosom of the Virgin, to be removed from the heavy responsibilities of this life."

He lifted a hand, but she seemed not to notice his motion.

"I am ready, Father. The days hang heavy on me, and I long to be with the saints."

"In time," he said. "All in good time." He walked by her side from the chapel. "And the woman?"

"Her time is near," Mother Manuela said. "Soon I can go back to my home."

"Soon," Monteiro agreed. "Keep me informed."

He left the woman who wanted only to die to her own miseries. *Well,* he thought, *if death is all she wants—* But he didn't complete the thought, for she was one of the faithful ones. She knew the mortal dangers of sin, and she believed, as did he, in swift and just punishment. Not many truly dedicated ones remained.

The population of the monastery was at an all-time low. Once every cell had been the home of a devoted monk, but in recent years the young ones had not come, and the old ones had died one by one. Now the building rang with emptiness, and only a few monks tended the gardens and the livestock atop the cliff. However, he did not have to concern himself with the daily running of the place. Few as they were, the monks handled the chores and kept food on the tables. His time was too valuable. He spent his time in devotions and in thinking.

To keep his mind off the temptation to begin the Frenchman's penance, he went to his private quarters. In one small chamber were his bed, a chest, a table with a water pitcher and wash bowl. The other, larger chamber was his own private chapel; its door was secured with a strong chain and padlock. Using a key that hung from his belt, he opened the padlock, then pulled the chain through the hasps, causing it to rattle. As he pushed the door wide, nirvana came to him. No longer was he a mere monk. No longer was he simple Father Monteiro. He fell to his knees and placed his hands, palms down and open on the floor in front of him, for the master was present, and he was the master's right hand, a being of might and importance. As such, he was above all of the petty rules. In the presence of the master, he shucked off all hypocritical piety and was free to be as the master intended.

His eyes fell on the cross that was the centerpiece of an altar on the far side of the room. It was black, and it was upside down. He crawled into the sacred place on his hands and knees and struck fire to light black candles. The glow of light showed a line of skulls along the front of the altar, the bones of those who, at Father Monteiro's direction, had made atonement for their sins. He knelt in front of the upside-down cross and whispered his loyalty to the master that only he knew. He could hear the master's voice, deep and loving: "You have done well."

He dared to speak, for he was on intimate terms with the master. "Someone waits for you below."

"Yes," said the deep voice. "Soon we will do our work, together. Soon, soon. Soon you will have your reward."

Into Monteiro's inflamed mind came visions of the tortures that he himself would inflict upon the Frenchman.

And not only the man. No, no, no, not only the man. He felt an ecstasy of anticipation as he pictured the body of the fair-haired one stretched before him on the rack.

"Master," he moaned, and in his adulation he was transformed. His nose was elongated, his yellow eyes widened. His teeth seemed to grow into huge fangs, and a snarl came from deep in his chest as the power of the master lifted him bodily from the floor and left him floating in bliss for long, long minutes.

"Master," he whispered, "I need the pale-haired one now."

"No," said the chilling voice.

"The other, then," Monteiro begged. "The other."

No answer came, but he was lowered slowly to the floor. He went into the other room, opened the door to the hall, and rang a bell. Within seconds an old, frail monk hurried down the hallway and bowed before him, looking up at him fearfully.

"Bring the kitchen slut," Monteiro said.

The old monk hurried off.

The girl was an ignorant and unschooled peasant from the neighborhood. It was against all of the ways of the old order to have a woman about the place, but Monteiro had done away with tradition and the rules. When she entered Monteiro's room, her eyes were wide in fear.

Monteiro fixed her with his yellow eyes. "There, there, fear not, for this is what you want. This is what you crave."

She shrank back as he reached for her frock and tore it from her body.

The trail leading Renno and Little Hawk upward from the village to the monastery was a steep one, running along a rocky gorge. Far below, a small stream wound its way through and over the rocks. A vulture soared high above the overhanging cliffs, a black speck against a leaden sky. The horses had been left in Guarda in the care of a stable keeper. Renno led the way, for at times the pathway was not wide enough for two to walk abreast.

The first view of the gray, slate-topped building

caused him to stop in his tracks. From that massive pile, hanging like a swallow's nest over the gorge, came an evil that washed over him and caused the hair on his neck to stand up. Even though he had seen the building before— in his vision in the cave of the Old Ones at Altamira—and was thus forewarned, he was not ready for the overwhelming malignancy that issued from the place.

"Not very cheerful, is it?" Little Hawk asked. "Shall we go on?"

"Hold," Renno said.

For long minutes they studied the building. Renno was memorizing its outlines, imagining the interior. He saw quickly that there were only two means of access to the abbey: the wooden basket that was lifted by chain and pulley from the trail to the gatehouse high above, and, almost assuredly, a path from the top of the cliff. He reasoned that because of its isolation, the place would have to be largely self-supporting. Nothing could grow in the gorge below, so there must be fields and outbuildings atop the cliff.

"I fear we must climb," he told Little Hawk.

Hawk looked at the sheer precipice rising above his head and grinned. "Unless, Father, the manitous will give us wings."

Renno surveyed the cliff, and while he was trying to pick out a safe route to the top, the swaying wooden basket was lowered from the gatehouse. A monk in gray robes alit and started down the trail toward them. Renno pulled Little Hawk into an alcove and waited until the man was almost upon them.

"Good day, Father," he said, stepping out.

The monk, his face wrinkled and old, went pale. He put one hand to his mouth. "God have mercy, you startled me," he said.

"The abbey, what is it called?" Renno asked.

The old monk scratched his chin. "Now isn't that odd," he said in a tired voice. "It had a name once. Saint something-or-the-other, but I can't remember. Now it's simply called Monteiro's Monastery."

"For Father Monteiro."

"Yes, of course."

"And is Father Monteiro in residence?"

"Oh, yes," the old man answered.

"Father, hear me and hear me well," Renno said. "We seek a woman with pale hair, a Frenchwoman."

"Yes, she is within," the monk confirmed. "Her time will come soon, as a matter of fact."

"Her time?" Little Hawk asked quickly.

"She is with child," the old man said, crossing himself. "First will come the time for the birth, and then the time for her death."

The man's enigmatic allusions to life and death chilled Renno's heart. This was no place to give birth—and no place to die, either. "Tell me, Father," he asked with new intensity, "how do I find this woman once I'm inside?"

"I'm afraid you don't, my son," the old man answered. "Visitors are not allowed. Once upon a time they were. Pilgrims came from far away to pray in our chapel. But Father Monteiro will have none of that."

"At the top of the cliff," Renno said, "is there a way we can get into the building?"

"Yes, but I wouldn't try it," the old man declared. "The way is locked and barred, and only those who work with the animals or in the fields can obtain entry."

"Thank you, Father," Renno said.

Suddenly the old man's expression changed as his face registered a new suspicion. "You're thinking of robbing us, aren't you?" he said.

"I want only my own," Renno answered. "The woman."

"No, you want the cross, the golden cross!" The monk backed away. "You're brigands!" He turned to run. Little Hawk caught him by his robe. The man's feet continued to move, but they merely slid on the rock of the ledge.

"We have not come to rob you," Renno insisted.

"Unhand me!" the monk begged in a terrified voice. "I must warn my brothers."

Little Hawk seized the monk and held him still. "We're not going to hurt you," he said.

"I am caught," the old man mumbled. "I am in the hands of minions of that devil, Monteiro." He struggled violently until he exhausted himself.

"We are not friends of Monteiro," Little Hawk explained, trying to calm the old man.

"We have no time for this," Renno said, feeling urgency in every cell of his body. "We'll have to find a place below where we can secure him."

Renno turned to start back down the trail. Little Hawk followed, half-carrying the frail old man.

"We will not harm you," he kept reassuring the monk. The old man relaxed. "I will walk," he said.

Little Hawk freed the monk and let him walk just ahead. But suddenly the old man whirled and, in a panic to get back to the abbey to give warning, tried to push past. The trail was narrow, and his foot slipped. He fell against Little Hawk and rebounded toward the edge of the cliff. Little Hawk reached out quickly and seized his robe, but the garment was frayed and the threads were rotted. It split and tore as the old man teetered on the brink before falling toward the gorge far below.

"Manitous!" Little Hawk gasped, holding the torn robe in his hand. "He tried to push past, I was only trying to stop him. He almost pushed me off, and then—"

Renno, too, felt guilt. If he had been a bit more patient, more persistent in assuring the old man that no harm would come to him or his abbey . . .

He shook off the thought. "The monk is with his God," Renno said. "It is not our fault."

"He was so frail and helpless," Little Hawk sighed.

"It is done," Renno insisted. "We cannot bring him back." He pointed toward the gray pile that was outlined against the evening sky. "Renna," he said. "Renna is there."

As the pains first began, Renna was frightened. Her daughter, Emily Beth, had been born in a luxurious town house in Paris with the finest medical care available. Now she was alone in a dark, chill cell.

Mother Manuela brought breakfast, and Renna told

her, "It has begun. I will need clean sheets and blankets for the baby. I will need warm water for washing and a bit of brandy if there is any."

Mother Manuela cringed in fear as Renna's facial muscles tightened and her hands went to her protruding stomach.

"I will need some help from you," Renna repeated. She had taken control of her fears and had subdued them, for she was Seneca. She had grown up in a village where birth was a natural, uncomplicated matter. In a time of emergency an Indian woman could squat, bear a child, and be up and walking in an hour.

"I know nothing of birth," Mother Manuela protested.

"I will tell you. You will have to catch the baby in your hands. Oh, and we'll need a sharp, clean knife to cut the cord."

Perspiration broke out on Mother Manuela's forehead and a look of horror came to her wrinkled face when Renna clenched her fists and withstood another strong contraction.

"Go, now, bring the things I have told you," Renna gasped, when the pain subsided.

Suddenly, with a gushing sound, her water broke. Mother Manuela fled from the room, leaving Renna alone.

Renno and Little Hawk had to retreat a half mile down the trail toward the village before finding a way to the top of the cliffs. It was a difficult climb, inside a jagged chimney in the sheer rocks, and they were both breathing hard when they reached the top.

A rocky ridge led to the walls of the abbey. A spur of the ridge formed a plateau for cultivated fields, and there were crude sheds to shelter cattle and goats. In the fading light no one was visible. They approached the abbey wall to find only one entry off the plateau, a huge door bound in iron.

"It would take a battering ram to break that down," Renno said.

A growth of ivy covered a portion of the gray stone

facing the fields. Little Hawk pointed upward, and Renno nodded in agreement. Both secured their weapons to their belts or around their shoulders; then Little Hawk began to climb. Renno followed, and they found themselves on the slate roof. The roof was in several levels. Careful exploration provided no way of entry.

The top level of the roof slanted away toward the abyss of the gorge. Renno was remembering the layout of the building: three windows with wide ledges just under the roof line on the side facing the long drop. He moved carefully toward the edge of the roof, lay flat, and let his head hang over. There, about eight feet below, was the lower ledge of a window. He turned and motioned Little Hawk to join him.

Little Hawk eased himself down toward his father. His foot slipped. He fell and began to slide toward the edge of the roof and the drop that lay beyond it. Renno braced himself and put out his arm to catch Little Hawk around the waist. For a moment it seemed that Little Hawk's momentum would carry both of them over the edge, but Renno—his fingers of his left hand clinging to a protrusion in the slate—managed to hold.

"Thank you," Little Hawk said in Seneca.

Renno, who was giving silent thanks to the Master of Life and to the God of Little Hawk's mother, said nothing. He pointed. Little Hawk lay beside him and looked down at the window.

"If you will notice," Renno said, "the wall slants inward."

It was true. From the window ledge the stone wall leaned back toward them.

"Anchor yourself well," Renno said, "and you can lower me over the side. I will then swing inward and drop to the ledge."

Little Hawk swallowed. "I am lighter than you, Father, and perhaps just a bit more agile."

"All right." Renno positioned himself. His toes had purchase on a ridge in one huge piece of slate. Little Hawk, his heart pounding, lay on his stomach with his feet extended out over the edge of the roof. They joined arms, using the warrior clasp with both hands, and ever so slowly, Little Hawk allowed his body to slip over the brink.

Renna's contractions were coming very close together and with great strength. She raised herself in the bed and squatted, and the power of the downward push told her that the child was very near.

The door opened and a frightened young girl whom she had never seen came into the room.

"Who are you?" Renna demanded.

"I am from the kitchen," the girl said.

"I will need your help," Renna told her as another contraction came.

The girl held a knife. "I have brought this, and others are bringing water."

There was a knock on the door. A stooped monk entered at Renna's bidding and placed a steaming bucket of water and clean sheets on the table beside the bed.

"Now you, girl," Renna asked, "have you aided in birth before?"

"No, *senhora*," the girl said, "but I have watched."

"Just do as I tell you," Renna said. "When the baby comes, you will cleanse him with a cloth and warm water."

"Yes, I can do that," the girl said.

A contraction began. "Come to me," Renna said. "Hold my shoulders."

"I think, *senhora*, that you should lie down."

"No," Renna said, "do as you're told."

The girl put her hands on Renna's shoulders and helped her to balance herself. Renna put one hand out to press against the wall. Her face went white as the hardest contraction of all doubled her over.

"He is coming," she said, as she felt the great, tearing expansion caused by the baby's head. "Put your hands under me. Don't let him fall."

The girl knelt, put her hand down, felt the head of the baby.

"Now," Renna gasped, as she pushed and her body convulsed and the baby fell with a wet plop into the waiting hands of the kitchen girl.

With a sigh Renna lay down. She closed her eyes, breathed deeply. Urgency cut into her and she pushed herself up on one elbow. She had no need to worry. The maid had cleared the baby's mouth and now was holding it by the heels. A sharp slap and the wail of the newborn's protest filled the room.

"It is a boy," the girl said.

"So I had planned," Renna said.

There was another knock. The girl put the baby on Renna's stomach and hurried to open the door. A monk was there with another pan of water and towels. He saw the baby, and a weak smile crossed his lips. "Truly a gift from God," he said.

Together Renna and the kitchen girl cut and tied the cord. Renna watched as the girl bathed away the birth fluids from the squirming boy who, in spite of the unfavorable circumstances of the past months, was whole, healthy, vigorous. The afterbirth was disposed of by placing it in the slop jar, and Renna felt soft, cleansing towels on her body. Then she held her child at her breast as he sucked greedily to start the flow of the clear, watery mother's juices that would turn to rich, white milk as he nursed.

Hanging from his father's arms, Little Hawk's head was just below the level of the monastery roof. He looked down. The wall did slope, as his father had said, giving him a view of the ledge. The ledge protruded about two feet.

"Lower me," he called up, surprised that his voice was calm.

He eased his grip and his hands slid down his father's arms. The strength of Renno's hands on his arms was reassuring.

At last they were joined only by their hands and Little Hawk's legs were hanging in front of the window. He could only trust in the manitous that the room below was empty, that no one would see him, for when he was turned loose of Renno's hands and dropped to the window ledge, he would be totally vulnerable.

"I'm going to swing now," he said.

"So."

He moved his legs, swung out over the terrible abyss, and then inward like a pendulum. He decided to drop on the count of three, and his heart was pounding wildly as he counted aloud, then said, "Now!"

He released his hold on his father's hands and fell . . . only a few feet. Landing in a crouch, he teetered for an instant, then lunged forward to cling to the window sill with all of his strength. He looked up, could see Renno's face outlined against the darkening sky.

The window was covered with wooden shutters from which the paint had long since weathered away. To his relief the shutters opened easily. His luck held. The glass had been broken, and he stepped down into a dark, small room that contained a bed, a table, and a small chest of drawers. The room smelled of dust and neglect, as if long unused. He went back to the window, showed himself, and whispered, "Wait."

He took the blankets from the bed and cut them into strips, then tied them together. When he had a rope which he felt was long enough to reach to the chimney pot atop the ridge of the roof above Renno, he bundled it up and, on the second try, managed to get it within Renno's grasp. When the rope was secured to the chimney, it just barely reached the top of the window.

"Come down," Little Hawk whispered. "When you are at the end, I can steady you."

Renno lowered himself over the edge. As he did so, Little Hawk could hear the old, flimsy fabric of the make-shift rope stretching and tearing. Reaching, he grasped his father around the knees and said, "Let go."

Renno landed off balance and teetered for a moment before Little Hawk could pull him into the room.

"Thank you," Renno breathed in Seneca.

"Let's not do that again," Little Hawk replied.

Renno looked around the room. "No one has slept in here for a long time."

The same was true of all the other rooms on the topmost floor of the monastery. Their careful explorations revealed only the unoccupied cells of monks who were long gone.

Chapter Nine

With her child at her breast, Renna dozed. The tug of the hungry little mouth was so reassuring that it was impossible for her to entertain negative thoughts. Relaxed, free of pain and the discomfort of a distended stomach, she was dreaming of the time—and it would be soon—when Beau would come for her and she would see the sky once again, away from the cold, stone walls of her prison. So content was she that when Mother Manuela entered the room and gave the scullery maid a curt order to leave, she knew only a bit of pique at having her serene moment disturbed.

The child continued nursing as the nun moved to stand menacingly over the bed. "You are no longer protected by your belly," she said in an iron-hard voice. "Now you will answer for your blasphemy and heresy."

"Leave me alone," Renna answered. "I'm tired. My baby is going to sleep."

"Your child is the wages of sin and lust!" the mother superior cried, her eyes glinting with madness.

Without another word the nun jerked the boy away, lifting him roughly by the heels. As the infant wailed in sudden discomfort, she reached with her right hand to the table for the knife that had been used to cut the umbilical cord. Before Renna—weakened by the birthing—could stir, the knife was moving toward the child's neck.

Renna screamed and struggled to overcome her frailty. Struggling to her knees, she felt a sharp pain in her lower regions but nevertheless lunged toward the murderous nun. Mother Manuela halted the progress of the knife toward the infant and stabbed out at Renna instead. Renna gasped and drew back. Holding the crying child upside down by its feet, the nun closed in on Renna, knife flashing.

Renno and Little Hawk, having found that the upper floor of the monastery was unoccupied, padded quietly down a stone stairway and entered a long corridor that led to a large, barred door. Opening it, they found it was the door onto the plateau. They left it ajar and returned to the staircase, where they descended one more floor.

Following another corridor, they heard from behind a partially open door a man's voice chanting in Portuguese, as if in prayer. Peering around the door, they saw a monk lying on his face so that his prostrate body formed a cross on the stone floor. He had a crucifix in his hand and was obviously at his devotions. Renno motioned Little Hawk to go forward. They were halfway down the corridor when they heard the scream.

Quick as were Renno's reactions, Little Hawk was quicker. Renno followed him as he led the way toward a closed, wooden door and flung it open. The scream came again as they saw Renna being threatened by a knife-wielding figure in dark robes. Trapped on a bed, she was on her knees, moving back and forth to throw off the aim of the knife hand. A naked, squirming infant was hanging upside down in the clutch of the attacker.

In an instant Little Hawk crossed the intervening floor space, and even before the attacker could turn to confront the intruders, Little Hawk's blade had slid deep beneath the dark robes. As the figure fell, the baby slipped from its fingers.

With a quick swoop, Renna caught the child in her hands. She fell back onto the bed and rolled to her feet, the infant in her arms.

It took an instant for her to recognize Little Hawk. "Brother!"

Little Hawk jerked the sword from the body of his victim, bringing with it the life of the nun.

"Sister," Little Hawk replied, "you make strange friends."

Then Renna's gaze fell on her father, and she leaped to throw her free arm around him. Renno clutched her tight, saw her eyes filling with joyous tears as she whispered in Seneca one of the old, traditional phrases of greeting. He put one hand on Renna's tousled, pale hair and caressed it softly. His eyes turned downward to the child.

"A boy?" he asked, his voice choked with his emotion.

"Yes," Renna said, nodding happily. "But how on earth? How did you come to be here, Father?"

Renno took the boy in his hand carefully, lifted him near his face, examined the unfocused blue eyes, the small nose, looked at each individual finger. "He is complete," he said.

"Will *you* tell me then, how you came here?" she demanded of Little Hawk, who was also looking closely at the boy.

"By design, Sister," Little Hawk said with a wink.

"But how did you know where I was? How could you possibly know?"

"You can thank the manitous," her brother said, inclining his head toward their father.

Renno could readily see that the baby had not long been a part of the world outside his mother's womb. The boy was still wrinkled and pink. His primary goal was to get his daughter and his grandson to safety. He had not come to Portugal on a crusade. Evil flourished in this grim building; but no harm had come to Renna or the boy, and he did not want to risk them by taking time to engage in punitive action. He was fully aware that they were aliens in a strange land.

"Can you walk?" he asked, lifting his eyes from the baby to examine Renna's face.

"With just a little help, yes," Renna said.

"Then we will go." He handed the child to Renna. "Wrap him well."

"Father, this is an evil place," Renna said.

"So," Renno agreed.

"That we have seen," Little Hawk said.

"I was forced to watch them kill by torture a young couple who had . . . made love," Renna said. "Perhaps others are there now. Father Monteiro—"

"Have they harmed you?" Renno asked. "Or the boy?"

"No, but they intended—"

"We have far to go," Renno said. "Where is Beaujolais?"

Renna told him, giving him her opinion that Beau was due to return for her at any time.

"How did you come to be a prisoner?"

It took a few minutes for Renna to relate the events from the time that the French ship was forced into the harbor at Porto. Renno frowned. If he took Renna and child back to Porto, there would still be suspicion, unless Beau had returned with clearances from the government in Lisbon. To complicate the matter, he and Little Hawk had entered the country without the sanction of the Portuguese government. In Spain they had been suspected of being French spies. In Portugal they would, no doubt, be suspected of being Spanish spies.

They had one other choice: to travel overland to Lisbon, where there was a French office. But if they took that option, they might very well miss Beau and leave him to wander around the hills of northern Portugal looking for Renna.

"Father," Renna said, breaking into his thoughts, "I wouldn't be able to sleep at night, thinking that there might be others in that terrible room. They were going to take me there. This horrible woman was going to kill my baby."

"This is not Monteiro?" Little Hawk asked, looking down at the body on the floor.

"That is Mother Manuela."

"A woman?" Little Hawk's face paled. He bent, lifted the hood, and saw the wizened face. He had never before killed a woman.

"Don't waste sympathy on her," Renna said. "She was going to kill my baby. She deserved death. Wanted it, in fact. She said many times that she was ready to escape the tribulations of life, and now she has been granted that wish. In my opinion, she will be surprised when she awakes in another world that is not of her choosing."

"She would have killed the child?" Little Hawk asked. "A woman? Of God?"

"She was a woman," Renna said, "but not of God. She was one with Monteiro in his evil. She did not participate in the tortures, but she knew of them and condoned them. She would have watched while they put me on the rack where I saw the young man die. I saw his flesh tear and heard his screams as his tendons and joints were broken asunder."

"I think that we should have a look," Little Hawk said. "I think that we should meet this Father Monteiro."

"We have what we came for," Renno objected, still unwilling to risk his new grandson's fate by engaging in battle with an unknown number of men. He had never run from a fight when it was unavoidable, but not even in his youth had he been so rash that he sought out strife.

Little Hawk remained silent.

Renna donned her clothing while Renno held the boy. "We'll need the blankets for my child," she said when she was dressed.

Little Hawk gathered up the blankets, and Renno led the way out the door into the hall and toward the stairs leading to the level that gave access to the plateau. The hallway was empty, but as they started up the stairs, they heard a clatter of feet behind them. Two robed men were climbing the stairs from below, and as soon as the new-comers saw them, they gave chase.

Renno recognized at once that these two men were no frail monks. One of them was armed with a short sword, the other carried a heavy mace with sharp spikes.

Little Hawk drew his saber and leaped to intercept the man with the sword. Steel clashed on steel. Renno dodged a wild swing of the mace held by the other man and tried to end the fight quickly by swinging the butt of his musket upward, aiming for the point of the attacker's chin. The blow missed. The robed man crouched, circled warily. Renno could have ended it with a quick shot, but he did not want to alert the rest of Monteiro's men.

The mace made a wicked whistling sound as Renno ducked and the weapon passed over his head. He whirled, following the flow of motion of the heavy blow, caught the man's arm with the barrel of his musket, and leaned forward to let the blade of his stiletto find passage between ribs to the soft core of the enemy. The heavy weapon fell from suddenly lifeless hands.

Little Hawk had pushed his less skilled opponent against a stone wall, and as Renno turned to watch, his son feinted a slash and then lunged. They heard the point of the saber impact the stone of the wall, having gone all the way through the enemy's body.

"Quickly," Renno said, leaping to help Renna up the stairs.

Monteiro had finished his black devotions for this day, and now he could wait no longer. He made his way quickly to the room of atonement and gave orders. The iron cage where Beaujolais had spent an uncomfortable night was lowered to the floor and strong hands dragged Beau out. He struggled but he was held securely by four strong men as he was stripped of his clothing and taken to the rack, where he was tied in place with strong ropes stretching his arms over his head.

"If you are truly a man of God," Beau said, "you will not do this."

Monteiro pushed back his hood, the better to see, and

his yellow eyes gleamed with malevolence. He felt a surge of anticipation as he approached the cogged wheel that moved the rack. He himself would do the honors. He turned the wheel, and the stop clicked past two notches.

His victim's face tensed but did not yet show pain.

Monteiro looked down at the well-formed male body, saw that the man was in the prime of life, long muscled, trim, smooth skinned, with patches of black hair on his chest and at his groin. He decided that the rack would be too speedy, too immediately damaging; its use would bring too quickly the final moment when the heretic fully grasped that irreparable damage was being done to him. That was the moment when the heretic lost all hope, and his pain became infinitely more intense—for even a brave man could withstand pain only so long as he had hope.

It was always a temptation to rush the supreme moment. But Monteiro resisted, slacking off on the wheel so as to amuse himself with the Frenchman at more leisure. He donned a thick leather glove and heated the tip of a needle-pointed instrument in the coals of the fire that burned night and day. Then he approached the handsome body, the white-hot tip of the instrument glowing.

Renno was leading Little Hawk and Renna along a corridor toward the exit to the plateau. Suddenly, ahead of them, a monk stepped out of a side room and, seeing Renno with his pistol at the ready, threw his hands to his face in fear.

Renno leaped forward and seized the monk, who, like the one they had encountered on the trail, was an old and frail man. "Be quiet, if you value your life," Renno growled.

"Praise be to God!" the monk said in a serene voice. "You have come to save all of us."

Renno was taken aback. He turned, motioned to Renna and Little Hawk.

"What will we do with this one?" Little Hawk asked.

"You are come to deliver us from the hands of evil?" the old man asked in a quavering voice.

"No, Father," Renno said. "That is not our function."

"But I have prayed," the old monk said in puzzlement, "and now you are come, and yet you are *not* here to free us of the evil one?"

Renno was touched, and he fought against his inclinations with quick anger. "Get out of the way, old man," he said.

"But what of the man-prisoner?" the old monk asked. "Will you leave him to that devil, Monteiro?"

"What man, Old Father?" Renna asked quickly.

"The Frenchman who came seeking you," the monk replied.

"Oh, Beau!" Renna gasped.

Renno took a deep breath. Suddenly the situation was altered. "Where is he?"

"The dungeon." The monk pointed.

"How many men are there?" Renno demanded, his hand tight on the monk's arm.

"Monteiro and six henchmen."

"Perhaps only four," Little Hawk said. "We have killed two already."

"The large, strong men—are they monks?" Renno asked the man.

"No, not men of God. They are Monteiro's hired ruffians, and those of our order who remain are helpless against them."

Renno put his hand on his son's shoulder. "Stay with your sister."

"No," Little Hawk countered. "There are more of them than of you."

"And I will not be left alone, either," Renna declared. "Besides, I can show you the way."

"Come then," Renno agreed.

Little Hawk took the baby in one arm and supported Renna with the other as she took the lead.

Beau bellowed in shock, pain, and surprise as Monteiro inserted the white-hot tip of his instrument under one fingernail.

Monteiro's skull-like face was parted in a grimace of ecstasy. His yellow eyes glowed.

"You may begin your confession at any time," Monteiro said, as he reheated the instrument.

"What would you have me say?" Beau asked. "I have told you that I was baptized in Mother Church, that I believe in the Holy Trinity—" His voice was calm, although his inner feelings were anything but serene. He watched, his head twisted to one side, as Monteiro approached.

This time the needlelike point, glowing with white heat, was driven quickly under Beau's index fingernail. His body tensed, every muscle rigid, as he roared out his protest.

One of Monteiro's henchmen snickered. "This one will not be brave. He will wake the dead with his screams."

"Monteiro," Beau gasped, "why? Can you tell me why you are doing this?"

"By so asking," Monteiro said, standing where Beau could see into his eyes, "you confess your sins. You confess that you are unaware of the laws of God, for if you have to ask why, you are in sin without knowing it. Such ignorance only compounds your guilt, for His word is everywhere."

"Tell me how I have sinned," Beau demanded. "This is the age of justice. No longer can a man be presumed guilty without proof. Tell me how I have committed heresy or blasphemy."

"This is my proof," Monteiro said, as he brought the instrument close and touched the skin of Beau's male member, raising a small blister.

Beau's physical pain was intense, but his mental pain was more excruciating, for a sudden picture of Renna at the mercy of the madman who stood looking down into his face made chills of horror course up his back.

"Monteiro," Beau asked, "where is my wife?"

Monteiro was intent on giving pain to another of Beau's fingers, but he paused.

"By now your child, the devil's spawn, is dead," he said, chuckling.

"My child?" The mental agony pierced Beau.

"It was a boy," Monteiro said. "Mother Manuela will

have taken care of him by now, and you will be followed to the rack by the evil whore of blasphemy whom you call your wife."

Beau sank back, for he was reduced to the point where there was no hope. He had failed in the primary duty of manhood—protecting his loved ones. Black despair made him almost indifferent to Monteiro's next thrust of hot metal under a fingernail. His bellow trailed off into a shrill, womanlike scream.

Renno saw no one as he and Little Hawk followed Renna. The monk who had told them about the Frenchman in the room of atonement was left behind, his hands raised in an attitude of prayer. The stairwell leading down to the dungeon level was dark. The stones of the steps were worn with the passage of many feet over the centuries. A lower corridor was lit only by flickering candles.

Renna halted outside an ironbound door and nodded. "Here," she said.

Renno put his musket against the wall and looked to the priming of his pistol as Little Hawk handed Renna the baby, checked his own pistol, and loosened his saber in its sheath.

"You will stay here," Renno instructed his daughter.

"Yes," she agreed, cradling the baby in her arms. "Be careful."

Little Hawk opened the heavy door slowly to reveal a huge, high-ceilinged room lit by the glare of torches. The air was smoky and heavy. A searing scream of agony came at the instant of the opening. Renno stepped onto a landing at the head of a short flight of steps leading down to floor level.

Beau was stretched on the rack and a figure was bent over him, holding an instrument of torture in his hands. Four others, hooded, wearing long black robes, were in various attitudes of attention as they watched Beau's body convulse with pain and heard his roar of indignation become a shriek.

Renno saw a cloudlike aura around the figure of the cowled man who had to be Monteiro. Gradually individual

figures came to be distinguishable, and he felt a shiver of
dread, for he had seen the cavorting things of evil before.
He had fought them during his encounters with the witch
Melisande and the Seneca shaman Hodano. He looked at
Little Hawk, lifted his pistol, nodded.

Two shots rang out. There was no warning; one does
not alert evil. Renno's shot was wasted, for he had aimed it
at Monteiro, and he had seen an imp of evil stand between
the mad priest and the ball. Little Hawk's shot dropped
one of the men. The other three were alerted. The two
Seneca were leaping down the stairs, leaving their dis-
charged pistols lying on the stone floor of the landing.
Little Hawk drew his saber, yelling a Seneca war cry.
Renno lifted a huge, two-bladed ax from a rack near the
foot of the stairs.

Monteiro screamed out, and the flickering imps of
evil swarmed around him protectively. The three remaining men hesitated, then surged forward to meet the attack
armed with sword and ax.

Renno led the way, crashing under the powerful
swing of an ax to bury his own ax in the chest of the
enemy. Little Hawk was as swift, parrying a thrust from a
huge, two-handed sword of Toledo steel to lance the body
of his opponent with his marine saber.

Only one man was left. Renno whirled, leaving him to
Little Hawk. Monteiro was armed only with the needle-
pointed instrument of torture.

"Renno!" Beau yelped in glad surprise.

But Renno's attentions were with Monteiro and an
old enemy, an enemy he had faced in the coils of a giant,
earthen snake in the Ohio lands, in the jungles of Jamaica,
and along the banks of the Father of Waters. The human
tools of the ancient evil ones were different, but the pain
was the same, as the imps of the black spirits launched
themselves at him, fastened long, rotting teeth into his
flesh without leaving wounds, tried to push through to the
core of his being with their cold, agonizing attack.

Renno called upon the powers of good, upon the
manitous of the Seneca, but the spirits of his ancestors
were far away, save for one, the far-traveling one, the

bronzed-skinned one who stood at Renno's side and
slashed at the clinging demons with a tomahawk that
lanced out beams of blinding light. Two Rennos, one of
them visible only to Renno, were engaged in deadly battle
with Monteiro and his spirit of darkness.

At first Little Hawk saw only that his father was face
to face with Monteiro. He himself had to give his attention
to the last remaining henchman, who was armed with a
slim, gleaming sword and knew how to use it. The man
was large, with strong arms, and his determined attack
drove Little Hawk back until he felt the stone of the wall
at his shoulders. He was hard put to parry the forceful
blows, but even as he was on the defensive he was studying the technique of the enemy. The man had a habit of
repeating himself. Stroke, lunge, slash. Stroke, lunge,
slash. Little Hawk fought his way along the wall and, as
the man lunged, moved gracefully to the side until he was
in the open. He let the enemy be the aggressor, falling
back toward the center of the huge room, taking the blows
with his saber. Stroke, lunge, slash. He timed his movement and stopped the enemy in midlunge, ducking under
the stroke to drive his saber upward into the heart. The
weapon was almost pulled out of his hands as his opponent
fell.

Little Hawk glanced over at his father, who now, it
seemed, was slashing at empty air as he wielded the heavy
ax. Father Monteiro, meanwhile, was fleeing an invisible
enemy. Little Hawk, feeling the winds of good and evil in
the air, gave chase.

As Monteiro raced up the stairs ahead of Little Hawk,
Renna stepped forward to meet him. She had put down
the baby and seized one of the flambeaux from an iron
holder on the wall. Now she aimed a blow at Monteiro's
head with all of her strength. Monteiro drew back, almost
backing into Little Hawk as the burning torch flew toward
him.

But suddenly the torch smashed into something as
solid as a wall of stone, showering sparks and fiery parti-
cles, and Monteiro was unharmed. In that moment Little

Hawk saw the things of evil that had protected Monteiro from his sister's blow—saw mossy, green teeth and baleful, fiery eyes and long, venom-dripping talons as they swirled about. Monteiro stretched out an arm, and suddenly Renna was flung against the stone wall, then Monteiro was past her. Renna sank to the floor beside her baby.

Little Hawk called out a warning to his sister as he leaped over her outstretched legs. He saw a swirl of black robes at a junction of the dim corridor and raced after them. He skidded around the corner, almost losing his balance on the damp floor. In front of him the corridor was empty save for two doors. He opened each with his saber at the ready, only to find dank, empty cells. There was no other exit from the corridor. Puzzled, he raced back to Renna.

"Are you all right?"

"Yes," she said, shaking her head. She had picked up her child. The boy was wide awake, his little hands seeking, his pale blue eyes blinking.

Little Hawk turned. Renno was leaning on the handle of the ax, the battle over. "Monteiro?" he called out.

"Gone," Little Hawk said.

"I'm not surprised," Renno replied. He looked around. "It seems that the dark shades lingered only long enough to give Monteiro a chance to escape."

"I saw them, too," Little Hawk replied.

"And I," added Renna softly.

A groan came from the Frenchman on the rack. "Beau!" Renna cried out, as she moved toward the stairs.

"No, sit down," Little Hawk told her, taking her arms.

"Beau," Renna cried out again. Then her legs gave way and she fell into Little Hawk's arms.

Renno's stiletto quickly cut the ropes that bound Beau's limbs, and Beau sat up, shaking his head. Suddenly he covered his genitals with his hands.

"Would you please hand me my clothing?" he asked weakly.

With Renno's help, he was quickly dressed. As he came up the stairs, followed by Renno, Renna threw herself at him, hugging him with her one free arm.

"Here, what's this?" he asked.

"Monsieur le comte," she said, "may I present your son."

For long moments, Beau's face was illuminated, free of the agony of his ordeal, as he looked at the red, wrinkled little face. Then he winced.

"They've hurt you," Renna whispered.

"Not seriously, my love," Beau replied.

She lifted his hand, looked at the fingertips and made a moaning sound of sympathy.

"They will heal," Beau said.

She drew close, and the movement caused a lance of pain where he had been burned. "I fear, however, that the joys of our reunion will have to be moderated for a while."

Little Hawk heard a movement at the head of the stairs. He tensed, then relaxed when he saw that it was only the old monk who had told them about Beau.

"The monster is not dead?" the monk asked.

"No," Little Hawk replied. "He escaped me in the corridor outside the door."

"Then he has certainly fled," the monk said, "for there is an escape door—a priest hole to the trail leading down the mountain." He crossed himself and lifted his face in silent prayer.

"He will not return," Renno promised, "not if you call upon God to support you."

"Perhaps we have done too little of that," the monk acknowledged.

Only four other monks were left in the ancient monastery. They begged to be allowed to serve a meal to the men who had killed the evil ones in the room of atonement. Renno agreed, for he could see that both Beau and Renna needed rest before traveling, and he knew, too, Beau's injuries must be attended to.

A search of the old building revealed no indication of Monteiro. The monks showed Renno the priest hole in the lower corridor. It made its exit from a hidden cleft onto the trail leading to the village. Monteiro was gone.

They slept in monks' cells, woke early, and ate a

hearty breakfast. Renno was eager to move on, but both Renna and Beau were weak from their separate ordeals. He chaffed with inaction but waited for two more days, giving Renna, especially, a chance to regain her strength. The five old monks were solicitous, for they were grateful at having been at least temporarily freed of the evil control of Monteiro.

When, at last, Renno and his little group set out down the trail toward Guarda, they were met with curious stares. In the village one old woman mustered enough courage to approach them. She spoke first in Portuguese and then in Spanish.

"There was lightning from a clear sky," she said. "Has the evil one, then, been vanquished?"

"He has fled, Old Mother," Renno told her. "Should he return, stand against him with your prayers."

The old woman crossed herself. She tottered back toward a waiting group of villagers to spread the news. There was much making of the sign of the cross, and curious eyes followed them as Renno retrieved the horses from the stable and then helped Beau and Renna—holding the baby—onto their mounts.

The four set out on the road toward Porto, where, Beau assured them, a Portuguese sloop awaited to take them all to the civilized climes of Lisbon. He promised there would be no problem about Renno and Little Hawk being in the country without papers. They would be listed as aides to the official ambassador from Napoleon.

They were halfway to Porto when their plans were changed abruptly by the appearance in the road ahead of a young man in well-made, expensive clothing that was obviously of French design and make.

"André!" Beau shouted, when he saw the young man. He got down off his horse carefully, favoring a certain portion of his anatomy. "What are you doing here?"

"I have come to warn you," the young man said. "General Andoche Junot is marching on Portugal with a French army of thirty thousand men. The antagonism of the people of Porto forced the ship to leave the harbor because it had brought you, a Frenchman. At any rate, the captain had given you up for dead. I remained behind to keep you from going into Porto, where you would surely be either killed or thrown into prison."

On an autumn day when the sky was free of the usual haze of humidity and the sun was a blessing, when the air was crisp, clean, and pure, Gao fell in love. He had planned merely to prove the fickleness of girls to his brother. He had presented the worked doeskin to Head-in-the-Cloud, and she had agreed to walk out with him. Now they were in the woodland where the leaves of the hardwood trees had turned to various shades of red, yellow, brown, and gold. One of the family dogs had followed Gao and was sniffing his way through the trees, somewhat frustrated by the multitude of opportunities to leave canine messages.

"When will the pecans be ripe?" Cloud asked, after a long silence.

"Soon," Gao said. For some reason words came hard. At first he had been quite glib as he walked at the side of Head-in-the-Cloud; then he began to smell the clean freshness of her black hair, felt her warm softness as her hip bumped his at a narrow point of the pathway. There was an awareness in him that infected his tongue with numbness.

"How lucky you are to be related to the English-woman," she said. "To be able to come and go in that big house when you like. Tell me, is it as wonderful as they say?"

"It's—a big house," Gao managed. "Have you not been inside?"

"Once, when I was much smaller, but that was before it was completely furnished. Is it true that some things were brought by wagon all the way from Knoxville?"

"Oh, yes, and even farther," Gao replied. "Some pieces came first to North Carolina by ship, and then by wagon all the way across the mountains."

"I wish I could see it again."

"I'll show you," he said, without thinking. Though he and Ta-na were keeping an eye on the orchards and livestock, the housework was done by Beth's servants, the freed Negroes, and the house was the undisputed domain of Cook.

"Oh, will you?" Cloud cried, turning to favor Gao with such a smile that he felt his face go warm and full with his flush. "When?"

"Right now, if you like," he said magnanimously.

"Let's do," she agreed with enthusiasm.

They took a path that would lead to the creek near Huntington Castle, came to the water after a brisk walk, and saw the big, frame house gleaming whitely through the trees. Gao was beginning to wonder just how he'd manage to get past Cook's vigilance when he saw Ta-na emerge from the stables. He felt a surge of guilt and doubt as Ta-na lifted an arm in greeting and came to meet them. There was a curious expression on Ta-na's face.

"Ta-na," Cloud said with enthusiasm, "Gao is going to show me the house."

"I see," Ta-na said doubtfully.

"Where have you been?" Gao asked weakly. "I was looking for you."

Ta-na looked at him. "But instead you found Cloud?"

Gao felt as if Ta-na were seeing through him. Was it true, what they said about the impossibility of an Indian lying to another Indian?

"Well . . . she wanted to see the house," Gao said, recovering his confidence. It was going faster than he had anticipated, but after all, he had set out to show his brother that Ta-na was wasting his time and making an idiot of himself by spending every evening with a girl.

"I suggest, then, that you show her the house," Ta-na said. "You have, of course, obtained permission from Cook?"

Gao had not, and he knew his brother could see that he had not.

"I'm sure it will be no problem," said Ta-na, smiling wryly.

"Come with us, Ta-na," Gao said, trying to change the subject.

"I am giving hay to the horses," Ta-na said. "Go ahead, show Cloud the house of Beth Huntington."

Cloud was looking from one to the other of them, her expression one of puzzlement at the increasing belligerence between the two boys.

"Come then, Cloud," Gao said.

He led the girl across the sloping lawn toward the house, forming his request to the old Negro woman in his mind. When they turned the corner of the house toward the separate kitchen area, he saw Cook standing beside a steaming wash pot of black iron that squatted on three short legs over a brisk fire. She was punching clothes down into the hot water with a stick. Two of the house girls were with her. The smell of lye soap filled the air. Gao pulled Cloud back behind the corner of the house, his decision made.

As he suspected, the servants had thrown the house open for airing on such a nice day. The French doors of the great room stood open. A gentle breeze ruffled the curtains within. He took Cloud's hand and went toward the porch. He halted on the steps leading up to the porch, looked around carefully. With three of the house servants in the back yard doing the washing, he guessed that he could escort Cloud quickly through the lower story of the house and be back outside without being discovered.

Suddenly a large wasps' nest fell from its lodging in the eaves above and landed at the feet of Gao and Cloud. A buzzing horde of angry insects followed the fall of the nest.

"Be still," Gao said quickly, for he was an experienced wasp fighter and he knew that wasps attack motion. But it was too late. Cloud jumped and cried out as a half-dozen red wasps landed on her shoulders and her head, and she lifted her hand immediately to brush them off. She was stung on her bare arm. She slapped at the offending insect and smashed it, releasing a scent that sent the swarm into a frenzy.

Gao had to move then. He took Cloud's arm and jerked her backward. The wasps followed, finding a place for their stings on the necks and arms of their tormentors.

One brave wasp warrior found the tip of Gao's nose before he could brush it away.

To Cloud's credit, she made no sound, did not cry out again after her initial surprise. They ran, flailing at the attacking wasps with their hands and when, at last, they had outdistanced the most persistent of the winged avengers, they were smarting from dozens of wasp stings each.

As they made their panicked retreat, Gao heard a burst of laughter from behind some ornamental shrubs. They turned to see Ta-na step into view, bent over and laughing uncontrollably.

"Show her the house, Gao," Ta-na gasped between gales of laughter.

As Gao burned with shame, he saw tears coming into Cloud's eyes.

"Stop it, Ta-na!" Cloud shouted.

Gao was beginning to be suspicious. Wasps' nests didn't generally fall by themselves. He glanced back toward the steps leading to the porch and saw, beside the fallen nest, a small rock of just the right size for throwing, and he knew Ta-na had thrown it. With his nose swelling and smarting from the wasp bite, his body burning all over, Gao charged.

Ta-na tried to avoid his rush, but he was weak from laughing. Gao ran into him with his head low, his shoulder bowling into Ta-na's stomach, knocking Ta-na backward, causing him to lose his balance. They tumbled to the ground and rolled, Gao coming up on top.

They had wrestled many times since they were toddlers, and never had either of them tried deliberately to hurt the other; but Gao had been shamed before Cloud, and his nose was stinging. He launched a blow with his fist that took Ta-na in the nose and brought an immediate gush of red.

Then the fight was on.

They faced each other, kneeling, fists flailing, until Ta-na landed a blow to Gao's sore nose and Gao, roaring, seized Ta-na by the tunic and pulled him to his feet, the better to land a mighty blow that took Ta-na high on the forehead and caused severe pain to Gao's knuckles. Ta-na landed a punch to Gao's middle that brought a gasp.

"Stop it, stop it now!" Cloud shouted from the side-lines.

Gao glanced at her fleetingly, saw the perplexed and distraught expression on her face as she watched the sudden violence. He wondered if she knew what this was all about.

He turned back to Ta-na, who was bleeding and had an eye that was beginning to puff up. Gao's own eyes hurt, too.

Still the fight went on until, gasping, Gao stopped, and Ta-na stopped, too. They looked at each other for a few moments, and then turned as one to see that Cloud was no longer in the garden.

"What you boys doin'?" Cook yelled from the corner of the house. "You ain't in Miss Beth's flower bed, are you?"

"No, ma'am," Gao said.

"Go on with you, then," the old woman said.

"Go on with you," Ta-na said. "Go show Cloud the house."

Gao grinned. A little trail of blood was running down the corner of his mouth. "Suddenly, for some reason, I no longer wish to act as a guide. Besides, as you can see, she has gone."

"Have you had enough, then?" Ta-na asked.

"Have you?" Gao asked, still grinning.

"Quite enough," Ta-na said.

"Do you still wish to spend all of your evenings with a girl who walked out with another boy at the first opportunity?" Gao asked, remembering the original purpose behind his actions.

"Come, let's see if Cook will give us some baking soda to put on your wasp stings," Ta-na answered.

Chapter Ten

Roy Johnson knew that his former friends and associates in Knoxville and Nashville called him a squaw man. He didn't lose any sleep over what other people thought of him. He didn't for a minute miss his life back in Knoxville, or the house he still owned there, with all his possessions. He had a home here in the village and a woman who cared for him as he cared for her. The house they shared wasn't fancy—the floor was packed earth—but the woman was first-rate. He didn't have many possessions here, just a few weapons, a tobacco pouch, and a pocket knife, but then a man didn't need much, when it came right down to it. The things of the white man's so-called civilization were all right in their place, but sometimes their absence didn't bother a fellow at all. Take the flatware that Beth had provided for Toshabe. It was a set of fine English silver, and Toshabe liked to take it down and look at it; but she and Roy didn't always eat with a knife and a fork.

Clothing? He still had a good suit and a couple of shirts, but his daily wear was that staple of frontier apparel, buckskins. To the comfort and simplicity of wearing them was added the value of love, for Toshabe had fashioned them for him, even though her eyesight wasn't what it once was. When she was stitching a new tunic for Roy, she sometimes had to hold the material and the needle at arm's length. At such times she grumbled that her arms were getting shorter, but she managed to see to the needs of her man.

The man was at peace. He missed the one whom he considered to be his son and he missed his blood grandson, but he had plenty of male company. For a good smoke and talk of the hunt and far places, he had El-i-chi. If he hungered for more cerebral conversation, he could visit Se-quo-i. And the two young sprouts who called him grandfather were always about, for which he was glad: with each passing year he had became a bit closer to Ta-na and Gao. He was one of the first to notice that the young warriors were acting a little odd. When El-i-chi recounted one night that the two boys had asked to be allowed to live in Renno's unoccupied longhouse, Roy nodded and told himself the lads were growing up.

It was Roy who first saw Ta-na's black eye. Roy was sitting in the sun in front of the longhouse whittling a whistle for little Ah-wen-ga when Ta-na came out of the house across the way. Ta-na saw Roy and turned to the side, but Roy called out and the boy, after some hesitation, turned and walked across the commons.

"Now that is a fine-looking shiner," Roy said.

Ta-na's eye was swollen, purple, and puffy so that the boy was looking at the world through one good eye and a mere slit.

"What does the other fellow look like?" Roy asked.

Ta-na grinned weakly.

Where Ta-na was, Gao was not usually far away, and this morning was no exception. Gao came out of Renno's longhouse and turned away, just as Ta-na had done. Roy had to call out Gao's name twice to get the boy's attention. He approached with his head held low. Roy peered into Gao's face and said, "Yep, looks like you ran into the same door."

The two boys were silent.

"Nothing to say, either one of you?" Roy asked.

"It is not important, Grandfather," Ta-na said.

"I think it's pretty important when my two grandsons have only two good eyes between them," Roy said. "Are you sure you don't want to tell me what happened?"

The boys were silent. Ta-na looked up, watching the soaring flight of a hawk. Gao looked at his feet.

"All right," Roy said. "If that's the way it's going to be." He fell silent, too, for Ah-wa-o had come onto the commons, little Ha-ace strapped to her back, Ah-wen-ga trotting at her side.

"Howdy, Ah-wa-o," he called out. "And you, little missy, I've got something for you."

Ah-wen-ga ran to him and looked at the cleanly whittled new whistle in admiration.

"Here, take it," Roy told her.

She grasped the whistle and blew a pretty note, took it out of her mouth, and said, "Nice."

"What on earth has happened to your eye?" Ah-wa-o demanded, putting her hand in Gao's hair and turning his face up so she could examine the damage.

"We bumped into each other accidentally," Gao said.

"You should have put a cold compress on it immediately," Ah-wa-o said.

"Ta-na eye bad!" Ah-wen-ga said, pointing with her new whistle.

Ah-wa-o looked at Ta-na, made a clicking sound with her tongue. "You both should be more careful."

"Yes, Mother," Gao answered, winking at Ta-na.

"I'm going to see your grandmother," said the little Rose, turning away.

Gao waited until his mother was a few paces away. "I'm going to the swimming creek," he said. "Want to come, Grandfather?"

"My boy, the sun feels too good right here," Roy said.

"You fellows run along." He reached down to pick up a stick and started whittling again.

"Coming?" Gao asked Ta-na.

"You go ahead," Ta-na replied.

A quick look of hurt crossed Gao's face, but he said nothing. He turned and marched off toward the creek.

"You boys had words?" Roy asked Ta-na.

"No," said Ta-na, not convincingly.

"I guess most brothers have a go at it now and again," Roy went on. "No real harm done, lessen one of them gets an eye put out or something. Funny thing, though, most of the time what brothers fight about doesn't amount to a hill of beans, now does it?"

Ta-na said nothing.

Seeing that Ta-na was uncomfortable with this subject, Roy tried another. "Should be getting a batch of letters from your dad and Miss Beth one of these days soon."

"I will look forward to it," Ta-na said blankly.

Roy studied the boy. Letters seemed to be a sore subject, too. In fact, letters *had* come from Renno, but so far as Roy knew, they'd all been addressed to himself. He couldn't recall one addressed specifically to the boy.

"You and Gao have a fight?" Roy asked, returning to the crux of his curiosity.

"Yes," Ta-na said.

"Kiss and make up, did you?"

Ta-na giggled. "More or less," he said.

"Not like you to let Gao go off by himself," Roy noted.

Ta-na was moodily silent. "Grandfather, are there ever times when you just want to be by yourself?"

"Matter of fact, yes," he said. "That the way you're feeling?"

"I have some thinking to do," Ta-na said.

Roy could see that whatever was bothering Ta-na, the boy wasn't going to tell anyone until good and ready to do so. He looked down at his whittling. "If you need somebody to, well, to sort of help you form your thoughts—"

"Thank you, Grandfather," Ta-na said.

"Yes, well, go on about your rat killing, boy."

"Yes," Ta-na said. He turned and left.

* * *

When he was out of sight, Ta-na headed toward the Cherokee village. He and Gao had fought, but basically it had been over Head-in-the-Cloud, and she was worth fighting for. Gao had no right to come between her and Ta-na.

Arriving at the lodge of Cloud's parents, Ta-na's heart was beating loudly in anticipation of seeing her. He called out at the door, and Cloud's mother came to tell him that Cloud had left the lodge.

"Do you know where she went?" Ta-na asked.

"She's with Gao. They said they were going to look for nuts."

The mother's voice held an unmistakable note of pride, which hurt Ta-na. She was, he supposed, happy that her daughter was being wooed not by just one son of a sachem, but by two. Didn't she realize that Ta-na and not Gao was the son of Renno, the *true* sachem?

He walked back toward the longhouse, keeping other houses between himself and the spot where Roy had been sitting. But the sun had lengthened the shadows, and Roy's spot, no longer sunny, was empty. Ta-na ducked into the house and gathered a blanket, his bow and quiver, tomahawk, knife, fire-making kit, some jerky, and two of the delicious nut balls made by his aunt Ena. Well-equipped, he slipped out without being seen and was soon in the woods, making his way across the little creek that ran behind Huntington Castle.

He passed the mulberry tree where he, Gao, and Beth had once been trapped by a bear and, trotting lightly under the weight of his travel kit, began to put distance between himself and the village. Had there been anyone to ask, he would have said that he was traveling with no definite destination in mind. In fact, he'd come this way before, many times, and with Gao. The trail was well used and it led to a rocky, tree-covered ridge that thrust itself up to a height of two hundred feet. He slowed his pace when he reached the foot of the ridge, for the going was steep.

He halted just below the crest on a natural shelf that

held enough soil for trees and grass. Above his head sandstone was exposed to a height of about thirty feet. Ages of wind and rain had shaped an overhang that formed an open cave. The view through the trees that grew on the shelf just below the summit of the ridge was toward the village. Far off he could see a smudge of smoke. The women would be cooking the evening meal.

He gathered firewood in copious quantities and piled it under the overhang. A foolish rabbit provided him his supper by jumping from under his foot in the deep grass to run only a few yards before halting, feeling that it was safe in its own surroundings. Ta-na made a good, clean shot, with the arrowhead acting more like a club against the back of the rabbit's head than like a piercing instrument. The blow left little blood, and the animal's entrails could be removed without mess and fuss. That there was no one with him to say "Good shot" didn't bother him.

His father, Renno, often went into the forest alone to think and to communicate with the manitous. He knew from his father El-i-chi that the manitous talked to Renno. He admired his blood father and tried in many ways to be like him, but he wasn't sure he wanted to talk with the spirits of the dead. The idea of it sent a shiver up and down his spine and he looked around quickly.

Dusk was coming, the end of a clean, warm autumn day. The sun was lighting the western horizon with peach-colored fire, and the blaze of the day's dying extended a quarter of the way around the arc of sky. The sunset reflected off the multicolored leaves. As if in sympathy with the end of the day, a large oak leaf fell, wafted down so slowly that Ta-na caught it in his hand.

Darkness came slowly. His eyes became adjusted to the dimness, and he could see the trunks of individual trees for a long time. Then there was only the glow of his fire, and the night was black all around him. A whippoorwill called from the woodlands below, and for a fleeting moment a bat was silhouetted against the lingering light in the west. The roasting rabbit smelled good. He turned it, saw that the skin was crisped and brown. Deciding it was done, he cut off a rear leg with his knife and blew on the meat to cool it. Soon he was chewing contentedly, savoring the feast.

Life was good. He could understand why his father, Renno, liked to be alone in the forest. There were no distractions, nothing to interfere with one's musings. He felt a strong urge to see Renno so that he could say, "Father, I know."

But he had not been asked to go with his blood father and his half-blood brother.

He pictured them, Renno and Little Hawk, so tall, so fair of skin, so light of hair. He looked at his own hand in the light of the fire. He was Seneca. Three quarters of his blood was the blood of red men. Three quarters of Little Hawk's blood was the blood of the people of Roy Johnson. Ta-na squirmed. He did not want to be disloyal to Roy, because he truly loved the man he called Grandfather, but it was just an honorary title. His real grandfathers were dead, and Roy Johnson was a white man.

Was white blood shared in common the reason why Renno seemed to prefer his son Little Hawk to the son he had named Swift Waters? They were always together, Renno and Little Hawk, and although there had been times when the two of them took Ta-na and Gao along on a hunt, there was not between Renno and Ta-na the closeness and understanding that seemed to exist between the two men whose skin was whiter. Of course Little Hawk was older, a man now, but the closeness of father and son had existed as long as Ta-na could remember.

Little Hawk's mother had died, as Ta-na's had died, when Little Hawk was quite young, but Renno had not given his first son away, as he had done with Ta-na almost from the moment of birth.

An owl called from the creek bottom below and a few minutes later Ta-na heard the dying shriek of a rabbit. "You, too, dine with Mister Rabbit," he whispered to the owl. "Eat well, Brother."

Yes, he had been given away. So he had two fathers. He had two mothers, for Beth Huntington had never neglected him. He chuckled, thinking of Beth, for there had been times, when he and Gao were pent up in Beth's

classroom, that he had wished Beth *didn't* favor him. Two
fathers. Two mothers.

And thinking of Ah-wa-o was sweet, for he knew that
she had nursed him as she had Gao. He told himself that
he was being unnecessarily sensitive. It had been Ah-wa-
o's fecund plenty that had determined his early fate. Had
Ah-wa-o not been in milk because of Gao, he might not
have lived. His own mother had been killed while they
were in the North, far from any other woman of his tribe
who could have been his wet nurse. He loved Mother Ah-
wa-o with all his heart.

And yet she had seen Gao's black eye first and had
shown concern. About his own shiner, which was every bit
as spectacular as Gao's, she had made no comment other
than "You both should be more careful." Not "You should
be more careful, Son Ta-na." She had not spoken to him as
an individual, only as a part of a pair. So it was that his
spirit was dark and shriveled in him as he remembered
other slights, real or fancied, and concluded that although
he appeared to have two fathers and two mothers, in real-
ity he had no one.

Feeling deliciously sorry for himself, he put more
wood on the fire. Full night was upon him now. The lights
in the sky were bright overhead, but there was no moon.
Beyond his fire the woods were a blackness. A small animal moved in the dry, fallen leaves, and he cocked his
head to listen. A wolf howled from far away. He knew this
section of woodland, had hunted it dozens of times, had
tramped it during the day and at night, but always with
someone, always with one of his fathers or . . . with Gao.

He told himself angrily that he didn't need Gao. Gao
had chosen his own company. He had lied, as well. He had
said that he was going to the swimming creek, and he'd
gone directly to Cloud's lodge.

Cloud. He didn't need her, either. He had said such
foolish things to her, comparing her eyes to the lights in
the sky at night, her hair to the perfumed flutter of butter-
flies' wings. Foolish, foolish Ta-na, whom no one really
loved.

He spent a long, shivery time thinking of following

his cousin Ho-ya into the west. Surely, since Ho-ya's party had been such a large one, he could trail them by asking for knowledge of their passage. Then he could be his own man, hunt his own hunt, leaving girls completely alone and giving his heart to no one. There would be no family connections other than a cousinly regard between him and Ho-ya and We-yo. Or, alternately, he could strike out on his own, go north into the Ohio country and find Tecumseh, there to fight for those of his own blood.

He was sunk deep into misery when he heard a noise on the rocky ledge above his head. It wasn't a big noise, but it caught his attention. It came again. It sounded like the scratch of large claws on stone. He reached for his bow and grabbed an arrow from his quiver. He could imagine a large animal, the panther of the forests, glaring down at him with baleful cat's eyes, ready to leap upon him. He waited, and the noise was not repeated, but the night had changed from a friendly, fuzzy-black warmth to a chill and menacing emptiness.

Now the noise came from his rear, from among the trees. He whirled and notched his arrow.

"Hold your fire," said Gao, stepping from behind a large tree into the light of the fire.

"You should have called out," Ta-na complained. "I might have shot you."

"I'm glad you didn't."

"How did you find me?"

"You left a clear trail past the creek. After it got dark, I just had to guess."

"I didn't ask you to come," Ta-na said.

"No, you didn't," Gao conceded. "Do you want me to leave?"

Ta-na recalled the feeling of loneliness. He laughed. "No, I don't want you to leave."

"Good. I wasn't looking forward to going back through the woods alone. I don't know why, but I was thinking, there in the dark, that this is a night for spirits."

"There's meat," Ta-na offered.

"So I see." Gao sat on the ground, lopped off the

other rear leg of the rabbit, and began to eat with grunts of appreciation.

"I was with Cloud," he said, with his mouth full so that Ta-na had to ask him to repeat. "All she could talk about was you, Brother."

"Then why did she walk out with you?"

Gao shrugged. "With girls, who can tell?" He gnawed at the bone for a minute, threw it into the brush, and wiped his mouth on the back of his hand. "At any rate, I have given up trying to talk sense into you. I will not interfere again." He looked at Ta-na seriously. "Brother, nothing is important enough to come between us. Not a girl, surely. If you choose to make a fool of yourself over a girl, I will merely wait until you recover from the illness."

Ta-na felt a gladness well up in him. He could doubt the affections of his mothers and his fathers, perhaps, but until Head-in-the-Cloud had come between them, he had never had any reason to doubt his brother.

"If you want to moon over a girl, all I ask is that you save a little bit of time to spend with your brother," Gao continued.

"More than a little," Ta-na promised.

"Good," said Gao. He yawned. "Do you intend sleeping here, or shall we go back to the longhouse where we can sleep like human beings in a bed?"

"I had intended sleeping here."

"I have no blanket."

"We have shared one blanket before," Ta-na said.

"Very well."

Before morning it rained, a cold drizzle, and they awoke to a murky dawn, thoroughly chilled even though they were huddled together under Ta-na's blanket. They went back to the village at the warrior's pace, running silently, once more content with each other's company. When they neared the eastern creek, they heard a girl's voice lifted in laughter. For practice, for curiosity, or just for the hell of it, they stalked the sound of the laughter and, peering through the branches of a spreading cedar near the creek, saw the source.

Gao felt quick anger, for the girl was Head-in-the-Cloud, and she was sitting on a mossy bank beside a junior Cherokee warrior who was at least three years older than he. He glanced quickly at Ta-na, for his anger was caused by concern for his brother. Ta-na's face was expressionless, reminding Gao of Renno.

They backed away silently as the young Cherokee put his arm around Head-in-the-Cloud; then the two eaves-droppers forded the creek upstream and ran into the back garden of Beth's big house.

"So much for love," Ta-na said.

Gao looked at him quickly, feeling sympathy. Ta-na was grinning broadly.

"Girls," Gao said knowingly.

"They never change," said Ta-na.

Over the evening meal Ah-wa-o scolded both of them anew about being more careful, until Ta-na—laughing at himself—wished that his mother Ah-wa-o would be more partial to his brother, at least in this matter.

The *Comtesse Renna* arrived in Lisbon in mid-November to find the capital in panic. The reason soon became known as well-to-do Portuguese swarmed around the ship at the docks, offering gold and jewels for transportation to Brazil. The generosity of the offers intrigued Adan, but his first loyalty was of course to Renno.

Things were becoming quite complicated. The French general Junot's advance forces were only days from Lisbon. The Portuguese royal family embarked for Brazil with an escort of British men-of-war, while Adan was unloading his cargo at pleasingly inflated wartime prices and purchasing Portuguese wine, wool, and other fabrics.

The success of his commercial venture did not assuage his concern for Renno. It was evident that the superior French armies would invade Portugal at their leisure. With the ports under French control, it would be difficult to get back into Porto to pick up Renno and Little Hawk.

In the time remaining to him, Adan visited the French offices in Lisbon. Here he learned that the comte de

Beaujolais had been in Lisbon and had sailed up the coast to Porto to retrieve his wife. If the fates were kind, Adan felt, he would find Renno, Little Hawk, Beau, and Renna all together and get away before the French arrived in the northwest.

He sailed the same day that the first French troops arrived in Lisbon but not before he was able to garner some encouraging news. Already the great Napoleon had divided Portugal like a goose being carved for dinner, and the partition was favorable to Adan's needs. At Fontainebleau, the French and the Spanish had decreed that the northwest of Portugal, including Porto, would go to the house of Bourbon-Parma. Thus Porto would not be directly under French occupation, making it easier—or so Adan hoped—to sneak in, pick up his friends, and head for the open Atlantic.

At Beaumont Manor, Beth Huntington was impatiently pacing the floor of an upstairs sitting room. Her brother, William, sat in a comfortable chair, a snifter of brandy in his hand.

"Really, Beth," he said, "you should relax."

She threw herself down into a chair.

"Would you like some brandy?" William asked.

"Yes, please," she said.

Beth had seen births, had watched We-yo's and Ah-wa-o's children being brought into the world, but somehow this time it was different. Perhaps it was nothing more than the fuss and bother that attended the event. A doctor had been rushed to the manor. Two midwives were bustling around calling out for clean sheets and hot water.

Beth had been in the room with Naomi, but with the midwives and the doctor and Estrela, who certainly was qualified to be here through personal experience in the craft of making children, it was too crowded.

Naomi was trying to be brave, but in the last months of her pregnancy she had grown enormous. Her stomach was so distended that for weeks she had done little more than sit uncomfortably in a chair. The doctor had assured them that everything was normal, that the girl was healthy and strong; but it was different when the girl who was experiencing the intimidatingly severe labor pains was your own daughter—for so Beth had come to consider Naomi—and when the child to be born was your own grandchild.

Beth, who had never known the feeling of carrying a child, felt sympathetic discomfort, a cramping in her stomach.

"Well," William said, "when you've been through it six times, as I have—"

"Oh, hush, William," she said. "You have six children, but you haven't yet felt the first pain."

He laughed. "The first one was awfully tricky. Every time Estrela would have a contraction I'd have stomach cramps."

"How much longer?" Beth asked, springing to her feet to resume her pacing.

"As long as it takes," William replied.

"Damn those men!" Beth exclaimed. "They should have been back by now. Little Hawk should be with her."

"Beth, I'm sure he would prefer to be with his wife at such a time."

So here was another worry: it was obvious that something had gone wrong. If it had been a matter of sailing to Lisbon, visiting with Renna and Beau, and then coming home, the *Comtesse Renna* would have been in port long ago. Something was wrong, and although Beth had confidence in Renno's ability, he was, after all, in an alien land where there was political unrest. She prayed as she paced, and her prayers were equally for Naomi and the child and for Renno and the others.

Beth was feeling angry and exhausted when, at last, Estrela came sweeping into the room. She was wearing a dark gown with an apron. Her sleeves were pushed back to reveal her arms to her elbows, and she was carrying a child wrapped in a swaddling cloth.

"A boy," she said, smiling broadly. "A fine boy."

Beth looked down at the wrinkled, pink little face and felt a flood of warmth.

"Naomi?" she asked.

"It was difficult," Estrela said, "but she is doing well."

William unfolded the cloth to reveal the child. He touched the pink, distended belly, saw the obvious signs of maleness, chuckled. "A fine lad," he said.

"I must see Naomi," Beth said.

When she opened the door to Naomi's lying-in room, she saw a bustle of activity around the bed, and her heart leaped. Something had gone wrong. She crept forward on tiptoes, her heart pounding. Naomi, who had been very, very brave in emulation of the Seneca women whom she had watched during the birth of a child, cried out just once.

"Oh, God, be with her," Beth whispered.

And then she heard a wondrous sound, a sound that at first puzzled her. It was the protesting wail of a newborn child. She rushed forward.

One of the midwives was holding a baby, smaller than the one that had been carried by Estrela, a baby still smeared with birth fluids. She ran her finger into the baby's mouth, removed mucous, then flipped the child upside down to encourage still another wail of greeting for the world.

"Twins," Beth pronounced.

Naomi's face was flushed with effort, but when she heard Beth's voice, she turned her head and smiled.

"Another boy," said the midwife. "Another fine boy."

Beth went to the bedside and took Naomi's hand.

"Two boys, Beth," Naomi whispered. "*Two!*"

"You've done very well, darling," Beth said. "Now you have some difficult work cut out for you. You have to think of names for two."

"No," Naomi said, "we will not name them, not until Little Hawk is here."

So it was that the twins, who were of different sizes, the first born being the larger, were called Big Boy and Little Boy.

Chapter Eleven

"The French army will, of course, make Lisbon their first goal," Beau said to Renno and Little Hawk.

They were having a council of war at a campsite in a hidden ravine near the road to Porto. The news that had been given them by the young officer, André, required planning. To continue into Porto would be dangerous, since Beau and André were obviously French, and Renno and Little Hawk were strangers who, by association with Beau, would be called enemy as well. It would in any case be futile to go to Porto, since the ship that had brought Beau from Lisbon had been forced out of the port.

"Unless, we could steal a boat and sail it down to Lisbon ourselves," Little Hawk suggested.

"I think we must travel by land," Beau said, "until we contact the French army. I assure you, Renno, that these papers"—he tapped the coat pocket where he kept his commission as Napoleon's representative—"will provide safe conduct, not only for those of us who are French but also for you and Little Hawk." He smiled. "And in a few weeks' time any friend of the French can travel wherever he pleases in Portugal."

"What I want to see most is the deck of a ship sailing for England," Little Hawk said.

"That is going to be a bit more difficult," Beau said. "It was to cut off commerce between Portugal and England that Napoleon sent Junot and the army. No English or American ships will be allowed in Portuguese ports once the country has been occupied." He lifted his hand. "But we will find a way."

"Beau," Renna said, "if you could talk to the emperor, tell him how my father and brother saved our lives—"

"Yes," Beau agreed, "if it comes to that, Renno, you will go with us back to France. Once there, I'm sure that it could be arranged for you to cross the Channel."

"Then we have a long way to go," Renno said.

"I would guess that we will come into contact with French forces well before we reach Lisbon," Beau said.

"We will sleep," Renno announced. "Tomorrow we will buy fresh horses in the next village."

So it was. The Portuguese did not consider Spanish gold to be an enemy. The new mounts were not the finest examples of horseflesh that Renno had seen, but the party of five—six counting the infant—left Guarda adequately mounted, to travel southward along the difficult road called the Excommunicated Way.

Although Renna's strength was returning rapidly, she became very tired after only a few hours in the saddle. Renno adjusted their pace to hers, and the miles passed slowly. Soon winter would be upon them, and it could be severe in the northwestern mountains. Renno, remembering the charts, knew that it was important for them to gain the lower country to the south before the advent of snow, but he did not want to put too much strain on Renna.

Monteiro had fled from his monastery in haste, but not without order and purpose. He had prepared for such an event long before the deadly strangers had arrived, for it was the nature of his role on earth that there be multitudes arrayed against him. But he would always prevail because his master was with him.

In a small cave below the abbey he abandoned his priestly robes and donned the dress of a countryman. There were weapons in the cave—a dagger, a slim rapier, and well-oiled pistols wrapped in sheepskin. There was also a supply of gold coin. Taking these, he picked up a horse he had boarded at the stables in Guarda and rode south. It was time for him to abandon the past, to find a release other than the torture chamber for his dark passions.

In the mountains south of Guarda, he encountered a shepherdess in long black skirts, greeted her courteously, and later left her ravaged body lying for the vultures in the bottom of a ravine. Finding the mountain pasture where the shepherdess's husband tilled a patch of rocky soil, he drove his rapier through the man's heart, disposed of the body, and took possession of the peasant's hut while he laid his plans.

He would have more scope for his work in a city, he decided, and Lisbon called out to him. There he would begin again, finding many who would do his bidding in exchange for gold. And obtaining gold was the least of his concerns: his master would make the necessary amount of gold available to him when the time came.

He was in no hurry. Actually, it was a relief to be delivered from the tedium of pretense required when he wore the priestly robes. He was free now to pay tribute to his master whenever he felt the need, and no mealy-mouthed, pious, craven-hearted monks were around to make him sick to his stomach with their hypocritical mumblings.

He gloried in the storms that swept over the mountain, for storms brought discomfort and destruction to the little people, those who called God their master and prayed to him with heartrending sincerity when all the time it was *his* master who dominated their lives. It was his master who brought death to their children ahead of their allotted time, who scattered their flocks with sudden storms, visited illness, poverty, and despair upon them. His master was the main influence in their lives, and the fools didn't have enough sense to realize it.

In the city he would find more sophisticated men—and women. His body was hungry again, and he regretted having killed the lonely shepherdess. He was preparing a travel pack to resume his journey south when he saw, far away on the trail called the Excommunicated Way, a party of five riders.

He could use an extra horse, and he would need the gold that would surely be in the purses of such well-to-do travelers. That there were five of them didn't bother him. He would drop two with his pistols, leaving only three, one of whom was a woman. He found a place of ambush and lay on his stomach, his pistols at the ready.

Renno was in the lead as the group rounded a curve in the trail. At that point the road ran along the bottom of a wooded ravine beside a mountain stream gurgling its way over rocks. The water was clear and sweet. Above the trail on either side the ground sloped sharply upward into thick trees. Ahead the ground rose to a ledge of rock, where the trail became narrow and exposed.

The day was a fine one, crisp and cool. Sunlight glinted off the stream, and as Renno's eyes swept the landscape ahead of him, it reflected off something bright—and perhaps man-made and polished. Although not expecting danger, Renno was alert by habit. He kept his eyes on the spot at the edge of the trees above the trail and saw another burst of reflected sun.

He pulled his horse to a halt, turned in the saddle, and said, "We will rest here."

"Don't stop because of me," Renna said.

"Let the horses drink," Renno said. "Rest."

He dismounted and led his horse to the creek, glancing surreptitiously toward the spot in the trees. He thought he saw a hint of movement. He tied the reins of his horse to a bush.

"I'm going to scout ahead," he told Little Hawk. "Stay here by the water until you hear my call."

"Shall I go with you?" Little Hawk asked.

"No," Renno replied. "I will be above you, on the slope. Don't look now, but in the shadows below the large tree, just above the point where the trail narrows, someone lies in wait."

"We will be ready."

Monteiro cursed when the party halted beside the stream, but he had plenty of time. They would come to him, for there was no other way for them to go. He shifted his weight to remove a pebble from under his chest, looked to the priming of his pistols. Everything was in readiness.

When one of the men left the little group resting beside the stream to disappear into the brush, he assumed the man was going to answer a call of nature. But when minutes passed and the man had not reappeared, Monteiro became concerned. He looked uneasily over his shoulder into the dark woods, for he fancied that he heard movement. He turned, trained his pistols into the shadows. A small bird fluttered up from the carpet of leaves, and he cursed himself for his undue alarm. Still, the man did not rejoin his party, and it had been a long time.

They had watered their horses. One of the remaining men lay full length on the bank of the stream, drinking. There was something familiar about him. Monteiro strained his eyes as the man finished drinking and rose. For a moment the man faced Monteiro and fear struck, for this was the Frenchman who had lain naked on the rack. That meant that the man who had disappeared was the one who was protected by the forces of the enemy, the one who was immune to Monteiro's spirit allies.

In great agitation Monteiro came to his feet and ran. He was not yet ready for another encounter with the bronzed, light-haired man who fought with his own spirits at his side.

*   *   *

Renno found the spot where Monteiro had lain in ambush. The grass had been flattened, and scuff marks revealed where boots had dug their toes into the earth. He tracked the unknown man into the trees, followed the spoor for half a mile until it emerged onto a rocky ledge and was lost. He was not ready to forget the incident, but perhaps it had only been one of the mountain people. They were rather standoffish. One of them could merely have been curious and, having spied on the group for a few minutes, gone on about his business. That was one possibility. There were others, and Renno would remain alert as they traveled southward.

He walked to the edge of the drop over the trail and waved his arms. Little Hawk saw, and soon the group was up and moving. Little Hawk led Renno's horse to the narrow point in the trail where Renno came sliding down the slope and mounted.

Sergeant Conrad Gautier, scouting with a detail of eight men for the lead elements of General Andoche Junot's victorious army, was riding hours ahead of the nearest body of French troops. He liked it that way. He was encountering no opposition in the scattered villages and farms of the mountains, and he had plenty of supplies with him. Sheep were available for the taking when the squad needed meat, and clean, sweet water ran through almost every little valley. Here, removed from the dominance and hauteur of the officers, he was enjoying his war. He had picked his eight-man squad himself, not only for their fighting ability but for their compatibility.

The scout unit had covered perhaps five miles of mostly unpopulated hills and valleys, and it was time to send a runner back to the main body to report. He chose one of the men, issued his orders, and sat his horse in a slumped, relaxed position as he watched the man ride off at an easy lope.

"I think we will stop for the day," he said, pushing back his hat and looking up at the clear, sunny sky. There was no need to get too far ahead of the slow-moving infantry. He could nap while the men prepared the evening meal.

"Sergeant," said one of the men, a bearded veteran of the march through Spain, "remember that smoke we saw beyond the western ridge?"

Gautier nodded.

"Too much smoke for one house," the man said. "Must be a village." He grinned knowingly. "Women, sergeant."

"And trouble," Gautier replied. "No, my friend, tonight we will rough it."

The unit had been together, without the loss of a man, since Junot crossed the Bidassoa River into Spain back in October. The men knew him well, knew that it was useless to petition or argue once he had made up his mind.

Gautier chose a comfortable place beside a stream, unsaddled his horse and rubbed him down, hobbled him and turned him loose to graze on the grass growing on the banks of the creek. He found a sunny spot, used his saddle for a pillow, and was dozing off when he was awakened by a hand on his shoulder. He sat up, instantly alert, not making a sound. The man pointed. Gautier turned his head and saw a rider approaching, a Portuguese countryman on a fine, black horse. He rose, pulled down his tunic, saw to his pistol, and walked to stand at the edge of the camp.

Ugly bastard, Gautier thought, as the rider halted a few feet away and dismounted.

"Good afternoon, Sergeant," the newcomer said, in only slightly accented French, "we are well met."

"Perhaps," Gautier said. "State your name and your business, my friend."

"My name doesn't matter, but I am called Monteiro." The man had squinting yellow eyes and black hair growing out of his nostrils. "What matters is that I am an agent of the emperor and have information for you."

"The devil you say," Gautier allowed. "I suppose you have credentials to prove your contention."

Monteiro snorted in derision. "Of course, Sergeant. Do you suppose I have traveled through half of Portugal, assessing the possibility of resistance, with a great sign on my chest reading 'I am a French spy'?"

"What is this information you have for me?" Gautier asked.

"Not far behind me is a group of Britishers who were put ashore at Porto to rouse the populace against the French army," Monteiro said. "There are four of them. Two masquerade as Frenchmen, and the others speak the language as well."

"Four?" Gautier asked.

"Four and a whore that they have picked up along the way."

"A woman?" Gautier smiled. "Is this whore so bad to look at?"

Monteiro leered. "As a matter of fact, she is quite comely." He made imaginary mounds on his chest. "Big," he said. "Her hair is pale, like moonlight."

Gautier brought his attention back to the men. "These men—they are armed, of course."

"Of course," Monteiro said. "They are spies. They will fight to the death to prevent being captured and hanged as the vermin they are."

Gautier was thinking that it would be most pleasing to ride back to the supercilious officers of the main body with four enemy spies. What happened to the woman, meanwhile, would be his affair and his alone.

"Come," he said to Monteiro, "Have some food, and tell me just where these enemy agents can be found."

"They are an hour, maybe two, behind me. My guess would be that if you ride now, you can come upon them just as they are making camp. That way you would catch them unprepared to resist."

"I have seven good men," Gautier said. "Let the British fools resist, if that is their object." Dead spies wouldn't be quite as impressive to the officers as live spies, but he'd settle for either. "Eat quickly," he told Monteiro. To the men he barked, "Saddle up. Prepare to ride."

Within minutes the squad was moving out, Monteiro at the sergeant's side to guide him.

After a while Monteiro hissed a warning to Gautier. "I smell smoke; we are approaching the spies' campfire."

The sergeant held up his hand to halt the squad. The sun was sinking behind the ridge to the west, and the trail fell into deep shadow as Gautier set the example by dismounting. The trail ahead disappeared into a grove of trees. Now Gautier, too, could smell the smoke of a fire. He whispered his orders.

"We will leave one man to guard the horses," he said.

"Since I am not a soldier," Monteiro said. "I will guard the horses."

"No," countered Gautier. "You will be at my side, *mon ami*, to tell me if those ahead are truly the British spies of whom you speak. Another will stay behind."

Gautier led the way, creeping from tree to tree. He was doing his best to move silently, but neither he nor his men were woodsmen.

To the ears of Renno and Little Hawk—men of the wilderness who could stalk to within arrow range of an anxious deer—the unskilled Frenchmen announced their coming from the moment they entered the copse of trees. The crunch of leaves underfoot, the scrape of a limb against fabric told Renno the story.

Little Hawk's realization was only a second later than Renno's. "At least four of them," he said.

Renno nodded. He motioned for silence, whispered, "All of you, into the trees over there." He pointed away from the direction of the oncoming sounds.

Renna asked no questions. She picked up her son in his blanket and ran into the concealment of the trees. Beau was at her side. Renno, Little Hawk, and André followed, leaving the little clearing around the fire deserted.

"Keep Renna and the child well back," Renno told Beau.

He positioned André and Little Hawk in the cover of large trees and waited.

When Sergeant Gautier saw the flicker of the fire through the trees, he hissed at his men, gave a low whistle, and led a crashing, noisy, lumbering charge that carried him and his six men into the clearing. He halted, swinging his rifle muzzle this way and that, aiming at nothing. Behind and around him his six men milled uncertainly. One of them looked at Monteiro, who was just stepping into the glow of the fire.

"So, where are these Britishers?" Gautier demanded.

"Frenchmen," Beau exclaimed. "They are French soldiers. Stay here." He moved forward, shouting, "Soldiers of Napoleon, hold your fire. I am coming out."

Renno watched carefully as Beau stepped into the clearing, leaving his musket leaning against a tree, holding his hands high. "Sergeant," he said loudly, "we are well met. We were hoping to meet French forces before we reached Lisbon, but did not expect to contact you so quickly."

Seven rifles were trained on Beau.

"If you will permit," Beau said, moving his hand slowly. "My credentials. I am—"

His name was lost in the crash of a pistol. Beau's hat flew off, and he fell limply.

Renno, seeing the man who had fired, immediately recognized the devil priest from the abbey, and he knew that he had to be very, very careful.

He fired, whooping a war cry to signal Little Hawk. One Frenchman went down. Six rifles fired almost as one, but the balls spent themselves in the trees as both Renno and Little Hawk leaped to the attack. They emerged from the trees, and Little Hawk's pistol spoke, making the odds more favorable by one. Out of the corner of his eye, Renno saw him leap to engage the leader of the Frenchmen with his saber, while he stood ready with his sword to take on others.

It was five against two for a few moments, but the Frenchmen, in their eagerness, impeded one another so that Renno was facing only two men. He whirled as if to retreat, and when his two opponents leaped forward, he crouched and lunged upward with his weapon to impale the leading attacker. He barely managed to free his sword from the falling body and escape a mighty downswing. He parried a lunge, heard a pistol explode, and saw André burst out of the trees. Another of the Frenchmen was down.

Sergeant Gautier was one of the finest swordsmen in his regiment. He was swearing with anger as he saw man after man fall to the outnumbered attackers, but he could not get past the guard of the young bronzed warrior who faced him so skillfully. He saw that the odds had been evened. Now it was three against three, for Monteiro was not engaging in the fight. No longer did he hope to take British spies back to his officers. He wanted the bastards dead. They had done what the Spanish and Portuguese armies had not been able to do: they had killed four of his men. Four good men.

He leaped forward to the attack, and at first it was a mystery why he came to such a quick, sudden halt. He felt only a dull blow at his middle, but he was frozen. He looked down and saw the blade of his opponent's saber buried in the vee at the bottom of his rib cage.

"My God," he said, as the point of the blade penetrated upward into his heart.

Little Hawk withdrew his weapon from the sergeant and whirled. Renno was backing his opponent toward the trees. André made a killing slash, opening his opponent's throat, just as Little Hawk turned toward him. Only one other Frenchman remained. The dark-clad man standing in the shadow of the trees lifted his hand, and Little Hawk saw that the hand held a pistol. He reacted instantly, for the pistol was trained at his father. His own hand moved with great speed and sent his dagger flashing toward Monteiro.

Since the man was intent on getting a clean shot at Renno, the dagger penetrated his defenses without his notice and slammed hilt first into the hand holding the pistol. The hand loosened and the weapon dropped, firing when it struck the ground.

Little Hawk, following the flight of his dagger, was

already leaping toward Monteiro, saber at the ready, when the evil man's eyes fixed on him. When he was only three steps away, Little Hawk felt something thump into his leg. He looked down, and his eyes went wide, for a thing of horror was clinging to him with distended claws ready to sink long, dripping fangs into his thigh. He lashed down at it with his saber, stumbled, and almost fell.

The attack preoccupied Little Hawk and gave his opponent a chance to choose his next move. Only one other Frenchman was on his feet, the one facing Renno. Monteiro turned and vanished into the trees—indeed *through* them, as if his evil powers enabled him to run full tilt without crashing into anything.

Now Little Hawk was in pursuit. He could hear Monteiro ahead of him and was able to follow him by the noise he made. Soon they were out of the trees, and he could see Monteiro running up the trail. Another French soldier stepped out into the trail, into Monteiro's way. Monteiro shouted a warning and swung his sword. The Frenchman fell back in fright, but not quickly enough, for Monteiro's blade severed his neck. Then Monteiro loosed his horse, climbed into the saddle, and freed the other horses as well, sending them cantering off into the twilight before he himself disappeared down the trail.

Little Hawk ran with all of his speed. One of the horses had stopped and was cropping grass beside the trail. It had been well trained, for it stood still while Little Hawk approached, took the reins, mounted, and set off after Monteiro.

By sheer luck Little Hawk had picked a fast horse. Within minutes he could catch glimpses of Monteiro and his mount as they passed from shadowed to moonlit patches of the trail.

Renno was occupied with an excellent swordsman when he saw Little Hawk disappear in pursuit of Monteiro. Fearing that his son was no match for the shaman of evil, he pressed his attack.

"Mercy," gasped the Frenchman, as Renno pushed him until his back was against a tree.

"Put down your weapon."

The Frenchman let his sword fall from his hand.

"André," Renno shouted, "guard this one."

He took in the situation at a glance. The clearing was littered with the dead. Beau was lying near the trees on the far side, and even as Renno glanced that way Renna ran out of the shadows with the boy in her arms and kneeled beside Beau. Renno's heart ached for her, for Beau had fallen like the dead; but another, more immediately urgent matter sent him running into the trees. He found the dead French soldier on the trail and ran on, for in the distance he could hear the sound of galloping hoofs. His own horse was back in the grove near the creek, unsaddled. His only choice was to run, and he ran as he had not run in years, all out, punishing his body.

Quickly his lungs were fighting for air and a pain lanced his side. He ran on, running through the pain, driving onward until his tortured lungs expanded, and he could breathe deeply, pumping life back into his faltering legs. He could no longer hear the sound of the running horses.

Monteiro knew that it was the young one who pursued. He had seen Little Hawk in action twice now, and he was not unimpressed; but he knew that he could face him. It was the pale older one who was more dangerous, fighting with a double at his side. This one riding hot on his heels would be alone; Monteiro felt that he could kill this one without help, but if it became necessary, he could call on his allies.

He chose his spot carefully—a place where the trail sloped down into a small valley and widened. He pulled his horse to a stop and turned it. He did not have long to wait.

The bronzed rider came plunging down the trail in full gallop. His horse went down on its hind legs, fighting to stop, as Monteiro, blocking the trail, kicked his horse forward.

Monteiro's sword hissed through the air, but the man ducked, then parried the backswing, kicking his own horse

forward. The animal's shoulder jammed into Monteiro's
mount and forced Monteiro to pull back from another full
swing of the man's blade. The man lunged, leaning far out,
and this time his blade made brief contact.

Monteiro yelped with pain, for the blade had sliced a
shallow cut into his side. His horse reared and he felt
himself falling. He threw both feet out of the stirrups and
slid off the horse's rump.

Little Hawk, seeing his opponent dismounted, leaped
from the saddle and pushed in to take advantage of the hit
he had made. He could see a dark stain on Monteiro's
shirt. But he had not reckoned with Monteiro's allies.
They came snarling at him out of the empty air, things
with fangs and claws, creatures of vile stench and fearful
sounds. He fell back, slashing at the monsters that were
besetting him. He could hear Monteiro laughing at him, as
he felt the creatures attacking, then felt pain without
wounds. He slashed out at one of the imps, his blade con-
tacting nothing, and he cried out in agony and frustration.

Suddenly a voice was speaking to him, a calm, strong
voice, and he willed himself to hear.

"This, too, is real," the voice said, and around him
was a glow of light.

Little Hawk caught a glimpse of a man that he took to
be his father, but then, as he slashed at one of the imps of
evil and felt the satisfying crunch of flesh and bone under
his blade, he saw that his companion wore the traditional
scalp lock of a Seneca warrior and was dressed in nothing
more than a breechclout.

"Thank you, Old Father," he whispered, as he slashed
his way toward Monteiro through the clinging, clawing,
slashing things that were no longer immune to his sword.

Monteiro leaped forward, his blade at the ready. Steel
clashed on steel. They came near, face-to-face, arms
locked, straining, and Little Hawk could sense the evil in
the yellow eyes. He gathered his strength and pushed
Monteiro away, sprang after him, going for a quick kill.
The lunge was frustrated by a skilled parry, and Little
Hawk had to leap quickly backward to escape having his

legs cut out from under him. All the while the shades of evil chattered and gibbered around him, but he no longer felt their teeth.

Monteiro's arm was getting heavy. He was panting for breath, and he began to realize that he could, after all, be killed. He roared his disbelief. He had his master's promise! He had his allies! They were all around the enemy, clinging to his legs, leaping upward to snap at his arms and his face, but to no avail.

"Where have I failed you?" he whispered as he barely avoided a killing slash aimed at his throat. He could no longer attack. He could only defend.

Then he knew. As Little Hawk's saber left a great, weakening, bleeding gash across his chest, he knew that not even the master was invincible, that there was, after all, a stronger power. He was in possession of this surprising knowledge only a second before the shining blade of the saber chipped its way past his ribs into his heart.

Little Hawk stepped back and leaned on his saber, his chest heaving as he caught his breath. He heard pounding footsteps, whirled, and saw in the dim moonlight that it was his father.

Renno came to a quick halt. Monteiro was a darkness against the earth.

"So," Renno said.

"Beau," Little Hawk gasped, "was he—"

"I don't know," Renno said. He seized Little Hawk's arm in a warrior's clasp. "You did not fight this fight alone?"

"No," Little Hawk said, remembering the appearance of the manitou with awe and gratitude. "*He* was here."

Renno nodded. "Thanks be to the manitous and our ancestor."

They caught the two horses, mounted, and rode back toward the clump of trees. When they came into the clearing, the ground was still littered with the dead, but to their pleasure Beau was sitting up, leaning against a tree. He had a white cloth around his head.

"The ball nicked him just above the left ear," André said. "He's all right."

"Praise be to the manitous and the God of my wife," said Renno.

"I don't think this place would be very conducive to sleep," André went on. He pointed toward the surviving Frenchman, who was sitting against a tree with his head hung low. "This man says that the main French force is about five or six miles down the road."

"It is not Junot himself, but one of his lieutenants," Beau said. "We must make contact with him."

"So that we will have to fight the whole French army?" Little Hawk asked.

"It was Monteiro who convinced this sergeant and his men that we were enemies," André said. "It is tragic that we were forced to kill our own friends, but when we make contact with the main force, we can explain. Then we will have passage to Lisbon."

"Will they listen to you, now?" Renno asked, squatting down beside Beau.

"If Monteiro doesn't reach them first," Beau replied.

"Monteiro will not be speaking to anyone," Renno remarked.

"This man," André said, "will support our statement that we were attacked."

"Yes," the soldier agreed weakly. "It was the Portuguese, the one called Monteiro, who fired the first shot."

"Tomorrow, then, we will go to meet them," Renno said.

They moved the camp a few hundred yards upstream to get away from the dead. At first light André and the surviving soldier began digging graves. Even with the help of Renno and Little Hawk the job was not completed until midmorning. When they rode past Monteiro's body, they saw that small scavengers had been at work. No one suggested that they stop and bury what was left.

For the first hour Beau rode with his head hanging. Renna rode by his side, reaching out to touch him now and then when it seemed that he was going to doze off and fall from the saddle.

"Father," she called out.

Renno reined in his horse and allowed Beau and Renna to catch up with him.

"We have to stop," Renna said.

Renno looked into Beau's eyes. They were half-closed. He lifted one of Beau's eyelids. The pupils were very small. Beau tried to focus, shook his head.

"We will rest," Renno decided.

"Don't stop," Beau objected. "I can go on."

"No, there's no hurry. If we wait, the French army will come to us."

Renna placed cool cloths on Beau's forehead. He slept. Little Hawk took advantage of the pause to scout into the hills, where he found sheep grazing untended. There was lamb cooking on a spit within an hour.

"Perhaps I should ride ahead for a few miles," André suggested.

"If you wish," Renno agreed.

"I'll take the French trooper with me," André said, "so that if we contact the army, he can vouch for us."

Renno nodded. He himself was content to postpone the encounter with more Frenchmen, but he had come to accept the necessity of making themselves known to the army. He would have preferred avoiding contact altogether, but to do so would have meant a long, hard trek into unknown circumstances in Spain, to the east. As André and the trooper rode away, he settled himself down beside his new grandson.

"The outdoor life agrees with him," Renna said.

Renno looked thoughtful. "My grandson does not yet have a name."

Renna laughed. "We've had no chance to think about it, have we?"

"We have been on the move," Renno agreed.

"He will be named for my father," Beau spoke up.

"Ah, you're awake, then," Renno said.

"I am firmly convinced that I will live," Beau answered.

Renno lifted Beau's eyelids one by one, and the eyes were clear and focused. "I would agree."

"For my father," Beau went on. "He will be Louis Philippe Joseph."

"A big name for so small a boy," Little Hawk put in.

"Well, I think it's a good name," Renna declared, "one that he can be proud of."

Petit Louis," Beau murmured. "My firstborn son."

"I want you to sleep now," Renna ordered, pushing on Beau's chest.

"Sleep? Not when I smell roasting meat," Beau protested.

They were feasting on lamb, and even Renna's ladylike chin was greasy, when they heard horses coming at a slow trot. Renno readied his weapon, but it was only André and the French trooper returning. André threw himself out of the saddle and ran forward.

"Did you make contact with the army?" Beau asked.

"No," André said. "We found the point where the army turned and marched southward."

"Southward?" Beau asked, puzzled.

"As if in great haste," André said.

"Well, then, there is nothing for us to do but follow," Beau said, looking at Renno for confirmation.

Renno was silent. With the morning he led the group away from the camp with all of his senses alerted. At midmorning they approached an isolated village. They saw no one in the streets as they rode in, but horses and wagons were tied in front of the largest building in the central square.

"It would seem that a town meeting is in progress," Beau said.

Renno led them through the village to the road on the other side. He wanted to have maneuvering room. Then he rode back into the village. Men were coming out of the large building, and he greeted two of them in Spanish.

"What news of the French army, friends?" he asked.

It would have been natural for the Portuguese to be suspicious of a man speaking Spanish, but evidently the news that had just come to the village was too good, too exciting, to be kept even from a stranger. "We no longer have to be concerned with the French army," said one of the men.

"We saw that they had turned and were marching south," Renno said.

"It is because the English have landed at Mondego Bay," said the Portuguese man. "They have landed with a great army, and the brave Nationals of Portugal are marching to join them. Soon the French will be driven from the soil of our country, praise be to God."

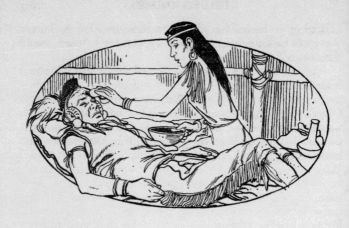

Chapter Twelve

Beside a clear stream in their pleasant valley protected by tree-clad hills, Ho-ya and his followers had turned their weapons of war and defense to peaceful use. The men had hunted, the women had dried meat and prepared skins for clothing and blankets. Construction of the communal longhouses was completed just as the last leaves fell and chill winds swept through the valley, presaging a cold winter.

The longhouses were smoky and noisy. Dogs shared shelter with their masters, and children wandered the length of the house, poking into the possessions of others with youthful curiosity. Inevitably disputes arose, for the people were accustomed to having their own family lodges.

As an unmarried man, Rusog Ho-ya took one of the smaller areas within the lodge, although his acknowledged position as leader of the settlement would have entitled him to more room. He shared the space with his sister, We-yo O-no-ga-nose; her daughter, Summer Moon; and the adopted infant, Jani.

Since the beginning of the long journey west, Ho-ya had changed, imperceptibly at first and then rapidly, as he grew in spirit to meet the challenges of leading his people. Others saw this, and though he was not yet called chief, it was to him that the people brought their petitions and problems. When two women disputed the ownership of a battered cooking pot, it was up to Ho-ya to find a solution. When a young lad came of age and aspired to become known as a warrior, it was Ho-ya who officiated at the informal ceremony. Chief in responsibility, if not yet in name, he often called upon his memories of his father and his two uncles, Renno and El-i-chi, for guidance in his decisions. That he was fair was proven by the growing respect shown him by those who lived in the two large longhouses.

Winter came to the hills with bone-chilling suddenness. The morning was bright, the sky clear, and children played around the longhouses lightly dressed. Shortly after midday clouds rolled down from the northwest and the temperature started falling. The first snowflakes came with an early darkness, and when daylight returned, the winds had drifted snow to a height of three feet against the walls of the longhouses. Women trudged through the new snow to replenish firewood stacks. The chill crept through the thin bark walls, and people huddled around the fires with their newly made skin cloaks draped over their shoulders.

The snow continued all that day. Young boys braved the cold and the restricted visibility to hunt rabbits in the woods. The little gray animals had betrayed their grassy nests by leaving tracks in the fresh snow. Once flushed out, they floundered in the softness and could easily be chased down. The fresh meat was always welcome.

Gray skies lingered after the snow stopped. The smoke from the smoke holes spiraled straight up in the still, cold air. Birds of the forest, including the long-billed woodcock, lost their fear of human habitation and sought food scraps on the kitchen middens. Woodcocks and doves fell to the arrows of the young boys and, in some cases, to well-thrown rocks. Paths were beaten down in the deep snow to the creek, where the women broke a thick sheet of ice to dip frigid water. Meandering pathways led into the woods, where both men and women went to answer nature's call. The stacks of firewood dwindled rapidly, and before the snow began to melt the women and the young ones were crunching over the hard crust in search of deadwood. The search took them far from the settlement, for the woodlands near the houses had been largely cleared of fallen limbs.

The snow melted into a sea of slush and mud. Water dripped from the roof and from the trees, and the damp cold penetrated, instilling restlessness among those who shared the longhouses.

"When the weather is more favorable, I will encourage them to build individual lodges," Ho-ya told his sister. He spoke loudly in order to be heard over the laughter and cries of a roiling pack of small boys, who were wrestling in the open space in front of their room. Two dogs, their ribs standing out to show that winter was a hungry time for domestic animals, barked and tugged at the clothing of the combatants.

We-yo laughed. "You will get no objection from me."

But it was not the dogs alone who went to sleep at night with inadequately filled bellies. The last of the corn, save for the precious supply of seeds for next year's crop, had long since been used up. Foraging was severely limited in winter. Children and women gathered fallen nuts and dug for a yellowish root; when boiled, it made a flavorful tea that gave a man the impression that his stomach was full. But game—other than the rabbits and small birds —was scarce, for in the cold the animals hid themselves away in cozy places. Hunters had to venture farther and farther from the settlement, and when a man came home with a deer, it was an event worthy of celebration.

Some among the settlers began to regret their decisions to leave the lands of plenty in the East. Ho-ya had little patience with their complaints. "Did I seek you out and ask you to follow me?" he demanded. "Did I hold a rifle to your head and say that you must come with me? No. You approached me, and you said that you wanted to leave the lands where the whitefaces breed like mice. You came of your own free will, and you can go the same way."

"Don't be too stern with them, Brother," We-yo urged. "They are hungry and frightened."

"You and I are not exactly living off the fat of the land," Ho-ya replied, patting his sunken belly.

"Your new thinness becomes you," We-yo countered, smiling.

Ho-ya was not constructed to be thin. He was thick in chest and waist, powerful of leg, and his arms were large and muscular; but now he was honed down to rawhide toughness with not an ounce of surplus fat on his stocky frame. We-yo, too, had shed her excess of the soft, womanly cushion that lies just under the skin. Her slimness was becoming, for it emphasized her half-round breasts, the length of her graceful neck, the sweep of her legs.

The shortest days of the year were upon them, and the nights were long, cold, and dark. It was the time of the year when ghosts walked and, in the traditions of the Seneca, longed to relive the happy days of their lives, sharing in the food, dancing, and games, enjoying the warmth of fire and home.

Because of the length of the nights, the people slept more, and they dreamed. Dreams were significant to a Seneca, and there were enough of them in the two long-houses to cause a demand for a shaman. It was dangerous to accumulate a heavy load of dreams without relieving the pressure by telling them to someone else; since dreams were from the core of one's being and very personal, it was not always desirable to tell them to one's family or to groups gathered at night around the fires. It was best to confide the dreams to an expert who could advise, for some dreams were meant to be obeyed, while others were warnings.

A delegation of young Seneca men and women came to sit around Ho-ya's fire to talk of the weather, and the hunting, and of the birth of a child during the past week. It was only after much such talk that the purpose of the delegation came to the fore.

"Ho-ya, Sachem, we have no shaman. We have no one to hear our dreams, and the ghosts have not danced."

"One cannot look at a man and say, 'You are our shaman,'" Ho-ya answered.

"There is one among us who dreams most powerfully," said a young woman. "His name is Running Deer, and he is of that clan. He speaks with animals."

"I will speak with Running Deer," Ho-ya agreed. "And we will dance for the ghosts."

Satisfied, the delegation went back to their own rooms. Ho-ya mused. "I am Cherokee," he told We-yo. "Many of our people are Cherokee. They do not call upon the Master of Life, and although our mother did, I have not spoken to him as have my uncles, nor has he stooped to speak to me."

"There is need for a celebration," We-yo explained. "Whether it is Seneca or Cherokee in nature does not matter."

"Some Cherokee laugh when a Seneca states that his dreams are piling up," Ho-ya remarked.

"But the need is very real for a Seneca," We-yo insisted.

"So be it," her brother conceded.

Ho-ya sought out Running Deer. He was a frail-looking man, whose stamina during the long trek had surprised everyone, including Ho-ya. Now the young man was engaged in carving a false face from a piece of black walnut wood, and already the distorted features of the mask were taking shape.

"There are those who say you have magic," Ho-ya began, disdaining the usual polite discussion of minor things.

Running Deer did not look up from his work.

"It is said that you speak with animals."

Running Deer nodded.

"And that you dream dreams that guide you."

Now Running Deer looked up. His eyebrows were thick, his eyes deep-set. "I have heard the people and what they say," he said. "I do not know all the charms and magic of a shaman of our people. When we were among our people, I felt no call to learn. It is only here, in our new home, that the manitous have come to me to tell me that I can help."

"I am pleased that the manitous speak to you," Ho-ya said with some skepticism.

"It is not necessary for you to believe that I speak the truth," Running Deer replied, beginning to work on his mask again. "It is only necessary that I know the truth."

"We will hold a feast," Ho-ya declared.

"That is good, for the ghosts are restless and chaff at the barriers that separate the living and the dead."

"And you will hear the dreams of those Seneca who wish to tell them?" Ho-ya asked.

"So it will be," Running Deer said.

It was not a sumptuous feast, but Ho-ya told the women to go into their reserves and be sure that the food, though limited in variety, was plentiful. Women brought out their newest garments and dug into their possessions to find the trinkets and trimmings that they had carried from their homes. New snow had fallen to cover the frozen ground to a depth of almost a foot, and the men played the snake game while women and children cheered them on. In the comfort of the longhouses the people danced, and not even the Cherokee, who did not believe in such things, seemed to mind that the ghosts shared in the gaiety and the food.

On the second night of the celebration Ho-ya gathered the entire group into his longhouse and called for their attention. "Here is Running Deer," he said. "You all know him. You know that on the trek he proved he had learned the ways of the healer, and now the manitous have spoken to give him guidance. Honor him, for he is to be our shaman."

He had done his duty. He had given the Seneca among them a hearer of dreams, and for days afterward Running Deer was kept busy as men and women cleared their minds of the load of dreams that had accumulated since leaving the village of Renno and the shaman El-i-chi.

The dancing and singing eased tensions. It seemed quieter in the longhouse, and Ho-ya was content.

When it became evident that the days were getting longer, people's spirits revived. The Seneca in the group organized the traditional events of the celebration of the new beginning, and the Cherokee, for lack of something more exciting to do, got into the mood of the celebration.

Running Deer conducted the rituals to help the Master of Life bring spring once more, carrying out with due solemnity the rites of cleansing and the many prayers. He remembered, too, the reenactment of the gambling contest, in which the Master of Life wins spring from forces of darkness, and with it the new green growth and the fruits of summer.

"I think, Sister," Ho-ya said, while the new festivities were under way, "that the timing of the most important festival of the Five Tribes was not an accident."

"Brother, I am glad, for I share with our Seneca mother her regard for the spirit world."

"My beliefs cannot always follow where yours go," Ho-ya countered, "but the festival of our mother's people does much good. It comes when the crops have been long since harvested, when the fishing and the hunting are at their worst—during the snow and cold, when everyone has been confined to the longhouses for many weeks. Like us, here in our two longhouses, the people who started this midwinter celebration had seen too much of each other, were restless with their confinement, and needed release. And then comes the dancing and the games, and everyone is reminded that the sap will soon rise and that the trees will burst with new leaves and the hunting and fishing will be good once more."

He nodded and smiled. "Yes, the old ones knew what they were doing when they invented this celebration, so we will make it a part of our tradition." He turned to We-yo and took her hand. "Come then, we will dance with the others."

*   *   *

In late February, winter struck again, this time with freezing rain and sleet, so that the earth was frozen solid, forming a foundation for six inches of crusted snow. The smoke from the longhouses eddied and swirled and clung close to the ground. The sun hid itself from man's sight behind low, leaden clouds, and the wind was an icy knife to cut through the warmest clothing.

Ho-ya was playing with Summer Moon and Jani beside a cozy fire in the longhouse when a young woman bundled in skins came running in, letting in the cold wind with her.

"Sachem," she called out to Ho-ya. "You come."

In the common area between the two longhouses stood an impressive figure of a man. He was very tall, half a head taller than Ho-ya, and bulky winter furs thickened his figure. His head was shaved except for a narrow strip running from his forehead back along his crown, where a roach made from a deer's tail arched up stiffly. This standing comb of hair had been dyed brilliant red. From the man's ears hung elaborate circles of carved bone with graceful dangles of painted leather and wood. It was evident he had traded with the whitefaces, either directly or indirectly, because a crimson silk scarf was knotted around his neck.

He stood in regal splendor, holding a stone-tipped spear in one hand, a steel-headed tomahawk in the other. Women had gathered to stare, to point, and to whisper in speculation. He remained motionless, moving only his head as Ho-ya, having hurriedly pulled a buffalo robe around his shoulders, came from the longhouse.

The stranger waited until Ho-ya had walked slowly to a point five paces away. Then he spoke in a dialect that was completely unfamiliar to the Cherokee. Ho-ya lifted his hand, palm outward, in the sign of peace. The gesture was not returned.

Ho-ya gave a greeting in Cherokee, then in Seneca. The tall warrior answered in his own strange language.

"Do you speak Spanish?" Ho-ya now asked, and for a moment he remembered the long mornings in Beth Huntington's classroom.

The stranger stood silent. Ho-ya had some French, a language that he had learned from his grandmother Toshabe. He gave greetings in that language, and this time they were returned, for the French explorers and trappers, the ragged men of the woods, had left fragments of their language along the rivers in vast areas of the North American continent.

"You are welcome here in peace," Ho-ya said in frontier French.

"Who is it that welcomes me to my own hunting grounds?" the newcomer asked haughtily.

"I am Ho-ya, of the Cherokee."

"I am Young Elk, war chief of the Osage Nation, on whose hunting grounds you trespass."

Ho-ya was polite, but firm. "We came to a valley empty of human life," he said.

"All who trespass on the hunting grounds of the mighty Osage Nation will go immediately or face the consequences," Young Elk pronounced, gesturing violently toward the east with his lance.

One by one Seneca and Cherokee warriors had emerged from the longhouses carrying their weapons. They ranged themselves behind and to the side of Ho-ya. Only one or two of them understood French; they translated for the others in loud whispers.

"We came in peace," Ho-ya declared, "to leave the lands of the whitefaces behind us. When we came into this valley, it was home to the beaver, the raccoon, the deer, and the fox. We have made this valley our own."

Young Elk's face darkened. His hand tightened on his lance. "You came not at the invitation of the Osage," he said, "but you will leave at the bidding of a chief."

"Where would you have us go?" Ho-ya asked.

"That is your affair. Go where the spirits lead you, except into the lands of the Osage."

"We are of one blood," Ho-ya began, without realizing he was repeating something his uncle Renno had said many times.

The Osage spat into the snow. "I know not what blood flows in your veins," he retorted, "but it is not my blood, not the blood of the Osage." He lifted his lance. Half-a-dozen Seneca and Cherokee warriors tightened their bow strings or raised their rifles. Steel tipped arrows and shot were aimed at the tall stranger.

"I am one," Young Elk said. "Do you need the help of all these with their whiteface weapons against one Osage?"

"I would have you as my friend," Ho-ya said.

"That cannot be as long as you trespass on Osage land."

"Surely enough land is here for all."

"So say those who have no hunting grounds," said the Osage. "Will you leave?"

"No, for we have made this our home, and we have no other," Ho-ya countered.

Young Elk lifted his lance again. "Then I will kill you."

Behind Ho-ya, dozens of tomahawks rose in defiance. "Hold!" Ho-ya ordered his men. "Put down your weapons." He turned back to Young Elk. "And if we fight?"

"You will die, and the others, seeing the futility of trying to steal game from the Osage Nation, will go back where they came from."

"And if I kill you?" Ho-ya asked.

"That will not happen," Young Elk said, dropping into a fighting stance, brandishing his lance.

"I have no lance to throw," Ho-ya said. "I have only this." He lifted his tomahawk.

"So it will be," the Osage said, tossing his lance aside and shifting his tomahawk to his right hand. Both men shrugged off their heavy furs. The snow in the commons had been packed into a hard, slick surface, but their soft, leather moccasins gave them reasonably good footing. For long moments they circled each other as the crowd of onlookers grew.

Out of the corner of his eye, Ho-ya saw that his sister had emerged from the longhouse with Summer Moon and Jani, all of them wrapped in warm deerskins. She was watching intently, her face pale.

With a piercing whoop Young Elk leaped to the attack, bringing his blade in from the level of his waist, trying to go under Ho-ya's guard. Ho-ya timed his move and simply shifted his body backward slightly so that the roundhouse blow sent the Osage blade whistling inches in front of his stomach.

"Ha!" cried Young Elk as Ho-ya's follow-up came within a blade's width of taking off a long, regal Osage nose. And then Young Elk had to backstep swiftly as Ho-ya came through with a backswing aimed at a vulnerable, out-thrust knee.

"You have fought," Young Elk declared.

"Did you think I had not?" Ho-ya demanded.

"It will be sad to kill one who handles the blade so skillfully."

Ho-ya feinted toward Young Elk's face, changed directions, then aimed the blade at the stomach. The Osage grunted with effort as he parried the blow. Then he backed away, going on the defensive for a few moments.

Ho-ya, seeing his chance, drove forward with several attacks. Too late he realized that the Osage had simply been luring him into attacking on purpose, so as to study the Cherokee's fighting methods. For now the Osage changed his tactics accordingly and mounted a flashing, varied attack that sent Ho-ya stumbling backward, hard put to evade and parry the lightning-fast strokes.

For an eternity it appeared that Ho-ya was hopelessly outclassed and that it was only a matter of time before he failed to evade or block one of the killing blows from the Osage's tomahawk. But he had been trained in the use of the Indian's finest weapon by experts, by Rusog, his father, and by his uncles, Renno and El-i-chi of the Seneca.

The Osage was very tall and wiry. Ho-ya was shorter and powerfully built like his father. If anything, in the early going, the Osage was slightly faster and lighter on his feet, but as steel clashed on steel and the sounds of their breathing became short and strained, the strength in Ho-ya's sturdy body began to tell. It was evident that Young Elk was tiring. The Osage pushed hard, trying to end the fight, but now Ho-ya matched his strokes and slowly, slowly, began to push the Osage back into a defensive posture again.

Heavy-armed, Young Elk just barely managed to block a blow that would have buried Ho-ya's blade in his face. He gasped with effort. His counterstroke was weak, so weak that Ho-ya brushed it aside easily and leaped inside as the force of Young Elk's blow carried his weapon around. Ho-ya was in a position to end it then, for the Osage was off balance, his throat exposed. Ho-ya launched the killing stroke, pulled it at the last split second, and stepped back, holding up his left hand in peace. He had to duck quickly to keep from being decapitated by Young Elk's backswing.

"You refuse my offer of peace?" Ho-ya asked.

The answer was a gasping attack that tried all of his skills. Sadly Ho-ya concluded that he would have to kill the Osage, after all. He ducked under a wild, awkward swing, blocked the backswing of Young Elk's arm with his shoulder, and sent his weapon toward the Osage's temple in a blow that would end it once and forever.

Ho-ya would never know why he did not deliver the blow, for he had found the opening, and it was obvious the Osage had no intention of abandoning the fight short of Ho-ya's death. But just before the sharp steel would have slashed into Young Elk's temple, Ho-ya turned his wrist. The flat of his tomahawk smashed against skull and the Osage dropped as if his legs had been cut from under him.

Shouts of approval arose from the watchers. We-yo ran forward and knelt beside the Osage.

"He is not badly hurt," she said.

"No," said Ho-ya. He motioned to two warriors. "Lift him. Carry him to my bed." He followed them and We-yo into the longhouse.

A great bump had grown on Young Elk's temple. When the warriors had stretched him out on Ho-ya's bed, We-yo bathed his forehead and bruised temple with a cold cloth. "He does not move," she said to Ho-ya anxiously, when the stimulation of the cold cloth did not cause the Osage to so much as twitch.

Ho-ya, tired from the battle, squatted on his heels by the fire, watching We-yo's ministrations to the unconscious man. He, too, wondered if the blow had been fatal, and he felt relief when the Osage groaned and moved one hand.

The first thing Young Elk saw when he opened his eyes was the most beautiful face he had ever beheld. It was feminine, round and bronzed, and it gazed at him with obvious concern. The eyes were brown, large and slightly tilted. He tried to sit up, and the world spun around him and a soft hand was on his chest, holding him.

"Rest for a minute, warrior," the voice said in French. He sank back. "Who are you?" he asked.

"I am We-yo," she replied, wielding a damp cloth soothingly around his brow. "Like Ho-ya, I am of the Cherokee. Now lie still."

Ho-ya came to stand beside We-yo. Young Elk's eyes widened. "You are not dead," he said.

"No," Ho-ya answered.

"But if you are not dead, then why am I alive?"

"If death is all you want," Ho-ya said, "seek it elsewhere, for I will not kill you now when I could so easily have done so before."

Young Elk shook his head to dispel the buzzing in his brain. He could not understand the reasoning of this man who called himself a Cherokee. He had made it clear that one of them had to die. Under Young Elk's code, there was no mercy for an enemy. The fierce warfare of the plains left no room for weakness: a man lived by killing his enemy or he died.

"We will have to fight again," he said, just as a fierce pain caused him to squint his eyes closed.

"Perhaps we will wait just a little while," Ho-ya answered, as the Osage passed into unconsciousness.

When next Young Elk opened his eyes, the beautiful one was still here. "I have food for you," she said. "Can you sit up now?"

"Yes," he said. He felt dizzy as he tried, but he managed. With his weak hands he accepted a bowl from the beautiful one and drank the meaty broth therein. "Good," he said, handing the bowl back to We-yo. He looked around. It was dark. Fires lit the longhouse and sent wraiths of smoke into all corners. He coughed. He couldn't imagine living in such intimacy with dozens of people. His house was small and round, and it was his and his alone, for he had moved out of his mother's house when he first became a warrior.

"Where is the warrior?" he asked.

"Here," We-yo said, pointing.

Ho-ya was seated beside the fire sharing his evening meal with a girl of about three. An infant lay in a cradle nearby.

"His child?" Young Elk said, indicating the girl.

"Mine," she replied.

"The boy?"

"Adopted."

"The man, he is your husband?"

"My brother."

"Your husband?"

"Dead."

Young Elk swung his feet off the bed and stood. After a few seconds the world was still, and he walked on legs that had suddenly grown longer, making him feel as if his head were in the timbers of the ceiling. He went to Ho-ya.

"By sparing my life, warrior, you have earned your own," he said.

"For that I am grateful," Ho-ya said wryly.

"I am sorry that you must go."

"We have discussed that point," Ho-ya replied.

"You must go, or I will bring my warriors and kill all," Young Elk declared.

"Perhaps I should have killed you," Ho-ya said.

"Come, and I will give you another opportunity," Young Elk replied, reaching for a weapon that was not there.

"Why do you insist that we leave this place?" We-yo inquired. Her voice was like the sound of a dove in summer to him.

He was truly sorry. "The Osage are many," he said.

"And we are few. We take up so little land," We-yo said. "And we have come so far."

Young Elk's head was still aching, but his thoughts became clear. "Perhaps there is a way."

"Speak," Ho-ya said.

"In exchange for this woman of the golden skin, you and the others will hunt in this valley, but not in the buffalo plains to the north," Young Elk said.

"A chief of the Cherokee does not sell his sister," Ho-ya declared.

Young Elk raised his eyebrows in surprise. "It is a strange thing, this Cherokee way of thinking," he said.

Ho-ya started to speak, but We-yo held up her hand. "It is true, Young Elk," she said softly. "A woman of the Cherokee is not a thing to be bought and sold."

"How, then, is a woman of the Cherokee obtained?" Young Elk asked.

"If the chief of the Osage cares to pay court to her in the manner of her people, if he is kind and woos her with words and deeds, then perhaps she listens with favor to his words."

"Words," Young Elk said. "I have no pretty words."

"You do not have to barter yourself," Ho-ya said angrily. "We will fight for our home if that becomes necessary."

"Those words I understand," said Young Elk.

We-yo smiled, her eyes hooded, hiding her secret thoughts. "As for you, Brother," she said, "I know what I am doing. You, Young Elk, come with me, and I will give you more to eat. I think that both of you have had enough fighting for one day."

"I will go to my own people," he said.

"You will sleep, and then in the morning the cobwebs will be gone from your head and you can go to your people," We-yo said.

Not since he was a child at his mother's skirts had a woman given him orders, and yet he did not protest. He accepted more stew and dried meat.

"This is what you eat?" he asked.

"When the hunters have not been successful," she said. "But in the new beginning we will plant corn and beans and squash and other good things."

"Things that grow in the earth?"

"Yes."

"We do not dig in the dirt like prairie dogs," he said.

"Yes, but you are a mighty hunter, and the buffalo, I take it, are many."

"As the grains of sand," he said.

"So many? Then why would you begrudge my people only a few?"

"You are sounding like a Cherokee again."

"But I told you, that is what I am. Do you not approve?"

His eyes told her that he approved very much, but he could not find words. He grunted.

"Very expressive," she said in elegantly accented sarcasm.

Young Elk slept on a bed of skins by the fire. He slept fitfully in the crowded longhouse. *Like living in an anthill,* he thought, just before he finally fell asleep.

He awoke to find the fire burned low. It was cold. He put on fresh wood, and then the woman was close by, stirring the fire expertly and putting a kettle on to boil. Soon they were enjoying herbal tea and rewarmed stew of dried venison. They were alone, for it was very early.

"The words you want to hear, how do I say them?" She smiled at him. "Tell me about your home."

He grinned. "It is not quite so crowded as this."

"Our Cherokee and Seneca brethren back east live in individual lodges," she said. "We built these longhouses in the style of the old Seneca of the North, because we had so little time."

"I am glad to hear that your people are sensible in some ways," he said. "Come with me. See my house."

She looked away. "Is it far?"

"Two days, because I have only one horse, and you will have to walk."

"I think I will decline your invitation with regret," she said, "for I do not fancy walking for two days in the snow."

"Then we will both ride," he said.

"That's an improvement."

"Eh?" He didn't catch the word.

She laughed. "Perhaps, Young Elk, when the snow is gone and the sun is kind, I will visit you and see your house and learn how your people live. I would like to see the buffalo that are like the grains of sand."

"Soon the green things will grow," he said. "Then I will come for you."

"You do not intend to have your warriors kill us, then?"

He was puzzled, for he did not understand her casualness in mentioning something that was a real possibility. Even more, he was puzzled at himself for spending a night in the overcrowded longhouse, leaving his horse hobbled in a little nook out of the wind with nothing to eat, possibly to freeze in the night. That thought gave him pause, because he himself did not fancy a two-day walk in the snow. He was confused. This woman—or the blow delivered by the powerful Cherokee—had softened his brain.

"Perhaps I will tell them not to kill you now."

"I'm so pleased," she answered.

"Now I will go."

"Come when the snow is gone and the grass grows green," she said.

"Yes."

She walked with him out of the longhouse.

The cold had moderated a bit overnight, and there was no wind. Their moccasins crunched on the hard-crusted snow. The sky was clear and blue, and the sun was just beginning to peek up over the trees.

"I will walk with you," she said.

"Yes."

They were silent for a long time as they entered the woods. Young Elk followed his own tracks to the creek, which was frozen. The ice was slippery, and We-yo slipped as they crossed. He took her arm and steadied her and the feel of her through her doeskins roused him, sent tendrils of need into his groin.

"If I tell you that you are like the moon when it is full and yellow, are those good words?" he asked, as he helped her climb the bank of the creek.

"Those are good words," she acknowledged.

"If I tell you that my house is empty, and that you would fill it?"

"Good words," she said, "but too soon spoken, perhaps."

A soft whinny came from a little cul-de-sac in a rocky ridge. Young Elk's horse stamped his feet impatiently. The Osage gave praise to the spirits, for he had been foolish in forgetting his horse. He put his hand on the animal's nose and said, "You will have food soon."

"Journey with care," We-yo said.

He touched her on the cheek. "I will come," he promised.

She watched him ride off in the snow, his shaved head gleaming, the horse stepping carefully as his hooves broke through the crust. She had not put on her heavy robe, and the cold was seeping into her bones. She ran back toward the longhouse but slowed to a walk, heedless of the cold, for she could remember every aspect of his face, the long, hawklike nose, the eyes that had just a hint of cruelty, the finely sculpted mouth. He was so tall, so proud of stance.

But he was a stranger from a tribe of warriors of the plains, and he had offered to buy her, taking her in exchange for something of value. She wondered what life would be like with him in his little house, wondered, indeed, what sort of house it would be and how his own people would react to a stranger. It would not be like going with a man of the Seneca tribe, for example, for the Cherokee and the Seneca were true cousins and brothers in blood. It would be more alien than her life would have been with the father of her child, for he was Mingo, and lived by the Iroquois traditions moderated by life in the area beyond the Ohio.

It frightened her to think of such strangeness, but as she entered the longhouse to find Ho-ya, Summer Moon, and Jani awake and ready for a morning snack, she felt warm inside, for the warrior's touch had been a burning on her arms and on her face. She felt as if his finger on her cheek had left the warmth of fire.

"Our guest has departed?" Ho-ya asked.

"Yes. He had his horse secreted across the creek."

"I wonder if all of his warriors will be mounted," Ho-ya mused.

"I would think so."

"We will have to build a stockade, as did the Iroquois of old."

"Perhaps we will not need it," she said. "He has agreed not to kill us. At least not until the snow is gone and the grass is green."

"As I told you, you will not barter yourself for peace with these Osage."

"No," she said, "but in the spring I am going to visit his house and his people."

"I will not have—"

She put her fingertips on his lip. "Do you remember White Blanket?"

"Of course I do."

"He was a man, and his touch made me feel like a woman."

"So?"

"I thought that part of me was dead, but it lives, Brother. It lived under the touch of the Osage. He, Young Elk, reminded me that I am still a woman."

"Manitous!" Ho-ya exclaimed. "As long as I live I will never understand women."

Chapter Thirteen

To be caught between two great armies, Renno decided, was not the most desirable of circumstances. His first inclination was to seek out the English. He was married to an Englishwoman, after all, and in spite of the fact that something just short of a state of war existed between the United States and England on the high seas, he and his family had always been welcome in Beth's native country.

There were complicating factors, of course. Beau's status presented a quandary, for even though Beau was a diplomat and carried the documents to prove it, it was a certainty that he would be held in custody by the British at least until the fate of Portugal had been decided in battle.

"My first concern," Renno told them as they sat in council around a campfire on a chill night, "is for the safety of Renna and my grandson. I think that the only course of action that makes sense is for us to travel toward the coast and make contact with the English."

"I respect your concern for my wife and child," Beau replied, "but I have my duty, Renno."

"Your duty is to Renna and the child," Renno countered.

"I agree that I have a duty to my family," Beau said. "However, I have a duty to my country and to my emperor, as well. I can do them little good by spending the duration of this war as a guest of the British." He shook his head. "You are free, of course, to join the British, but I will take Renna and Louis with me to the south, to make contact with my own people."

"And perhaps others like those who were going to kill you as a spy without giving you a proper hearing," Renno argued. "No, I will not allow you to endanger Renna and the boy in that manner."

Beau bristled and drew himself up to speak, but Renna spoke first. "Beau, our daughter is in England."

"Yes, but—"

"How long would it be before I could see her, before she could be back with her own family if I went with you to Lisbon?"

Beau opened his mouth but did not speak. He spread his hands in mute appeal.

"If you must," Renna said, "go to Lisbon. I will not stand in the way of your duty, but wouldn't it make sense for me to go to England? I miss Emily Beth. When you are back in France, we can join you by traveling under the flag of diplomacy in the same way we went to England."

Beau leaned forward and took one of Renna's hands in his. "To be separated from you—"

"I know," she said.

Beau straightened his shoulders. "I bow to the wisdom of my wife," he said.

They clung to each other in the firelight, husband and wife, arms entwined, bodies pressed tightly together for warmth and love. Renno, watching, ached for them. He knew his daughter; he knew that she would never beg Beau to come with her, however much she might wish to.

She knew, as did Renno, that Beau was loyal to his country and to Napoleon and that to ask him to forsake what he saw as his duty would only make his inevitable decision more painful.

With the morning it was time to part. Renno mounted and guided his horse alongside Renna's. Sitting her horse easily, little Louis in her arms, she was watching Beau ride away with André at his side.

Renno leaned over to her. "Let me carry the boy," he said gently.

"Thank you." She checked Louis's blanket to be sure he was well covered before handing him to her father.

With Little Hawk scouting the way, they rode all morning, the sun at their backs, then into the sun as the day waned. The Atlantic shore was not far away, and after two days of riding they caught their first glimpse of the cold, blue waters extending westward into a bank of low clouds on the horizon.

They turned south on the wide and well-traveled coast road, riding at a leisurely pace. Now and again bands of Portuguese men overtook them, riding hard to join the Nationals fighting alongside the English against the French invaders.

They could see the first redcoats from afar, two columns of scarlet-clad horsemen coming around a curve in the coast road. Little Hawk reined in his horse and turned to Renno, who came forward and took the lead.

When the lancers were a hundred feet away, riding confidently in the center of the road, Renno halted his horse and held up his hand. Then he waited as the patrol came closer, led by a striking young man who sat straight and tall in his saddle, his rust-red hair protruding from his hat and covering the nape of his neck.

Lieutenant Randall Farnsworth was the third son of an impoverished Scottish peer. He had found his place in the army, and although he was young, just twenty-five, he had begun to build a reputation for daring and perhaps a bit too much initiative for a lieutenant in the cavalry. He had fought with Wellesley in Denmark and had brought himself to the attention of Sir Arthur when he and his men held a Danish countercharge against overwhelming odds until reserves could be brought up.

At first Farnsworth intended to ride past the man in Portuguese dress, but as he drew closer, he saw the bronzed lightness of the face. No swarthy Portuguese this one. Nor was the younger man, who pulled his horse alongside that of the man who was holding up his hand.

Farnsworth raised his own hand and signaled his patrol to halt. It was then that he saw the young woman. She had her pale hair secured in braids so that her broad brow and her expressive blue eyes were emphasized. Her mouth was full, her face so perfectly proportioned that Farnsworth could not take his eyes off her even as the older man spoke.

"Good afternoon, Lieutenant," Renno said in a cultured, upper-class British accent. "We are well met."

The lieutenant turned his eyes from Renna. "And who may you be, sir?"

"My name is Renno Harper. This is my son Little Hawk, and my daughter, Renna." Renno noted that a sergeant, by his looks a veteran, had moved out of the column with two men, to flank Renno and Little Hawk on both sides.

"We ask safe conduct to a port where we can find transportation to England," Renno went on.

The lieutenant was staring at Renna again but returned his gaze to Renno's. "I am Lieutenant Farnsworth. May I inquire why you are here in the heart of Portugal?"

"You may." He smiled. "However, it is a long story, and we have been traveling far. In brief, we were stranded on the shores of Portugal. Our attempts to reach a friendly port have so far been stymied by the presence of the French army."

"What do you know about the French army?" Farnsworth asked, his eyes once more wandering toward Renna.

"Elements of Junot's forces were marching north toward Porto when your force landed," Renno said. "They then turned back toward the south."

"You saw them?"

"We saw an advance patrol."

"Exactly where?" Farnsworth demanded.

"I have no map," Renno said. "Two days' ride to the east."

"I think, sir, that you had better come with me," Farnsworth decided. "Sir Arthur will want to question you."

"Sir Arthur?" Renno asked with a smile. "Wellesley, here?"

"You're acquainted with Sir Arthur?"

"We have met," Renno said. He turned to Renna and Little Hawk. "I think that we will be on our way to England soon."

Leaving the patrol in the charge of his sergeant, Farnsworth escorted Renno, Little Hawk, and Renna down the road to the south. After a ride of just over an hour they began to hear the sounds of a large encampment. From the top of a hill they saw the British expeditionary force arrayed before them in orderly rows of tents. Wheeled cannon were arranged in tiers in an artillery park. Horses grazed in a meadow. From a forge somewhere came the ring of steel on steel. A sergeant bawled orders as a detachment of men drilled in an open area among the rows of tents.

Renna drew the stares of hundreds of male eyes as Farnsworth led them through the encampment to a large tent guarded by young men in splendid regimentals. An aide spoke with Farnsworth, then disappeared into the tent. Within seconds Sir Arthur Wellesley himself emerged. He was bareheaded, and as he looked up, he shaded his eyes against the afternoon sun.

"By Jove, it is my American friend." He motioned. "Come down, come down. I'm consumed with curiosity."

Renno and Little Hawk dismounted, and Farnsworth jumped down to assist Renna from her horse. She handed the baby to him, and he cradled it gently as she stepped down.

"Thank you, Lieutenant, that will be all," Wellesley said as Renna took the baby into her arms again.

Farnsworth remounted and, with one last, lingering look at Renna, cantered away.

Wellesley took Renno's arm. "How the devil did you and your son end up in Portugal?"

"Sir Arthur, it's a long story. Before I tell it, may I present my daughter."

Wellesley beamed at Renna. "Most charming," he said. "And you make me even more curious." He called out, and a grizzled old sergeant popped out of the tent. "Sergeant, find decent quarters for this young lady and her child and see to her needs."

"Sir!" barked the sergeant. He bowed to Renna. "If you'll come with me, ma'am."

"Now then," Wellesley said, "I can wait no longer." He led them into his tent, where they found camp chairs. Within a miraculously short time, cups of hot tea were served.

"Before you begin," Wellesley said, "perhaps you'd better tell me what you know about the whereabouts of the French army."

A large map lay on a campaign table. Renno went to it and, orienting himself quickly, traced his finger down the Excommunicated Way to the point where they had encountered the French patrol. "We ran into them here."

"How many?" Wellesley asked.

"We saw eight men, including a sergeant."

"Weren't they suspicious of you?"

"Belligerently so," Renno said.

Sir Arthur raised an eyebrow. "Just how belligerent were they?"

"It was necessary for us to kill most of them," Renno said in a flat voice.

Wellesley exploded wind through his lips in surprise. "What, the two of you and the girl?"

"We had with us my daughter's husband, the comte de Beaujolais, and a young French officer."

"My word," said Wellesley. "I don't understand."

It took a while for Renno to explain. When he had

finished, Wellesley was still puzzled, wondering how Renno had known that Renna and the child were in Monteiro's monastery.

"Just call it a lucky accident," Renno said. "We were traveling toward Porto and just happened to encounter someone who had seen a pale-haired woman being taken to the monastery." That was as close as he could come to an explanation.

"Well, my friend," Wellesley said, "it is an amazing tale indeed. Now you want transport to England with your son and daughter?"

"Yes, sir, that is my request," Renno said.

"It can be arranged," Wellesley said. He nodded and his orderly refilled their tea cups. "A ship will be leaving in a few days. In the meantime, I'd consider it a great favor if you'd show my lads where you last saw the French. You know the ground, and I'll have to admit that I'm a stranger in a strange land."

Renno didn't answer immediately. It crossed his mind that assisting the British could conceivably endanger Beau. But Beau was probably already safe behind French lines.

Little Hawk looked at his father and grinned. "It would be better than waiting around camp," he said.

Renno nodded in agreement.

Wellesley called his aide. "Get me Captain Lillington." He turned to Renno. "Forgive me, I haven't even asked if you are prepared to ride out again immediately. If you're too tired—"

"We are ready," Little Hawk said.

Captain Lillington was an older man who had made a career of the army. He sorted out fresh horses for Renno and Little Hawk, and by the time the sun set out over the Atlantic and the early winter darkness had come, they were miles from the main encampment.

Although she was surrounded by an army of thousands of men, Renna felt very much alone. She talked to her infant son at her breast in a soft whisper, telling him how brave his father was to journey alone in search of the French forces, and how much she herself missed him.

She had been assigned a tent at the edge of Wellesley's headquarters complex. There was water in the tent,
and she sponged off her perspiring body as best she could
without totally disrobing; she was reluctant to expose herself since the canvas of the tent seemed so thin. When she
had finished, she felt refreshed and very hungry. Little
Louis had gulped a milky snack and was sleeping peacefully on the bed when she heard footsteps outside the tent.

"Madam," called a voice. "I have your tea."

She opened the flap and saw Lieutenant Farnsworth.
He was carrying a tray on which sat a tea service and a
bowl of small cakes.

"If I may?" He pushed past her into the tent, put the
tray down on a small table, and bowed. "I hope you enjoy
it," he said.

"Thank you."

He stood looking at her, his lips slightly parted, his
eyes squinted. "Is there anything else, madam? Anything
at all?"

"A bit of soap, perhaps?"

"Of course." He laughed. "I'm afraid that it will be
rather coarse. Army issue, you know."

"That will do nicely," she said.

He walked to the open flap of the tent, his back
straight, moving as if he were on parade. He turned. "The
evening meal will be served at six."

"Good. I'm starved," she said.

He looked distressed. "Oh, I'm sorry. I didn't think.
I'll go to the mess right now—"

"No, please," she said. "The tea will hold me until
six."

"Are you sure?"

"Yes. I don't want to be a bother."

"Never," he said earnestly. "You would never be a
bother."

Farnsworth brought the evening meal as well. It was
soldiers' fare—bully-beef stew and a hard biscuit—but,
brought under a silver cover, it was steaming hot and the
smell was delicious.

"Cook borrowed one of the general's trays and servers," Farnsworth said. "It wasn't difficult. The general's orderly has taken a liking to me, God knows why. But I'll have to pick up the service as soon as you're finished."

"I am grateful," Renna said.

"I have soap for you, and a comb." He handed her the two items, wrapped in a clean towel, and as he did so, his hand brushed against hers.

"Thank you, Lieutenant."

He hesitated, lingering. "I'll be back in an hour," he said at last.

"Yes. That will be fine."

Farnsworth walked away from the tent. He had been reluctant to leave her. He knew so little about her, knew only that she was American, and that she was obviously married, for she had the child. He also knew that he was devastated by her—in love as he'd never been in love before. The hopelessness of it served only to make his emotions more powerful.

When he returned for the tray, she handed it out to him, said good night, and quickly closed the flap. He took the tray back to the general's mess.

The old sergeant who was Wellesley's orderly was at his meal. He winked at Farnsworth. "Had your tucker, lad?"

"No," Farnsworth replied. He was not hungry.

"Have a seat. There's plenty," the sergeant invited.

"Thank you," Farnsworth said, taking a seat. "I will have a cup of tea."

"So you've taken it on yourself to serve the wee lass," the old sergeant said.

"Just being courteous," Farnsworth said. "The general has sent her father and her brother out on patrol with Lillington. I thought she'd be more comfortable seeing a familiar face."

"Familiar since six hours ago?" the old sergeant asked.

Farnsworth flushed.

"My lad, she's a married woman with a child," the sergeant cautioned.

"That doesn't mean that I can't be considerate of her."

"And her husband is a bloody wog," the sergeant growled. "A frog eater."

Farnsworth's flush became deeper. He was reluctant to believe that it was true.

"Not only that," the sergeant said, "but he's a blue blood, her husband, a bloody count, no less." He affected an atrocious accent. "The bloody comte de Beaujolais. That makes her a countess, lad, and that fare is much too rich for your belly."

Farnsworth drank his tea in silence. He still was not hungry, but it would be a long night, so he accepted the bully-beef stew and, deep in thought, forced himself to eat. *No, it can't be true. Not a Frenchman. Not, as the sergeant said, a bloody wog.*

Refreshed from a good night's sleep and hungry, Renna was delighted with the morning meal of tea and bread, which Farnsworth delivered on the general's silver salver. She thanked him, and the lieutenant blushed.

Farnsworth was by no means the first young man to be smitten by her. It was flattering, of course, but she would do nothing to encourage him. She avoided eye contact and stood primly while he put the tray on the table and turned to face her.

"I thought perhaps you'd like to see the camp when you've finished eating," he said.

"Thank you, no," she replied. "I have the baby to look after."

"Another time, perhaps."

"Perhaps."

The day seemed to stretch on forever. While little Louis slept, she walked a bit, up and down in front of her tent, listening to the sounds of the army and watching men come and go from headquarters. She was pleased to see Farnsworth when he brought the midday meal. For a time she forgot her resolution to be cool and distant, for she was lonely. When he came for the tray and servers after lunch, she followed him outside.

"By your accent I'd say you're a Scot," she remarked.

"That I am," he confirmed with a wide smile. "From the north country. And you, lady? I know that you are an American. What is your state?"

"No state, actually," she said. "I grew up in the Cherokee Nation, on the western frontier."

"No," he said in surprise.

"My people are Seneca."

"Indians?"

"Yes."

"Are all American Indians as beautiful as you?"

She turned away. "I have not met all of the American Indians," she said. "Thank you, Lieutenant, for once again bringing my meal."

On the second day, when Renno and Little Hawk had not returned, the tent seemed smaller and the hours longer. Farnsworth suggested once more that she might enjoy seeing the encampment, and this time she agreed. She declined his offer to carry little Louis.

He led her past the headquarters tent to a parade ground where groups of infantry were at drill. Sergeants bawled out orders, and hundreds of booted feet thudded the earth in union. It was an impressive sight.

Farnsworth stood proudly at Renna's side. When other men looked at her with admiration, he straightened his shoulders even more and let a little smile play over his lips.

"I have heard that you and your husband were stranded in Porto," he said. "I'm very curious as to how you happen to be with your father and your brother now."

She laughed. "Have you an hour to listen?"

"I have as much time as it will take."

He seemed to be a considerate man, Renna thought, young but trustworthy. And he was someone to talk with, to help shorten the long day while she awaited Renno and Little Hawk. She told her story as they strolled toward the artillery park. Here, too, men were conducting training drills, hitching teams of horses to the caissons, dashing to a designated point to pull the horses back on their haunches and wheel the big guns into firing position.

"We'll be moving out soon," Farnsworth explained. "It's said that Junot and his army are to the south, between us and Lisbon."

"May God go with you," Renna said. But she was thinking that Beau would be in Lisbon, and she prayed that he would be kept safe.

"I can understand if your sympathies are with the French," said Farnsworth, "since your husband is French."

"I am torn by this foolish war," she answered. "True, my sympathy is with my husband, but I wish—" She paused on the verge of saying something that could have been construed as criticism of Napoleon, for it was her personal belief that it was this one man's ambition to rule large portions of the world that kept war clouds hanging darkly over Europe.

"Well, I imagine you'll be on your way to England before we move," Farnsworth said.

"Yes."

"And then?"

"We'll stay with friends until my husband is back in France and sends for us."

"In London?" he asked.

"Near London. At Beaumont Manor."

He beamed. "But I know Lord Beaumont," he exclaimed. "My family has cousins who live quite near the manor. I have attended social functions as a guest of William and Estrela, Lord and Lady Beaumont."

"My daughter is with them now," Renna said. "So you can see why I'm eager to get back."

"Your daughter?"

"Yes. She's three years old."

"And doubtless beautiful, like you."

Renna laughed. The fact that Farnsworth knew William and Estrela had altered his status from solicitous, considerate host to friend of the family. The light of devotion was still in his eyes, but he was a gentleman who, she felt, would know and keep his place.

"Randall Farnsworth," she teased, "you will have to watch your tongue. I must warn you that my husband is quite jealous."

"I will keep that in mind," said Farnsworth, bowing slightly.

Later, after he had escorted Renna to her tent and retired to his own, Farnsworth poured some brandy and sipped it pensively. *Your husband may be jealous, but soon there's going to be a sizable little war centered around him. In war, men have been known to die.*

Beth Huntington, incensed, paced back and forth across the drawing room at Beaumont Manor. "If the Congress of the United States had set out purposely to ruin me," she stormed, "they could have done no more damage."

The object of Beth's ire was an Act of Embargo passed by the Congress at the request of President Thomas Jefferson. The law declared that no ship of the United States could sail for any foreign port. In order to leave port for coastal trade, a ship had to give a bond and swear that its destination was another port of the United States.

In announcing the action, the British newspapers quoted Jefferson as saying, "If we had suffered our vessels, cargoes, and seamen to have gone out, all would have been taken by England or its enemies, and we must have gone to war to avenge the wrong."

"He has taken the livelihood of every man who goes to sea," Beth complained. "This is total destruction of the shipping industry. We would rather take our chances with search by the English. I, for one, have given orders to prohibit the employment on my ships of any deserter from the Royal Navy. And Napoleon's threats against any traffic with England are so much bluff, for he lacks the ships and the men to enforce them. I do not mind submitting to the licensing system of the British, for my business is mainly with England and her colonies in the Caribbean; and in doing business I have had the protection of the Royal Navy on the high seas and the guarantee of secure entry into British ports. Now, instead of that, I have no choice but to sit and wait for ruin."

William was a man who had always prided himself on being able to see both sides of a question, even when patriotism was involved. "I wonder," he said, "if the American seamen who were aboard the U.S.S. *Chesapeake* when the *Leopard* fired a broadside at her would agree that trade should go on as if nothing happened."

"Oh, William," Beth said, "there will always be firebrands on both sides."

"I think Mr. Jefferson reacted rather wisely to the *Chesapeake* incident," William argued. "He merely went home to Monticello and spent a quiet summer while others called for war."

"Well, he has declared war on the shipping industry," Beth replied.

"I think, little Sister, that you will survive, and without missing a meal," William said.

Thomas Jefferson was tired, and his teeth were going bad. An infection spread into his jaw and he was confined to his quarters. To an old friend he wrote,

> My head is well silvered by eight grandchildren. I have one daughter only remaining alive. At the close of my present term I shall return to their bosoms, and to the enjoyment of my farms and books, a felicity which the times in which my existence has happened to be placed, has never been permitted me to know. I have one other great consolation that after forty years of service to my country I retire poorer than when I entered it.

As the infection in his tooth and jaw began to lessen, he took more interest in day-to-day matters. In January of the new year, congressional Republicans would meet to choose their candidates for the presidential election in the fall. Many were entreating Jefferson to declare for a third term, among them Jefferson's prime adviser, Secretary of State James Madison.

"You know, Mr. President," said Madison, "that the Constitution does not prohibit a third term."

"No," Jefferson said, "it is silent on the matter. However, James, two terms were enough for George Washington. He felt, as I do, that it would be unwise to make the presidency an office for life, lest it degenerate into an inheritance. I intend fully to follow the sound precedent set by my illustrious predecessor."

Jefferson knew that Madison coveted the office, and it had become well-known that James Monroe, newly returned from London in a huff after Jefferson's rejection of his treaty with Great Britain, was a candidate. Monroe was in a bitter mood, blaming his old friends Jefferson and Madison for cavalierly dismissing the treaty over which he had labored so long.

Jefferson was in a delicate position, for he knew that Madison expected his support. But Monroe, too, claimed friendship. Jefferson at first tried to solve the problem by standing aloof from both candidacies, calling Madison and Monroe the "two principal pillars of my happiness."

But John Randolph of Virginia, often a thorn in Jefferson's side, was backing Monroe. That, as much as anything else, forced Jefferson to abandon his professed neutrality. He made it known in certain circles that he wanted James Madison to follow him into the White House. So at the Republican congressional caucus in January, Madison received eighty-three of eighty-nine possible votes.

"I want to go home, James," he told Madison after the nomination. "I long for the privacy of Monticello. I am no longer able to push myself from morning to night in the thankless job of cleaning out the Augean stable every night, only to find it filled again in the morning."

He still had time to serve in the presidency, however, and one of the things that gave him great satisfaction was to appoint Meriwether Lewis governor of the Louisiana Territory.

"No man deserves recognition more," he declared. "It is fitting that he who led the first expedition into the fastness of the western lands should govern them."

*   *   *

Renno could see no advantage to be gained by leading Captain Lillington to the scene of the swift and deadly battle with the French patrol. Lillington's objective was to determine the whereabouts of the main French force, so after studying the maps, Renno led the patrol southeast to intersect the French line of retreat.

News of the British landing had spread throughout the countryside, so that the patrol was greeted by cheering men and laughing women in the small villages along the route. On the morning of the third day, the patrol encountered Portuguese who had seen the advance elements of the French army. Getting information was complicated, for it was difficult to find a native who spoke anything other than Portuguese. Renno managed with a combination of Spanish and sign language to determine that the bulk of the French army was still marching south, in the direction of Lisbon.

Lillington pushed his men hard, moving so fast that Little Hawk and Renno had little time to scout the roads in advance of the patrol. At a small village named Leira, they found a junction of two main north-south roads; here the villagers told them that the rear elements of the French army had pulled out only the day before.

"Captain," Little Hawk said, "we are at least fifty miles from Wellesley's encampment. It is obvious that the French are falling back on Lisbon."

"We don't know that for a certainty," Lillington said. "We will ride on."

The patrol moved toward Vimeiro, coming ever closer to Lisbon. Little Hawk was taking his turn at the point when the first French presence made itself known to him by the flashing of the sun on metal. He left his horse hidden in a copse of trees and went forward on foot, taking advantage of natural cover until, in the end, he was crawling on his stomach to peer over a small undulation of land. Fifteen French cavalrymen were dismounted and in cover on both sides of the road. It was a natural spot for an ambush.

Little Hawk eased away, taking care to make no noise,

for the nearest of the Frenchmen was a mere fifty feet away from him. He galloped back to warn Lillington.

"How many did you say?" the captain asked.

"I counted fifteen. They are armed with rifles, pistols, and sabers. I'd guess that there are at least two more men detailed to tend the horses. They're hidden in the woods south of the point of ambush."

"Show me," Lillington demanded, unrolling a map.

Little Hawk pointed to a spot where ridges hemmed in the road on both sides.

"Can we flank them?" Lillington asked.

"The ridges rise sharply on either side of the road," Little Hawk said. "A horseman would be moving very, very slowly and would be exposed to fire from the positions alongside the road."

"Take too damned long to circle the ridge and come at them from behind," Lillington said. He sighed, tugged at his belt. "There's nothing for it but to take the wogs from the front."

"You'll lose at least half your men," Little Hawk objected. "The best you can manage on the road is four abreast." He traced the road with his finger. "You'll come into range of their rifles when you round this curve, and for three hundred yards you'll be targeted. In the time it will take you to cover the ground, fifteen men can fire and reload at least three times."

"Young man," Lillington replied, "you just show me the ground and let me make the command decisions."

"Captain," Renno put in, "we have accomplished our mission. We have found the northernmost French outpost. The main body of the army can't be far to the south. My guess would be that they're deployed in front of the village of Vimeiro to protect Lisbon."

"I will decide when we've completed our mission," Lillington said.

"So," Renno said. He nodded to Little Hawk. "Show the captain the ground."

*   *   *

Renno rode at Little Hawk's side as they neared the last curve that hid them from the eyes of the fifteen Frenchmen lying in ambush.

"The road straightens now," Little Hawk said. "Then comes a three-hundred-yard straight stretch to the ambush."

Renno nodded, reined in his horse, and the two of them waited for Lillington to come up to them. "When you round this curve," Renno said, "you will be within range of the French rifles."

"Lead on, then," Lillington said.

"My son has shown you the ground," Renno said. "We go no farther on this road."

"Damn you," Lillington shouted, "do you disobey a direct order?"

Renno positioned his rifle across his legs and spoke quietly. "We are not under your orders, Captain. We are here as a favor to a friend, to your commanding officer."

"I'll have you put in irons," Lillington blustered, turning in his saddle.

"Try it," Renno said, lifting his rifle, "and you will not live to finish giving the order."

Lillington's face flushed with rage, but Renno's penetrating stare cooled his passions. "You're right," he conceded. "You are not under my orders. Stand aside then, and let soldiers do their job."

Renno and Little Hawk pulled their horses off the road to allow Lillington to form his column of thirty men into fours. The captain sent a disdainful glance toward Renno as he gave the order to advance. The column went forward into the curve at a walk, and then Renno heard the captain give the order. The horses broke into a canter, and as the leading men emerged onto the straight stretch of road, the French rifles opened up.

Renno motioned to Little Hawk, dismounted and secured his horse, and then ran into the trees. Little Hawk followed. When they reached a point where they could see the road, it was littered with fallen men and horses. A wounded animal lifted its head and shrieked in pain. The French rifles fired again, and more men went down. Lillington was leading the charge, leaning far forward in his saddle, brandishing his saber. He fell just as he reached the French position. His men continued the charge, their numbers almost equal now to those of the French ambushers. The Frenchmen started to flee and were ridden down. Sabers flashed. A horse, shot in the stomach, reared and threw his rider. In the hand-to-hand combat that followed, it seemed for a while as if there would be no victor; then it was quiet. Four Englishmen were standing; two others were wounded; the rest lay dead.

"You were wise not to have any part of this," Little Hawk said.

"I have fought against men like these," Renno replied somberly. "Brave men who obeyed orders every bit as senseless as that given by Captain Lillington. I have killed them, and even as I killed them I admired their bravery. But they were the enemy. Rightly or wrongly my father, Ghonkaba, and my grandfather, Ja-gonh, had said 'These are your enemies.' I fought. I made the white man's war my war. But this—" He gestured toward the road where one of the wounded men had managed to sit up, holding his stomach with blood oozing out through his fingers. "This is not our war. It is not our lot to fight for these white men. The French are not our enemy, but theirs."

Other thoughts crowded into Renno's mind, disturbing recollections that he did not voice. He had fought against the British when the cause was freedom for Americans—white Americans. He had fought against the Chickasaw when they had been deluded into visions of grandeur by the Spanish. He had killed Spaniards and Frenchmen and renegade Americans. Looking back, he could feel that he had been given no alternative by the manitous but to kill. In retrospect he had few doubts. He regretted having had to kill in the Chickasaw war, but he had killed to protect his home and the home of his brothers, the Cherokee. But why had he fought in the Ohio Territory? There he had maneuvered against brothers of the blood who wanted only to drive the white man from their lands.

He did not know why his thoughts traveled back in time to the fallen timbers and the slaughter of the hopes of the tribes of the Ohio. Perhaps it was the senselessness of Lillington's charge. Lillington's action would have no lasting effect on the outcome of the war in Portugal, but for those who lay dead on the muddy road there was no greater finality. Was all war as inane? And worse, had he himself fought the wrong enemy?

Chapter Fourteen

One of the four men who were on their feet after Captain Lillington's charge was a young corporal. When Renno and Little Hawk joined the survivors, he was leaning on his rifle, breathing hard. His eyes stared into the infinite distance. He seemed dazed.

"Corporal," Renno said, "the wounded men need tending."

The young man straightened. "Yes, sir," he said. He turned to his exhausted men and gave orders.

"You have dead to bury," Renno said. "While you perform that duty, we will ride ahead and have a look."

Renno put his horse into motion, and Little Hawk followed. "Father, I'm surprised," Little Hawk said. "Are we to become involved after all?"

"It will do no harm to look," Renno said. "We may see something worth reporting to Sir Arthur, who may listen to reason even if his junior officers do not."

The road dipped into a wooded hollow, where they saw the tracks of the French horses. All were gone. The guards, having seen the fate of their comrades, had wisely decided to leave the field.

"They'll lead us to the main units," Renno suggested.

"Or to another ambush," Little Hawk replied.

"If you were the French commander, how would you protect your rear?" Renno asked.

"With roving patrols, ambushes, and a rather sizable rear guard."

"We encountered an ambush, but we have seen no roving patrols."

"Perhaps the French commander did not have the quality of training that I had at West Point," Little Hawk said with a sarcastic smile.

Renno returned the smile. Little Hawk's education, cut short when he was expelled from the military academy after taking an interest in the commandant's daughter, had not been outstanding. But his inborn tactical sense was second to none.

They rode on, and for the next three miles, the only sign of the French was the tracks of their passage. Then, at the junction of two roads, the jingling of metal and the creaking of leather gear alerted the two, and they hid in brush beside the road as a patrol of ten men passed them, moving to the west. The tracks of the horses belonging to the destroyed ambushing force also turned west.

They let the patrol pass out of sight before taking the road again. Renno rode the lead, all senses alert. The ground rose ahead of them in a long, steady sweep up a shallow ridge. A group of cavalry came over the crest of the hill. Renno and Little Hawk took to the fields, hiding in a ditch until the Frenchmen were past.

"We are very close," Renno said.

They left the horses hobbled in the ditch and made their way carefully to the top of the ridge, using every available bit of cover. A valley opened up before them. On the far side, where the ground began to rise again, they saw the French army deployed in defensive formation. On the slope behind the army lay a small village.

"I have never seen so many thousands gathered in one place," Little Hawk declared, awe in his voice. He whispered, although the nearest Frenchman was a good mile away. "They have picked their position well. Any attack would be across open ground, giving the French cannon and riflemen a good field of fire. Casualties would be enormous."

Renno nodded grimly. In the past British officers had shown a sanguinary tendency to accept any challenge, however foolish, and to send their troops face on into enemy guns. It was not his war, and the British troops under Wellesley were not his people, but it saddened him to think of good men charging that long mile into the muzzles of the French guns.

"The disposition of artillery and infantry is easy to understand," Little Hawk said, surveying the field. "Now, where's the cavalry?"

"My guess would be in the woods past the village," Renno replied. "From there they could sweep out to give support on either flank."

"There's a small unit guarding the road at the top of the rise," Little Hawk said.

"We have seen enough," Renno decided. "How many, do you estimate?"

"A short corps, say fifteen thousand men."

Renno nodded and began to slide backward off the hill. The horses were as they had left them. They made their way through the fields and woodlands, came back onto the road two miles to the north, and returned at a lope to the site of the ambush. The corporal and his men were burying the last of the dead. Renno could see that the survivors were spent.

"Corporal," he said, "the French army is less than ten miles away. There will be patrols. My son and I are going to ride ahead to report to Wellesley. I would advise you to follow as swiftly as possible, keeping a watch at your rear.

If a patrol should overtake you, try concealment instead of confrontation."

"Yes, that's good advice," the corporal said.

Renno set a fast pace and was pleased to see that Little Hawk stayed at his side. They rode into the night, slept for a few hours, and were on their way again before dawn. The horses were lathered when they reached the English camp.

When they thundered up to the headquarters area, Wellesley's orderly, Sergeant Blankenship, greeted them.

"Sir Arthur?" Renno asked.

"He'll see you immediately," said the old sergeant, taking their horses as they dismounted.

Wellesley was at his map table when they went into the tent side by side. "Ah, good," the general said. "Come and show me."

Renno found the little village of Vimeiro on the map and stabbed at it with his fingers. "They're deployed to protect Lisbon," he said. "It's Junot's corps."

"That would be at least fifteen thousand men." Wellesley looked thoughtful.

"That was my estimate, sir," Little Hawk agreed. He leaned forward and traced a line. "They have dug defensive trenches here and here. The cannon are situated to have a clear field of fire over this large, open area to the west of the ridge. Their rifles will cover that last few hundred yards of the approach."

"It's not like Junot to plan a defensive action," Wellesley said. "Tell me about the country here and here." He indicated the flanks of the French position.

"It's hilly and wooded to the north," Renno said. "We did not penetrate to the south."

Wellesley was deep in thought.

"If you don't mind, sir," Renno said, "we'll see if we can find something to eat and see my daughter."

"Oh, yes, of course. I take it you rode here ahead of Captain Lillington and his men?"

"I regret to report, sir, that Captain Lillington and all but six of his men are dead." Renno explained, his hard, blue eyes boring into Wellesley's. "He led a very gallant charge against an entrenched defensive position."

"Bloody hell!" Wellesley nodded grimly. "Thank you, my friend. I can see why George Washington valued your services."

Little Hawk led the way out of the tent. Renno was stooping to pass through the flap when Wellesley called his name. He turned.

"Did you also make pointed tactical recommendations to General Washington?" Wellesley asked.

Renno smiled. "I was a lot younger then, General, and I had not seen as many men die senselessly."

Wellesley answered the smile. "If you and your son would care to come with me, I can promise you that you will not see me spend my men wantonly and recklessly."

"I have my daughter and my grandson to consider," Renno said.

"They'll be in good hands, well away from the action." He took two steps toward Renno, bent his head forward earnestly. "I don't intend to march my men bravely into the mouth of the cannons. I want you to find me a position between Junot and Lisbon, a good defensive position. Then Junot will come to me on my terms, not I to him on his."

Little Hawk put his hand on Renno's arm. "I have never seen such a battle." His voice was intent with curiosity.

"It is not our fight," Renno countered. "And aren't you eager to return to Naomi? In one piece?"

"I can bear with a brief delay," replied Little Hawk, "and we will watch from a safe distance."

Renno nodded. "We will march with you," he told Wellesley.

"Your daughter and grandson will remain here in the base camp," Wellesley said. "They will be perfectly safe."

Renna stood on a little rise, with Louis in her arms, as Wellesley's army of nineteen thousand men picked up their tents and equipment. Renno and Little Hawk were long gone, having left the encampment before light at the head of the advance patrols.

Slowly, ponderously, the army marched out, becoming a long red snake of movement. As the artillery rumbled past, men called out greetings to Renna, waving and saluting, for they had seen her walking with her child around the camp.

Though she missed her daughter, Renna surprisingly did not begrudge the time that would now elapse before they all took ship for England. She felt closer to Beau—being in the same country with him—than she would feel later, once they were at sea. But it was no secret that Wellesley's aim was to move the British army into Lisbon and return the capital city to Portuguese control. Beau would be in Lisbon at the French offices. She prayed that he would not become involved in the fighting; he was a diplomat, not a soldier.

She watched for a long, long time. Now the supply wagons rolled past her position and behind them a rear guard of cavalry. A single horseman detached himself from the column and galloped up the slope toward her. The rider lifted his horse over a stone fence in a smooth, graceful flow of motion. It was Randall Farnsworth. He drew his horse to a halt and dismounted.

"You have come out to see us off," he said. "How nice of you."

"It's a very impressive sight." She looked into the distance along the column of wagons, artillery, and marching men.

"I wish that I were staying here to look after you."

"We'll be fine," she assured him. "Sir Arthur has left Sergeant Blankenship with us."

"The general values you highly, to leave his personal orderly behind."

"We are appreciative," she acknowledged.

Farnsworth glanced toward the tail end of his column, which was moving off down the road. "I must go," he said, looking at her with obvious longing.

"God be with you."

"And you." He leaped into his saddle, lifted his hat in salute, and then was gone.

Renna went back to her tent. Sergeant Blankenship had tea ready when she arrived. He fussed over the service, and she didn't have the heart to tell him that she was perfectly capable of serving her own tea.

"How's that, mum?" he asked, beaming. "Hot enough?"

"Just right, Sergeant," she said.

"I'll be bringing your evening meal at six."

"Thank you."

"And, mum?"

"Yes?"

"It's going to be a long wait, sitting here wondering what's going on with the army. If I may make a suggestion?"

"Of course," she said.

"There's a town nearby, quite a pretty one, and the villagers are friendly. I thought perhaps that you and the wee lad would fancy a walk on the first nice afternoon."

"That sounds wonderful, Sergeant," she agreed.

As it happened, the next afternoon was sunny and pleasant. Sergeant Blankenship escorted her proudly down the main street of the little village. The people smiled, nodded, and bowed. Blankenship bowed widely in return.

"I've heard some of the officers say, mum, that the food at the inn is quite good."

It was, and it was a pleasant change from army fare.

As the days became weeks, a walk to the village and a midday meal at the inn became routine. Renna fashioned a carry board, Seneca style, for little Louis, and with Blankenship at her side, always fatherly and polite, she explored the near countryside. Louis grew pleasingly and was soon taking small amounts of soft foods to supplement Renna's milk. In the fashion of her mother and of Seneca mothers, she chewed meat for Louis until it was pulverized, then placed it in his mouth. He smacked and worked his toothless jaws, blinking in pleasure at the new treat.

*   *   *

Like two great beasts extending claws, the armies reached out. A British patrol clashed with a small French unit and sent it scurrying back toward the main body in the valley. Wellesley took advantage of the enemy's temporary blindness to move his army to the east in an encircling movement, coming up from the south to a site that had been chosen in advance by Renno and Little Hawk.

"An excellent position," Wellesley declared, riding side by side with Renno to examine the ground. "Very good, yes."

He immediately set about positioning his troops. Renno and Little Hawk rode north to look down upon the French army from the rear. Obviously Junot was aware that Wellesley had circled around him, disdaining the frontal assault over the killing ground to the front of the French army. And as Wellesley had guessed, defensive warfare was not Junot's choice. The speed with which he set his army in motion, reversing its direction to move toward the British position, made it seem that he welcomed the chance to attack.

Before the attack came, it was preceded by a thunderous artillery battle. Wellesley had placed his guns in protected pockets to cover the front of the army. Junot had to make do with whatever positions were available to him on the rolling approach to the British defensive stand. In spite of the great smoke and thunder of it, the French bombardment did little damage. Then Junot moved his infantry and sent them forward into a hail of cannon and rifle fire.

Renno and Little Hawk were a mile away, on the left flank of the British army atop a little knoll. The battlefield was laid out before them as if it were an exercise on a model table. Little Hawk felt a tingle of awe and anticipation as the French infantry stepped out smartly, rifles at the ready. He sighed when the first bursts of English cannon fire knocked gaps in the orderly line and caused the formations to waver like tall grass blowing in a storm.

"I have come to believe that we are witnesses to one of the great stupidities of man," Renno said.

"But this is the way wars are fought," Little Hawk

answered. He pointed. "Look, now Junot sends his cavalry to the flank."

In a cloud of dust the cavalry swept forward. From the trees behind the British lines Wellesley's cavalry moved to blunt the French charge.

"Anthony Wayne's American Legion marched in perfect formation toward the rifles in the fallen timbers," Renno said. "They were brave men, and these are brave men. Such men should not be used up so heedlessly."

"If you were Junot, how would you attack?" Little Hawk asked.

Renno was silent for a long time. When he spoke his voice was soft. "First of all, I would not be here, trying to seize land that was not mine; but if I were, I would train my men not to march in perfect lines into the guns but to move rapidly, taking advantage of any cover, falling to the ground behind a bush or a small rise, running, weaving to throw off the aim of the riflemen. Then, when we were near, I would have them fire from a prone position, to give back some of the fire that they had been taking. Fire, load, move, roll, and fire again."

"I think the white generals would say that your method would not be an honorable way to fight," Little Hawk said.

"Tell *them* about honor," Renno said, pointing to the growing number of French dead littering the field behind the wavering but still advancing lines. "We can only be thankful that Beau is not among them. Let us hope he is safely far away."

Now the battlefield was wreathed in smoke, and for a long time nothing could be seen. When a wind rose to whip the smoke away, the French forces were in full retreat.

Randall Farnsworth led his men in the charge that blunted the attack of the French cavalry. Like their infantry comrades, the French horsemen were outnumbered, but they fought well. They were veterans. They had known battle in many European fields, and they had led the way for the army across all of Spain. They gave ground grudgingly and left the field covered with their dead, the grass sprinkled with their blood.

By evening it was apparent that the French had been badly beaten. The battle for Lisbon was over, and Junot's forces were in full retreat. The French army could have been destroyed completely if Wellesley had had fresh reserves, but he had committed his entire force to the fight, and he had taken his own casualties. The men were spent, exhausted, incapable of giving immediate chase.

Farnsworth gathered his remaining men and took the roll. His casualties were light. He went to his commanding officer to report the readiness of his troop.

"Lieutenant," the colonel said, "if your men are capable of it, you may move into Lisbon immediately."

"We are ready, sir," Farnsworth answered.

"You will be the advance of the entire army," the colonel said. "We can't know at this time if the French left forces in the city, so you will proceed with caution. Do not engage a superior force. Mainly, I want you to show the flag, to let our Portuguese allies know that we have carried the day here. If the French have abandoned the city, throw a cordon around the government buildings and hold them until the main force arrives."

Farnsworth was delighted. He knew that he had handled himself well during the battle and that his men had fought like veterans. Now he was to have the honor of being the first to enter the Portuguese capital. He could envision promotion to captain and perhaps even a decoration.

The men grumbled good-naturedly when Farnsworth gave orders to move out but cheered lustily when told that they were to be the first into Lisbon. They marched out smartly, made camp that night just two miles from the outskirts of the city, and entered the old town with first light. They were well into the city before people began to be up and around, at which time their reception became a procession of triumph, with cheers and kisses blown by pretty girls. There were no French soldiers to be seen.

Farnsworth discovered that, so far as government was concerned, he had ridden into a vacuum. Since the Portu-

guese royal family had long since fled to Brazil, many
rank-and-file civil servants had left the city as well. The
French had been in Lisbon, but they were gone now—
they, too, having fled at the news of Junot's defeat at
Vimeiro.

Farnsworth obeyed his orders, positioning his men
around the government buildings. He made rounds regu-
larly as the day lengthened. One group of his men had
found an English-speaking government worker who was
eager to talk to his British ally.

"Soon they will come back, the royal family," the civil
servant said. "And then the government will work again."

"And in the meantime?" Farnsworth asked.

The man shrugged. "I am but one man," he said. "A
diplomat."

It was not the first time that Farnsworth had thought
of Renna's husband, a diplomat. "And what of the French
diplomats?" he asked. "Did they also flee?"

"Oh, yes," the man said. "They left only a few men
behind when they went with the French troops."

"They left men behind?"

"To destroy the papers of state, you know?"

"Where are the French offices?" Farnsworth demanded.

The man pointed to a graceful old building at the
edge of the governmental complex.

"Thank you, my friend," said Farnsworth. He called
his color sergeant. "Give me three men, Sergeant. I want
to go calling on some Frenchmen."

The entrance door to the French offices was locked.
One of the lancers smashed it in with his rifle butt. Inside
the floors and walls were marble, and their footsteps echoed in the corridors. A quick search showed the ground-
floor offices—some of them magnificently ornate in their
decor—to be empty. Farnsworth led the way up a wide,
long staircase to the second floor.

When an exhausted messenger brought the news of
Junot's defeat to Lisbon, the first reaction among the
French diplomatic corps and occupation officials, who

were in the process of setting up a functioning government, was near panic. The military governor called in the ambassador. The ambassador returned to the French offices mopping perspiration from his brow and looking worried.

"It is estimated that the British will be here within twenty-four hours," he announced. "We must destroy all records. I will ask for volunteers to stay here in the offices until that task has been completed."

There was dead silence. The ambassador wiped his brow and frowned in exasperation. It was a full minute before Beau sighed in resignation and stepped forward.

"Thank you, monsieur le comte," the ambassador said.

"I will need two men to help me," Beau said. He pointed to two members of his personal staff. The men went pale. "You have nothing to fear," Beau assured them. "We will be finished with the job long before the British arrive."

While the ambassador led the exodus of the offices in great haste, Beau and his two helpers began to empty the files and the desks. Soon fires were burning in several fireplaces, but it was slow work.

"It looks as if the entire French staff did nothing but create paperwork," Beau complained as the day ended and the fires burned on into the night.

He allowed his helpers to sleep a few hours but woke them with the dawn. They had denuded the first and second floors of any documents that might provide information to the enemy. Most of the endless reams of paper would be, Beau thought, an excellent weapon against the British, for an army would be required to read through all of them, and the translators would be rendered useless for fighting, having been bored into helplessness without gaining an iota of useful information.

Only the offices on the third floor remained, and these had been occupied by lesser functionaries. His nervous helpers pointed this out to him, and he told them to go.

"Come with us, monsieur le comte," one of them implored. "The English cannot be far off now."

"I'll have a quick look on the third floor," Beau said. "Rest assured I'll be directly on your heels."

As Farnsworth turned into a corridor on the second floor, he came face to face with two French civilians, who immediately threw up their hands.

"We are your prisoners, sir," one of them said, "and I remind you that we are members of the diplomatic corps."

"And so you will be treated," Farnsworth replied. "Your names, sirs."

Neither of the names was the one he wanted to hear. "How many others are in the building?" he demanded.

"Only the two of us, sir."

Farnsworth turned, gave orders. His three men began to search the rooms of the second floor.

"Lieutenant," one of them called back, "same thing up here. They've been burning papers."

"Very well." Farnsworth looked hard at his two captives. "You are alone, just the two of you?"

"That is correct."

A soft thud came through the ceiling of the room from the floor above. "If you are alone in the building, what is that? A large rat?" He pointed his pistol threateningly.

"There is one other," one of them confessed. "He is a representative of the emperor himself."

Farnsworth's heart thudded. "And his name?"

"Le comte de Beaujolais."

Beau dumped the contents of a file box onto the top of a desk and thumbed through it. The papers had to do with routine housekeeping matters for the offices. Deciding not to waste time in burning them, he moved on to another room. He was examining the contents of a desk drawer when he heard a small sound from the corridor outside. He froze. He heard the sound again, a man walking very carefully. Beau was unarmed. He moved quickly to the door and threw it open. A British officer in a scarlet tunic faced him with a pistol pointed at his breast.

"Good afternoon," Beau said. "Apparently I delayed my departure too long."

"Your name," said the grim-faced officer.

"I am Beaujolais."

"Count Beaujolais?"

"Yes."

Beau saw the Englishman's eyes change, slit themselves. He saw the man tense, and his eyes fell to the hand that held the pistol. His own eyes widened as he saw the man's finger tightening on the trigger.

"Wait—" Beau said as the pistol exploded and something of great force smashed into his chest.

The three troopers came pounding up the stairs and along the corridor. Farnsworth was standing in the hall. He pointed to a body lying just inside an office.

"He was reaching into his coat," he explained. "I feared that he was going for a weapon."

"A frog eater by the looks of him," said one of the troopers. He kneeled down, loosened the collar, and felt the man's neck, but he wasn't sure how to find a pulse. "Do you think the fellow's done for?" he asked.

Farnsworth came and stared down at the Frenchman. "Of course," he said. He had fired point-blank at the man's chest, and blood was oozing out from under the body. The man looked peaceful in death, his handsome countenance marred only by a heart-shaped birthmark on his neck.

Farnsworth looked around. "Where are your prisoners?" he asked.

"They're locked safely in one of the rooms."

"Post a guard and hold them until the main body arrives, so that the intelligence officers can question them."

"Yes, sir, but it looks as if they've burned everything," said one trooper.

"Except on this floor," Farnsworth said. "We'll seal it off. The general might want to have someone look through the papers that are left."

"What about him?" the trooper asked, pointing at the fallen man.

"Leave him," Farnsworth said. "We'll have the body detail remove him later."

He saw that the troopers had helped themselves to some minor loot, but he said nothing. That was the way of war. On the next long march, when the items became heavy, they would be discarded. He wandered around the now-empty building, and his thoughts were of a pale-haired woman a hundred miles to the north. Now nothing stood between him and his desire except a period of carefully calculated concern and consideration on his part. Perhaps she would leave for England before he saw her again. Well, he knew where to find her in England. It would be best for him if she learned quickly of the death of her husband, so that her grief would be past when, at last, he was free to go to her at Beaumont Manor. She would go through a period of grieving, but he was a patient man.

Five British men-of-war lay in Mondego Bay, their sails rigged loosely to dry. Cannon poked their round snouts from the gun ports. Small boats came and went from shore. The shouts of a mate bawling orders carried over the water.

A letter from Sir Arthur Wellesley had assured passage to England aboard the troop transport *Norfolk* for "the honorable Renno Harper and a party of four, which includes a babe in arms." Renno and his group, with the effusive thanks of Sir Arthur Wellesley still ringing in their ears, had come up from Lisbon some days previously, only to find that the sailing of the *Norfolk* was to be delayed. Renno, familiar with shipboard accommodations, decided they should wait ashore in tents.

The new year was well under way. Little Hawk was once again impatient to see Naomi and his child, for her time of delivery was long past. To be a father without knowing the sex of his offspring, he said, was a frustrating experience.

"It was a girl, brother," Renna teased, "for girls are much nicer than boys."

Little Hawk took it in good spirit. "I would accept a little girl who looks like her mother."

"I look forward very much to meeting my new sister," Renna said. "I'm sure, since you love her, that she must be very nice."

Renno chaffed at the delay, and when the appointed time for sailing approached, he told Renna and Little Hawk to get ready to board ship. But before they could be ferried out to the *Norfolk,* a courier rode in from the south on a lathered horse with orders to hold the *Norfolk* still longer for important passengers.

"Bloody hell," Little Hawk said, using one of the more profane English oaths at his command.

It turned out that the three important passengers were all generals, Sir Arthur Wellesley among them. When he arrived a day or so later, he was in a testy mood, but he greeted Renno and Little Hawk in an affectionate manner.

"It seems, my friends, that we will travel to England in company," he said. He cut an impressive figure in his scarlet tunic, with its heavy ropes of gold. A glint of white showed at his throat behind the high, gold-leafed collar. His hair had grown long, hanging past his ears and down his broad forehead. His nose was long and powerful, his mouth rather small and bow shaped on both upper and lower lips.

It was not until the *Norfolk* was at sea that Renno learned exactly why Wellesley had been called back to England, along with Sir Hew Dalrymple and Sir Henry Burrard, the two generals who had been sent to Portugal by the War Office as Wellesley's superiors. The facts came out over a dinner in Wellesley's quarters.

"We whipped them handily, my friends," Wellesley explained to Renno and his son and daughter. "Wellesley beat them, and then Dalrymple signed a convention with them that in effect gave them safe passage back to Spain." He sipped from a glass of Spanish red wine, his expression dour. "By God, I had them in the palm of my hand. I could have destroyed a corps, and there would have been that many fewer Frenchmen to fight at a later date. But no! The War Office was not content with victory; they had to send *Sir* Hew Dalrymple to Portugal to snatch defeat from victory."

"General, as I remember, the War Office has made such brilliant decisions in the past," Renno commented.

"Napoleon has stepped into a barrel of molasses by his invasion of Spain," Wellesley continued. "Spanish patriots who go against cannon and rifles with clubs are making the little crop head wonder why he wanted to antagonize a former ally. And we turn loose a corps of veterans to march back into Spain and give him reinforcements. It is beyond belief. And now we must return to London to explain the convention signed by Dalrymple. Sir John Moore is in command of the army that was mine."

He swallowed the last of his wine. "But enough of my problems, my friend Renno," he said. "It has occurred to me that this voyage will be an excellent time for me to hear from you more about the New World."

"Don't encourage him, Sir Arthur," Renna spoke up. "If an Indian likes anything better than listening to tall tales, it is the telling of them."

Wellesley laughed. "The taller the better. Have at it, Renno."

When the *Norfolk* reached her moorings in Portsmouth Harbor, they made their farewells to Sir Arthur Wellesley, and Renno went to hire a coach. Little Hawk and Renna watched as the three generals—all of them grimly silent, their shoulders squared and chins high—left the docks on horseback.

Soon Renno had made the arrangements, and their coach was under way, bouncing and swaying over the rutted roads toward Beaumont Manor.

Little Hawk was almost frantic with anticipation. "I should have hired a horse," he moaned when the coach became mired in the mud and required the help of the male passengers to free it.

Nevertheless the miles passed, and early one spring evening, when the days were already becoming long, the coach turned into the lane leading to Beaumont Manor. The wheels had not stopped rolling when Little Hawk leaped out and headed for the house at a run. A servant, having heard the coach on the graveled drive, opened the

door and was almost bowled over as Little Hawk pushed
past into the front hall, calling out his wife's name.

It was past dinnertime, and Little Hawk heard the
sound of a harpsichord issuing from the drawing room. He
charged forward, calling out again. Then Naomi came
rushing out to the hallway. Little Hawk tried to stop, but
his momentum carried him into her. He wrapped his arms
around her and clung to her, barely managing to keep both
of them on their feet.

"Oh, oh, oh," Naomi was saying over and over.

He pushed her gently to arm's length and let his eyes
feast on her. She was thin, her waist small. Her skin
glowed with health and the excitement of seeing him.

"Manitous, you're beautiful," he whispered as he
pulled her to him and covered her mouth with his own.

Beth, moving only slightly more sedately than Naomi,
had followed the younger woman into the hall in time to
see Renno and Renna come in the front door. She ran to
meet them and threw herself into Renno's arms.

"Thank God," she said, kissing Renno quickly. She
turned to Renna, put her hands on Renna's cheeks and
kissed her lightly on the mouth. "And you!" she said gaily.
"How beautiful you've become."

Little Louis picked that moment to register his protest at having been bounced around in a coach all day.

"What's this?" Beth asked, lifting the flap of blanket
that protected the baby's face. "A boy?"

"A boy," Renna said.

"Blue eyes, like his grandfather and his mother."

"Black hair like his father," Renna said.

"But you haven't heard our news," Beth said excit-
edly.

The news had to wait, for now William and Estrela
had to be greeted and everyone was trying to talk at once,
everyone except Little Hawk and Naomi, who had stepped
around the corner of the hall and were not talking at all
because they were joined mouth to mouth and soul to soul.

"So now we are all together," Estrela said. "How
wonderful it is."

"All except Beau," Renna corrected.

"Of course, forgive me," Estrela said.

Around the corner, Naomi pulled her face away from Little Hawk's hungry kiss. "Wait," she begged. "You've made me quite breathless, and I have something to tell you."

He grinned and patted her flat stomach. "I can guess."

"Guess then," she said.

"A boy."

"Wrong," she said.

"A girl?" He smiled broadly. "That doesn't disappoint me at all."

"Wrong again," she said.

"What?" He was puzzled.

"Wait," she said again. She took his hand and pulled him back into the main hallway. "Father Renno," she said, "would you come, please? There's something I want to show you."

Renna rushed forward. "You're Naomi."

"Yes." The two embraced as Renno came to their side.

"What is this you want to show us?" he asked.

"Come along, all of you," Naomi said, taking Little Hawk's hand.

The twins were in their cribs, under the watchful eye of the woman who had been nanny for all of Estrela's children. Little Hawk pushed past and, seeing only one of the cribs, picked up the baby carefully. The diaper fell away. "But it is a boy," he said. He looked at Naomi questioningly. "You said it was not a boy."

"And so it is not *a* boy," she said. She picked up the other twin. "*Two* boys," she said.

"Manitous," Little Hawk whispered in awe. He held one boy alongside the one that Naomi was holding. "They are very much alike, but this one is smaller."

"That's Little Boy," said Estrela.

"And that would make this one Big Boy," Little Hawk said.

"I didn't want to pick names for them while you were away," Naomi said.

Little Hawk looked into the eyes of the woman he loved. "I can think of no better gift than these two that you have given me," he said.

"Hear, hear," said Estrela. "May there be many more."

Little Hawk grinned shyly. "Let me get used to these two first, Aunt Estrela."

Chapter Fifteen

~~~~~~

Randall Farnsworth's hopes of seeing Renna before she left Portugal were dashed when Sir John Moore, left in command of the English expeditionary force after the three senior generals were called back to London, received orders to march into Spain. Farnsworth found himself at the forefront, leading patrols through mountainous terrain toward the Spanish city of Salamanca.

But Farnsworth did not see Salamanca. A Spanish partisan, ragged, hungry, and frightened but determined to drive all invaders from his country, French or English, aimed his ancient musket and put a heavy lead ball in Farnsworth's shoulder.

The wound was not considered serious in itself. An army surgeon removed the sizable piece of lead, wound a bandage around Farnsworth's shoulder, and ordered his evacuation to a field hospital back in Portugal. Farnsworth started the trip on horseback. But the wound went septic almost immediately, and Farnsworth finished the trip in a horse-drawn ambulance, raving with fever and delirium.

At the field hospital an overworked doctor took one look at the young cavalry officer, shook his head, and consigned him to the dying tent.

Farnsworth lay burning with fever while men expired all around him, but he refused to die. When news came of his promotion to captain, he could barely acknowledge it. In his delirium he dreamed of the pale-haired woman from the New World. When, to the surprise of many, he dragged himself off the cot and walked out of the dying tent, the doctor took another look at his wound. Contrary to first impressions, the wound was septic but not gangrenous.

"Well, Captain," the doctor concluded, "I think with a bit of cleaning, after we've removed some of the proud flesh, that you're going to live after all."

"You're not going to touch me," Farnsworth declared. He was still feverish, and his worst fear was that the doctors would decide to take his arm.

It took four husky medical orderlies to hold him on the operating table while the doctor started snipping away at the dead flesh around his wound. Farnsworth bellowed with rage, fever, and pain, and then passed into unconsciousness. When he awoke, he still had both his arms. He was in a tent that smelled less of the dead and the dying, and his shoulder was cleanly bandaged.

He had lost weight. His uniform trousers no longer fit snugly across his flat stomach. When he stood, they tended to slide down onto his hips. His ribs stood out. His eyes were sunken, and the flesh was stretched tightly across his cheekbones.

"So, my boy," the doctor told him, "it's home for you. Back to England it is."

He made no protest. He walked to the ambulance but was satisfied to put up with the bumpy ride into Lisbon and to the port, for if he stayed on his feet more than a very few minutes, the world began to blur and blackness crept upon him.

He began to take some exercise during the voyage

northward through the Bay of Biscay, and by the time the ship docked at Portsmouth, he was able to walk for a quarter hour without becoming overly tired. Doctors at the army hospital examined his wound, nodded in satisfaction, and told him he'd be well enough to go home in a matter of weeks. He had a bed in a room with half-a-dozen other wounded officers, both army and navy, and was given access to the grounds. As the days warmed, he walked in the sun, growing stronger every day.

Then came the day when the bandages were removed for the last time. The healed skin around the wound was red and sensitive, but there was no suppuration. Farnsworth could move his arm with only minor pain, and the doctors assured him that with time he would have full use of the limb. When he was released from the hospital, he claimed convalescent leave, drew his back pay, bought a horse and saddle, and set out for the home of his cousin near London.

Day by day, week by week, Renna waited for word from her husband. Even though Europe was divided by war, letters could still travel from Paris to England via roundabout routes, the one most commonly used being through neutral Switzerland. But day after day, week after week, Renna was disappointed. She told herself that it would take time, that in all probability Beau had been forced to travel by land, since the English were in the Portuguese ports.

Enough news of the war reached Beaumont Manor for Renna to understand the realities. If Beau found it necessary to make his way back to Paris overland, he would have to negotiate a tortuous path around the battlefields in Spain. Sir John Moore's forces had been joined in that country by an army of thirteen thousand men under General David Baird. In addition to being faced with British armies, the French were learning that the ordinary people of Spain were fiercely patriotic. Even though Napoleon had deposed the Spanish royal family and put one of his brothers on the throne, Spanish partisans continued to harry the French forces.

Renna was concerned for Beau, but she was not in despair. Each night she made it a point to talk to Emily Beth about her father and to assure her that soon they would be back with him. In the meantime, William, undisguisedly pleased to have his sister and his old friend with him once again, outdid himself in inventing new ways to entertain his guests, thus postponing the inevitable time when Renno would say it was time to go.

Adan Bartolome arrived at the manor wondering how he was going to be able to bear the burden of reporting that he had been unable to locate Renno and Little Hawk, or Beau and Renna in either Lisbon or Porto. When he saw Renno, he gave a great shout and embraced him.

"There I was, sailing from Lisbon to Porto and back again looking for you, and all the time you were here, living the good life," he complained without real rancor.

Adan's presence brought merry times to the manor. Always cheerful, sometimes almost childishly enthusiastic, Adan was like a tonic to Estrela, and his continued good spirits kept the others laughing. He made Beth feel better because he was optimistic about business matters.

"How long can President Jefferson afford to enforce a law that paralyzes the commerce of the nation?" he asked Beth. "Besides, the embargo will drive up to profitable heights the value of any cargo I take back to Wilmington." He winked. "I can only imagine the, ah, shall we say, business opportunities that the embargo affords those who are willing to take some small risk."

"I don't think, my dear brother," Estrela said, "that Beth wants to become a smuggler."

Adan laughed. "I would never ask such a lady to commit a crime." He winked again. "However, I might ask her to look the other way."

Adan departed soon afterward, for he was eager to reach the home port with his cargo while the supply of imports from England was at a low. Since the *Comtesse Renna* had been at sea when the Embargo Act was passed by Congress and ratified by the president, she would enjoy free passage to Wilmington.

*   *   *

With the coming of the warm days of spring, the family went on outings. Beth suggested a journey to a spot that still had great meaning to her and Renno, the ancient battlefield at Hastings where once they had said good-bye.

Renno welcomed the trip and the memories it revived. He and Beth had made love on the grassy lea where once heavily armored men had fought and died, and he had known the pang of loss when, his farewells made to Beth both orally and physically, he had escorted her back to Beaumont Manor for what they had thought would be the last time.

Thinking of those times brought back the bittersweet recollection of An-da, Sweet Day, mother of Ta-na. Each of the women to whom he had been married had a special place in his heart, but he had loved An-da in a way that he had never loved another, for she was of his blood. She was Seneca, and she had given him a Seneca son.

He missed Ta-na now, wishing he could show the lad this historic battlefield. But he was glad that the boy had remained in America, among his own people, so that his time of training to be a warrior would be uninterrupted.

Renno and Beth walked the rolling hills about the battlefield hand in hand. She had grown more regal with maturity, but she had the looks of a woman ten years younger than her forty-two years. Her flame-colored hair gleamed with health, and around the green fire of her pupils, her eyes were flawlessly white.

Thinking how once he had lost her, Renno silently thanked the manitous for seeing to it that his youthful good-bye to her had not been final. How kind the manitous were to have brought her into his life again, as the wife of his maturity. She was the woman with whom he would grow old.

England in the springtime was serene, a land of flowers and neat, green fields. The tidiness of it all contrasted with the sheer wildness of the Cherokee lands and, for that matter, the entire vast, unmanicured sweep of the New World. With the lengthening days, the sun rose at what was, to the Americans, an indecently early hour. A million birds woke them, their songs coming in through the open windows on the crisp, wondrous mornings. In the evening daylight lingered past bedtime. Soon it would be summer. Renno felt restlessness growing in him, but every time he began to think that it was time to go, William offered some other plan for something to do.

"I'm an Englishman born and bred," William said one morning, "and I've never seen what many consider to be England's greatest architectural artifact."

Organizing a trip of more than one day for the entire extended family was not a simple thing. A caravan of vehicles was required for the Beaumont family—two adults and the four children still at home; also Renno and Beth; Little Hawk, Naomi, and the twins; and Renna with her two children, along with a company of servants and nannies. They traveled to London and past, westward to the plain at Salisbury, to Stonehenge, mysterious and stark.

On the day of their arrival at the nearby village of Amesbury, the weather had turned, and they disembarked from their carriages in a chill and penetrating rain.

The rooms at the inn were warm, the beds soft. With the morning the group from Beaumont Manor had the dining room all to themselves. Outside the skies were still gray. The landlord opined that a great storm was moving in from the Atlantic. Although Estrela's brood clamored to be allowed to see the object of the long journey, William said firmly that the three-mile jaunt to the henge would wait until better weather.

After breakfast, while the children were engaged in a noisy game of darts, Renno sat with Beth by a window.

"Do you fancy staying indoors all day?" Beth asked.

"I'm open to suggestions," Renno told her.

Bundled into warm clothing, they leased horses from the inn's stable and rode through the gray day to the top of a hill. Below them, looking small and insignificant, stood the brooding stones. As they trotted toward the ancient structure, the wind increased, driving swirling, dark clouds before it.

At close range the henge showed its true size. They dismounted and walked into the circle formed by the massive rectangular blocks set on end and topped by equally substantial horizontals. The wind howled and eddied, whipping Beth's skirts, and a sprinkle of rain stung their upturned faces. Renno let his eyes wander around the horizon. Nothing moved save the wind-waved grass and the tops of a few scattered trees.

Voices rode on the wind, and Renno felt the hair on his neck rise. The wind and the stones both contained infinite wonder. It seemed impossible for mere men to have carved these monoliths, to have moved them in their countless tons, to have positioned them so artfully as to convey a meaning that was lost. The voices wept, and they penetrated into his being to sing songs of loss and sacrifice, of anguish and ruin. His mind returned to the cave in Spain, and he felt here the same despair and heaviness of spirit he had felt there. For like the cave drawings, these stones told him that nothing was permanent, that his own world, like all others, would pass and be forgotten.

He stepped forward and, with arms extended straight out from his shoulders, chanted to his own manitous. The words, spoken in the language of the Seneca, were swept away by the wind. Minutes passed. Finally he dropped his arms to his sides and turned to Beth, who had stood silently watching him all the while.

"What is it?" she asked. "What is wrong?"

The voices moaning in the wind told him that her beauty, like all else, would wither, and that once again they would be parted—the next time forever.

He rejected this last melancholy thought. He knew in his heart that they would one day reach a final place together, the Place across the River, the place in the west where his ancestors awaited.

She put her arms around him. "You must tell me."

"It is nothing," he answered. He had been shown the end of all things that were dear to him. He had seen the passing of the Seneca and the Cherokee and the triumph of white expansion. He saw shame and suffering, and his thoughts went out to his family, to his son Ta-na, to his brother, his sister, his mother.

"Renno?" Beth coaxed.

"I feel a tremendous sadness here," he said.

"So do I."

"They were a warrior race," he said, "and strong in their belief. They did the labor of giants, and for what?"

"But they left this as proof of their greatness," she replied. "And their blood, diluted though it may be, runs in the living veins of a great nation."

He looked up into the roiling clouds. When his Seneca people had been absorbed into the Cherokee nation, when the Cherokee had been submerged into the sea of white, would there be someone to say as much for the Indian? He shook his head, trying to dispel the sense of doom. Beth's hand in his was a sweet warmth. He looked into her face and began to slough off his malaise.

He could not control the future. He could not stave off the end that had been promised by the voices in the wind. But for now he was alive and strong, and his wife was warm and beautiful. He had his son, his daughter, his daughter-by-marriage, and his grandchildren with him.

"You're cold?" he asked.

"I have a few toes that are not yet frozen into icicles."

"Come," he said.

"What was it?" she asked. "What did you feel?"

He shrugged. "I felt the cold, and the seclusion of this place."

"Some say the Druids built it, and that they made human sacrifices here."

He made no comment. He helped Beth into the saddle, and soon they were thawing their hands and toes in front of a roaring fire in the inn and warming their interiors with steaming cups of tea.

That night, after coming together in love, they lay awake. Beth broke the silence.

"It's time to go home, isn't it?" she asked.

"To Huntington Castle? To the village?" He could not keep a touch of bitterness from his voice; the day's events had disoriented him, and he hardly knew where home was.

"If that is not our home, what is?" she asked, her voice puzzled yet patient.

He took her hand. "I have asked much of you. I took

you from your place, from your country, and from the business you built in North Carolina. I took you far away from what you know as civilization, and you did not complain."

She laughed. "Well, my dear husband, living in Huntington Castle is not exactly roughing it." She turned onto her side and put her arm around him. "My home is where you are, even if your mother doesn't think that I am a good Seneca wife."

He chuckled. "My mother is quite fond of you, and my brother dotes on you."

"I would like to see them," she whispered. "Ta-na and Gao. El-i-chi and Ena and Ah-wa-o. Rusog and Roy. All of them."

"Even my mother?"

"Even your mother," she said.

"And is your house my home?" In the quiet time that follows the act of love, he had felt a hint of the distress that he had known as the voices of the past spoke to him at the henge. He was no longer the leader of his people. Rightly or wrongly he had given over that responsibility to his brother.

"Our house," she said.

"Built with your money."

She lifted herself on one elbow and said severely, "We'll have none of that. You're forgetting that Spanish gold established my business. Spanish gold saved Beaumont Manor and gave William a new start. You took us to that gold, Sachem. You made it possible for us to bring it back. Everything we have, all of us, is because of you. So don't you dare say that the money that comes from the Huntington Shipping Company belongs to me and not to you."

He laughed. "You almost convince me," he said.

"And what did you do with your share of the gold? You bought tools, weapons, useful things and some luxuries for your people."

He was silent for a long time. In a moment of weakness he had been tempted to blame the people, to fault them for having let him step down as sachem so easily. The moment passed quickly. It had been his decision and his alone. When he spoke his voice was low. "It will be good to see them."

"Yes, it will."

"Then we will go before the storms of autumn."

"But you can't leave just now, Renno," William protested. "We've scheduled the christening ceremony for Naomi's twins for two weeks from tomorrow."

"So," Renno said.

"Moreover, the embargo is still in effect. You'll have difficulty finding an American ship that is defying the law, and the United States won't let an English ship land at an American port," William said.

"We can sail for one of the Caribbean islands," Beth said. "My guess is that by the time we get there, Mr. Jefferson will have realized that his Embargo Act is rather stupid and will have repealed it. If not, I'm quite sure that Yankee skippers have figured out a way to beat the embargo."

"We'll talk about it after the christening," William declared.

They were having tea in the south garden. Nearby, what sounded like dozens of children were at play. Actually they were just Estrela's three youngest and Emily Beth. "We'll miss you all so much," Estrela said. "But we have one consolation." She patted Renna's hand. "You and the children will be staying with us, won't you?"

"Until Beau sends for us," Renna said, "if we haven't worn out our welcome."

"Never," Estrela said. "My girls love your little Emily."

The butler came out onto the lawn. "Sir, there is a young gentleman at the door asking to see Mistress Renna."

Renna's face flushed, and she leaped to her feet. "Is it the count, my husband?"

"No, madam," the butler said. "His name is Farnsworth, a Captain Randall Farnsworth."

Renna's excitement faded quickly. "Very well. I will

receive Captain Farnsworth in the parlor," she said. "If you'll excuse me?"

"Shall I come with you?" Estrela asked.

"No, thank you, Estrela."

"Isn't this the young man you met in Portugal?" William asked. "How the devil did he find you here?"

"I told him I'd be staying with you," Renna said. "He said that he knew you."

"Of course," Estrela said, "Farnsworth. We do know him. He's a Scot, a cousin to the Blands. He has been a guest in our house."

"Tall lad, red hair?" William asked.

"Yes," Renna said, turning away to walk swiftly toward the large back porch.

"Well then, if he knows us, why didn't he remember his manners and ask to see me?" William grumbled.

"I'm afraid that Renna has acquired an admirer, my dear," said Estrela.

William snorted. "Damned impudence."

Farnsworth was standing in the parlor, hat under one arm, shoulders straight. He was still gaunt. He smiled as Renna swept into the room.

"Countess," he whispered, leaping forward to take her hand and brush his lips to within a fraction of an inch of her knuckles.

"You've been ill," Renna said, noting his thinness, his sunken eyes.

"Nothing serious," he said. "However, it did prevent my coming to you sooner."

"And you've gotten your promotion," she said.

"Yes, thank you for noticing." His face became serious. "Countess—Renna—I fear that you will not welcome my presence when you hear what I have to tell you."

Renna heart leaped. "Do you have news of my husband?"

"Yes," he said. "That, dear lady, is why I came."

"Tell me," she said. "Tell me quickly."

"I went into Lisbon with the first British troops to

enter the city," he said. "Thinking of you, I made my way as quickly as possible to the French offices."

"Yes, go on," she said, as he paused. "You are frightening me, you know."

"I would face the most terrible enemy rather than the prospect of causing you pain," he said.

She was pale. "Tell me at once," she whispered. "Please."

"Portuguese partisans had raided the French offices after Napoleon's troops withdrew from Lisbon," he said. "They killed any Frenchman they could find."

"Please, God, no," Renna gasped, reaching out to place her hand on the arm of a chair for support.

"Your husband died defending the offices against Portuguese irregulars," Farnsworth said. "Actually they were nothing more than bandits and looters."

"Are you sure it was Beau?" she asked, grasping at a straw of hope.

"I'm afraid that members of the diplomatic community who survived the partisan attacks identified him," he said. "Your husband had a heart-shaped birthmark on the left side of his neck, did he not?"

Renna sank to her knees. Many times she had traced the outline of that mark with her fingers, had touched it with her lips.

"Renna," Farnsworth said, stepping forward to put his hands on her arms. "Forgive me for having to tell you."

She felt the world sinking out from under her, felt her knees go weak. Farnsworth's arm was around her waist. She allowed him to guide her to a chair.

"He is not coming back," Renna whispered. "He is never coming back." In her black misery she was reminded of another, earlier loss. Twice now death had taken the man she loved from her.

"I wish there was something I could do—something —anything," Farnsworth said.

"It was considerate of you to think of me," she said. "Now, if you'll excuse me—"

She ran from the room.

*　　*　　*

Michael Soaring Hawk Harper and Joseph Standing Bear Harper were christened by a minister of the Church of England in the family chapel at Beaumont Manor. The minister was not required to pronounce the difficult Seneca words for Soaring Hawk and Standing Bear. The kindly, bespectacled old man had trouble enough understanding why the boys had been given two names, one chosen by their mother to be acceptable in the world of the white man, the other, the Indian name, in honor of the clans of their paternal ancestors.

Randall Farnsworth was present at the ceremony. Dressed in his best regimentals, he stood beside black-clad Renna.

"The man's becoming a permanent fixture around here," William said testily to Estrela when Farnsworth showed up on christening day.

"Be patient, husband," Estrela admonished. "Having him here may give Renna comfort."

At first Renna felt supreme indifference to Farnsworth's frequent visits. In her grief she withdrew from everyone, and not even the presence of Emily Beth and little Louis could penetrate the pall of sorrow that oppressed her. Her milk dried up, and Estrela had to go into the village and hire a wet nurse for the baby.

Little Emily began to suffer from her mother's neglect. She chose Beth as an object of affection, clinging to the older woman for comfort and protection, until one day Beth came to Renna's rooms, where she spent most of her time in retreat.

"I won't try to tell you it will be all right," Beth said to her. "I suspect it will never be all right. But I also think the hurt will fade with passing months. In the meantime, darling Renna, your actions affect others, not just yourself."

Renna remained stiffly silent.

"I understand," Beth went on. "William and Estrela and your father and brother understand. It is Emily who wonders why her mother hates her so."

Renna, stung to the quick by Beth's words, said, "Hate? Oh, no. Never."

"She is a child, and all she knows is that her mother has not held her in her arms. She knows only that when she tries to seek you out, you avoid her and push her off on others."

"My poor darling," Renna said. "I must go to her."

And so it was that Renna began to overcome the malicious decay that can be one result of surrender to grief. She forced herself to be gay when she was with her daughter. They took long walks around the estate. They watched the workers plowing and planting the fields, found a fox den, and one bright early summer day saw the vixen bring her kits out of the den to play in the sun.

With the christening ceremony behind them, it was Renna who now kept Renno and the others from sailing for America.

"In the end," Renno said, "there is no pressing reason to return other than our desire to see those we have left behind. Renna's need is greater at the moment."

Renno, like William, had doubts about the continuing presence of Randall Farnsworth. "What is the man doing?" he asked Beth. "Is he paying court to her while she wears the widow's black?"

"Husband," Beth said, "she's an adult woman. She is mature enough not to do anything unwise or precipitous."

"Something about that young man doesn't ring quite true to me," Renno declared.

Beth laughed. "What speaks most loudly about Captain Farnsworth is his obvious devotion to Renna. And that is what you read in him, and being a father, you are skeptical of him. Fathers *always* think there's something 'not quite right' about men who woo their daughters."

"If that's what he's doing, it is far too early," Renno said.

"I agree, and I think he realizes it, too," Beth replied. "Right now, all he is to her is a friend, and she needs that badly enough."

Not satisfied, Renno made it a point to bring up the

subject with Renna by asking if, in any way, young Farnsworth was intruding on her grief.

"Not at all," Renna reassured him. "Actually, he makes me feel closer to Beau to be able to talk with someone who was in Lisbon when—" She did not finish the thought.

Farnsworth knew that sooner or later Renna would recover sufficiently from her grief to question him about her husband. The question came on a day when she had consented to walk with him around the gardens.

"Captain Farnsworth, what happened to my husband's body?"

"The Portuguese authorities gave him a Christian burial," he said, giving the answer he had prepared. Actually, he had no idea what had become of Beau's body. The last time he saw Beau, the Frenchman was lying in his own blood on the floor of the French offices.

"Where, do you know?"

"A small churchyard," he answered. "Oh, yes, it was called the Church of Our Lady of Lisbon. Quiet little place, not far from the French offices." He had seen the church in passing.

"Perhaps I could send money for a headstone," she said.

"Oh, I'm sure that the Portuguese took care of that."

"Still," she said, "one can't be sure."

"I suppose it wouldn't hurt," he said. "If you'll write the letter, I'll see to it that it gets sent to Lisbon by military mail. That way you can be sure it will arrive."

She had the letter ready when he took his leave at the end of the day. He opened it as he rode back toward his cousin's house. In addition to the letter, which spelled out the count's name, there were bank notes for fifty English pounds. He tore the letter and the envelope into small, unrecognizable pieces and scattered them along the roadside. The fifty pounds went into his pocket. He felt a slight twinge of conscience. He was not a thief. He assuaged his guilt by telling himself that when Renna's grief was past and she was his wife, all that was his would be hers. He would repay her for the fifty pounds many times over, if in nothing else but devotion.

Immediately upon hearing of Beau's death from Farnsworth, Renna had written to Beau's older brother in Switzerland, Louis Philippe, duc d'Orléans. A beautiful letter came in reply, in which Louis Philippe grieved for his brother and then went on to state that the son who had been born in Portugal was now heir to Beau's titles and property. Renna read the letter aloud to the entire family.

"Well, little one," Beth said to the baby boy, "now you have a title that is bigger than you. How do you like being the comte de Beaujolais?"

"Just how secure is the right of inheritance in France now?" Renno asked.

"There is law in France," Renna said, "and Napoleon was quite fond of Beau. I feel that it is my duty to my son to take him back to France so that he can take his rightful place."

"I had hoped to return to America," Renno said, "but I do not see how I can if my daughter remains here, with thoughts of going into harm's way."

"Then you must stay," Estrela insisted.

The growing animation in Renna, especially when Randall Farnsworth visited, was a relief to the entire family. She was still moody, and she of course still wore black, but her pleasure in his conversation was genuine. She began to treat him like a valued confidant.

"Don't they make an attractive couple?" Estrela asked William one day as Renna and Farnsworth walked past. Farnsworth had his hands clasped behind his back, and his head was inclined toward Renna attentively.

"He's a third son," William said. "Hasn't a farthing of his own outside of his army stipend."

"I wasn't trying to make a match," Estrela said. "I was just making an observation."

William had to admit to himself that they did, indeed, make a handsome couple. And Farnsworth seemed to be dotty about Renna's children. He was fond of saying that he'd known little Louis almost from the day of his birth.

So, slowly, William came to feel that it was a shame that Farnsworth was not a member of the landed gentry. If he were, when Renna's period of mourning was past, his marriage to Renna would solve a lot of problems, including the one presented by Renna's persistent determination to take her children back to France. Better to be the wife of an honorable Englishman than a widow of property in Paris, where every fortune hunter in France would lay siege to her, and where at any moment public opinion could turn once more against the old royalty to which Louis was an heir.

In one thing Randall Farnsworth had been unwittingly truthful as he gave Renna the false account of Beau's death. He had said that Portuguese irregulars had come upon Beau in the French offices; that part was technically true.

The British officer and his men in their red tunics had been observed as they entered and left the building that had housed the diplomatic representatives of France. The building was then empty and thus attractive to those inclined to help themselves at the expense of the enemy.

Two young Portuguese men, who slowly worked their way up to the third floor of the building, were disappointed by the lack of portable loot. They had found precious little that was salable when they entered the room where Beau lay. One of the young men turned away immediately, saying that it was time for them to leave the building. The other was more adventurous, and more greedy. He knelt beside what he presumed to be a dead man and felt for Beau's wallet. Reaching inside Beau's coat pocket, he was startled by a low moan escaping Beau's lips.

"He's alive!" the young man said, jerking his hand away.

"With so much blood, not for long," the other said.

With trembling hands the looter lifted one lapel of Beau's coat, avoiding the warm, wet blood that soaked a large area. He found Beau's wallet, opened it, was disappointed when he found only three small gold coins. He dropped the wallet onto Beau's chest.

"Help me," Beau whispered in French.

"Let's get out of here," said the other looter.

"Perhaps we should help him," said the one at Beau's side.

"You help him. I'm leaving." He started to go.

The man who was kneeling by Beau leaped to his feet and followed his friend out of the room. Before venturing into the street in front of the building, they looked both ways carefully. A policeman was at the corner, his hands behind his back. They waited till his head was turned, then walked in the other direction.

"That man up there," said the one who had taken Beau's coins, "he was alive."

"God will decide his fate."

"There are times when God does his work better with some small bit of help from below." He stopped, shifted from foot to foot irresolutely, then, with sudden determination, walked toward the policeman.

"You are a fool," his friend called after him.

"Perhaps, but the man was alive," the other said, over his shoulder.

The policeman listened with interest, and much to the relief of both looters, he asked no questions.

Beau opened his eyes to a whitewashed stucco wall and ceiling. Light came into the room from a window that reached almost to the floor. He was covered by a clean sheet and his chest was an ocean of pain. He moaned. A nursing sister in an odd, winged headdress bent over him and whispered soothingly in Portuguese.

The doctor who came within a few minutes spoke English. He lifted Beau's eyelids one by one and grunted in satisfaction. "You are a lucky man," he said.

"I don't feel lucky," Beau said. "I feel as if my chest has been caved in."

"Two broken ribs and some damage to surface flesh and muscle," the doctor said. He reached for something on the table beside Beau's bed. It was a heavy, gold medal honoring Saint Denis. Beau recognized it, for he had worn it around his neck from childhood.

"This saved your life," the doctor explained. "The rifle ball struck it and glanced off to smash bone and plow out of your side just under one of your ribs."

Beau took the medal in his hand. It was seriously deformed. He lifted it to his lips and, muttering a prayer to his patron saint, kissed it as weakness came suddenly with a surge of pain in his chest and he slept once more.

Chapter Sixteen

West of the Father of Waters, the time of the new beginning showed its green face briefly. Trees began to bud, and new grass lifted tender tips on the banks of the stream. But the mild days were a false promise. The hunters had just time to range out and return with fresh meat before winter struck again with howling winds out of the northwest and with frosts that hurt new growth.

When next the Master of Life conquered the forces of cold and darkness, We-yo remained skeptical. But as the days passed and the wild plums burst into frantic bloom, she ranged the valley with the other women of the village, foraging for new greens. They found good growths of poke, and when We-yo boiled her first batch, Ho-ya and Summer Moon ate the tangy green until their stomachs bulged.

The horses began to fill out from the gauntness of winter as the new grass carpeted the earth. Now the days were longer and the sun warm. Rains came with the voice of the thunderers and the flash of lightning, but it passed and life was good. Far-ranging hunters returned laden with the hides and meat of buffalo.

We-yo had not forgotten the Osage Young Elk, who had said he would come again in the time of the new green. When she spoke of him to her brother, Ho-ya reminded her that Young Elk had promised to return with warriors to drive the newcomers from Osage hunting grounds. Nevertheless, We-yo found herself looking forward to Young Elk's return with anticipation. As she went about her work, planting the seeds that would give them the fruits of summer and see them through the next winter with stored corn, she looked up each time someone approached.

He came with a nearly full moon, riding into the valley as the sun sank toward the western rim. He boldly entered the village leading six fine, young, healthy horses, trotted directly to the central commons, and halted. The horses snorted, shifted their feet. Young Elk sat as still as a statue and waited.

Ho-ya stepped out of the longhouse. He had taken time to don the costume of a Cherokee chief. His knife and his tomahawk were at his sash.

"I greet you, Cherokee," said Young Elk.

"I welcome you and honor you, Young Elk," Ho-ya said. He stood with his arms crossed on his chest, his chin high.

Young Elk swung his right leg over the horse's neck and landed lightly on his feet. "Your women dig in the dirt, planting seeds," he said.

"So," Ho-ya agreed.

"And I see no preparations for your departure."

"This is true."

Young Elk walked to stand three paces away from Ho-ya. "I have come for the woman," he said.

"I have told the great chief of the Osage that my sister is not for sale," Ho-ya said.

"Let the woman speak for herself," Young Elk said.

"Five of these horses speak for me. I have brought them as the wife price."

We-yo, who had been standing just inside the door of the longhouse, stepped out. She had changed from the clothing in which she had worked the fields all day. She wore carefully bleached doeskin, and a red ribbon secured her one large braid.

"I greet you, We-yo of the Cherokee," Young Elk said.

"I welcome you, Young Elk," We-yo said. "Will you eat?" She had known great doubt as she peered around the door during the exchange between the Osage and her brother, but as she looked into Young Elk's eyes, she saw strength there, and something else, something she had not seen in the eyes of a man since the death of Summer Moon's father. Where there had been doubt, there was a kind of exhilaration mixed with a warmth that caused a weakness in her loins.

"I have come for you," Young Elk told her.

We-yo felt her heart pound. Her decision had been made. "I am ready," she said.

"The wife price," Young Elk said, handing the bunched reins of five horses to Ho-ya.

"We need time, my sister and I, to discuss this matter," Ho-ya replied.

"There is no need for discussion between us, Brother," We-yo said. She stepped to look up into Young Elk's face. "But I have two things that I must discuss with Young Elk."

"Speak," the Osage said.

"This valley is the home of my people, and they will be allowed to live in it in peace and friendship with the Osage," she said.

"So you have said, so will it be," Young Elk declared solemnly.

"You will be father and protector to my daughter, Summer Moon, and to my son, Jani. You will call them your own."

"I will value the little ones as highly as the children that you will bear me," Young Elk said.

"So you have said, so it will be done," We-yo said.

"Good. Then we will go," said the Osage, taking her hand.

Ho-ya stepped forward. "Is this the wedding custom of the Osage?" he asked, his voice rising.

"I have paid the wife price, and this one has given me her hand," Young Elk answered.

"That is not the way of the Cherokee," We-yo told him. "Will you honor our customs, Husband?"

"So it will be," Young Elk agreed.

For the Cherokee and the Seneca, a marriage was a time for celebration; but the dancing that took place two days later, under the light of the rising full moon, was subdued. The singing tended to be slightly plaintive. The unity of the group was about to be diminished: one of their own was leaving.

They left the next day, Young Elk leading the way, sitting tall and straight on his horse with Summer Moon riding in front of him. He held the little girl in place with one arm as the horse went forward at a gentle walk.

Following on her own horse, Jani in her arms, We-yo listened to her husband's voice as he instructed his new daughter in the language of the Osage. Summer Moon repeated the words as Young Elk spoke them: sun, sky, cloud, horse. We-yo said them under her breath. She, too, was eager to learn.

They camped for the night after riding over a range of hills. There was good water, and Young Elk built a cozy fire. From her belongings We-yo produced blankets. Summer Moon was asleep quickly after a meal of dried meat. We-yo fed Jani, laid him down, and went to the stream to bathe. When she came back, Young Elk had spread his own blanket near the fire. Her blanket was in position to be a cover. She sat down on the blanket, her eyes downcast. He sat facing her.

"We will be home tomorrow night," he said.

Home. The word had more than one meaning to We-yo. It brought forth memories of her family, of her father and mother, her grandmother and her uncles. The long-house in the valley had not established itself in her mind as home. And now this man who had purchased her with five horses was taking her to a strange place that, like the longhouse in the valley, was not home.

"We will sleep this night," Young Elk said.

She looked up, watched him as he lay down beside her and pulled the blanket to his shoulders. She eased down onto the blanket and lay on her back.

"The lights in the sky are fiery tonight," she said.

"Yes," Young Elk grunted.

"There is a chill in the night air," she said.

He made a sound and his hand touched her, guided her to turn onto her side, facing away from him. He pressed against her, and she could feel the hardness of his muscular chest, his strong legs cupped into the back of her own.

"Do I warm you?" he asked.

"You warm me well."

"Sleep," he said.

But it was a long time before she could force her eyes to stay closed. She was achingly aware of him. His arm was around her waist, and at the crease of her buttock he was pressed tightly to her and she felt his manhood grow into a hardness. She waited, fire and ice in her stomach, but his breathing steadied and grew long and deep, and the masculinity that pushed at her softness relaxed.

A group of women carrying water pitchers watched them ride through the shallow waters of a clear stream. The Osage village was sited in a meadow near a grove of trees. The lodges were of two types, oval and rectangular, with straight walls and sloping roofs. Some of the roofs were matted, others were covered with buffalo skins. The largest of the rectangular lodges was not unlike a small Iroquois longhouse. Like the longhouse, the Osage houses were constructed to exploit the automatic ventilation that was the result of one entrance and a smoke hole.

After they had dismounted, Young Elk handed the horses to eager young boys and led We-yo to one of the medium-sized houses. It was rectangular. The roof rose to a height of about ten feet. Inside the one room measured

fifteen by twenty feet. There were raised benches that
served as beds, and near the dead ashes of a fire lay a few
ceramic pots and a cooking stone.

"Home," Young Elk said.

"Your family?" We-yo asked.

"No," he said.

"We will live here alone?"

He nodded.

From outside a female voice called, and other voices
could also be heard.

"We must go out to meet them," Young Elk said.

Cradling Jani in her arms, We-yo took Summer Moon
by the hand and followed Young Elk out of the house.
Several people, male and female, had gathered. When
Young Elk spoke, his words came so fast that their meaning was lost to We-yo, but she understood when he said
the Osage word for wife, when he turned and motioned
her to step forward.

"My mother," he said, and a gray-haired, wrinkled
crone stared at We-yo with baleful eyes.

"Mother of my husband," We-yo said, "I will be a
dutiful daughter."

The old woman did not understand the words. Her
eyes narrowed, and her antagonism was evident. Young
Elk spoke harshly, slashing the air with his hands.

"Come," the old woman said. "Come."

Young Elk nodded at We-yo. She followed the crone,
Summer Moon running along beside her. Near the creek
the old woman picked up a piece of deadwood, brandished
it, chattered in Osage.

"Firewood?" We-yo asked, having learned that word
from Young Elk.

"Firewood," the crone said, sweepingly indicating a
direction. She took Jani from We-yo's arms.

Soon We-yo had an armload. Summer Moon carried a
few small limbs, grunting with exaggerated effort. They
returned to Young Elk's house, where his mother handed
Jani back to We-yo and departed.

We-yo had a fire going when Young Elk entered with
a fresh cut of buffalo meat in his hands. There were no

metal cooking pots. We-yo rigged a spit and began to roast the meat.

"Tomorrow I will go in search of fresh greens," she said.

He answered her in Osage.

"Teach me," she said. She pointed to the meat and said "buffalo." He gave her the Osage word for it. The language lesson continued until the meat was seared on the outside, leaving the center hot and juicy. They ate with their hands, with the aid of Young Elk's knife. Summer Moon bit hungrily into the red, rich meat.

It was quiet in the village. The meal had settled in We-yo's stomach as she put Summer Moon and Jani to bed.

A little black dog had crept into the house to clean away the scraps of the meal. "Brave-as-a-Lion," Young Elk said, pointing to the dog.

"Is he brave?" she asked.

Young Elk laughed. "He would flee a rabbit, but in his heart—"

"Here, Brave-as-a-Lion," We-yo said, handing the dog a sliver of meat. "I know how you feel."

"Now it is time," Young Elk said.

She nodded, rose, removed her tunic, dropped her skirt. His eyes widened in pleasure as he examined her firm, shapely body. She stepped into his arms, and he lifted her easily, carried her to the bed. To her surprise and her great pleasure he was patient, tender, considerate, and, in the end, so virile that he awakened in her feelings that she had almost forgotten. In the goodness of it she cried out and his release brought from his throat a growl like that of a contented animal.

He slept. She sat cross-legged on the bed watching the dying flickers of the fire. Summer Moon and Jani were sleeping soundly, Jani making a sound like a little bee, while Summer Moon mumbled in her sleep. The house had been made cozy by the fire.

"Home," she said, and there was a new meaning to the word. In accepting this place as her home, she had effectively cut herself off from her past. There was a sadness in that, for she had been Cherokee. Her mother, Ena, had been Seneca; but Ena, too, had left her people. She had not ceased to be Seneca in her heart, but in her new world she became Cherokee. We-yo was Cherokee in her heart, but now she knew that she would be Osage.

She would teach Summer Moon and Jani the traditions and lore of the Seneca and the Cherokee, but they would be Osage and, thus, the blood of Seneca sachems and Cherokee chieftains would be lost and diluted into the greater whole, the Osage nation.

"Well, so be it," she said, for the man beside her was strong and kind to her, and he had, by his treatment of her and her children, taken her heart into his hands. She would be Osage, and she would let nothing come between her and the man who slept beside her. She remembered the feel of him inside her, the intensity of her response to him, and there was a melting inside her that caused her to flush with joy.

She was awakened by the shrill, harsh voice of Young Elk's mother. She heard her name, but understood little else as she dressed and strode through the door to face the torrent of words.

The old crone was jabbering in shrill tones, waving her finger angrily at We-yo and shaking her head. For whatever reason, the woman obviously thought We-yo was unworthy.

We-yo faced her, hands on hips, her dark eyes boring down into the weak, watery eyes of age. "Hear me, old woman," she said harshly.

The woman raised her voice.

We-yo put her face nose to nose with the crone and said in Osage, "Shut up."

The old woman fell silent with her mouth hanging open.

"Old woman," We-yo said in her native tongue, "I will hear no more condemnation from your lips. I am the wife of Young Elk, the wife of the chief, and you will remember and treat me as such. In return I will treat you with the respect due your age and position."

The old woman didn't understand all the words, but

she inferred the meaning from We-yo's tone and her blazing eyes. She took a step or two backward.

Young Elk stuck his head out the door. "What is all the noise out here?"

"Nothing, Husband," We-yo said. "It was just your mother and I coming to an understanding."

That spring Ta-na and Gao were accepted into the ranks of warriors, although they were not yet of an age to be considered men. There had been no serious war involving Rusog's Cherokee since the Spanish-inspired conflict with the Chickasaw tribe, but since the land was big and the dangers were many, it was deemed necessary to have warriors ready for any eventuality. Aside from the danger of flare-ups of old enmities among the southeastern tribes, there was the looming presence of white settlements to the north and to the east.

Senior warriors, both Seneca and Cherokee, conducted lessons in armed conflict. Ta-na and Gao's progress fell under the scrutiny of two highly qualified men: their father, El-i-chi, and their uncle-by-marriage, Rusog.

Since the time Gao and Ta-na had seen Head-in-the-Cloud sitting on a mossy bank, with the arm of an older man around her, Gao noticed that Ta-na carefully avoided any contact with not only Cloud, but with girls in general. He understood Ta-na's disillusionment, though Ta-na took pains to hide his pain. They had been together, after all, from babyhood.

Gao, too, was disillusioned with girls, at least temporarily. And since he felt that he was partly responsible for Ta-na's unhappiness, he did his best to keep his brother occupied, while he himself abstained from the walking out with pretty maidens. He decided that it was best to keep one's life simple, that is, to keep one's mind off girls. But he did not take into account that nature has a way of speaking very strongly to young men regarding one particular subject.

Head-in-the-Cloud was poised on the brink of sixteen. Her long, strong legs, her narrow waist, her small but comely breasts, and her lovely, round face were assurances that she did not lack invitations to walk or to visit the swimming creek. She was never without a willing escort on the springtime foraging expeditions, but none of those who invited her, none of those who became her guardians while she gathered greens in the woodlands and along the creeks, was able to capture her heart. She felt an unease within herself. Something was missing in her life; that something was a lad named Ta-na-wun-da.

Although, in her youthful arrogance, she was unwilling to take the blame for Ta-na's continued avoidance of her, she had come to suspect, over the months, that her acceptance of the doeskin from Gao and her walking out with him might have been the cause of the barrier that Ta-na had set up between them. At times she would tell herself that if Ta-na were so shallow and selfish that he did not want her to be cordial to his own brother, then he was not worth bothering with. Then she would relent and compose words of apology to Ta-na, words she was too proud to deliver to him, even if he were to give her the opportunity.

Although some Cherokee girls did not wed until they were older, the majority of Cloud's contemporaries were either already married or spoken for. Only Cloud remained undecided in the face of more than one opportunity.

"You must cease walking out with so many different ones," her mother warned, "lest people begin to talk about you."

"It is not the girl who walks out with several men you should worry about," Cloud replied, "but the one who walks always with the same man."

Her mother made a sound of exasperation through her lips. "You will not be able to string along half the young men in the village forever," she warned. "Men such as Red Horse will not be trifled with."

Red Horse, son of a senior Cherokee warrior and wise man, was the older man with whom Cloud had been sitting when she was seen by Gao and Ta-na. Of all the men who came to Cloud's lodge, he was the one whom Cloud's mother most favored.

"Don't worry, Mother," Cloud said, "I will give you grandchildren soon enough."

She left the lodge and was pleased that no young man was in the area. Many times when she emerged, one or another of them just "happened" to be passing or talking with someone nearby. She ran down toward the swimming creek. It was not quite warm enough to swim, but some of the younger ones were wading and hunting crayfish in the shallows. Crossing the creek, she went into the woods, wanting only to be alone. As she passed by the tree that had been the trysting place for her and Ta-na, she felt a little tug at her heart. Ta-na was being hateful and selfish.

Seated beneath the tree, she let the warmth of the spring day soak into her. A squirrel chattered at her from high up in the new leaves, and nesting birds were busy with bits of straw and twigs. She was half-dozing when she heard the snap of a twig and looked up to see Red Horse looking down at her with hunger in his eyes. He sat beside her.

"Why are you alone?" he asked.

"Because I wanted to be alone."

"Now you are with me."

"Now I am with you," she said. At first, having a full warrior pay court to her had been heady. His experienced touch had kindled fires in her, and at times it had been his restraint, and not hers, that had kept them within the bounds of propriety. Gradually, however, she had come to look upon him as old, much too old, already a man of some twenty years.

"I hunger for you," Red Horse said.

"I want none of that," she answered.

He reached for her and pulled her to him. "Let us press our mouths together in the manner of the white man."

"No, I don't like that," she said.

"There was a time when you liked it," he said, holding her as she struggled to free herself. He turned her face toward his and tried to kiss her. She bit his lower lip painfully, one sharp canine penetrating and leaving a welling of blood on his lip.

"Little vixen," he said angrily, using his strength to pin her to the ground. His mouth sought hers, and she tasted his hot blood. His hand was pawing at her breasts.

She did not scream. She fought him with all of her strength, kicking, trying to bite and scratch him. He held her arms and smothered her struggles with his strength and his weight.

Ta-na and Gao had been for a run. They carried knives and tomahawks not because weapons were needed in areas so close to the village, but because warriors always went armed. They were returning toward the village when Ta-na heard movement from the woods ahead. He halted. Something sizable was moving heavily, rustling last autumn's leaves, snapping twigs.

Gao cocked his head. "Wild boar?" he asked, whispering. He took his tomahawk from his belt and moved forward, placing his feet with great care.

Ta-na followed, looking over Gao's shoulder. Suddenly, under a big black walnut tree, he saw the back and legs of a warrior and, over the warrior's shoulder, the contorted face of Head-in-the-Cloud. He needed no time to make his decision. Rushing past Gao, he threw himself on the warrior's back and locked his arm around the man's neck. He put pressure on the throat.

The man shouted out in surprise and released Cloud's arms, then threw himself backward in an effort to rid himself of his attacker. But Ta-na was not that easy to dislodge. He had his neck hold secured with his right hand on his left wrist, and he hung on as the larger and older man threshed around, rolling this way and that.

The man was gasping for breath, but Ta-na's grip constricted his throat. The warrior managed to come to his feet, but Ta-na still held fast.

Suddenly strong arms were pulling at him. "Ta-na, stop, you're killing him!" Gao yelled.

Ta-na's anger was a red haze. He heard Gao's voice as if from far off, and he tightened his hold. He felt Red Horse's body go limp, and then he heard the words.

"Stop. You don't want to kill him. Stop, Ta-na."

And Cloud's voice, "Please stop, Ta-na."

He loosed his hold and let Red Horse fall to the ground. The older man gasped for breath and his body shuddered as his lungs filled.

"He was hurting you," Ta-na said, looking at Cloud's weeping face. "Are you all right?"

"I am not hurt."

Ta-na was shaking in the aftermath of his violent passion. "And you came into the woods with him," he said, remembering how his heart had ached when he saw her with Red Horse on the mossy bank.

"No. He followed me. I was alone."

The older warrior was trying to push himself up with his hands. Gao took his arm and helped him sit up. The man was breathing raspingly. He touched his throat and his eyes hardened. His hand went to his tomahawk and he leaped to his feet. "Come, motherless one," he said, "and let's see if you are as brave coming at Red Horse from the front!"

Ta-na's tomahawk leaped into his hand. He took one step forward and crouched.

Gao, too, drew his blade and moved to flank Red Horse. "You will have to fight two," he said.

Red Horse shifted his eyes back and forth uneasily. "He tried to kill me."

"He punished an animal who was attacking a girl," Gao said. "Go, now, and it will be forgotten, if Cloud concurs."

Red Horse rubbed his throat again. Slowly he lowered his tomahawk and, without another word, turned and walked away.

"Come," Gao said to Cloud, "we'll walk you home."

"Please, Gao," Cloud said in a small voice, "I want to talk with Ta-na."

"Eh?" Gao asked, looking at his brother.

Ta-na nodded. Gao left them.

"You wanted to talk," Ta-na said, still keyed up.

"To thank you for coming to help me."

He shrugged.

"To ask you why you have been avoiding me."

He looked into her large, brown eyes, saw stars in their depths. "When I saw you with Red Horse, I knew that you preferred him."

She looked down, avoiding his eyes. "I have been foolish," she whispered. "These months, all this time, every day, every evening I have been wishing that you would come."

He was hesitant, for he had been hurt once and he was not eager to experience that kind of pain again.

"Ta-na," she said, "it is you, no one but you, that I will walk with forever."

He saw tears forming in her eyes, saw, too, that a bruise would be forming on her neck from Red Horse's roughness. He stepped forward and put his hands on her shoulders, and she leaned into him, pressing her hips to his, lifting her face. He kissed her.

Perhaps, if a Huntington ship had not run the embargo with a letter from El-i-chi to Beaumont Manor, Renno would have procrastinated longer. As it was, the season of the roaring Atlantic storms would be upon them before they reached the United States.

El-i-chi's letter was short. Through him, Roy and Toshabe sent their love. Things were the same in the village, except that Ena and Rusog's twins had left home and family to seek new land west of the Father of Waters.

"Ah, Ena," Renno said in sympathy for his sister.

It seemed to him that the defection of We-yo and Ho-ya from their people was additional confirmation of his failure, for if those of his own blood could rebel against everything he believed, then perhaps it was he who was wrong.

At any rate, it was time to go. His place, in a time of war and rumors of war, was with his people. The old trouble between the United States and England was festering and swelling. England persisted in boarding American ships, to impress American citizens into the Royal Navy and to search forcibly for British deserters.

Renno polled the others. Beth, too, was ready, she said. Life on an English estate palled after a while; although she loved her brother well and would never fault him for continuing the traditions of his ancestors, her home was an ocean and half a continent away, in Huntington Castle.

It seemed not to matter to Little Hawk and Naomi. They were so much in love, so touchingly unable to get enough of each other, that they would be content anywhere as long as they were together. Only Renna would be left behind.

Adan had scheduled the sailing. A convoy of wagons had gone from Beaumont Manor to Portsmouth carrying Beth's purchases. Adan had brought the largest ship, the *Beth Huntington*. "And just as well," he said laughingly as he saw the extent of Beth's personal cargo, "or I wouldn't have room for a payload."

Two things happened quickly, both of them pleasing to Renno. First, one evening at dinner, Captain Randall Farnsworth had an announcement. Sir Arthur Wellesley, only lately having been rewarded for his service in Denmark and Portugal by being elevated to a peerage as Viscount Wellington, was forming an army to go back to Portugal and thence into Spain.

"Napoleon has two hundred thousand troops in Spain," Farnsworth said, "and it looks as if he plans to invade Portugal again."

"And how many men will Wellesley, or Wellington as he is now to be known, have with him?" William asked.

"A well-trained force of twenty-five thousand British troops," Farnsworth said proudly.

"Not very impressive," Beth said.

"With a bit of reinforcement from the Portuguese and the Spanish, we'll handle them," Farnsworth assured her.

The second thing that pleased Renno involved his daughter and hinged on a conversation that same night.

The family was enjoying cigars and brandy after dinner when Renna noticed Farnsworth signaling to her that he wanted to talk with her. They walked into the front garden. It was still light, that peculiar light of an English evening when the sun delays its plunge to the west and the birds, twittering, are settling down into their nests and nooks.

"It grieves me to think that I will be separated from you," he said without preamble. "So, although I respect your mourning for your husband, I must speak."

"I don't think you should say anything, Randall," she replied softly. "Don't say something we'll both regret."

"I could never regret having said that I love you."

She looked away quickly. She knew full well that both William and Estrela had come to favor Farnsworth's obvious attempts to win her affections. She herself wondered at times if it wouldn't be wise to give up her plan to return to France with her children.

"I will not ask for your hand," Farnsworth said. "Not now. Only God knows what will happen in Portugal and Spain. What I will ask, Renna, is that you delay your return to France until I come home from this campaign. Sooner or later, my darling, the whole of Europe is going to go up in flames. This Napoleon is expending the blood of France and her allies without regard for the future, and meantime the resolution of his enemies grows. I would not want you and the children to be in France when the fall of the empire comes."

"I can't make you any promises," Renna said.

"Think about it. Be prudent for the sake of the children. Wait for me. From this campaign will come glory and position for me, and then I will be able to ask you once and only once to be my wife. If you say no then, I will respect your wishes."

He was going into danger. He had been wounded terribly the last time he was in Portugal. Her heart wept for him. She was confused. She knew that she did not feel love for him as she'd felt love for Beau, but he was so kind, so considerate, so devoted.

Her decision was sudden, and she had to admit to herself even before she spoke that she was relieved. She had not realized how much she'd been dreading going back to France with only the children to keep her from being alone in a land that, since Beau's death, had become ever more distant, ever more alien to her.

"I will not go back to France," she said.

"Thank you."

What she did not tell him was that she had made another decision, which pleased Renno very much. When the *Beth Huntington* sailed from Portsmouth Harbor, Renno had all four of his grandchildren aboard, and his beautiful daughter as well.

The reasons for Renna's decision were twofold. There was the actual dread of parting from her family yet again, and of being alone in France. And then there was a feeling of guilt, guilt because she had considered Randall Farnsworth's suit for her hand with Beau dead less than a year. Perhaps she had formed her decision as a test. William and Estrela could tell Randall where she was when he returned from Portugal. She would be either in Wilmington, where Beth maintained a comfortable house on a cliff overlooking the Cape Fear River, or she would be at Huntington Castle in the Cherokee Nation. If Farnsworth loved her enough, and if it was meant to be, then he would find her. In the meantime, she had eased her guilt.

During his time of healing, Beau was questioned by both Portuguese and English authorities. He was frank and truthful with both. They were all civilized people. The war in Spain was killing thousands, but Beau was a diplomat, and his captors were gentlemen. The English intelligence officer who questioned him even made inquiries about Renna and her family, but the English army that had landed in central Portugal was now deep inside Spain and there was no one left in Portugal who remembered the pale-haired woman with the infant in arms. Beau could not imagine anything bad happening to Renna, so he assumed that she and her father and brother had gone back to England. He looked upon his encounter with the English officer who shot him as if it were an act of God, a senseless accident.

Soon Beau was walking, holding his upper body very stiff to prevent the healing ribs from paining him. He asked the Portuguese if he was a prisoner and was told that they would respect his diplomatic status. It was not clear to him as to what extent they would honor his former position as special envoy from Napoleon, but when he was able to move more freely, they allowed him the use of an office in the building that had once housed France's deputation to Lisbon. He waited for several days before he recovered a small hoard of gold coin that had been hidden away for emergency use. With money he could hope to make his way out of the country.

There was only one way, and it was a long, long road. It led through Spain, past the battlefields where two hundred thousand soldiers of the empire were trying to subdue the ragged Spanish armies. With the gold he purchased clothing, a horse and saddle, weapons, and a compact kit for traveling. No one tried to stop him. During his stay in Lisbon and during his convalescence he had learned enough Portuguese to get by.

He followed the route of the English army into Spain; when he reached the area of confrontation, he waited for a quiet time and then slipped through British lines to the French. For the first time in a year he heard his native language. It was spoken in the accent of provincials, members of a rough-and-ready cavalry unit; but they were Frenchmen. When he told his story, they congratulated him on his escape from Portugal and passed him back to headquarters command, where he spent several days telling all that he knew about conditions in Lisbon and in that part of Spain through which he had traveled.

He was surprised when he was given the opportunity to tell his story to Napoleon himself. The emperor was leading his army in person, for he was growing tired of the hemorrhaging of French blood in the dry hills of Spain.

"But, Beau," Napoleon said, "the information you have in your head is invaluable. You have seen the disposition of the English from the rear, and you can guide my army directly into Portugal."

"I had hoped, sire, to be able to go home to try to locate my family."

"My boy," said the little general, "we all have to make sacrifices. Give me but a month of your time, and we will be in Portugal and you shall sail home from there."

The fortress at Gerona withstood the French siege for seven months.

James Madison had not seen Thomas Jefferson so angry since a jury had declared Aaron Burr not guilty of treason.

"I am sick of these eternal evasions and defiances," Jefferson thundered. He was talking about the smuggling that was going on in defiance of his Embargo Act.

"Along the border with Canada," he said, "the traffic has risen to insurrectionary proportions."

"Well, Mr. President," Madison said, "we can't guard the entire border. There's just too much of it."

"They build rafts and carry contraband up Lake Champlain and across the St. Lawrence. They guard their smuggling with small armies of men."

"The governor of New York has called out the militia," Madison said. He knew that the president was shocked by the situation in which he found himself, for Jefferson had admitted that the Embargo Law was "the most embarrassing one we have ever had to execute."

"Mr. President," Madison said, "Perhaps it is time to admit defeat. Perhaps it's time to ask the Congress for repeal."

Jefferson paced, deep in thought. Madison knew what was on the president's mind, for it was on his, too: in a few short months, Jefferson would be going home to Monticello, and then Madison might well be in the White House, dealing with the consequences of Jefferson's decision today.

Jefferson stopped, shook his head once. "No, James," he declared. "I am determined to see it through."

"Even if it strains the Constitution?" Madison asked.

"Let's pray that we don't strain it irrevocably."

As Adan Bartolome steered the *Beth Huntington* around the shoals of the Cape of Fear in the dead of night and entered the Cape Fear river on a rising tide, he was not concerned with the constitutionality of Jefferson's Embargo. He wanted only to land his cargo safely and spirit it away into the Huntington warehouses before the federal authorities knew what was happening. He had done it before, and he was successful once again.

THE WHITE INDIAN—
BOOK XXV
WAR CLOUDS
by Donald Clayton Porter

Returning to America aboard the *Beth Huntington* with his wife, children, and grandchildren, Renno encounters the consequences of Jefferson's Embargo Act and must decide how to deal with a law that strains the fabric of the Constitution. His son, Little Hawk, grows restless and joins the ship's captain, Adan Bartolome, in a plan to circumvent the embargo and transport warehoused cotton. But their scheme is complicated by a British officer, Gunner Griffiths, who impresses Little Hawk, James Ridley, and other able-bodied men aboard the *Beth Huntington* into service on a British cruiser.

Renno and Beth visit Thomas Jefferson and James Madison with the hope of setting in motion action that will free Little Hawk and the others, only to find themselves embroiled in the events that will ultimately lead to war. Soon after, Renno learns that his mother is nearing death, and he leaves for the land of the Seneca and Cherokee.

In his absence, Ta-Na and Gao head north in Renno's place to become scouts for William Henry Harrison. There they are taken captive by the followers of the Shawnee chief Tecumseh, whose plans for Indian unity have taken root. Meanwhile, Renno becomes caught up in a quest to discover the cause of the death of Meriwether Lewis and is unaware of the grave danger that threatens Ta-Na and Gao.

Read WAR CLOUDS, *on sale in 1994 wherever Bantam Books are sold.*

FROM THE PRODUCER OF WAGONS WEST
AND THE KENT FAMILY CHRONICLES COMES
A SWEEPING SAGA OF WAR AND HEROISM
AT THE BIRTH OF A NATION

THE WHITE INDIAN SERIES

The compelling story of America's birth
against the equally exciting adventures of
an English child raised as a Seneca.

☐	24650-X	White Indian	$4.99
☐	25020-5	The Renegade	$4.50
☐	25039-6	Tomahawk	$4.50
☐	25868-0	War Drums	$3.95
☐	27841-X	Seneca Warrior	$4.99
☐	28285-9	Father of Waters	$4.99
☐	28474-6	Fallen Timbers	$4.50
☐	28805-9	Sachem's Son	$4.50
☐	29028-2	Sachem's Daughter	$4.99
☐	29217-X	Seneca Patriots	$4.99
☐	29218-8	Hawk's Journey	$5.50
☐	29219-6	Father and Son	$4.99

Available at your local bookstore or use this page to order.

Bantam Books, Dept. LE3   2451 S. Wolf Road, Des Plaines, IL 60018

Please send me the items I have checked above. I am enclosing $_____
(please add $2.50 to cover postage and handling). Send check or money order,
no cash or C.O.D.'s, please.

Mr./Ms._____

Address_____

City/State_____Zip_____
Please allow four to six weeks for delivery.
Prices and availability subject to change without notice.   LE 3 6/93